Finders Keepers

Kathleen White

For my family

Thank you for believing in me.

Prologue

I could hear the steady beat through the thick, concrete walls as I passed the building, and I couldn't help but cringe. The crap they passed off as music was a total disgrace. Hell, I'd have taken The Beatles over it any day. All I could do was hope that the next decade would have something decent to offer.

If I lived that long, of course. For all I knew, I could be dead before the seventies were over.

The cold steel of the sawed-off barrel against my hand helped to steady my nerves. It was hard to believe I walked away from a full college scholarship for this, but books just couldn't compete with the need to kill the things that didn't want to stay in the ground. As soon as I heard the reports of activity in this area, I'd hopped on the company-paid jet.

And here I was in what passed for a city in the Midwest, with the clouds threatening rain at any moment and terrible music to accompany my thoughts. Lucky me.

Finally, as I neared the end of the building, the music was overshadowed by a scream. Even that sounded better than what was seeping through the walls of the club. I withdrew the twin shotguns from beneath my coat, the bayonets already fastened securely to the ends of the barrels. With a sigh, I turned to face the alley and mentally prepared myself for whatever horror was waiting within.

It only took a moment for me to take stock of the situation, and I found myself gripping the weapons a little bit tighter. The reports had been right. One of the creatures had a girl pinned down against the litter-strewn ground and, if it could talk, would have been calling her breakfast. To her credit, she was fighting it off as best as she could.

It was difficult to discern her age. She almost had more dirt and grime on her face than the monster trying to kill her. Add in the steady stream of obscenities pouring out of her mouth and the way she handled the small switchblade, and it was nearly impossible to tell.

I'd have to figure it out later. Time to earn my paycheck.

As I rushed forward, I felt the bayonets sink into dead flesh. My muscles strained as I hauled the thing off of her and swung it to the side, pulling back on the triggers. The shells tore through the decaying muscles like a hot knife through butter, and the beast was hurled across the alley. It slammed into the wall with a gut-turning thud and slid down to rest among the garbage.

"And this time, stay dead," I muttered as I watched it closely.

I was ready to empty both barrels into it if it so much as twitched. Satisfied that it was taking my advice seriously, I turned my attention to its potential meal. She was shaking, which was to be expected, but she watched me suspiciously. I guessed that she was probably in her late teens, maybe a year or two younger than I was.

"What the hell are you doing out here?" I demanded before I realized my tone. After all, she was almost eaten alive. "Did you get kicked out of the disco or something?"

"Disco sucks," she said flatly. To her credit, her raspy voice only trembled a little.

"Ain't that the truth," I agreed as I wiped off the bayonets and holstered the guns.

"Who the hell are you?" Apparently, it was her turn to make demands. "And what the hell was that thing?"

"Well, that's a nice thank you," I shot back. "Next time, I'll just let the damn zombie eat you instead."

As I turned away, I shook my head. Sometimes I wondered why I even bothered helping these people. It wasn't like they'd have done the same. Most of them couldn't even help themselves. Maybe it was the money. I snorted at that thought. Maybe if I kept telling myself that, then I'd get a raise that would make it worth my time.

In retrospect, I shouldn't have been angry at her. She was out there

2

alone and had almost been killed, but my adrenaline was still going, and I'd just put my ass on the line to save hers. Not that the zombies were actually challenging anymore. It was the rumors that there were worse things out there killing people that bothered me. I'd managed to avoid them so far, but things have a way of catching up with you.

"Where are you going?"

I paused in mid-stride when I heard her voice and I realized that she sounded terrified.

"Home," I told her. "Well, as close to home as I've got right now. I think you should do the same. Who knows if there are any more of them wandering around? They tend to travel in packs." I turned around, surprised that she hadn't moved from her spot on the ground. "Well, what are you waiting for? Get the hell out of here."

"This is my home, asshole." She shot me a scathing look before staring down at her hands, her matted, black hair obscuring her features. "Just go. Thanks for saving my ass and all that. Just so you know, I had it under control."

"That's why it was about to finish you off?" I knew I had taken the bait on that one, but I couldn't help myself. "Don't be stupid, kid. You'd be dead if I hadn't shown up. Just admit it."

"I had it under control," she repeated.

"Sure, whatever."

I didn't see the point in arguing about it. We were both alive. That's what mattered, right? I decided to start over.

"Look, the name's Trina. It's my job to take down monsters like that. Not really that glamorous, but it pays the bills." I looked her up and down. She probably hadn't eaten a decent meal in weeks, if not months. "I've got some cash on me if you want something to eat. I probably have enough for a motel too if you want to get cleaned up."

Her grey eyes were studying me again. She obviously wasn't the trusting type and she knew that I was armed. I managed half a smile, hoping that it would put her at ease.

*****

The rain fell in icy sheets, soaking the pavement of the sidewalks and streets. The weather seemed even more miserable in the sickly yellow light of the street lamp. I turned the corner and stepped into the alley, unsurprised by the sight waiting for me.

"Shit Soph," I said, disapproval in my tone. "Don't you have enough sense to get out of the rain?"

"Nice to see you too," she said. She seemed to have difficulty getting to her feet, but I kept my expression neutral as she used the brick wall beside her to help her stand. The last thing she wanted from anyone, especially me, was pity. "It rains sometimes. Welcome to life. What the hell do you want, anyway?"

After visiting her for three years, I knew better than to be offended by her attitude. I almost looked forward to her caustic responses. Almost.

"It's payday," I told her. "I figured you might like a hot meal and a warm bed. But if you'd rather stay out here and get soaked, suit yourself."

"You just want to get laid."

"You know me," I said with a laugh. There hadn't been any accusation in her tone, not that I'd expected any. "What do you say? A nice dry bed or this?" I gestured to the alley surrounding us. "Limited time offer."

I watched her hesitate for a moment, but knew it was just for show. She hated charity and had to convince herself that the offer was what she wanted instead of what she needed. She was always stubborn like that. After taking only a single step forward, she doubled over, her entire body shaking from the coughing fit that left her gasping for breath. When it had passed, she straightened again and wiped her mouth with the back of her hand. Even in the dim light, I could tell it was streaked with blood.

"That sounds like shit," I remarked. "Let's go before you die on me or something."

"I'm fine," she insisted.

I wasn't buying it, but it was one more thing that wasn't worth arguing about. She wanted to play the tough street rat, and that was fine with me. As we walked out of the alley, I glanced back and noticed her steps were unsteady. She was also using the wall for support.

Thankfully, the motel was right around the corner. I had already booked the room for a few nights, so I didn't have to deal with the attendant with Soph in tow. The last thing I needed was some minimum-wage clerk spouting innuendos.

As soon as we had entered the room, Soph headed for the heater and turned it up as high as it would go. I dropped onto the bed with a satisfied

4

sigh and kicked off my boots before stretching my legs off the edge of the mattress.

"I'm gonna go grab a shower," she said after a few minutes. "It ain't all that often that I get the chance."

"Suit yourself," I said.

I let my eyes roam over her curves as she sauntered towards the bathroom, sure that she was moving seductively on purpose. The idea of joining her came to mind, but I dismissed it. We'd have plenty of time to catch up over the next few days. Instead, I stood up just long enough to slip off my trench coat and toss it onto the small table beneath the window.

My gaze lingered on the bathroom door as I reached down to remove the holsters of my guns, and I placed them on the floor next to the bed. I could feel a frown tugging at the corners of my lips when another fit of coughing echoed from within the bathroom.

Soph should have known better than to bullshit me like that. She knew I could always tell when she was lying, but she was determined not to admit any weakness, even in front of me. Never mind the fact that she might very well be on her way to the grave. Then again, women are naturally stubborn. I think it's something in our genetic code.

Soon enough, the sound of running water ceased and I forced the concern from my expression. She emerged from the bathroom with a bundle of soiled clothes in one hand while the other held one of the white motel towels around her body. I sat on the edge of the bed as she dropped the used garments to the floor and walked over to me.

"I need to get my clothes washed before I put them on again," she said.

"It's payday," I reminded. "We'll buy you new ones."

"And what am I supposed to wear until then?"

I could hear the challenge in her voice and she almost smiled when I lifted my hands to grasp the edge of the towel.

"I don't think you really need to worry about clothes right now."

*****

"Another day, another hundred and fifty bucks."

I absently kicked a stone across the sidewalk as I headed towards the alley. It was the beginning of summer and I was sweating up a storm in my coat, but there was no way in hell I was about to take it off. I might get a few odd looks for wandering around with it on in the middle of the night, but it was better than getting arrested for carrying the weapons that it hid.

The same crappy music was playing in the club as I passed it, but the eighties were just around the corner. They couldn't come soon enough. I made the turn at the end of the building and stopped. The alley was empty and I couldn't wrap my mind around what that might mean.

"Hey Soph! You here?"

I wasn't really expecting an answer, but I moved forward anyway. Hopefully, I could find a sign of recent inhabitants. For all I knew, she might have gone out to find something to eat. I hoped she wasn't dead.

The squeal of tires drew my attention and I looked over to the street as I slid a hand into my coat. My eyes narrowed as I watched the black muscle car stop at the entrance to the alley. I couldn't determine the model from this distance, and the fact that the only street lamp on the block had long since burned out didn't help matters. The sound of Black Sabbath pouring from the speakers drowned out the sounds from the disco. It was a welcome change.

I couldn't help but stare as the driver stood up through the open T-tops. She disappeared long enough to turn down the stereo, but there was no mistaking the familiar grey eyes as she came back into view.

"Trina? Is that you?"

Her raspy voice and telltale smirk were enough to confirm her identity and I took a cautious step towards the car, hardly believing what my eyes were telling me.

"No fucking way."

The words had come out as a whisper, and I didn't realize I had spoken until I saw her lift a black eyebrow. How could she have changed so much in two years? It just didn't seem possible.

"I'm wastin' gas waiting on you," Soph said. "Get your ass in the car already."

Well, I had come out here looking for her and she had found me instead. I hesitated only a moment longer before climbing into the passenger seat. It wasn't until we were a few blocks away that I finally turned my head to study her.

Her health had improved drastically, but she looked almost as pale as I was. I probably could have blamed that on the dark eyeliner framing her eyes, but that theory didn't seem to hold water. I felt my hand inching towards one of my guns as she drove. Something was off about her, but I couldn't place it.

"Spill," I demanded.

"A lot can change in a couple of years," she said with a shrug.

"Don't bullshit me, Soph," I pressed. "Who's the new sugar daddy?"

"There ain't one."

"Sugar mama?" I guessed.

Her laughter made me tense even more. Her voice was still as raspy as it had been when I first met her, but her laugh was strong and vibrant. It made a chill run up my spine.

"Can we stop for something to eat?" I asked, changing the subject for now. "I'm buying."

"We'll stop, but I'm paying this time," she told me. "And don't try to argue with me. You've paid for enough stuff for me over the years. The least I can do is buy you dinner." Her gaze drifted over to me and her smirk faded. "I ain't seen you in two years and already you're reaching for your guns? I thought you trusted me."

"I do," I assured her as I released my grip on the weapon and forced a grin. "It's just been one of those nights."

I leaned back and tried to relax. I'd been killing zombies for too long, I told myself. This was Soph. There was nothing to be worried about. I should just be happy that she was healthy again. I couldn't bring myself to believe that, but I could chalk it up to paranoia.

We stayed at the diner only long enough for me to eat something. I kept my mouth shut when she didn't order anything and assumed she had eaten before meeting up with me. She paid the check, and we headed for her place.

I wasn't sure what to expect when we arrived at the apartment complex. It looked expensive, even for the middle-of-nowhere Kansas. Once inside, I took in the décor with one sweeping glance. It had to cost more than what I made in a month. I let a grin slide over my lips as I watched her drop down onto the leather sofa.

"No disco ball?" I teased.

"Disco sucks," she countered with a laugh.

"How the hell did you land this place?" I asked as I sat down beside her.

"Pure talent."

"Right." My humor faded as quickly as it had come. "What's going on, Soph? You can't hide shit from me. I know you too well."

"Can't we just be happy that we get to hang out again?" she asked. She would have looked hurt if that damn smirk of hers wasn't firmly in place. "We can talk about what happened tomorrow. For now..." Sliding over to me, she straddled my legs and pressed her body against mine. "I ain't seen you in two years so let's go ahead and make up for lost time."

Even as my arms wrapped around her, I could feel the indecision gnawing at me, but I pulled off my gloves and dropped them on the cushion beside us. Her skin was cool to the touch as my hands found their way under the back of her shirt, but I told myself it was just because of the air conditioning. My eyes closed as our lips met and I withdrew one of my hands, bringing it up with the intent to entwine it in her hair.

My fingertips brushed against the side of her neck, and everything clicked into place. I rested my palm against the side of her throat, just to be sure that I wasn't about to make a mistake. I let my hand fall back to her waist, my other one coming out from behind her to grasp her hips, and I roughly pushed her off of my lap.

She was on her feet before I was, but that didn't surprise me. In one motion, I pulled out one of my guns and flipped the safety off of it as I aimed it at her head. At least now things were starting to make sense.

"What the hell, Trina?" she snapped, her tone angry and hurt.

"You tell me," I said evenly. "You've got no pulse, Soph."

"I told you I'd explain it tomorrow," she said as she took a step forward.

"Stay back," I ordered.

"You're being stupid. Put the gun away before I take it from you."

"You'll explain right fucking now," I said. "Give me one good reason not to pull this trigger."

"Because no one else wants to put up with your shit," she retorted.

"Five seconds," I warned.

"Will you just chill for a minute?"

"Four."

"Trina..."

"Three."

"Please…"

"Two. Last chance."

"Fine," she said as she dropped back onto the sofa and folded her arms over her chest. "It ain't like I'm a different person."

"You're dead," I pointed out. "So, yeah, you are. What the hell are you?"

I had heard rumors years ago that there were things worse than zombies out there. Never before had I ever come face to face with one. Zombies were easy to deal with. They didn't think. They didn't talk back. And they didn't sit there with their mascara running down their face when you pointed a gun at them.

"Look, I didn't have a choice." Her usual, hard demeanor had given way to a pleading look in her eyes, and I had to remind myself that she wasn't the living, breathing girl I had rescued those years ago. "This crazy bitch thought I was her kid that died in the plague. I was sick, dying. How the hell was I supposed to fight her off? I could barely even keep my eyes open anymore. I woke up like this."

"And I'm supposed to feel sorry for you now?"

"You're supposed to be my friend." She looked away as she continued. "You were the only friend I had out there. I don't know what I am now. I ain't alive, but I'm still here. Can't eat food or drink beer." Her voice lowered, and I had to strain to hear her next words. "Only thing I can handle now is blood."

Bingo. That sealed the deal. I didn't wait for her to say anything else. I couldn't risk spending one more minute in that place. The door slammed against the wall as I pushed it open and rushed up the stairs. I hoped that she would take the hint and just let me go, but I wasn't that lucky. I heard her footsteps behind me and spun to face her, leveling the gun on her again.

"Stay the hell away from me," I said coldly.

"Trina, please…"

"No, Soph." I stared at her, trying not to think of all the good times we had shared. "You remember what I do for a living? I kill corpses that aren't smart enough to stay in the ground. What are you again?"

"I don't know!" she insisted.

"Well, I do," I said. "You're a vampire, Soph. A goddamn,

bloodsucking vampire. The only reason I'm not taking you down right now is because we used to be friends. But if you ever come near me again, or if I find you chowin' down on someone, I'll put a bullet in your skull so fast-"

"Used to be?" she interrupted. "I thought you'd at least try to understand." She kept talking even as I turned my back on her and started walking away. "Trina, wait. I need your help with this one. You're the one that knows about all this undead shit. All I have are a bunch of books that chick gave me and half of them I don't even understand."

"It helps if you know how to read."

"Fuck you."

I'd hit a nerve. Good. I wanted to hurt her. Maybe if I hurt her enough she wouldn't come looking for me. Maybe if I hurt her enough then I wouldn't feel the emptiness that was starting to spread through my chest.

"Fine then," she called after me. "Go back to your crusade. Have fun with it. So much for having one person I could trust in this whole damn world."

I didn't respond. I just kept walking and didn't look back. The only reason I had kept coming back to this part of the country was to check on her. I couldn't help but risk a glance as I turned the corner, and I half expected her to be right there behind me, maybe even ready to kill me. Instead, all I could see was the heartbroken expression on her pale features.

*****

Six months had passed before I was able to swallow my pride. I stood at the bottom of the steps with my hand poised to knock, but I still wondered whether this was the right decision. I winced at the pain shooting up my arm as my knuckles fell upon the door and managed to straighten my shoulders a split second before it opened.

"Didn't expect to see you again," Soph said as she leaned in the doorway. "What do you want?"

"Can I come in?" I asked.

She offered a shrug in response as she moved aside. The interior hadn't changed much in my absence, and I felt my pulse quicken when she closed the door. Anyone with sense would be at least a little afraid of walking right into a vampire's home. I took a seat on the couch but didn't look up when I heard her voice.

"You smell wrong."

10

"Says the corpse," I said without thinking. I sighed and leaned forward to rest me elbows on my knees. "I'm dying Soph."

"Sorry about your luck."

"And you're still pissed off at me," I realized. "Great."

"The last time I had a problem, you pulled a gun on me," she said.

"I know." I couldn't bring myself to meet her gaze, so I stared at my hands instead. "I panicked, alright? I guess I went a little overboard."

"A little?" she repeated incredulously. "You told me you'd put a bullet in my skull if I ever came near you again and now you want me to feel sorry for you? Piss off, Trina."

I deserved that one. There was no denying it. I had to try to make peace with her, though.

"Soph…"

"No," she interrupted. "What do you want from me? You think I'm gonna put out just because you're dying? Or am I supposed to nurse you back to health? I don't think so. Get one of your other bitches to do it."

"There aren't any others. Like you said, no one else will put up with my shit." A bitter laugh escaped my lips as I shook my head. "Besides, there's no getting back to health at this point. If I'm lucky, I might have two or three more days before I keel over. I just need you to make sure I stay dead."

"Don't ask me to do you any favors."

"I figured you'd at least jump at the chance to put me out of my misery."

It was a cheap shot and I knew it. I looked up as she walked past and I followed her with my eyes as she walked into the kitchen. A pair of studded, leather gloves on the end table captured my gaze and I looked at her again. I was certain that she hated me, but the fact that my gloves were still sitting here contradicted that. I pushed myself up from the sofa and grabbed them on my way into the kitchen.

"Get out."

She didn't turn to face me. I didn't blame her. Her palms rested on the counter as if it were the only thing holding her up at the moment, and I dropped the gloves onto the marble surface beside her.

"Why did you keep them?" I asked.

"The same reason I still keep beer in the fridge."

"You wanted me to come back." I couldn't keep the astonishment out of my voice. When she nodded, I could only stare at her. "Then why are you trying to throw me out?"

"Because you're just gonna leave me again," she said quietly. "You stormed out of here last time and now you came back just to die on me. I can't handle it. You were the only one I had. I finally got over what happened between us, and I don't think I can go through that again."

"At least this time, we can part on better terms." It was the only thing I could offer at this point, but she was shaking her head. "Look, it's not like I want to die. It's going to happen anyway. I got careless and one of them got a lucky shot on me. I'm already contaminated and there's no cure. The only thing I can do now is make the most of the last couple of days I have left and hope that you'll make sure I don't come back as one of them."

I stepped over to stand behind her and wrapped my arms around her waist. She tensed at my touch, but slowly relaxed and leaned back against me. I hadn't realized just how much I had missed her, and it was hard to reconcile the fact that after another day or so, I'd never see her again. I could have stayed like that with her forever.

As we stood there, she whispered the words that would change everything. Maybe I had come to her just to hear them, but I hadn't expected her to actually say them aloud. I both hoped and dreaded them, but I knew my answer before they were spoken.

"What if you don't have to die?"

One

It had taken six months of hard work, but things were finally returning to normal. Repairs had been made to the barracks, and a new fence had been installed around the perimeter of the facility. The personnel had to make adjustments, and while there was still tension between the human and vampire staff members, very few fights had broken out.

Mikhail gave the file a cursory glance before sliding it back across his desk.

"Waste of time," he said. "The worst this guy's done is cheat on his wife. He's not worth the effort." Looking up at the clock on the wall he continued. "We'll pick this up later. I have an appointment in five minutes."

"Sure thing." Jerome lifted the folder and left the room.

Mikhail offered a nod before turning his attention to the computer screen. Spring was in full swing and the open window offered a pleasant breeze. He could hear the sound of methodical gunfire from the ranges, but he remained focused on the information before him.

"Right on time," he muttered as the phone rang. Lifting the receiver, he leaned back in his chair. "What did you find out?"

"One of these days it would be nice to get a simple 'hello'," Rhonda said with a sigh.

"Fine." His eyes narrowed as he looked at the monitor again. "Hello, Rhonda. How are you tonight? And by the way, have you found out why the hell I'm paying these two assholes every month?"

"Your company has apparently been paying them for almost forty years," the accountant said. "Have you been able to get into the files?"

"Finally," he said. "Someone took a lot of time to encrypt the hell out of them. At one time, all twelve of them were active. Now, there are only two, but they've been working since the seventies."

"What happened to the others?"

"It varies," Mikhail said. "A few retired, a few were killed in action, and a few just disappeared altogether."

"It stands to reason that these two will probably follow suit," Rhonda said. "If they've been active for four decades, then it's likely that they're preparing for retirement."

"I don't know," Mikhail said thoughtfully. "Something doesn't feel right here. Each of these guys had a specialty, and I'm talking off-the-wall shit here. No last names are listed on their files, but out of the two remaining, one has been getting paid to hunt zombies and the other one is just listed as 'Various'. I'm willing to bet that they're not exactly human."

"It sounds like you've found more information on them than I have," she said. "The only thing that I see is that they're paid salary while everyone else has expense accounts when they're on the job and a flat fee when it's completed." There was a pause on the other end of the line and the sound of keystrokes. "One of them has a company-paid penthouse in London."

"What about the other one?"

"Nothing," Rhonda said. "The only thing I have is a first name and bank account. I tried contacting the bank, but they won't release any more information."

"This is bullshit," Mikhail said flatly. "We need to get them in here. I want answers. We're paying them for something and apparently, they're getting special treatment. That's not how we operate."

"I recommend meeting with them here," the accountant said. "I'll call in extra security personnel, and that way I'll have the figures right in front of me."

"Fair enough," he conceded. "Let's hope the contact information is accurate. How are the rest of the numbers looking?"

"Business is good," Rhonda said. "Even with the policy changes over the past few months and the repair expenses, you're still making a decent profit. I took the liberty of transferring some of the funds into a high-interest savings account. It'll come in handy in case you have any unexpected maintenance in the future."

"Smart move," he agreed. "I'll be in touch."

Without waiting for a response, he hung up the phone and selected one of the files on the computer, reading the information to himself. Name, Alex S. Alias, Malice. Location, London, UK. There was no phone number listed, but a link to what he assumed was an e-mail address. It's better than nothing.

The mouse icon hovered over the link for a moment before he clicked on it. Instead of rerouting to his mail client, a video box popped up. Mikhail's left eye twitched as he waited for it to connect, and he kept his expression an otherwise emotionless mask when he saw the man on the other end. Damn. Sometimes I hate being right.

The man was younger than expected – late twenties, early thirties at most – and his features were unblemished except for the scar that crossed from his forehead to just below his right eye. He seemed about to offer a greeting, but instead stared at the unfamiliar face on his screen.

"You're not Jack," he said.

"Observant." He risked a smirk but wiped it away almost immediately. "Alex, I presume?"

"Where is he?"

"I wish I knew," Mikhail said truthfully. "I'm running things now."

"Is that so?"

"Last time I checked." He sighed and shook his head. "Look, I didn't contact you so that we could bullshit all night. My accountant and I have been sorting through the records, and your name came up. I'd like to meet with you so that we can discuss your arrangement with the company."

"I'm not some lapdog to come at your beck and call," Alex said. "I'll stop by when I can fit it into my schedule."

"That's not how it works," Mikhail said. "I don't know what kind of arrangement you had with Jack, but I'm in charge now. I know everyone on our payroll personally. I've taken the time to meet with them in person over the last six months, and you're one of the only ones I haven't spoken to yet."

"Sorry about your luck." He leaned closer, offering a smirk of his own. "I'll meet with you, but it'll be on my terms, and because I want to meet the one claiming to be my new boss."

"Listen, Malice," he said, his patience fading. "We can do this one of two ways. You can meet me in Philadelphia next week so we can get this sorted out, or I can take you off of our payroll. I suggest you take Option One."

"Let me make one thing perfectly clear, sheep."

As Mikhail watched, the image became distorted. The man's features began to shift, his mouth and nose replaced by a black muzzle crawling with glowing tattoos. As the connection began to break into static, he distinctly heard the creature's voice. Each word was clipped short, as if the beast was snapping his jaws after each one.

"I. Am. Not. Your. Bitch."

*****

At nine o'clock on a Wednesday night, most office buildings in Philadelphia were dark. The regular nine-to-five staff had departed to spend the evening with their families and loved ones.

At Evans International, the building was crawling with activity. The security team was running one final check on their equipment while the occupants of the top floor were making preparations for a potentially volatile meeting.

Rhonda Evans looked up at the associates surrounding her desk, her expression grim as she gathered a small stack of files. Rising from the leather chair, she handed the folders to her personal assistant and headed for the door.

"O'Donnell," she began, addressing the Chief of Security. "How many do we have tonight?"

"We're at double staff," Sean said. "I made sure that we mixed the coverage as an added precaution."

"Smart move," Ian agreed. He straightened his leather jacket before turning his attention to Rhonda. "I'll wait up here until they start to filter in, but don't even think of asking me to put on a suit."

"I think we all know you better than that," the accountant stated. "Make sure Euro is downstairs to meet our guests. I want to know what exactly we're dealing with before they get on that elevator." She turned to her assistant before speaking again. "Miss Bonner, is everything ready?"

"Yes, Ms. Evans," Marielle said. "I had catering bring in coffee and pastries as a courtesy. Also, Euro provided alternate refreshments in case any of them prefer that instead. It's all in Conference Room One."

Rhonda nodded her approval as they stepped out of the office. Crossing the black tile floor, she caught sight of one of her business associates exiting the elevator.

The mercenary looked much the same as he had the last time they had met. The only difference was that his previous military-style garb had been replaced by a custom-tailored, charcoal grey suit. His brown hair hung loose, drifting past his shoulders, and he absently brushed a strand away from his face as he stopped before them.

"Mikhail," Rhonda greeted, extending a hand. "How was your flight?"

"Not bad," he said. He grasped her hand long enough to shake before letting his arm fall back to his side. "Those private jets are something I could get used to. Either of them show up yet?"

"So far, no." Rhonda glanced at Ian, noticing the scowl on his face, and then returned her attention to Mikhail. "We still have about half an hour before they're expected to arrive. As per our agreement, we have plenty of security personnel on location."

"They better be armed," he said.

"We are," Sean assured him. He frowned, listening to the transmission through his ear piece, and pressed the button in the sleeve of his suit coat. "Stand by. I'm en route." Returning his attention to the others, he continued. "It looks like we have our first arrival, but there seems to be a situation."

"What kind of situation?" Rhonda asked.

"She brought a friend with her and is refusing to come up unless she's allowed to accompany her."

"Human or other?"

"Other."

"Mackenzie," Rhonda began. "Go down there with O'Donnell and handle it. Try to get her up here by herself, but if he's adamant about bringing her friend, then we'll make an exception."

The pair stepped into the elevator without a word. As they reached the ground floor, the doors whispered open with a chime. Even from the corridor, they could hear the sound of raised voices. Ian could distinguish the words clearly and his eyes narrowed as he cast a glance at his partner.

"Make sure you have your gun ready," he advised. "She sounds pissed. Expect trouble."

The Chief of Security gave a barely perceptible nod and folded his arms over his chest, one hand slipping into his blazer to grasp his service weapon. As they neared the main lobby, the first visitors came into view.

The pair seemed too different to be together. The only thing they had in common was the pallor of their skin. One of the women was a striking blonde, her blue eyes clearly showing her frustration. A grey trench coat was open in the front, revealing part of the tailored suit beneath it.

The other woman, who was currently arguing with Euro, was clad mostly in black leather. A tank top ended just above the leather pants that hung on her hips. Black eyeliner framed her eyes, matching the color of both her lips and hair. A backpack was slung over one shoulder, but the shift of her grey eyes to red caused Ian to quicken his pace.

"Is there a problem?" he asked, glancing between Euro and the couple.

"Who the hell are you?" The demand came from the leather-clad woman, her attention snapping over to Ian and Sean.

"Yes, there is a problem," her companion replied calmly.

"Well, let's see if we can resolve this without any incidents," Ian stated with a glance at Sean. "Did you bring the access list down with you?"

"Right here," Sean replied. Releasing his hold on the gun, he pulled a folded sheet of paper from one of the inner pockets and opened it. "Can I have your names, please?"

"Trina," the albino said. "This is my girl, Soph."

"I'm sure you were informed that this is a private meeting." Sean tried to keep his heart rate down, knowing that showing even a hint of fear to this pair would cause more problems than he needed at the moment. "In the interest of confidentiality, we have to ask that she wait downstairs until business is concluded."

"This is bullshit," Soph snarled.

"Chill, babe," Trina told her before addressing Sean again. "We're a package deal. Either she comes up with me or we say 'to hell with it' and go home."

"What's in the bag?" Ian interrupted.

"Kittens," Soph said with a smirk.

"Books," her companion stated with an irritated glance in her direction.

"We're gonna to have to take a look for ourselves," Euro informed them.

"If you put one hand on my stuff, I'll rip it off and shove it up your ass," Soph promised.

Ian lifted a hand to pinch the bridge of his nose, wincing at the phantom migraine that he could almost feel. Had he been mortal, he knew this situation would have warranted at least a dose of aspirin. Reaching for his phone, he sent a quick text message and waited a moment for the response.

"Alright," he said finally. "We can sort this out upstairs. The elevator will take you to the top floor and we'll have someone up there to meet you."

*****

"It would have been nice to have the empath here," Mikhail remarked.

"Well, she's tied up trying to get her business started," Rhonda said with a shrug. "Besides, her family is coming into town tomorrow night." Turning her attention to her assistant, she continued. "Miss Bonner, escort our visitors to the conference room when they arrive."

"You're going to let her handle them alone?" Mikhail arched a brow.

"She'll be fine," Rhonda said as she started down the corridor.

They walked past the elevators and had almost reached the corner when the metal doors opened with a chime. The tail-end of the conversation within drifted to them, and they took a moment to listen to what little they could hear.

"The point is, I'm not about to lose my job over your 'pissed at the world' attitude. Tone it down a bit."

"Fine," her companion conceded, although her tone was reluctant. "I'll try to behave."

Mikhail froze, turning slowly as he recognized the raspy, feminine voice. His eyes narrowed, one hand sliding into the folds of his suit jacket. Rhonda paused, realizing that she was apparently talking to herself, and frowned. Her gaze drifted between the arriving couple and her associate, taking stock of the situation.

"Sophia." It wasn't much of an explanation, but the mercenary declined to elaborate. Instead, he stared at the dark-haired woman, open hostility in his eyes.

"Can we at least try to get this meeting started before you shoot anyone?" Rhonda's tone was impatient, and she kept her voice low in hopes that it would go unnoticed by their guests.

As Mikhail gave a curt nod, he watched Marielle greet the pair, and then turned to resume his course.

"Holy shit, man," Euro said as he watched the figure enter through the automatic doors. "It's your evil twin."

"And here I thought I was the evil twin," Ian said.

He was certain that he had never met the man before, but the similarities were unnerving. The same sandy, blond hair crowned his head, but the crystal blue eyes that regarded them were fierce and predatory. His visage was marred by a thin, hair-line scar that crossed from his forehead to just below his right eye. Even the manner of attire was the same.

"I killed stupid," Ian read the bold white lettering on the man's black t-shirt. "Haven't seen that one before."

"Trust me, he deserved it." The visitor pulled the headphones from his ears as he regarded them, his expression conveying the fact that he was less than impressed. "Two corpses and a sheep. Just how I wanted to spend my night."

"We're thrilled to have you here," Sean said dryly. "Name, please?"

"Alex." The single word came out as a growl and his eyes flashed yellow for a brief moment before returning to their previous hue.

"This'll be fun," Ian muttered. "The meeting is taking place in Executive Conference Room One. We'll escort you up."

"Should I feel special?"

Ian ignored the remark as he turned and headed for the elevators. Sean lingered for a moment, lowering his voice as he addressed Euro.

"Lockdown procedures," he ordered. "I want to make sure no one accesses the top floor until this meeting is over. No one is to enter the building at all. Disable the elevators and lock all card readers as soon as I give the signal."

"Got it."

*****

Rhonda scrawled a few notes on the legal pad in front of her before glancing up at the others. Marielle was seated to her right at the large, round table with a similar notepad in her hands. Mikhail sat opposite of Marielle, doing everything he could to keep his expression impassive. Occasionally, he would lift his gaze to regard Soph. If the woman recognized him at all, she didn't show it. Instead, she sat on the floor against the wall, rummaging through her backpack.

Trina cradled a glass in a gloved hand and lifted it to sip the crimson liquid within, waiting patiently for the meeting to begin. She kept an empty seat between herself and her new employer, but she glanced around to take stock of the other occupants. Her gaze strayed to the seven suited men placed around the perimeter of the room, guessing them to be a security detail in case the encounter went sour. Only two of the figures possessed a heartbeat.

The door opened and Ian entered, followed by Sean and the man they assumed to be Alex. Ian took a seat beside Marielle and Sean moved to stand with his team.

Alex paused, glancing over them before striding over to the table. He reached forward, grasping the plate of pastries, and took it with him to an unoccupied seat before finally sinking into the chair.

"Coffee and donuts?" he asked skeptically. "That's it? No steak and beer?" He shook his head slightly before nodding towards Soph. "At least you hired a stripper so I guess this isn't a total waste of my time."

"I'd watch my mouth if I were you," Trina said, her eyes narrowing. She cast a glance at her wife, mainly to convey that she should remain quiet. It didn't work.

"What the hell did you just call me?" she demanded.

"Ladies and gentlemen, please," Rhonda interrupted sternly. "The sooner we get started the less time this will take. Mikhail, if you would…"

"I'm going to make this simple," Mikhail began. "I'm running Jack-O-Lantern now and I want to get a few details cleared up. Trina, we'll start with you."

As he opened one of the files, he watched her nod while Alex simply rolled his eyes and replaced his headphones in his ears.

"You've been listed as active since the early seventies," Mikhail stated. "It says here that you specialize in hunting zombies. Is that correct?"

"Yes," she said. "Not too many of them around these days, though. The last time we suspected an outbreak was in the late nineties."

"But your salary hasn't been reduced," Rhonda added. "Actually, it looks like it's been going up by ten percent every three years."

"Blame inflation," Trina said with a shrug. "It's not my fault the economy sucks."

"Given the amount of activity versus your salary, I believe it would be in my client's best interests to renegotiate your contract," Rhonda said.

"My contract is fine the way it is," Trina said evenly.

"How can you justify your current salary when you said yourself that there is little for you to do?" Rhonda pressed.

"Zombies were my main specialty," she said. "I was also called in to handle problem vamps until someone got the bright idea to start training the humans."

Alex pretended to tune them out. His fingers adjusted the volume on his MP3 player to the point where he was sure even the humans could hear the music. Grabbing a pastry from the tray, he took a bite out of it while slowly spinning in his chair.

His attempt to alleviate the boredom was interrupted as a crumpled piece of paper struck him in the back of the head. He stopped suddenly, a brow arching as he regarded Soph. She had a leather-bound book on her lap and a spiral notepad on the floor beside it. Glancing from the notepad to the paper, Alex quickly determined the source of the disturbance.

He took another bite of the pastry, chewing it for a moment before hurling the rest of it at the woman on the floor. Her hand shot up to catch it and she grasped it just long enough to throw it back at him.

"What the fuck is this? Romp-a-room?" Mikhail demanded.

"Don't look at me," Alex said with a shrug. "The hooker started it. What the hell is she doing here anyway?"

"Soph helps me out every now and then," Trina said, quickly losing patience.

"Then why isn't she listed in your file?" Mikhail asked.

"Because Jack-O-Lantern still has the 'No Girls Allowed' sign posted on the clubhouse," Soph stated. "I heard it was a pain in the ass for you guys to make an exception for Trina."

"Great," Alex muttered. "She's a feminist too. Watch out people. She'll be burning her bra any second now."

"Do you ever shut up?" Soph retorted.

"Do you want to try to make me?" he said.

"Can we at least pretend to be professional?" Rhonda said irritably.

The others looked at her, and there were a couple disgruntled musings, but the bickering had ceased for the moment. Trina shook her head as she rose to her feet.

"I'm done with this," she said. "You want to discuss my contract? Fine. We'll discuss it when this asshole isn't here."

She glared at Alex, who simply smirked, and then turned towards the door. Soph gathered her books, quickly replacing them in her backpack as she stood and followed.

"By the way, Soph," Alex began as he watched them leave. "The nineties called. They want their fashion back."

There was a snarl from the other side of the doorway, but Trina's calm – if annoyed – voice was heard above it.

"He's not worth it, babe."

*****

Eyes the color of sunset slowly gazed out over the city. Her wings shifted nervously as one hand rested on the cool head of the sculpted eagle. From her perch, she could see buildings stretching out beneath her and her lips turned into a frown.

Glass, metal, and the occasional stone structure, were observed silently as she sighed. This was all wrong.

She glanced up at the statue a few feet above her, the significance of the figure escaping her comprehension. She had chosen this building as a brief resting point because it seemed to be one of the few that still held some life to it. The cold, unfeeling glass and metal ones were too alien for her to feel comfortable.

Crouching down, she strained to see the strange metal constructs moving along the dark, stone ground. The red eyes at their backs caused her to shudder, and she wondered why she had arrived here when she crossed the shimmering doorway.

A slight breeze drifted over her, sending her hair across the feathers of her wings. She straightened, taking a moment to check the current, and then leapt from the edge. Stretching her wings out, she caught the wind and let it carry her away from her temporary refuge.

*****

"Never again," Trina said.

"I should have shot him," Soph said, ignoring the remark. "He would have deserved it."

"This is why I don't take you to meetings," she told her. "For once, it'd be nice if you could keep your goddamn temper in check."

23

Soph rolled her eyes as she pressed down on the accelerator. A quick glance in the rear-view mirror showed the lights of Philadelphia growing smaller as the car picked up speed. A speck of movement caught her attention, and she turned her head to stare up through the open back of the car.

With the top down on the convertible, she had an unobstructed view of a vaguely humanoid figure in the sky. Before she could focus on it, she heard Trina's voice again.

"Christ, Soph! Watch the road!"

She faced forward again, cat-like reflexes correcting the direction of the vehicle as she narrowly avoided hitting the guardrail. The angry blare of a horn behind her prompted a low growl as she looked in the mirror again.

There was no sign of the figure and she returned her attention to her companion.

"Stop being a baby," she said. "It's not like I'm going to kill us if I crash this thing."

"Yes, but getting in a wreck on the side of the Schuylkill Expressway isn't on my list of things to do tonight."

"Other than wasting half the night driving to and from Philly for a bullshit meeting, what is on your to-do list tonight?"

"Well," Trina began, leaning back in the passenger seat. "We've got a few hours before sunrise. Might as well grab some dinner and call it an early night. I'm sure we can keep ourselves occupied at home."

Soph offered a low, raspy laugh as a sign of agreement, and a comfortable silence fell between them. Trina seemed content to let the earlier issue drop. It was one of the things Soph loved about her. She'd voice her disagreement with whatever had been done, but once it was said, it was over.

Soph, however, had more of a temper. She could stay angry for months on end, sometimes playing out her discontent violently. That was one of the reasons they had moved away from the city to the quiet house on the outskirts of Malvern. They had plenty of land surrounding the home and few neighbors to complain about her temper.

They were three miles from their exit when Trina leaned forward. Despite the high speed at which they were traveling, she placed her hands on top of the windshield and stood, staring ahead in the distance.

"What to have some fun?" she asked, glancing down at her. When

Soph arched a brow, she looked forward again. "We got a disabled vehicle about a mile ahead on the right. At least two people inside; maybe more. It's hard to tell from here." She dropped back into his seat. "Pull over and let me out. I'll call you when I'm coming through the woods."

Soph eased back on the accelerator and pressed down on the brakes, bringing the car over to the shoulder. Before the convertible had even come to a complete stop, Trina was out of it and climbing over the guardrail.

She glanced up long enough to watch Soph speed off and then dropped to the ground. She made good time as she rushed away from the highway, her steps taking the route that she had traveled many times before.

It wasn't until she was a mile from their home that he finally slowed to an easy walk. Her mind thought forward to what would be waiting at the house and she let a smirk cross her lips. Maybe tonight won't be a total waste after all.

Once she had crossed the property line, she checked the time on her phone. She should be there by now, she thought. Before she could press the button to call her, she caught a strange scent on the air.

Trina stopped, her eyes darting around as she tried to determine what she was sensing. She had walked through the woods enough to distinguish each animal that made the trees its home, but this was completely foreign.

Closing her eyes, she inhaled deeply, listening at the same time. There it is. Blue eyes snapped open and she turned to the left. Definitely a heartbeat, but it almost sounds human. There were "No Trespassing" signs throughout the property, but apparently, they had done little to deter whoever was hiding out there.

The scent was wrong, though. She knew she was heading in the right direction; at least, that's what her senses were telling her. One hand withdrew one of her sawed-off shotguns – more out of habit than necessity – and she stalked between the trees in search of the elusive trespasser.

A soft rustle of leaves drew her gaze towards the sky, and she caught movement within the branches. Too big for an animal, she realized. She debated for a moment, trying to decide whether to pursue whoever was up there or to call out and see if it might come down.

A long, golden-hued feather drifted down to land on the ground in front of her, and she dropped to a crouch to examine it. What the hell? She picked it up in her free hand, turning it over before staring up into the trees again. She sniffed the feather and found that it lacked the same scent that most of the resident birds possessed. Instead, it matched what she had been following.

The vibration of her phone interrupted her search and she read the message quickly. Shaking her head, she abandoned the diversion and started towards her house again. After replacing her shotgun beneath her coat, she tucked the feather into one of the inner pockets and finally made the phone call.

"It's show time, babe."

*****

"Next time, we meet with them separately," Rhonda stated.

"I was hoping there wouldn't be a next time," Ian said. "I swear, if I could still get headaches, I'd have a migraine right about now."

"Lucky you, then," Mikhail said as he rubbed his temples. "That was complete and total bullshit."

There were no arguments. Rhonda poured two glasses of brandy and handed one to the mercenary before dropping into the leather chair behind her desk. Mikhail gave a brief nod of thanks and winced as he heard the sound of high heels crossing the floor, each footstep increasing the throbbing sensation in his skull.

A bottle of aspirin was placed on the desk and Marielle waited a moment before speaking.

"Sean just called back," she said. "He just spoke with the officer that Euro sent over and the place is empty."

"I can't believe someone broke into it again," Ian said. "Why do we even have security over there if people can just walk right into the owner's apartment?"

"Well, here's the weird part," Marielle continued. "The lock wasn't picked at all. They think that it was unlocked from the inside. Also, the motion sensors on the other floors weren't activated. Whoever was inside took the stairs up to the roof and left from there."

"And we're sure it wasn't the owners?" Rhonda asked.

"Positive," she said. "Sean spoke with Cassandra. The family is still in Zalyndrya until tomorrow night. It wasn't them."

"Have fun figuring that one out," Mikhail said before downing the brandy. "I'm heading to the hotel. Maybe tomorrow I might actually get

26

something accomplished before I fly home."

"I scheduled a meeting with Trina," Marielle offered. "I figured that it would be easier to get the details of her contract settled if you meet with just her. She even agreed to leave her wife at home."

Hearing the sound of the phone on her desk, she turned and hurried from the room. Ian watched her depart, a slight grin playing about his lips.

"And that is why she's worth every penny of her salary," Rhonda stated as she glanced up at Ian. "Now if I could only get her ex to stop staring at her ass every time she leaves the room, I'd be happy."

Two

Mikhail had taken the first flight back to Boston as soon as the next meeting had concluded. While it had gone much smoother than the first, it had given him a lot to think about. He decided that his first order of business when he returned home would be to dig a little deeper. Not just on the pair he had dealt with over the past two nights, but on all twelve names in the file.

It was a logical assumption that none of the secret operatives knew about each other. The animosity between Alex and Trina was enough proof of that. The recent memory of that first meeting brought him to another subject that he didn't want to deal with: Sophia.

He'd been fresh out in the field when he'd first encountered her. Mistaking her for his target at the time had almost cost him his life, but the operative he'd been shadowing hadn't been as lucky.

Shaking his head, he pushed that issue to the back of his mind.

His car was waiting when he stepped out of the baggage claim area and Jerome handed the keys to him. The Cadillac CTS-V was a definite step up from the older model that he had once owned, and he felt at ease when he slid behind the wheel. Turning the key in the ignition, he frowned at the gauges.

"How much did you drive this thing while I was gone?" he asked. "I know I had a full tank three days ago."

"Had to go pick up Caleb from Maine," Jerome replied. "Your car runs better than mine."

"It should. I'll have to stop on the way back to the office."

Letting the subject drop, he checked the time and mentally calculated how much of it he could allot to the tasks he had waiting on his desk. I should still be able to get everything done tonight, he thought as he pulled into the gas station. The pair stepped out, and he handed Jerome some cash.

"Pay for thirty in the tank and get me a cup of coffee," he told him.

29

"Pay for the gas first."

A cool breeze scattered a stray newspaper, sending it across the lot as he waited for the pump to activate. It didn't take long to refuel, and he quickly replaced the gas cap, but his calm was broken as he felt the hairs rise on the back of his neck seconds before he was addressed.

"You've cleaned up well, Mikhail."

He turned towards the speaker, his hand quickly withdrawing one of his guns from the folds of his coat. The weapon was almost raised completely when he recognized the melodic, accented voice that had addressed him, and he replaced the gun in its holster as he shook his head slightly.

"You shouldn't sneak up on people like that," he muttered. "Especially when you know they're armed."

"It's not as if you haven't tried to shoot me before," Lalasa said with a soft laugh.

"Yeah, you've got a point." He almost grinned as he briefly thought of their first meeting, and then he took note of her appearance. Her Glamour was in place, hiding her true features beneath a mask of humanity. Something still seemed out of place, though. Her smile, although genuine, seemed strained, and he got the distinct feeling that this wasn't just a social call. "Where's your husband?"

"He is in Philadelphia visiting Cassandra," she said.

"So, why are you here without him?"

"Do you always ask so many questions when you haven't seen someone in several months?" A slight smile returned to her lips as she arched a brow.

"You're being evasive," he stated, turning to lean back on the car. "Which means something's going on, but you don't want to talk about it in a gas station parking lot."

"Perhaps."

Movement out of the corner of his eye caught his attention and he turned his head to regard the wolf stepping around the front of his car. Returning his gaze to Lalasa, he watched her eyes flick over to the approaching mercenary before settling on him again.

"I suppose this is not the best time." she said.

Jerome slowed his pace, glancing between them uneasily. He was obviously unsettled by her presence, but as he took stock of the situation, he realized that neither of them seemed threatened by the other. His eyes widened briefly as he noticed the wolf nudging his employer for attention.

"Jerome, you remember Lady Konistav," Mikhail said. When she arched a brow at the use of her proper title, he smirked. "I did my homework."

"So, I see," she said before turning her gaze to Jerome. "Well met."

He offered a tense nod in response before handing a cup of coffee to Mikhail.

"Alright, get in and we'll talk about this back at my office," Mikhail stated. Casting a glance at Shade, he paused. "If he screws up the leather, you're paying for it."

"Naturally."

Jerome sullenly climbed into the back seat as Mikhail stepped around to the other side of the car and opened the back door for the wolf. As soon as Shade was inside, he closed the door and slid into the driver's seat before bringing the key to the ignition. He glanced over at Lalasa when the vehicle didn't respond.

"Think you can turn down the magic a bit?" he asked. "These newer models are computerized."

She inclined her head slightly, the amber ring on her finger flashing once as she dismissed her Glamour, and her half-elven heritage was revealed.

"Better?"

"Much," he said as he turned the key again.

*****

Black cowboy boots were propped up on the railing as Soph leaned back in the chair on the back porch. A large, leather-bound book was open on her lap, a notepad resting on the arm of the chair. Her brow furrowed in thought as she read the paragraph again, trying to grasp the meaning of the words.

More than once, she almost threw the book across the yard in frustration. She was able to guess at a few of the words, but the rest of them stubbornly refused her attempts at translation. After a few more minutes, she set it aside and picked up another one. Thankfully, this one was mostly written in English.

Before she could get started, she heard a rustling in the trees along

31

the field. Glancing up, she searched for the source of the noise, her darkly-painted lips turning into a frown. It's a bit early for her to be back, she thought.

Soph set the book aside and stood, the heels of her boots echoing across the wooden floor as she approached the short flight of stairs. Her eyes narrowed as she caught a glimpse of movement, and she almost considered going inside to retrieve her gun. She dismissed the thought almost instantly and descended the stairs onto the grass.

She focused on the small tree house nestled in the branches of one of the tall maples, certain that the sound had come from that area. Pausing, she listened closely, catching movement within the elevated structure. Her steps took her forward again, and she stopped a few feet away, her hands resting on her hips.

"Whoever is up there has five seconds to get down here before I come in after you," she said.

There was a nervous rustling from within, followed by silence. I should go up there anyway, she thought. Now that she was close, she could hear the sound of a rapidly beating heart. They're scared. Well, they should be.

"Last chance," she warned.

When no response came, she stalked forward and easily climbed up into the branches. As soon as she stepped through the open doorway, her gaze settled on the figure crouched in the corner. Its presence wasn't as surprising as its appearance, and a dark eyebrow lifted as she regarded it.

Her eyes adjusted easily to the shadowy interior, and the first thing she noticed were the wings wrapped around the form. She assumed it was an attempt to hide from her sight, but her boots sounded on the floor as she took a step forward.

"The whole ostrich technique doesn't really work," she said.

She wasn't expecting a response. After all, it was unlikely that the bird-creature would even understand her. Contrary to that thought, the wings opened, revealing the visitor. Pale orange eyes regarded Soph, set within a face that closely resembled a human's. The girl's golden hair spilled over her shoulders as her wings folded over her back. She made no attempt to move, but her eyes darted to the second doorway behind her.

"What the hell are you?" Soph asked, her own eyes wide with

surprise.

"I..." She hesitated, fear coming off of her in waves. "My apologies. I was simply hoping for a place to rest. I did not mean to intrude."

"At least you speak English," Soph said. She couldn't place the accent, but whatever the girl was, she apparently had the ability to communicate. "That still doesn't tell me what you're supposed to be."

"You are not familiar with my people," she said, frowning.

"Well, I ain't never met someone with wings."

"The rest of my people do not have them. Mine were an accident."

"You think you can start making sense sometime soon?" The novelty of the strange creature was starting to give way to impatience, and Soph began to debate the pros and cons of killing her just to save herself from further annoyance. "I'm going to ask you one more time, and you'd better have an answer this time. What are you and what the hell are you doing on my property?"

"The second question I have already answered," she said quietly, edging towards the opening in the wall. "As for what I am... Have you never met an elf before now?" Shifting uncomfortably under the steel grey gaze, she struggled to find the right words. "I had to leave my home."

"So, you ran away or they kicked you out?"

"Both, I suppose."

Soph pondered her words for a moment. Something about them touched a nerve and her usual, cold stare softened ever so slightly. She knew what it was like to be lost with no one to turn to. Granted, it had been at least forty years since she had been in that position, but she remembered all too well how bad it could be.

"I guess it ain't hurting nothing for you to hang out up here," she said finally. "Not sure how long you can stay, though. I'll have to think about it."

"If you require payment," the elf began timidly, "I can trade some of my possessions in exchange for lodging. I have very little money, but I do have a few items of value."

"This ain't a pawn shop." Before she could elaborate, her cell phone rang and she lifted it to her ear, her gaze never leaving the elf. "Yeah?" She paused, listening. "I'm out back in the tree house. We have a problem." Another pause. "Right. I'll meet you down there." Replacing the phone in the case on her studded belt, she focused her attention on the strange visitor.

"Stay here. I'll be back in a few."

Ducking out of the small building, she climbed back down to the grass and walked a few yards away. Trina came into view as she exited the back door of the house, and her steps brought her to stand before Soph. She glanced past her, catching the unique, but familiar scent on the wind.

"What's going on?" she asked, her gaze returning to Soph.

"Before you freak out, let me explain," she began. "We've got a girl up in the tree over there, but I think she's running from someone. I don't think she has anywhere to go, so I was going to let her chill here for a little while."

"This isn't a halfway house," Trina stated. "Get rid of her. We don't need a runaway poking around. Take her to one of the shelters in the city if you want to let her live."

"That's a bad idea," she said, shaking her head. "You need to see this." Turning towards the woods, she called out. "Come on down. I want you to meet someone."

"This better be good," Trina muttered. "I swear, you can scare the shit out of people before killing them, but as soon as you see someone on the road to being homeless, you turn into Miss Bleeding-heart-"

She trailed off as the figure emerged from the tree house, blinking once to make sure her mind wasn't playing tricks on her. The girl seemed to be in her late teens, but her youthful appearance wasn't as surprising as the lengthy span of the golden feathered wings that had spread out to slow her descent. She landed softly before the appendages folded over her back, but she did not approach further.

"Soph..." Trina began slowly. "What the hell is that?"

"She's an elf!" Soph said excitedly. "How awesome is that?"

"An elf," Trina repeated. She stepped towards the petite figure, her eyes taking in every detail before she stopped a few feet away from her. "Really?"

"Yes, m'lady," she said quietly, keeping her gaze lowered. "I told your friend that I am willing to trade some of my possessions for safe lodgings if you wish."

"How old are you?"

"I..." She looked up at her, trying to understand the relevance of the question, but her expression was impassive. "I am two hundred and four

34

summers, m'lady."

"Two hundred and... Holy shit." She turned and headed back over to Soph, taking her by the arm as she led her further away from their visitor. "This better not be one of your practical jokes."

"It's not," she insisted. "I don't know how she got here, but it won't hurt anything to let her stay for a few days. She looked like she was just going to hang out in the tree house, so I was thinking she could stay there."

"Do you think she might have anything useful on her?"

"She might. If she wants to give some of it up, I ain't planning to argue."

*****

Mikhail shed the suit coat as soon as he had closed the door to his office, and he draped it over the back of his chair before sitting and motioning for her to do the same. Neither of them had missed the nervous glances at the appearance of the ancient vampire and her lupine companion. Apparently, they had not been forgotten.

"Alright," he began. "What's the problem?"

"I find myself in need of your services," Lalasa said.

"And I find that hard to believe."

"Rhonda informed me that you might have someone on your roster that would be of assistance," she explained. "I am searching for someone who I believe has found her way to your world."

"Details." He pulled a legal pad out of the desk drawer as he lifted a pen. "Start with a physical description and how dangerous she is."

"She is about a head shorter than I am," she told him.

"So, about five feet tall. Go on."

"Light blonde hair and her eyes..." She paused, frowning. "I'm trying to find the right word in your language. They have a tint of orange, but a lighter shade of the color."

"We'll go with orange for now. Any distinguishing characteristics?"

"Well, she is Elven, but a bit different than the rest of her people. She had a mishap when working with a spell beyond her ability and now carries a set of wings. She was given access to my library in order to find a counter, but she has fled the castle with one of my spell books and several enchanted items."

"Are you concerned about her safety or do you just want your property back?"

"Both," she said. "Krysanna is young and naïve. She spent the first two centuries of her life in the secluded forests of Evemyst. She knows little of the outside world of Zalyndrya, let alone how to survive in your world. She must be found as soon as possible."

"Two hundred years is young?" He lifted a brow skeptically and pressed the button to turn on the computer monitor. "Evans was right to send you to me. Apparently, I have someone who specializes in finding things or people. Unfortunately, he flew back to London last night, so I'm going to have to put him on the next flight here."

"Add it to my bill."

He nodded his assent and opened the file. A few quick keystrokes entered the password and he scanned the information. Clicking on the link provided, he waited for the device to connect before he was presented with the live video feed.

"Now what?" Alex glared at him.

"I have a job for you," Mikhail said. "Top priority and top pay. How soon can you be in Boston?"

"Top pay?" he repeated. He seemed to consider it for a moment before leaning close to the webcam. "I'll be there in five minutes. Make sure your guards don't give me any shit."

The connection was severed abruptly, and Mikhail lifted the phone on his desk to advise his staff. Setting the item back in the cradle, he returned his attention to Lalasa.

"I need a list of the property that he's supposed to recover."

"Of course," she said. "The spellbook is one of the most important items. It's also how I knew she had come here. It contains the incantation to open a portal between worlds. I've spent a long time perfecting that one and it has several fail-safes included. It would be practically useless to anyone here, except that we don't know how many people my brother had taught our language to. Aside from that, Krysanna also took a couple of translation aides. One is a bracelet that translates written words. It must be recovered with the book. The other is one of the ivy pendants for vocal communication."

"If she has so many of your things, shouldn't you be able to find her yourself?"

"Ordinarily, yes. However, there is a ring that prevents the wearer from being tracked by magical means. That one belonged to Karian." She offered a slight smile. "I would have found you quicker last year if he hadn't been wearing it at the time."

"Lucky me."

Their humor faded as Lalasa glanced to the door, her eyes widening. Shade was on his feet as quickly as she was, and they both stared at Alex as he entered. Mikhail glanced between them, one hand inching towards his gun.

Shade padded over to the newcomer, whining softly. Alex glanced down at the wolf, his expression softening for a fraction of a second before his gaze lifted to rest a cold glare on Lalasa.

"Your pet?" he asked.

"My friend," she clarified.

"I see." The answer seemed to satisfy him and his hand rested on Shade's head as his attention shifted to Mikhail. "Let's hear about this job."

"I need you to find someone," Mikhail began, glancing at the notepad. "Approximately five feet tall, blonde hair, slender."

"A petite blonde," he mused. "So, am I supposed to kill it?"

"She is not to be harmed," Lalasa said firmly.

"Right," Mikhail agreed. "Find her and bring her back here, along with anything in her possession."

"Does she have any distinguishing characteristics?" Alex asked.

"If you see a chick with orange eyes, then you've found her," he said.

"Fight or flight?" Alex seemed to be making mental notes, storing the information for later use.

"Flight," Lalasa said. "She will fight if cornered, but she is more likely to flee if she feels threatened. She was last detected in Philadelphia, but she is not the type to remain in a city like that. She has probably taken to the woods if she has been able to find any." She extended her hand, a few whispered words conjuring a quiver of arrows. "This was found in my apartment. It might aid you in your search."

"Anything else I need to know?" he asked as he took the weapon.

"That's it," Mikhail said.

Alex lingered only long enough to offer Shade a scratch behind the ears before he departed. Lalasa watched him leave and slowly turned her

37

gaze to Mikhail.

"You did not give him all of the information," she said, a note of disapproval in her tone.

"He's been acting like he's hot shit," he said with a shrug. "It's time to see if he can back it up. You know something about him, don't you?" When she nodded, he frowned and leaned back in his chair. "Care to share with the rest of the class?"

"He is of the wolf," she explained. "They were extinct in Zalyndrya before I was even born. I'm not sure what their role is here, but in my world, they were the guardians of the forests. It is said that they had a close bond with the elves."

"I don't see him having a close bond with anything," he snorted.

"How long has he been employed with your company?"

"His file said that he started in the mid-seventies."

"That's odd," she said thoughtfully. "His kind is stronger than normal humans, but they are still mortal. He should have the same life span as your people. I wonder..."

She fell silent for a moment, considering the possibilities. Several theories presented themselves, all of them equally likely, but she shook her head slightly.

"A riddle for another time," she decided, her attention returning to him. "Is all well with you? You seem a bit troubled."

"Just stress."

"Obviously," she said with a soft laugh. "You can't deceive me, Mikhail. If you don't wish to speak of it, then simply say so, but consider this first. Part of my duties back home is to provide counsel when it is needed." When he opened his mouth to retort, she raised a hand. "However, my offer is not out of any sense of obligation or duty. I consider you to be a friend. If you want to talk about it, I'm more than willing to listen and advise as needed."

"I'll keep that in mind," he said.

*****

The sound of the steel door closing was the only indication that a visitor had arrived. Marielle looked up from the computer as she watched the figure stride across the floor. Despite his tall, muscular frame, his boots made no sound on the tile as he approached the desk. A casual smile rested easily on his lips as he regarded her and she did her best to conceal her surprise at his unexpected presence.

"Miss Bonner," he began. "I must say, you are looking quite lovely this evening."

"It's good to see you again, Mr. Konistav," she said, genuine warmth in her tone. "I'd watch it with the flattery, though. I don't think your wife would approve."

"Perhaps," he agreed with a grin. "Although I believe there is a saying around here that might be appropriate. One can peruse the menu so long as he does not sample the buffet." When she rolled her eyes, he shook his head slightly. "On second thought, I suppose that was not the best choice of words." He cleared his throat deliberately, although his humored expression did not change. "Is Rhonda in tonight?"

"She is, but she has an appointment in ten minutes. I'll let her know you're here."

Lothan offered a brief nod, his dark blue eyes unblinking as he watched her lift the phone from the desk. His sensitive hearing was able to pick up both ends of the conversation and he distinctly heard Rhonda swear when the Personal Assistant announced his arrival. There was a brief pause before the accountant responded and ended the call.

"One of those nights?" he guessed when Marielle replaced the receiver on the cradle.

"One of those weeks," she said with a sigh. "You can go right in."

"I heard."

Marielle's smile returned when he gave her a wink, and she motioned towards the double doors at the end of the cavernous lobby. Her attention then returned to the information on the computer monitor.

Within the private office of Rhonda Evans, Lothan's carefree demeanor vanished. One look at the accountant told him that something had definitely gone wrong. The cuffs of her white shirt were unbuttoned and the sleeves rolled up to just below her elbows. A grey blazer lay discarded on the back of a nearby leather chair, and her eyes glanced up for a fraction of a second before returning to the various papers scattered before her.

"I figured you'd be giving Cassandra advice on how to run a café like an empire," the accountant remarked, absently motioning to one of the chairs across the desk. "Since your wife ran off to Boston for the night, wouldn't that leave you to tell her what not to do?"

"I am confident that my daughter can handle a simple decision such as that," he said, ignoring the sarcasm. "I assume there is a report on the unauthorized access to our residence?"

"Of course," Rhonda assured him. "Given the nature of the situation, it's already been transferred to an encrypted electronic record, and the original document has been shredded."

"I will pretend that I know what that means and assume that only a select few will be informed of what happened."

"That sums it up nicely."

"Good." Lothan finally stepped around the chair and dropped into it. "Have there been any incidents at any of the other properties?"

"Everything has been quiet," she said.

Three

The shadows split apart as a figure emerged within the heart of Philadelphia. Alex continued along the dimly lit street, stopping only when his destination came into view. The uniform on the doorman confirmed his decision, and he crossed the road with sure steps before entering the building.

A chandelier spread illumination throughout the vast lobby, reflecting on the highly polished marble of the floor. Reaching into his pocket, he withdrew a faded passport and flipped it open for a moment before replacing it and selecting another, identical item.

"Is the penthouse suite available?" he asked the woman at the desk.

"I'd have to check," she said hesitantly, casting a disapproving glance at his attire. Her acrylic fingernails tapped on the keyboard as she pulled up the room information, and she returned her attention to him as she spoke again. "It's vacant at this time. Would that be cash or credit?"

"Credit," he stated with a grin as he presented the card linked to the expense account.

"I'll need to see your ID," she added. Taking the offered passport, she continued. "And how long will you be staying with us, Mr. Whitman?"

"Well, I have a lot of matters to attend to," he said thoughtfully. "Let's go with a month and I'll let you know if I need to extend it."

The woman hid her surprise as she entered the reservation and credit card information. The idle tapping of his fingers across the counter seemed to increase her agitation, and she wanted nothing more than to finish the transaction and send him on his way. To think that she had almost called security to escort him from the building. The near mistake caused an imperceptible shudder to course through her.

"Everything is ready for you, Mr. Whitman," she said finally, extending the keycard, passport, and credit card towards him. "Is there anything else I can do for you?"

"I'll need access to a private internet server," Alex said. "And you might as well turn on all of the pay-per-view features. I may want to relax later. Reserve a limo to pick me up in forty-five minutes."

A satisfied grin spread across his features as he stalked past the desk towards the elevators. He was certain that his new employer had purposely withheld information, and that knowledge didn't sit well with him.

His mind replayed the brief meeting with the strange client as he entered the penthouse suite, and he absently turned the locks before switching on the lights. Too many things didn't fit. The woman obviously had power at her command, so it made little sense that she would need him – or anyone in that company for that matter – to help track down the elusive blonde.

It made him ponder his quarry and his previous grin slowly faded into a thoughtful frown. *What's so important about this girl that she wants her found and brought back alive?* It was more probable that she was after whatever the mark was carrying, but that one detail – the insistence that she wouldn't be harmed – nagged at him. *Well, if they wanted her found so badly, they should have given me all of the information,* he decided. *Then again, when dealing with a vampire, I really shouldn't expect anything different than this.*

That brought him back to his observations of the unlikely client. He had picked up her scent as soon as he had neared the office, but it was alien to everything he had previously encountered. The traces of polluted molecules that seemed to hover around every metropolis were absent from her form, and he couldn't quite place the spicy, floral scent that seemed infused with the ancient earthy aromas. At first consideration, he conjured the image of a castle set in sprawling acres of green.

Shaking his head, he dismissed the musings for now and opened up his laptop case. While he waited for the device to boot up, he crossed the room to gaze out the massive windows. The lights and noise of the city stretched out around him and he took a moment to solidify his plans. A glance at the arrows only added to his determination.

I'll find your little blonde, he decided. *But I'm going to do it my way.*

*****

Items were scattered about the floor of the tree house, and Krysanna sat along one wall, motionless except for her eyes as they scanned a page of

42

the book that rested on her lap. A subtle movement caught her attention, and one hand went to the dagger at her side as she looked up quickly. She relaxed slightly when she recognized the one who had entered, although her fingers remained on the hilt of the weapon.

"Didn't mean to startle you," Soph lied, leaning in the doorway. "We decided that you can stay for now, but Trina wants to know what you have that you think you can offer in return."

The elf nodded and set the book aside, her gaze sweeping across her possessions while she glanced up at the woman every few seconds. She doubted that the meager amount of money she had brought with her would be worth anything in this strange world, but she withdrew a few coins anyway.

"I do not have much," she began quietly as an idea came to her. Removing the gold bracelet from her wrist, she lifted it for her host to see. "I know it does not look like more than a simple trinket, but the enchantment upon it makes it more valuable than it would seem."

"If it's worth so much, why are you ready to give it up?"

"If it will ensure that I am permitted a safe haven, then it is worth the sacrifice," Krysanna said. "Do you know what it is like to have nowhere to turn? Have you ever felt the fear of being hunted with little chance of escape? Even if you agree to a few short days, then I will gladly part with this in order to make preparations."

Soph studied her but didn't immediately respond. In truth, she could relate to the elf's plight, but she wasn't about to reveal that to her. There was no deception in Krysanna's words, and she realized that this was the first time that she had heard her speak so boldly.

"What kind of preparations?" she asked cautiously.

"I need to find a world similar to my own," Krysanna told her with a glance down at her book. "When I opened the portal to escape Zalyndrya, it brought me here. There must be a way to alter the destination. I can read this easily without the aid of the bracelet, but I had brought it along in case I needed to translate any foreign script."

"So, you're saying that your little bracelet will let you read things in a language you don't know?" Soph asked, excitement building inside of her. When the elf nodded, her smile widened. "Tell you what, hand that over and you can stay as long as you have to."

Krysanna stared up at her, hardly believing her good fortune. Hope surged within, and she smiled for what might have been the first time since her ordeal had begun.

*****

"Is your car still in the shop?" Ian asked.

"It's supposed to be done tomorrow," Marielle said, not looking up.

She knew he was sitting on the corner of her desk, just at the edge of her vision, and for a moment, she felt the warm familiarity of his presence. Silently chiding herself, she pushed the feeling aside and continued searching through the records displayed on the screen.

"So, I take it you might need a ride home?" he pressed.

"I was planning on taking a cab."

"Save your money. I'll take you home. I'm heading that way anyway."

"I can afford it."

"I'm sure you can," he agreed. "But I don't see the point in that. Why take a cab when we're both heading in the same direction?"

"You're not letting this go, are you?" she asked with a sigh. "Shouldn't you be out checking with your informants?"

"Already did," he stated. "Don't change the subject. What time are you off?"

"Midnight."

"Then I'll meet you downstairs in twenty minutes."

She looked up to see him crossing the room towards Rhonda's office and shook her head slowly. A dozen arguments against his suggestion echoed in her mind, countered by a dozen reasons why she wanted to accept his offer.

Marielle had been careful to keep their friendship from slipping back into the romance they had enjoyed several months before, but each day she found it harder and harder to keep from crossing that line. While his Camaro would be much more comfortable than the average taxi in the middle of the city, she had to wonder which option would be safer. When it came to Ian, she risked losing much more than just her heart.

*****

Mikhail leaned back in his chair and rubbed his eyes with the heel of his hand. Hours of staring at the computer screen had caused weariness to creep in, and for a moment, his vision wouldn't adjust to his surroundings.

44

Methodical gunfire from the firing range hammered at the dull ache building in his head, and he rubbed his temples in an attempt to ease the pain away.

A notepad rested on the desk beside the computer, several notes scrawled quickly across the paper. Of the twelve secret operatives, he had discovered that only two were still active – Trina and Alex. Nine of the remaining mercenaries were deceased, some from wounds suffered in the fields, others from disease, and a couple without any obvious explanation. Death certificates had been issued and a digital copy was attached to each entry.

That left one remaining file. As Mikhail leaned forward to read the information, he was surprised that this one man had managed to retire to a relatively peaceful life. Carl B. Codename: Reaper, he mused. Born 1952, active from 1970 to 1995. Married once; wife died in 1997, but no cause mentioned. He pondered that for a moment before continuing on. One daughter, single and living in Philadelphia. Carl moved to Florida in 2001, one year after his daughter graduated high school.

He continued to skim through the file, frowning when he came across the picture of the subject. Something about the man seemed oddly familiar, like a face seen in passing, but he couldn't place it. The photograph must have been taken shortly before his retirement, and Carl appeared to be the picture of health. It wasn't a stretch to assume that his current status with the company had something to do with his wife's death.

Pushing that thought to the back of his mind, he scrolled down, searching for one detail that had yet to present itself. An eyebrow lifted in speculation when he found what he wanted.

Specialty: Vampires. He snorted and shook his head slightly. Would have been nice if we'd known about him last year. Hell, we could have used his help with that. The only contact information listed was an address in Florida and a link to a generic e-mail address. Mikhail toyed with the idea of sending him a message but dismissed the idea. Let him enjoy his retirement. He worked for us for twenty-five years. No sense in bothering him now.

The phone on the desk interrupted his thoughts and he lifted the receiver without even looking at the caller-ID. Loud music assaulted his ears, and his eyes strayed down to the digital display, unsurprised that the call had come from a blocked number. Most of the field operatives kept their numbers hidden to keep from being tracked when on an assignment.

"Jack-O-Lantern," he greeted sharply, already irritated with the caller.

"And here I thought I was calling Pizza Hut," Alex remarked on the other end of the line. "I must have the wrong number."

"Where the hell are you?" Mikhail demanded, feeling justified in his annoyance.

"Well, I'm doing research on this assignment," he said. "You see, sometimes, people will hide in the last place you would expect them, so I took a ride down to Delaware Avenue. I have Candi here with me and guess what? She's a petite blonde. She's studying to be an investment broker and suggested that I diversify my portfolio. So, I have four of her friends here to help out."

"You're at a strip club," he said, clenching his teeth to keep his mounting anger in check. "I'm not paying you to sit there and shove money into some stripper's G-string."

"I'm building good Karma for you," Alex countered. "We're putting these girls through college. You should feel good about it."

"I'm going to feel really good about firing your ass if you don't get the hell out of there and start doing your job."

"Well, you said to look for a petite blonde," he said, false innocence in his tone. "And I've managed to find five of them. All we need is a set of orange contacts and voila!"

"I also said to look outside of the city," Mikhail reminded him. "Now stop dicking around and get out there."

He dropped the phone back onto the desk and turned to stare out the window. His gaze flicked to the rifle leaning in the corner of his office and he curled his fingers around it before heading to the door. An hour or so on the firing range would help calm his nerves.

*****

Marielle glanced at Ian as he pulled into the garage beneath her building. She waited until he had parked and turned off the engine before speaking.

"What are you doing?"

"I'm walking you up," he said as he pulled his keys from the ignition.

"You don't have to do that," she protested.

"I know."

She let a sigh pass through her lips but chose not to argue with him.

Instead, she did her best to ignore his footsteps beside her and edged away from him as they stepped into the elevator. Silence hovered between them as they rode up to her floor, broken only by the soft chime announcing their arrival.

"This 'just friends' thing isn't really working out as planned," Ian said, following her into the hall.

"Please don't start with that right now," Marielle said, frowning.

"I'm just saying that friends at least talk to each other," he said with a shrug. "You keep getting more and more distant, and I'm trying to figure out why. When did you stop trusting me?"

"It's not that I don't trust you." She paused, glancing down. "I just don't trust myself with you. I don't want to get involved with you again. I mean I do, but I can't take that risk."

"You know I'd never hurt you," he said softly.

"I know," she admitted. "You tell me that often enough, but I'm always going to wonder. You can't know the future, Ian."

"Then we'll take it slow." He stopped, turning to face the door to her apartment, and his expression became suspicious. "Are you expecting someone?"

"No," she said, confusion clouding her features.

"No sign of a break-in," he said, lowering his voice. "The locks are all intact, but someone's in there. Give me your keys and stay behind me."

She nodded mutely, handing over her key ring as quietly as possible. Stepping back, she watched Ian slide the key into the lock, the soft click of access almost inaudible. Marielle held her breath, trying to prepare herself for whatever violence might be waiting inside the comfort of her home.

Through the slowly opening crack of the door, she was able to glimpse the figure sitting on the couch, a paperback novel open in his hands. She let out the breath she didn't realize she was holding and placed a hand on Ian's arm as she slipped past him.

"Dad," she said with a warm smile. "What are you doing here?"

"Just checkin' up on my girl," he said, setting his book aside. "Figured I'd surprise you with your birthday right 'round the corner and all."

Carl Bonner regarded them with the same brown eyes that his daughter had inherited, and his voice still held the slow, southern drawl that years in Philadelphia had been unable to erase. Despite his age, he still

47

appeared fit, not even a groan escaping his lips as he rose to his feet. His hair held more grey than brown, but hadn't yet begun to thin.

"And who might this be?" he asked, his gaze settling on Ian.

"Dad, this is Ian," Marielle said.

"Isn't he the one you broke up with?" His lips turned in a slight frown as he gave her escort a disapproving look. "You didn't get back together with him, did you?"

"He gave me a ride home since my car is in the shop," she told him, feeling like a teenager all over again. "How long have you been here?"

"Well, my flight got in about three hours ago," Carl said. "I got my hotel room and figured I'd stop on by to see you when you got home."

"You don't have to stay at a hotel," she said. "I have a spare bedroom so you're welcome to stay here."

"Well, that's mighty fine of you to offer. I guess I'll go pick up my things and head back over here then." He looked at Ian and forced a grin. "Nice to meet you. You be safe on your drive home. I'll be seeing you around."

"Likewise," Ian said evenly.

*****

"Malice, it's Reaper."

Alex leaned forward in the booth as he heard the voice on the other end of the phone. The occasional call from his old associate was to be expected, but usually those conversations were more to reminisce about the good old days. It had been a long time since he had heard such an edge to the man's voice.

"Well, I'll be damned," he said, putting on a fake accent for the caller's benefit. "Why, I ain't heard from you in a coon's age."

"There's only one thing worse than a Brit trying to talk southern," Reaper remarked. Alex could picture him shaking his head as he spoke. "And that's a corpse trying to get cozy with my daughter."

"Where are you?"

"In Philadelphia. Heading down Locust Street towards Broad," he said. "Just crossed Fifteenth."

"Take a left on Broad and park it," Alex said. "I'll meet you on the south side of City Hall."

48

The shadows split apart as Alex emerged, scanning the area for any signs of his former colleague. A figure rounded the corner, and he started forward, his expression neutral. The two regarded each other for a moment before a grin spread on his lips, one hand extended.

"So, is retirement all it's cracked up to be?" he asked with a familiar clasp of hands.

"Florida's nice," Carl said. "It beats the hell out of the winters up here."

"Maybe I'll drop in sometime," Alex said. "Tell me about your vampire problem."

He had little patience for formalities; business was more important. If he planned on taking a side project in addition to his current assignment, then he wanted to get started as soon as possible. He still had no leads on the so-called "petite blonde" he was supposed to find, but maybe helping out an old friend would give him a chance to step back and regroup.

Carl pulled out his phone, unlocking it before pulling up the photo gallery. Scrolling through until he found the first one he needed, he stiffened. The father in him wanted his daughter to be safe and happy, while the former mercenary lent experience to the opinion that her safety was more important than temporary happiness.

"His name is Ian Mackenzie," Carl said as he handed over the phone. "Works for Evans International. From what I've gathered, he's some kind of bodyguard for Rhonda Evans herself. My daughter is her personal assistant, so they see more of each other than I'd like."

"I've met him," Alex said, scrolling through the images. "Doesn't seem too bad for a corpse, but I wouldn't want my daughter dating him if I had one. Problem is, his boss is in tight with the one signing my paycheck, so we have to play this carefully."

"Who's running things now?" Carl asked. "I heard Jack went missing last year."

"Some little shit who used to go by the code name Pumpkin," he said with a shrug. "He's working his way onto my shit list. Asshole gave me this job, but he's holding back intel. He'll learn, though. He's already picking up a tab for a penthouse suite and a few nights at the strip club."

Carl laughed at that. He shouldn't have expected differently. Malice always had a way of getting what he wanted through his own creative methods. In a way, Carl was a little envious. For a few fleeing moments, he almost missed working together, but those days were long gone. Retirement suited him just fine. He'd been able to raise his daughter in peace, and she'd seemed to turn out okay. All in all, he had little reason to complain.

The disappearance of his former employer was concerning, though. Even if he was technically retired, Carl still held a lot of respect for the man, and Jack's sudden absence hit him hard. At least his retirement checks had continued with the new management. The man running things now apparently decided to keep that in place, and he hadn't called the former operative up to Boston.

"Tell me about your blonde," he said. "Maybe I can do some digging."

"There's not much to tell, yet," Alex said, handing the phone back. "There's more to her than they're telling me. The client was there when I took the assignment, and there was something off about her. She's another corpse, but she didn't smell local. Either she's been living in the woods this whole time, or she's not from anywhere I've been. I'm trying to find the link between her and my job, but I'm coming up with nothing. She was really familiar with the new boss, though. Like they were close friends or something like that."

"They're all connected," Carl said thoughtfully. "She's in tight with the kid who's running things now, he's got ties to Marielle's boss, and Evans' bodyguard is trying to get cozy with my kid. Malice, this runs deeper that I think either of us can see. It's like that tower puzzle game-"

"Jenga?"

"Yeah, that one," he said. "Pull the wrong block, and the whole thing is going to come tumbling down on your head. You don't want to be in the middle of that mess if it goes to shit."

He had a point, Alex thought. He needed more information, but he had to make sure he maneuvered the pieces into the right positions to come out on top. It was going to be a challenge, but that's what made it all the more thrilling. As his grin returned, excitement flashed in his eyes.

"I'll keep that in mind," he said. "Send me the details on your daughter's admirer, and I'll see what I can do."

"The priority is to keep her safe," Carl said. "If I could just kill the bastard, I would, but we have to be subtle about this."

"Subtlety's my middle name." Alex let out a quiet laugh, shaking his hand again. "I should get to work, then."

*****

"Your dad didn't seem too happy to see me," Ian said.

They didn't have much time to discuss it; Marielle's father would return soon, and she still had to make sure the guest room was presentable. Ian had followed her around the condo, helping as much as he could along the way.

"He's just worried about me," she said, straightening after putting fresh sheets on the bed. "You know how dads are, don't you? He still thinks I'm his little girl, no matter how old I am, and he means well."

Ian didn't argue, but he had a feeling there was more to it than that. There was something off in Carl's voice, something that hinted that he knew more than he was willing to tell them. It sent warning bells ringing in his head, and a sense of unease ran through him. Maybe he could find a way to get some background information on the man. As he continued to try to figure out what seemed strange about him, it hit him.

Carl Bonner was a solider. His movements were eerily as precise as Mikhail's, his mannerisms both casual and calculated. Beneath his attempts at southern charm, he had plenty of battles behind him, and that alone was enough for Ian to proceed with caution.

"Was your dad in the military?" he asked, helping her straighten the comforter over the bed.

"Not that I remember," she said. "He used to travel a lot on business before I came along, but then he settled down and ran a small shop down in Wilmington. Why?"

"He just carries himself like he would be," Ian said.

He let the subject drop there, deciding not to press for more information. If his suspicions were correct, then he needed to keep her as far away from his own personal investigation as possible. The last thing he wanted was for her to get caught in any potential crossfire. Checking the time, he headed into the living room and grabbed his jacket off of the back of the sofa.

"Guess I should get going before he gets back," he said.

"Thanks again," she said. Her smile was a little reluctant, and she still seemed reserved in his presence, but it was a start. "Be careful out there."

51

"Anytime, Marielle," he said. "If you need anything, all you have to do is ask."

She could feel heat rising to her face, but thankfully, he didn't comment on it. As she watched him leave, Marielle let out a sigh. During the course of the past year, her life had become far more complicated than she liked. She missed the evenings when all she had to worry about was making sure Rhonda's schedule was organized.

Things were so different now. In the blink of an eye, she found herself surrounded by vampires and mercenaries, some nicer than others, and it had taken a while for her to come to terms with her new reality. She wasn't entirely there yet, but she'd long since stopped avoiding sleep to keep nightmares at bay. The more time she spent with Ian, the easier it was for her to forget what he really was and what he could do. Some nights, she wanted nothing more than to curl up on the sofa and watch movies with him, but then her sense of self-preservation would kick in, telling her that he was more dangerous than she could imagine.

Her thoughts were just as much of a mess as they'd been the night he'd confessed to her, but the fear had slowly dissipated into subtle reminders of caution. She missed the good times; she missed him.

A knock at the door stirred her from her thoughts, and she took a deep breath to clear her head. Ian's question nagged at the back of her mind, and as her father greeted her with a smile, she studied his movements and mannerisms. She never had a reason to doubt what he'd told her about his life before she was born, but after everything she'd experienced, questions were brewing.

*****

The answer had to be there; there were no other options. Krysanna read the passage for what must have been the seventh time, but there were no new revelations in the words. Her earlier sense of dread and frustration returned, tears threatening to spill over. She was so close; there was just one element missing if she could figure out what it was.

Dusk was quickly approaching, and she summoned a few globes of light to illuminate the tree house. She scanned the text again, trying to find some clue as to what she had overlooked. Still, she found nothing new, and she finally closed the book, leaning back against the wall.

She knew she should sleep, but she didn't want to waste the time when she had move on soon. Her people required little sleep – one night out of every three was enough – but she'd pushed herself to her limits. Exhaustion was settling in, and her eyes drifted closed as her wings wrapped around her body.

She awoke a few hours later, feeling a bit better after resting, and she stood to stretch as her wings spread behind her. Her stomach reminded her of the need for food, and she closed the distance to the entrance of her refuge, looking out over the nearby woods. Perhaps she could find some berries that were edible. Leaving the safety of the enclosure sent a wave of fear crashing over her, and she took a few steps back.

Finding her way back wouldn't be difficult, but there were too many unknowns outside of her temporary shelter. The safest option would be to remain in place and use the last of her meager supplies to sustain her for another day. It was by no means a permanent solution, but it was better than being caught unawares by whatever dangerous creatures roamed this world.

"You awake up there?" a familiar voice called from below.

Krysanna edged over to the opening again, one hand resting on the wall as she looked down. Soph offered a smile but waited to start climbing up. The elf tried to return the expression, her lips turning upward just a hair, and stepped back a few paces to make room for her host.

"Wasn't sure if you'd eaten yet," Soph said. "But you were sleeping earlier. I wasn't sure if you were gonna sleep at all, since I haven't seen you do it since you got here. Here, something to hold you over until we figure out what else you might be able to stomach."

Krysanna accepted the paper bag with a murmur of thanks, her gaze lowered. She gave a quick glance up at Soph before looking inside, finding a clear container with a combination of greens and other vegetables mixed together. Her smile brightened a little; the meal would more than satisfy her needs.

"Many thanks," she said.

"No problem." Soph stood there for another few moments before looking behind her. "I'll leave it, then. If you need anything else, just come knock on the back door."

The elf could hardly believe the kindness this woman had shown, and she thanked Di'Litha for her good fortune. She had a safe haven and a decent meal to keep her going while she studied her books, and she couldn't ask for more.

Four

"I need a favor."

Sean hated hearing those words and hearing them from Ian wasn't a good sign. With a sigh, he looked up from the report on his desk and leaned back as Ian took a seat across from him. Sean studied him for a minute before speaking, his brow furrowed in thought.

A lot had changed between them since the previous year. He recalled the twinge of resentment he'd felt at the knowledge that Rhonda wanted a personal security detail who wasn't connected to his team, and it had taken time for him to get past that sting to his pride. He had a good group of officers under him, but Ian had been an unknown. Only after learning the truth did Sean finally understand her reasons.

There were some things for which humans were ill equipped, and keeping the accountant safe from pissed off vampires if a negotiation went south was one of them. Her decision to keep Ian on board made sense now, and Sean felt a small sense of grudging respect for him. He might even go so far as to say that they'd formed a hesitant friendship.

"What can I do for you?" he asked.

"I need access to some financial files," Ian said. "And I need it to stay quiet."

"Why don't you just ask Rhonda?" Sean asked, frowning.

"Didn't I just say that it needs to stay quiet?" Ian said. "If I ask Rhonda, then she's going to want to know why, and I don't have a good answer. She deals with facts, not speculation, and speculation is all I have right now."

Sean could relate. He recalled the phone call he'd made to Marielle to request a few background checks off the record, and apparently, Ian was in a similar situation now. Being the Head of Security had its perks, and he had no problem accessing restricted files. The trick was to get in and out before the IT security staff caught on and put a stop to it.

"What's the name?" he asked, logging into the database.

"Carl Bonner."

"Wait. Isn't that Marielle's dad?" Sean stared at him, his hand resting on the mouse but refusing to move. "Why the hell are you looking into him?"

"Because I think there's more to him than he's telling me," Ian said. "And her. He's hiding something, and I want to make sure it isn't something that can come back to bite us in the ass."

"That's not a good enough reason," Sean said.

"Like I said, all I have is a gut feeling about this," Ian pressed. "Maybe I'm being paranoid over nothing, but I can't shake it. He's living off of retirement benefits, but Marielle said he ran a shop in Wilmington when she was growing up. She didn't remember much about his previous job, but she said he travelled a lot because of it. When he stopped by last night, there was something about the way he carried himself. He's a soldier, Sean. He wasn't military, but I look at him, and I see the guys up in Boston, like they're cut from the same cloth."

There were too many questions running through his mind, but Sean could see Ian's point. The story seemed fine on the surface, but the details beneath it didn't add up to a complete picture. He had to make a decision, though. The sooner he found what they needed and logged out, the lower the risk of getting caught, and as a consequence, quickly fired.

"There's no guarantee that Rhonda's handling his money," he said. "But if she isn't, then maybe we can get a lead on where to look next." He clicked through a few screens, pausing to read the details here and there before looking up. "I might have something."

It wasn't much, but it was better than nothing. Sean turned the screen so that Ian could read the details, and he leaned back in his chair again. There was an automatic transfer set up at monthly frequencies, starting just a few months ago at the start of the year, but few other details. Ian read it twice, making sure that he had the information correct.

"So, this just started this year," he said. "Which means whoever is paying him just became one of Rhonda's clients recently. It's a start."

Sean turned the monitor around again and logged out, checking the

56

time. It looked like they were in there only long enough to get what they needed without raising any red flags, and with the sheer number of transactions that went through every day, the chances of discovery were minimal. He took a deep breath as he leaned back in his chair again.

"She's picked up a lot of new clients," Sean said. "It's going to be tough narrowing it down. There have been a good number of company mergers, so this could have come from any of them."

Ian swore under his breath. It would take too long to go through every single new acquisition, but finding a better method was going to be a problem. There had to be an easier way if he could just find it. Asking Rhonda was a bad idea, asking Marielle could be disastrous, and he wasn't sure if any of his other contacts would be able to find anything. A thought occurred to him, and he stood quickly, heading for the door to the office.

"Thanks, Sean," he said. "I owe you."

As he stepped out into the corridor, he glanced at his phone. There was no signal this far below ground, but he had a pretty good idea of who might be able to dig deeper for him. They'd traded favors in the past, so this shouldn't be too big of an issue. Once the elevator doors opened to the building's lobby, he brought his phone to his ear.

"Euro, it's Ian," he said. "I'm heading your way. Are you on break soon?"

*****

Trina lounged on the sofa, occasionally glancing at Soph out of the corner of her eye. Her partner was curled up on the armchair, her eyes darting across the pages of a weathered book as she paused here and there to take notes. She didn't exactly mind that Soph had started to make some progress with her little project, but her interest was bordering on obsession, which left little time for them to just relax together like they used to.

"I'm going to be taking assignments again soon," she said. "I was hoping you might put that aside so we can enjoy the time we have before I'm on the road."

Soph looked up, blinking once. The enchanted bracelet had been the breakthrough she'd been waiting for, but she hadn't considered that she was completely ignoring Trina in her attempts to learn more about what the books contained. She was torn – there was so much for her to learn, but her wife had a point. There would be plenty of time to study once she had the house to herself.

Closing both the old book and her notebook, she set them aside on the small table beside her and moved to join Trina on the sofa. Neither of them had been paying much attention to whatever had been playing on the television, so she wasted no time in reaching over to steal the remote.

"Anything good on tonight?" she asked, flipping through the channels.

"Doubtful," Trina said. She was quiet for a few seconds, gathering her thoughts before she spoke again. "How long do you think your elf is going to stay out there?"

"No clue," Soph said with a shrug. "She doesn't seem like she wants to go anywhere at the moment. Pretty sure she's running from someone or something, but I can't get anything out of her about it. I kinda don't want to push her for info, though. It'd probably spook her and she'd run off again. There's no telling what kind of trouble she can get herself into if she's out there on her own."

"You're really worried about her, aren't you?"

It was more than a little surprising, the more Trina thought about it. Soph had always been one to take care of herself, often at the expense of others. To see her show such concern for a complete stranger was definitely a change, and Trina wasn't sure if it was a good one or not. Time would have to tell on that one, she decided. As long as the elf stayed out in the treehouse, then the chances of her discovering any of the things Soph and Trina kept hidden were minimal.

"I guess I feel like I can relate to her in a way," Soph said. "Remember where I was at when we first met? I was out there on my own. No one tried to take me in or keep me safe, and maybe she's in that situation now. I don't want anyone to go through the shit that I went through out there."

"I was around," Trina reminded her.

"Yeah, but it wasn't like you were always there," Soph said. "You helped when you were there, probably kept me alive longer than I would've been, but when you weren't there, it was just me and the streets. You ever have to worry about where your next meal is coming from, or if someone's going to stab you in your sleep because you have a blanket and they don't?"

Trina was silent at that. All in all, before she'd taken up with her employer, her life had been pretty damn good. She'd been an athlete in high school, preparing for college with a full-ride scholarship on the table, but she'd given it up without even stopping to think about the consequences. Watching one of her friends become some undead bastard's lunch had made that decision for her.

She absently wondered if her parents ever looked for her after she left. Years had passed before she'd set foot in her hometown, and she'd kept her distance from her childhood home. It was possible that they'd still be alive, but she couldn't bring herself to make any attempt at contact. That life was over. She wasn't the same woman she'd been back then, and even if a fleeting glimpse of her would bring her parents momentary peace, it would only cause pain in the long run.

Shaking her head – as much in response to Soph's question as to clear away the unwelcome thoughts – she looked at her with a mixture of interest and sadness. It wouldn't do any good to dwell on the past, but Soph was opening that door this time around, and all she could do was wait for her to continue.

"She needs someone right now," Soph said. "I don't want her to end up like I did. I mean, things worked out okay in the end, but I get the feeling that she isn't going to be interested in solving her problems the way we did."

She turned and stretched out, resting her head in Trina's lap. Her eyes drifted closed as she felt fingers delicately thread through her hair, and a soft sigh of contentment escaped her lips. During moments like this, it was almost easy to forget her past and what she'd become. Most nights, she was an unapologetic killer – they both were – but right now, they were just a couple enjoying an evening without any further distractions.

"Do you want to kick her out?" she asked after a few minutes.

"No," Trina said. "I just don't want her digging too deep around here. If you're right, then any indication that we're not human is going to send her running. We don't know anything about her, really, and that leaves me with a lot of questions. Where did she come from and why is she even here? I think you're right that she's running from something, but do we really want whatever it is to show up here?"

It wasn't as if Soph hadn't considered that possibility, but she doubted that whatever Krysanna was running from would find her all the way out here. They were far enough away from any neighbors to avoid any unwanted attention. The person or thing that had the elf so terrified had little chance of tracking her down at all. After all, Soph was pretty sure those wings weren't just for show, and it was harder to track someone who could fly than someone who was stuck on the ground.

"Not worried about it," she said. "Besides, if anything shows up and tries to start shit, I'll kick its ass. Relax, babe. I've got this."

Trina could only hope that she was right. Rumors of what had happened up at her company's headquarters last year were still fresh in her mind. There wasn't a solid connection to what she'd heard about and the wayward elf in her backyard, but she'd never really experienced strong magic like they'd spoken of after everything went to hell in Boston. She wanted to take Soph's word for it, but something clawed at the back of her mind, refusing to allow her to lower her guard around their guest.

*****

He had to admit that the hotel had gone all out when they'd designed his suite, and he leaned back comfortably on the plush sofa as he scrolled through his notes. Alex still wasn't thrilled at the prospect of tracking down some strange girl with orange eyes with only the barest of details, but he knew he was good at his job. His track record spoke for itself.

The problem was that the scraps of information he had weren't even enough for an outline, let alone a partial picture of who he was tracking. His thoughts turned to the client, trying to figure out her motives. He couldn't place her scent, which was enough to put him on edge, but she wasn't feigning concern for the girl's safety; she was genuinely worried. It was an odd thing to see from a vampire.

Asking for help was out of the question. Not only would his pride not allow it, but if he had to ask his employer for more information, then he might end up looking at a pay cut. Then again, the company was picking up the tab for both his room and his night on the town, so it evened out for the most part. He wasn't about to admit that, though.

Brushing his finger across the screen of his tablet, he decided to put that project aside until he could figure out a better plan. Reaper's troubles demanded his attention, and he had enough time on his hands to at least get some basic information about his new mark. He pulled up the Evans International website, tapping through various pages in search of something that might be at least somewhat useful.

It came as no surprise that there was little personal information about the staff, aside from the CEO's personal profile, but there had to be better records somewhere. Most likely, they were kept on site, either in a digital format, hard copies, or both. Getting in wouldn't be a problem, but getting what he needed and getting out again before security caught up to him would be tricky. He always loved a challenge.

Dimming the lights just enough to send shadows sprawling across the room, he smiled to himself and closed his eyes. A few steps forward brought him into the darkness, and brief disorientation spiraled around him before he felt solid flooring beneath his boots. Alex opened his eyes to survey his surroundings as he withdrew a small flash drive from his pocket. The hood of his sweatshirt hid his features as he crossed the room to the desk near the large double doors, and he paused, considering which route to take.

There would be more information in the CEO suite, but that would take more time than he was willing to spend in the place. Ducking behind the desk, he slid the drive into the USB port and waited for it to work its magic. As the screen came on, the password came across in a series of dots before the desktop came into view.

His fingers flew over the keys as he dug into the files, copying whatever he thought might be useful before grabbing his flash drive and locking the computer again. So far, so good. He cast a glance at the double doors again, weighing the pros and cons of lingering in the hopes of digging up more than he already had. Shaking his head, he opted for his initial plan, and he slid the drive back into his pocket as he darted into the shadows again.

The familiar sight of his hotel room filled his vision, his hand grasping the storage device as if it were the most valuable item in his possession, which might not have been too far from the truth. Even without going through the CEO's own files, her personal assistant was sure to have access to enough to suit his needs. All he had to do was sift through it until he found something worth the effort.

As he fired up his laptop, he glanced at his cell phone and read the message from his employer that he'd ignored for the past two hours. Mikhail wanted to screw with him, but he didn't know Alex, and he'd certainly underestimated his ability to be a complete dick when the mood struck. This was one of those times, and he honestly didn't feel like dealing with anymore bullshit when he was close to grasping something that might help with his former colleague's problem.

His phone vibrated with an incoming call, which also went ignored as he scrolled through the various files. Considering that Evans was involved in the financial aspect of his company, there was no telling how many skeletons she had lying around. Even if he didn't find what he needed here, there was a good chance that he'd be able to dig up enough of them to tuck away for future negotiations.

Reaper's daughter's file was as good a place to start as any, and he pored over every detail available as he scrawled a few notes on a notepad beside him. Her background was standard enough – decent education, a little bit of work experience, and her general responsibilities regarding her current position. None of it was even the least bit useful, though. He was, however, able to obtain her address, as well as her emergency contacts, including her father.

Professional courtesy dictated that operatives refer to each other by their code names, regardless of whether or not their legal names were known. As he read the fabricated history of his old friend, he had to suppress a laugh. It was believable on the surface, boring enough to prevent the average person from looking closer, but after traveling in the circles he did, Alex knew where to spot the smallest detail that didn't belong. The shop in Delaware, where Carl Bonner supposedly worked before retirement, didn't even exist, but no one seemed to give it more than a cursory glance. Then again, the file was focused on Marielle, not her family.

The security staff was his next priority. Her vampire boyfriend was some sort of bodyguard for the woman in charge, and it was the next logical step to find his file. Alex scanned the options, deciding to start with the head of the team and go from there.

Sean O'Donnell's file was a little more interesting, detailing his education at Valley Forge Military Academy and a brief attempt at continuing with the Army. The records were detailed enough for Alex to know that they weren't complete bullshit, and he scrolled further down to his emergency contacts, of which there were few. A sister in Texas and a woman who lived with him were the only ones listed.

There was little information on the sister, and he clicked on the details for the other one. His eyebrows rose as he looked at the picture, warning bells ringing in his head. She didn't look threatening – quite the opposite with the warm smile that rested on her lips – but the green of her eyes was darker than any human's that he'd met, and they lacked the telltale ring of the edge of a contact lens. Cassandra Konistav, he read. Her background was even more confusing, and he minimized the window to look up the town that she'd supposedly once called home. He was only a little surprised to find that it didn't exist.

It was a puzzle for another day, and he resumed his search in the hopes that something would turn up eventually. After two hours of scouring the files, all he had was a name and more bullshit pretending to be recent history regarding Ian Mackenzie. The good news was that he had access to Marielle's schedule, so he could always just drop in while she was out and search her condo undisturbed.

This time, when his phone lit up with an incoming call, he grabbed it and stared at the name on the screen before accepting the call.

"Where the hell are you?" the voice on the other end demanded.

"At the moment? Philadelphia." Leaning back, he stretched his other arm over the back of the couch. "Isn't that where I'm supposed to start looking for this girl?"

"My patience has its limits, Malice," Mikhail warned. "And this isn't a client that we want to piss off. You're not going to find the girl in a strip club or any of the other places you like to hang out. She might not even be in the city anymore with all the time you've wasted dicking around out there."

"Is there a point to this call?" he asked.

"It's get off your ass and get the job done before I cut your expense allotment so far down you'll have to find a cheap motel instead of whatever high dollar hotel you've decided to fuck around in." If his tone weren't enough to indicate how angry he was, the profanity did the job. "I want a report in three days. Don't screw this up."

"If you wanted me to take this seriously, then maybe you should have given me the full story," Alex said evenly. "Any other job, and I would have had a full file, including a full description and last known location. I'll get it done, but since you want to play stupid games with me, then I'm taking my sweet time with it. I could be relaxing in my flat right about now instead of grasping at straws. How important is it that I find her?"

"The client is a valuable ally," Mikhail said. "And she's paying damn well for this."

"Then give me what I need so that I can do my damned job."

*****

Euro was waiting outside the hospital when Ian arrived, leaning against the wall as he took a drag of his cigarette. Stepping forward, he met his friend halfway, clasping his hand with a smile. There were a few questionable stains on his scrubs, and Ian arched a brow.

"Rough night?" he asked.

"It looks worse than it is," Euro said.

"I can't believe you're still working here. After last year, and with all of your connections, you could have any job you want." Ian shook his head slightly. "How long do you think you're going to stay?"

"Maybe I actually like helping people," he said. "Bet you didn't think of that, now did you? I've been tossing around the idea of going back to school, maybe move up to being a doctor. It's not like I don't have time to do it at my own pace."

Being immortal had its perks, and taking his time continuing his studies was one of them. Although, when it came to having eternity stretched out before them, there were plenty of downsides to the deal, but Euro had long ago decided to try to keep a positive outlook. If he focused on the negative, he'd only fall into the same trap some of his old associates had. He'd cultivated his connections over the decades, and he had at least one or two people in his pocket for almost any situation.

"I'm guessing you're not here to restock," he said as he dropped his cigarette in the bin.

"You'd be right," Ian said. "Marielle's dad is in town."

"Sounds awkward."

"Awkward doesn't even begin to cover it," Ian said. "Something isn't right about him. As far as Marielle knows, he worked at a quiet little shop over state lines before he retired, but a place like that isn't going to pay the kind of retirement package that goes into his bank account every month. I pulled some strings and checked the accounts at work, and his is a new one. It came along with a bunch of them from a company merger, but I can't find anything else on it."

"When did his account officially fall under Rhonda's portfolio?"

"First of the year," Ian said. "Which means either that's when the

64

merger took effect, or it happened in the months before New Year's, and it didn't actually kick in until January first."

Euro considered the possibilities as he pulled out his phone, tapping the screen a few times. He could think of at least a dozen different companies that had changed hands over the past year, and he tried to narrow it down to the last quarter. That still left him with too many potential businesses, and he shook his head.

"I can make a few calls, but it might take a few nights," he said, sliding his phone back into his pocket. "Anything else that might help narrow this down?"

"I have a suspicion, but nothing to back it up with," Ian said. When Euro nodded for him to continue, he hesitated before speaking again. "It was something about the way he carried himself, like he's ready for a fight at any time. It kind of reminded me of the guys up in Boston."

"I'll look into it," Euro said. "I didn't really think any of them ever made it to retirement, but I could be wrong there. It's a start anyway."

"I just hope I'm wrong about this," Ian said. "Marielle's been through a lot in the past six months, and I really don't want to be the one to tell her that her father's been bullshitting her all her life."

"Who says she has to know?"

"I already screwed up with her by keeping things from her," Ian said. "I'm not going to make the same mistake this time around. Besides, I think she has a right to know who he really is, if he hasn't been honest about it. I can understand wanting to keep his family out of that part of his life, but he's retired now. There's always going to be a chance that someone he pissed off along the way is going to come knocking or go after his family. She can't protect herself if she doesn't know that she needs to."

"Can't argue with you there," Euro said. "I'll let you know as soon as I find a lead."

"Thanks," Ian said, finally allowing himself to relax. "I'll take you out on your next night off to pay you back for it. Sound good?"

Euro laughed with a nod and checked the time, realizing he should have been back ten minutes ago; it was a wonder no one had come looking for him again. Ian watched him head back through the automatic doors, and he felt like he had a better handle on the situation than he'd had earlier in the night. Carl Bonner was hiding something – something big – and if it put

Marielle in any sort of danger, then Ian had a problem with it.

Five

Relocating to Ridley Park from a world that was so different from what she'd seen on Earth wasn't nearly as difficult as she'd anticipated, and Cassandra couldn't resist a smile as she checked the herbs in the garden she'd insisted on planting in the backyard. The project kept her occupied during the day, and she'd taken to experimenting with different plants she'd picked up on Zalyndrya to see if they would be able to grow in the different soil. The native plants were growing nicely, but it was too soon to tell if the foreign ones would thrive or perish.

A little bit of magic would help things along, but she was careful to use minimal energy, finding a balance that might help the new additions without overpowering any of the others. It was a nice distraction, but she was growing restless day by day. Of course, she'd spend some of her spare time learning the area, but it was a far cry from the daily routine she'd followed back home.

She stood, brushing some of the dirt from her jeans, and returned to the house. Sean had a day shift, so he'd be home in the evening. The thought brought another smile to her lips, and she turned on her phone as she climbed the stairs. Once the screen brightened, she checked the messages, surprised to see one from her brother.

Dinner tonight? I'll cook if you want to come over. Before she could answer, another text flashed across the screen, and she glanced at the clock before reading it. *I guess you can bring your boyfriend, if you must.*

Why are you awake? she responded. *I thought you'd be asleep this time of day.*

I don't actually have to sleep, he texted. *I might nap in a little while, but you didn't answer my question. Do you want to come over tonight?*

An invitation to his home was rare, especially because he spent so little time there. It felt like he was always on the road, and while she knew it was part of who he was, Cassandra lamented the missed opportunities to reconnect. They weren't exactly near-strangers anymore, but there was so much about his life that she still didn't know, things she tried to avoid bringing up out of concern for his happiness.

We'll be there shortly after sunset, she said.

She placed the phone on the desk in the room she shared with Sean and grabbed a towel on her way to the bathroom. Convincing her boyfriend to accompany her would be no simple matter; he still wasn't too fond of her brother. He'd agree eventually, but he wouldn't be thrilled about it. Some rifts took longer to mend than others, and it was something that the two of them would have to work out on her own. She wasn't going to get in the middle of their mutual dislike of each other. Cassandra had no issue with addressing things if they became too intense or started to lean towards violence, but as long as both men tried to resolve their issues with words, she would sit back and allow them their space.

*****

Sean wasn't excited about visiting Cassandra's brother, but he kept his opinion to himself as they rode the elevator up to the twenty-sixth floor of the building. He had to admit that the man had done well for himself in the short time he'd been on Earth, but he couldn't bring himself to approve of the methods. Then again, he didn't approve of much when it came to Karian.

When the doors whispered open with a chime, he took Cassandra's hand and approached one of the only two doors on the floor. After a few seconds, a series of soft beeps came from the other side of the door, and it opened to reveal their host, who regarded them silently for a moment. After offering Sean a curt nod, his attention turned to Cassandra, and he gave a warm smile as he stepped aside.

The interior of the condo was decorated mainly for functionality, but there were just enough hints of personality beneath the surface to show that it was a home. A table of polished cherry wood occupied the dining room, along with a matching china closet that contained various items reminiscent of Zalyndrya. In the living room, two leather sofas dominated the space, and the wall adjacent to the door held various colors of a mural in its very beginning stages. The patches of paint weren't enough to guess what the final product would be, but each stroke had been carefully placed.

68

"Whatever you're making smells delicious, Karian," Cassandra said, following her brother into the kitchen.

"Well, I do remember how to cook," he said. "I might not do it too often, but I like to think that I haven't forgotten in so short a time."

Watching the twins exchange pleasant conversation, Sean tried to relax. He couldn't quite believe that the man in the kitchen laughing with Cassandra was the same one who had nearly killed him. Beneath the surface, he knew better than to let his guard down, though. There was little love between them, and he couldn't shake the feeling that Karian was looking for an excuse to finish what he'd started.

As the pair brought the food out to the table, Cassandra motioned for him to sit, silencing him with a look when he tried to protest. He took a seat where one of the two plates had been placed, and he hoped that he was hiding his discomfort well. A glance from Karian, coupled with a smirk, told him that his acting skills needed work. Sean responded with a glare, but he schooled his expression into something marginally more pleasant when they returned to the table.

"I hope it tastes alright," Karian said, sitting beside his sister as he opened a small, opaque bottle. "I couldn't taste it to be certain, but it was a simple enough recipe to follow."

"I'm sure it'll be wonderful." Cassandra's smile brightened the room, and she served Sean and herself portions of chicken parmigiana and spaghetti. "I've wanted to try this for months, but I haven't made it myself, yet. I may need to have you copy the recipe for me before we leave."

"Let's make sure that you find it palatable first," Karian said.

His smile was guarded, and the tension in his muscles refused to dissipate. As Sean observed him, he found it impossible to see him as anything other than the predator he was. Maybe it was the years he'd spent on Zalyndrya, of which Sean knew little, that had shaped him into the perfect candidate for his condition, but if he allowed himself to think about it, then he'd have to admit that providing Karian with even more skills meant to wound and kill was terrifying.

"Your English has really come along," Sean said, trying to temper the unease. "You must have worked really hard to master the language."

"It was a requirement of the job offer," Karian said. "I'll admit that I had help, though. Before I returned, Lalasa worked an enchantment to help me learn quicker. There's no way that I would have become as proficient as I am without her assistance."

"Are you on better terms with them now?" Cassandra asked. Hope settled on her expression; she wanted nothing more than for her brother to see the side of the ones who raised her that she knew.

"It's complicated," he said, taking a sip from the bottle. "Lalasa tries, and I appreciate that, but it's not enough to erase a lifetime of bitterness. I can't say that I hate her anymore, but I wouldn't call us friends, either. Lothan, on the other hand, is an asshole, and he can go work on his tan for all I care."

Cassandra's smile faded, but instead of anger, there was a dull ache. It was painful to hear that her only living family still harbored harsh feelings towards her adoptive parents, but she knew that it would never come easily. It would take many more years, perhaps decades, for the wounds to heal.

"He saved your life," she reminded.

"That's debatable," Karian said before changing the subject. "Have you decided on a new project?"

"I have a few ideas," she said. She didn't want to leave the discussion there, but she followed the new topic with minimal objection. "I was thinking of opening a coffee shop or a bakery, but with later hours than most places like that. I've noticed that the only real places for people to socialize at night are bars and diners. I'd like to offer something a little more comfortable for those who prefer a more relaxing atmosphere." She paused, almost leaving her thoughts there, but continued instead. "You could always help me with it. It'd be hours that you can work, so that wouldn't be an issue."

"I already have a job, Cass."

"I know, but I just thought that you might enjoy something different," she said.

"You don't approve," Karian said. When she didn't answer, his expression softened. "I know you mean well, but I'm fine. Really, I am. My job isn't as quiet as a nice little shop, but it's what I know, and I'm good at it. Not to mention that it pays very well. Maybe one day, I'll think about something a little less exciting, but for now, I'm going to continue along this path."

She chose not to push the issue, and Sean placed his hand on hers in a silent gesture of support. Karian would follow whatever path he felt suited

70

him at the time, and his decisions were his own to make. Nothing she could say could force him from it, and pressing too hard would only send him back into seclusion. They'd lost sixteen years; she was not going to allow any more to slip through her fingers.

"Do you at least have friends?" she ventured.

"Again, complicated."

Sean watched the exchange but remained silent. Cassandra had voiced her concerns to him many times, and he'd offered what little advice he could, but neither of them could really place themselves in Karian's position. Cassandra was still learning the things she'd missed over the years, and Sean knew even less about the man than she did. Lack of knowledge fed the frustration, making understanding all the more difficult, but he could tell that she really only wanted to see her brother happy.

"I don't have the kind of life that makes it easy to get close to people," Karian continued. "I'm on the road more than I'm home, and it wouldn't be fair to expect a friend to sit and wait to hear from me on the rare occasions that I'm in town. I go out and socialize here and there, but I'm not looking for a strong connection with anyone."

"Ian might like to get to know you," Sean said. "You two seemed to get along before, so maybe you should give him a call."

Karian turned his head to regard him, his expression thoughtful. He hadn't outright refused, and Sean took that as a good sign. The suggestion had merit, and Sean could see him considering it, but he didn't expect a decision.

"I'll give it some thought," Karian said.

The rest of the meal passed with comfortable conversation. They avoided any other potentially volatile subjects, focusing instead on Cassandra's ideas for her possible project and the daily routines of Sean's occupation. As the evening wore on, Sean found himself starting to enjoy the company. Despite their issues in the past, Karian had been a considerate host, and it certainly helped that no threats passed between them.

After packing up the leftovers for them to take with them, Karian walked them to the door, hesitating before pulling his sister into a hug. It was still a little awkward between them, but hopefully that would fade over time. He exchanged a brief handshake with Sean and waited until they'd stepped into the elevator before closing the door.

71

He'd enjoyed the visit, but spending the time with them had tested his willpower. Thankfully, neither of them had seemed to notice the hunger gnawing at him, and the single bottle of O Negative had barely eased it. Grabbing his leather jacket, he left the condo and opted to take the stairs down to the ground floor. His motorcycle remained parked in the garage beneath the building as he crossed the lobby and exited through the glass doors, pausing to decide which way to go.

Starting down the sidewalk, he headed in the general direction of Broad Street. His boots were silent on the pavement, his hands sliding into the pockets of his jacket as he observed the city around him. It was teeming with life, and the occasional pedestrian that he passed tempted his hunger. He'd grown used to the pull, though, and he knew that he still retained enough control to choose his next meal without difficulty.

He stopped outside of one of the hotels, a hint of a smile on his lips as he walked into the lobby and towards the restaurant. Taking a seat at the bar, he slipped out of his jacket and turned his head to survey the other customers. When the bartender approached, he ordered a bottled beer, and he waited for her to walk away after presenting it to withdraw a small vial from the inner pocket of his jacket. He emptied the crimson liquid into the bottle, tucking the vial away as he swirled the beverage to mix it.

Snippets of conversation drifted towards him, the same idle chatter of people who had nowhere else to be at the moment. His gaze drifted over a few of them, making assessments along the way. There was a woman who briefly caught his attention, but she looked a little too similar to one he'd taken home the week prior, so he continued his silent perusal.

Movement to his left caused his head to turn, and he looked over the man who leaned on the bar beside him, presumably waiting for the bartender. Karian estimated that he was only a little older than he was, but the lack of anything that would indicate that he'd just come in from outside gave a good indication that he was staying at the hotel, probably for business.

Brown eyes met his as the man turned his head, and Karian turned on the barstool to face him, resting his elbow on the bar as his hand curled around his beer. The stranger gave him the same once over he'd done on his own, and Karian arched a white brow, his lips turning in a crooked smile. This was almost too easy.

Small talk had never been his best skill – it was hardly necessary in his line of work – but he listened with feigned interest as the other spoke of the meetings that he'd been attending all day. Karian doubted that he'd remember any of it later; he'd already forgotten the man's name. Still, he didn't argue against the suggestion to take the conversation somewhere a little more private, and he downed his drink before following to the elevators.

He still hated the machines, but he could swallow down the claustrophobia long enough to reach their floor. It certainly helped that his companion was more than willing to keep him otherwise occupied during the ride. They broke apart as the doors opened, but the separation lasted only until the door to the hotel room snapped shut.

Midnight came and went, and a few hours later, Karian slipped out of the room and ducked into the stairwell. He'd had enough control to keep his breakfast alive this time, and he was a little proud of himself for it. With his hands in the pockets of his jacket again, he descended the stairs and exited into the lobby, while the doors to one of the elevators whispered open.

His nostrils flared at the unfamiliar scent, but he kept walking, glancing at the man who exited as he passed. With senses alert, Karian crossed the lobby of the hotel, nodding once to the doorman, and stepped out into the comfortable night air. His exceptional hearing picked up the sound of footsteps following him, along with the strange scent, but he maintained a casual pace. Movement out of the corner of his eye caught his attention, and his muscles tensed when the stranger fell into step beside him.

He almost reminded Karian of Ian, with similar build and blond hair that was slightly wet from a recent shower, but he carried himself differently. The fluid grace of a predator, combined with the way he appeared coiled to strike at the slightest hint of a threat, kept Karian on guard, but he had no intentions of starting trouble on his own.

For two blocks, neither of them spoke; neither seemed willing to break the silence. His plans for returning to his condo moved aside to make way for the new development, and he kept his gaze forward as he continued towards City Hall. The late hour ensured that there were almost no other pedestrians along Broad Street, and the man beside him finally addressed him.

"Someone had a good evening."

Karian couldn't place his accent – he hadn't heard it before – but he

73

recognized the words as English, which hardly came as a surprise. It was the dominant language of the area as far as he knew. With a short breath of a laugh, he opened his mouth to respond.

"Jealous?"

"Hardly," Alex said. "I just couldn't help but notice that you reek of sex."

"And you reek of wet dog," Karian said. "What's your point?"

"Did you at least get the name of tonight's entrée?"

Karian stopped in his tracks, green eyes narrowing as he turned his head to regard him. The man stopped as well, a knowing smile on his lips as he met his gaze. There was no fear, even after revealing that he was aware of Karian's condition, and he almost looked amused at the reaction he received.

"What do you want?" Karian asked evenly.

"The winning lottery numbers would be nice," he said. "I just like to keep tabs on the local corpses."

Alex watched him process his words, hoping for an even more entertaining response, but Karian just watched him, his expression cautious. With a trace of disappointment, Alex started forward again, and Karian continued alongside him. One thing had struck him as curious, though – the vampire had a familiar accent himself. It was a connection to his client, and he needed to learn more.

"Interesting city," Alex said. "You never know who you might run into or where they've been."

Karian didn't respond. His mind turned over the small details he'd observed, trying to fit the pieces of the puzzle beside him into a clear picture. The man wasn't human, but he was certainly alive. After another block, the little tidbits clicked into place, and Karian glanced at him again.

"You're a wolf," he said.

"And you're not as dumb as you look," Alex said. "You're not going to get all pissy about it, are you? I really don't have the patience for that tonight."

"Not at all," Karian said, allowing himself to relax just a little now that he'd figured out what he was dealing with. "Your kind are actually quite respected among my people. I see no reason to change that."

It was Alex's turn to stop and look at him in surprise. For all of the supposed drama between their different species, which he'd seldom actually witnessed, the vampire had nothing negative to say regarding their differences. He would have been suspicious, but Karian's words were genuine.

"What brings you to the City of Brotherly Love?" Alex asked, crossing the intersection once the light changed. When Karian didn't answer, he tried another tactic. "Okay, then. Are you going to give me your name, or should I just pick one for you?"

"Silver," Karian said. Giving his real name was out of the question. Even though he called this city home, he wasn't too keen on the idea of Alex knowing more about him than he was willing to provide.

Alex considered him for a moment. He'd heard that name recently, and he tried to place it as City Hall stood before them. The rumors surrounding his former employer's disappearance and the events that followed replayed in his mind, along with the news of a new recruit training several months earlier.

"You're the new guy," he said after a moment. "Don't look so shocked. Word gets around when someone joins the company under unusual circumstances. That and I have a tendency to dig up information when I want it."

"Are you going to keep me guessing as to who the hell you are?" Karian asked.

"Malice," he said. "And before you ask, I'm only in Philly for a little while on assignment."

"That's probably one of the things I enjoy the most about the job," Karian said. "I think I prefer being on the road and in different cities to staying home. Then again, I've never been the type to stay in one place for very long."

Despite their mutual distrust, an air of comradery settled over them. Neither of them really knew what to make of the other. Both were in the same business, but different species, and both knew better than to get close to anyone, especially a colleague. There was no animosity, though, and it was a refreshing change. Karian still had trouble dealing with most of the staff in Boston, especially those who had been present when he'd been held captive. It was likely that he'd never see Alex again, but a few minutes of connecting over a common thread suited him just fine.

"It's not a bad city," Karian said. "It takes some getting used to, but there are worse places to work." Before he could say anything else, his phone vibrated in his pocket, and he pulled it out to read the message across the screen. "My apologies, Malice, but it looks like we're going to have to catch up another time."

"I'm sure we will," Alex said, watching him turn and head back down Broad Street.

He mentally catalogued every little detail he'd gleaned from the brief interaction, sorting them into neat little compartments. The strange accent wasn't the only link he found to his client; physiological curiosities added to the small list of coincidences. He saw no shadow and heard no sound as his colleague turned the corner, and he pondered the significance as he started back towards his hotel.

Alex had dealt with enough vampires to know what to expect from one, but even the ones he'd encountered in the meeting with his current employer were on par with every other corpse he'd encountered along the way. His client and Silver were different, and he wondered if a new strain of the curse had started to emerge. He'd need to tap a few more resources to find an answer, and he changed course at the next intersection. If his reliable contact still lived in the city, then maybe he could learn more before he ventured deeper into the mystery.

Six

Marielle scrolled through her emails once she'd arrived at work, marking appointments on Rhonda's calendar. It was going to be a full week, she realized with some disappointment, and she wouldn't be able to take an extra day off to visit with her father. His visited so rarely, and she seldom had time to make the trip to Florida to see him, but she couldn't blow off her job when the business was becoming even more successful.

Some of the lower profile clients were assigned to other accountants with the firm, freeing up some of Rhonda's time for wealthier guests and prospective customers, but that meant little as far as Marielle was concerned. Checking the schedule for the night, she sent a few confirmation emails and started building new profiles for the ones who would be meeting with her boss within the next several hours.

An interoffice message popped up on her screen, grabbing her attention, and she opened the small window to read it. One more meeting added itself to the calendar, and she forwarded the details to Rhonda. This one was a little more interesting than the others, but her boss wouldn't deny them, even if it meant pushing another client back just a little.

Over the course of the past several months, she'd come to terms with the reality of the business. Knowing that most of the people who walked through the door were either undead, or representing someone who was, had initially jarred her with fear, but now she'd regained her footing enough to greet them as she'd done before she'd learned the truth. Some of them were even friendly to her, more so than the few human clients she'd encountered during her employment. The fear hadn't vanished completely, but she managed it better than she'd done in the past, and her innate professionalism often won out over human emotion.

One of the double doors opened behind her, and she glanced over her shoulder as Ian emerged from the office, a casual smile thrown in her direction, which widened when her heartbeat sped up slightly. Heat rushed to her face, and she returned her attention to her computer, printing out documents for the next appointment.

Ian leaned on the edge of her desk, reading the screen while she gave a valiant attempt at ignoring him. With everything going on during her shift, she wanted to avoid the obvious distraction he provided, but he was undeterred, and he made no attempt to remove himself from her presence while she worked.

"Busy night?" he asked when she finally looked at him again.

"Yeah," she said. "Three prospective clients, two current clients who want to discuss their portfolios, and I just heard from Sean that Lady Konistav is supposed to be here before midnight."

His eyebrows rose at that. It wasn't that he'd expected more notice of her arrival, but he hadn't heard that she was even in town recently. Maybe she'd just arrived, or maybe Cass had chosen to keep the information to herself. Not that it was really his business, but he wanted a chance to catch up with her again.

"I just hope she shows up early," Marielle continued. "Karian has an appointment at two, and I'm pretty sure things are still a little tense around them. The good thing is, according to my notes, Lothan isn't going to be here, and I think that Karian's a little more comfortable around Lalasa than he is with Lothan"

Ian agreed, although he couldn't imagine Karian being comfortable around either of them; he barely tolerated Ian on the few occasions they'd met since he'd returned to Earth. There had to be a way to bring him out of his shell, but he couldn't figure out how to manage that without pushing him further away. They hadn't even really spoken since the night he'd driven Karian back up to Boston, and he found himself actually looking forward to seeing him again.

"Any familiar names on the potential client list?" he asked.

"Trina and Sophia Skovgaard," she said. "They should be here around one. Hopefully, there won't be any issues this time. Things didn't go so well when they were here to meet with Mikhail."

"Yeah, I remember," he said. "I'll make sure to stick around for that one. Anyone else?"

"No one that I recognize," she said. "But I don't have full profiles on the others yet. I'm still waiting for them to send in their initial portfolio documents, but at this rate, they'll probably just bring hard copies of everything instead of emailing digitals."

It made even more work for her, but she didn't really mind. Marielle prided herself on maintaining structure with her organizational skills, and fitting all of the documents together into something that made sense, while being easily accessible to her boss, was one of her best talents. She welcomed the challenge and enjoyed the satisfaction when everything came together in the end. She was sure Rhonda appreciated her work; her paycheck was a good indicator of that, even if she rarely said so directly.

The door to the stairwell opened on quiet hinges, and Ian glanced over towards the elevator lobby as he straightened. He could count on one hand the number of visitors who preferred to climb the stairs to the top floor of the building instead of taking the elevator, and his first guess proved correct when Lalasa came into view.

Silent footsteps brought her closer, and she greeted them both warmly as Marielle stood, stepping around her desk to meet her. The empress had chosen a subtle outfit for the meeting, one that could have helped her pass for a local if it weren't for her features. With the technology surrounding the building, and her previous experiences with Rhonda's security system, she'd forgone her glamour, and while at first glance, one might have thought she was human, the delicate point of her ears revealed otherwise.

"It's good to see you both well," she said. "I trust things have remained quiet since last year?"

"Likewise," Ian said. "And yeah, it's pretty much back to normal around here."

"As normal as it gets for us," Marielle added. "I've already told Ms. Evans that you're here, so she'll be with you shortly. Can I get you anything while you wait?"

Lalasa shook her head, her violet eyes resting on the double doors as one of them opened and Rhonda stood in the doorway. Deep brown eyes complimented her dark complexion as she regarded them, her gaze calculating. With a glance at the three of them, her attention settled on her employees.

"Marielle, if my one o'clock arrives early, let them know that I'll be with them as soon as possible," she said. "Ian, find Sean and make sure we have security measures in place for that one. I don't want a repeat of what happened last time they were here." Her attention then moved to her client. "Lady Konistav, please come in."

While Ian headed towards the elevators, Marielle returned to her desk, and Lalasa followed the accountant into her office. The décor hadn't changed since the last time she'd visited, and she settled comfortably into one of the chairs in front of the large desk. Rhonda took a moment to browse through her notes, ensuring that everything was in order, before lifting her gaze to her guest.

"It's good to see you," Lalasa said with a gentle smile. "Has business been well?"

"You too," Rhonda said. "It's been busy, but busy is good. With Mikhail's company signing on with us, I've had to hire more staff to keep track of some of my other clients. I'm in a position now where I can focus on my high-profile clientele and regulate some of the less involved clients to the other accountants on my staff. Marielle does a wonderful job of keeping things in order. Honestly, I'm glad she decided to stay on board. I doubt I could find another assistant who would be able to do the job half as well as she does. How are things on Zalyndrya?"

"Busy as well," Lalasa said. "We have the Spring Festivals on the horizon, which means the city will have plenty of visitors and vendors. Tensions are rising with Evemyst; I fear that we'll be unable to complete negotiations before the treaty expires. Abnalia, one of my advisors, has chosen to remain with us even if that happens. Some loyalties run deeper than blood."

"Indeed," Rhonda said, shifting her focus for the reason for this meeting. "I'll try not to keep you, then. All of your accounts are in order, the investments we've made on your behalf are doing well, and if you decided to relocate here, you could live off of the interest alone for at least a couple of centuries."

"And my daughter's accounts?" she asked.

"Lady Konistav-"

"I think we've moved beyond formalities," Lalasa said. "Please, call me by name if you wish."

"Understood," Rhonda said. "Lalasa, your daughter is an adult, and confidentiality laws require that I refrain from sharing the details of her finances without her express, written permission. I know that you're concerned, but without her authorization, I can't tell you anything."

"I had to ask," she said. "I appreciate your adherence to ethics, though. I need to transfer funds to an associate to pay for services. That's the real reason I'm here."

Rhonda turned to her computer, pulling up information as she nodded. Moving through the screens quickly, she accessed the list of accounts, and her gaze lifted to regard Lalasa.

"I would suggest using your general expense account," she said. "It won't affect your primary savings, so your interest accrual there will remain untouched. Where would you like to send the payment?"

"I've hired Mikhail's organization to find someone," Lalasa said. "Send a seventy-five thousand deposit to his account. Once the task is complete, I'd like another fifty thousand to transfer as well."

"Done," she said, processing the transaction quickly. "As for the remaining payment, I'll draw up the paperwork for you to sign. You'll need to declare an agent to notify me of when you want the rest of the money sent over. They will be the only one able to authorize the final transaction."

Lalasa found that comforting, and despite the memories of how she'd come into Rhonda's acquaintance, she was grateful for the woman's skill and knowledge. The rest of the meeting passed without issue, and she signed her name where indicated in an elegant script. Sliding the papers across the desk, she lifted her gaze to Rhonda.

"You truly are exceptional at this," she said. "I'm sure it can be uncomfortable dealing with my kind, but your professionalism and efficiency are impressive. You seem to enjoy it, and it suits you well."

Rhonda stared at her, momentarily taken aback by the praise. She prided herself on her work but hearing such a compliment from a woman who had not only seen a millennium pass, but oversaw an entire empire, left her at a loss for words. Looking away briefly, she let her surprise pass, and then looked at her again.

"Thank you," she said. "I've always been good at numbers, and my father gave me the opportunity to make something out of it. I like to think that I've made him proud with the way I've handled our family's business."

"I'm sure you have," Lalasa said. "And you should be quite proud as well. I've learned that money can be a volatile subject around here, and it's obvious that those of us who have to plan for a very long future trust you with managing it for them. I doubt that I'd have found anyone better to assist with our finances on this world. Thank you for your dedication, Rhonda."

"It's a pleasure," she said, standing. "Having clients who appreciate the work that goes into this makes a difference."

Rhonda walked her out, and they parted ways with a handshake before she headed back into her office. Lalasa stopped at Marielle's desk instead of leaving immediately, and the woman looked up at her.

"I'll be in the area for the next week," she said. "My husband will be joining me tomorrow night, and we'd love to have you and Ian over for a visit. I'll be extending the invitation to Cassandra and Sean as well, and to her brother if he's interested. I'm sure he'll decline, but it wouldn't do any harm to make the offer."

"I would love to, but my father is visiting from Florida," Marielle said. "Maybe next time?"

"He's welcome to join us if he wishes," she said. "I'll ask Lothan to at least try to maintain some level of decorum. I'm not sure when I'll have the opportunity to visit again, and it would be nice to see everyone before I return home."

"I'll talk to him," Marielle said, glancing past her as one of the elevators chimed to announce a new arrival. "I can let Cass know tomorrow, and we'll go from there."

"I look forward to hearing from her, then," she said. "Safe travels."

Lalasa passed the next pair of clients on her way to the stairs, offering a slight nod of acknowledgement, but she took note of the way the woman clad in black stared at her. Stopping, she regarded the two for a moment, her head tipping to the side with a silent question. The blonde murmured an apology for her companion's poor manners before taking the other's arm to guide them towards Marielle, and Lalasa watched them for a moment before pushing open the door and starting down the stairs.

"Trina," Soph hissed, turning her head to stare at the closed door of the stairwell. "Just wait a second, will you?"

"Fine," Trina said, turning to face her. "What's the problem?"

82

"What the hell was that?" she whispered. "She didn't have a heartbeat, but she didn't have a shadow either, and did you get a good look at her? Did you hear her accent?"

"I wasn't really paying attention to her," Trina said. "We're not here to stalk other clients; we're here to see if I'm going to hire an accountant to help with things to make it a little easier for you while I'm away. Can we please focus?"

"But Trina," Soph pleaded, looking between her and the entrance to the stairs. "Didn't any of that seem weird? What if she's the one Krys is running from?"

"It's not like she knows who we are or where we live," Trina said patiently. "And you're making assumptions over a few seconds and a glimpse of some stranger. Can we please just go have this meeting and get it over with?"

Soph opened her mouth to argue but let the matter drop. She cast one last glance at the closed door before continuing towards the desk, her black cowboy boots echoing on the tiled floor. As they reached the one final barrier between them and the purpose of their visit, the woman stood to greet them.

"I'm sorry we're a bit early," Trina said, trying for a smile.

"It's no trouble," Marielle assured her as she held out a leather folder. "Ms. Evans will be with you shortly. In the meantime, would you please fill out these forms?" She gestured to the glass table across the lobby. "You won't be waiting very long."

Taking the portfolio, the couple relocated to the table and scanned over the forms. The documents were standard, with a few alterations to consider the uniqueness of the clients, and Trina completed them quickly. As she closed the folder again, Marielle approached to retrieve it.

"Ms. Evans is ready for you," she said. "If you'll follow me, please?"

As they followed her into the office, Soph noted the extra personnel in the room. Ian stood against the wall behind Rhonda, while a man in a dark suit had posted just inside the door, both having arrived through the back elevator ahead of time. That one was human, she realized, hiding a grin as Marielle directed them to the chairs across from the accountant and set the folder on the desk.

"Do you have security on hand for all meetings with prospective clients?" Trina asked once Marielle left the room.

"It never hurts to be careful," Rhonda said. "You've met Ian Mackenzie, my personal security detail, and occasionally, I find it necessary to have additional personnel present. I'm sure you understand."

Trina glanced at Soph. They understood all too well why Rhonda had requested a security presence. Their previous meetings had been less than peaceful, and Trina couldn't fault her for taking care to ensure her own safety. There were certain hazards that came with associating with their kind, after all.

"Before we begin, allow me to explain a little bit about this company and the services we offer," Rhonda continued. "It's been a family business for several generations, and I stepped into this role when my father retired. We've enjoyed remarkable success, and the simple fact that I'm still alive should be enough of a testament to the satisfaction of my clients. I'll admit that my rates are not cheap, but for the service, operating hours, and personal attention that you'll receive, I'm sure you'll find that my price is reasonable."

"Fair enough," Trina conceded.

"I assume you two are married?" Rhonda asked, moving forward with the business at hand.

"We only recently made it official," Trina said. "But Soph has been using my last name for the past thirty years."

"Will you be maintaining your funds in a joint account?"

"That's the plan," Trina said.

They covered the basic details before moving on to the specifics of the services they would need, and Rhonda answered their questions confidently and thoroughly throughout the meeting. By the time everything was settled, both Soph and Trina were satisfied with the package she offered, and after only a few minutes of quiet discussion, they placed their signatures on the final documents.

"I look forward to working with you in the future," Rhonda said, standing. "Do you have any other questions?"

"I have one," Soph said. She'd kept her mouth shut throughout the rest of the discussion, per the agreement she'd made with Trina earlier, but there was one thing that had been nagging at her ever since they'd arrived. "Who was the woman who met with you before us?"

"Ms. Skovgaard," Rhonda began cautiously. "Confidentiality comes standard with my services. I'm not at liberty to disclose the identity of my other clients. I'm sure you understand."

Soph's disappointment was obvious, but Trina slipped a hand into hers and gave a gentle squeeze. The confidentiality clause also worked in their favor, and neither of them could argue the logic behind it.

"That's all, then," Trina said. "Thank you for your time and help."

"You're very welcome," Rhonda said. "If you need any other assistance, please feel free to take my card on the way out. Marielle will be happy to schedule any other appointments you might need."

*****

Marielle closed the door quietly, hoping not to wake her guest when she returned home. With the current workload, her schedule had begun to run later, but hopefully, it wouldn't last forever. The occasional busy week was common, and the more success her employer found, the more benefits she'd receive in turn.

The television was still on in the living room, and she turned the corner to see Carl look up at her from his place on the sofa. His expression was concerned as he gave a brief glance at the clock, but she rolled her eyes and set her purse down. It was almost reminiscent of her teenage years, when she would come home just a few minutes past her curfew, but thankfully, there was no lecture this time.

"Dad, it's almost five in the morning," she said. "What are you doing up?"

"Couldn't sleep," he said. "I thought you worked for an accounting firm? What kind of hours do they keep there?"

"Rhonda tries to make herself available for people who aren't able to come in during regular business hours," she said, skirting around the reality of the job. "Besides, for what she's paying me, I'm not about to complain about working late nights every now and then. You didn't have to wait up for me, you know. I'm not sixteen anymore."

"I'm allowed to worry."

"Not if it keeps you up all night," she laughed. "Trust me, Dad. I'm a big girl. I've got this." She stepped into the kitchen to make a cup of tea, reappearing in the doorway while she waited for the water to boil. She could always just use the microwave, but there was something about a nice hot cup of tea from the kettle. "What are your plans for tomorrow night?"

85

"Nothing that I'm aware of," Carl said. "Are you working late again?"

"I don't have to be in until around midnight, but I was invited to dinner with some friends," she said. "I initially declined so that I could spend some time with you before you go home, but they said you're more than welcome to come with me, if you want."

"So, I might actually meet someone other than your 'not boyfriend'?" he asked with a grin.

"We're not together," she insisted, even as she felt the familiar blush stain her cheeks. She could only hope that it was dark enough where she was standing to prevent him from seeing it. "We tried dating, and it didn't work. Ian is just a friend, and yes, he was invited too."

That was all he needed to hear to make his decision. In most instances, he wouldn't have intruded on his daughter's time with her friends, but if the vampire planned to be there, then Carl wasn't about to leave Marielle without any kind of protection. He didn't allow his thoughts to show on his face, but his smile vanished the second she returned to the kitchen, and he sent a quick message to his associate before tucking his phone away again.

There had been no news from his former colleague on the vampire situation, but he was trying to be patient. He couldn't expect results within twenty-four hours, but Ian apparently had no intentions of going away anytime soon. The inability to handle it himself was beyond frustrating, but he couldn't afford to risk his daughter learning the truth about his past. It would crush her; she'd probably hate him for the things he'd done.

Then again, she'd dated a vampire, but maybe she hadn't known what Ian was. She hadn't been through the same training that he'd completed, and she'd never found herself in the position where the only way to walk out alive was to kill one. Carl hoped that she never would. Marielle meant too much to him for him to ever want her to start down that path, and he'd do whatever it took to make sure she never would.

"I wasn't sure if you wanted any, but I brought you a cup anyway," she said, carrying two steaming mugs as she sat down on the other end of the sofa. "It's chamomile, so maybe it'll help you sleep. It helps me most of the time."

"Have you ever thought about moving down to Florida with me?" he asked as he took one of the mugs. "The winters aren't as rough as they are up here, and I'd get to see you more often."

Marielle looked down, suddenly interested in the tea and the way the cup warmed her hands. They'd discussed this before, and every time, she'd given him the same answer. She picked up something else in his voice this time, though, an edge of concern in addition to the faint hope that she might change her mind.

"I really like it here," she said softly. "I have a great job, and I'm doing really well for myself. I'd love to be closer to you, but this just isn't the right time for me to think about moving. I can't just drop everything and relocate to Florida."

"I know," he sighed. "Can't blame me for asking though. I miss you, kiddo. It'd be nice to have you around more."

"You could move back," she said. "I have the extra bedroom, and you could use that until you decide if you want a place of your own. It wouldn't be any trouble."

"Can't take the cold up here," he said. "I guess we'll just have to visit each other more often. Don't you get vacation time with this fancy job that you have?"

"I know, I know." She managed to laugh again, the tension fading. "I'll get better about coming to visit, I promise. So, about tomorrow night?"

"I think I can fit it into my busy schedule of doing nothing," he said. "Might even find it in me to pick up a bottle of wine or a six-pack, depending on what kind of friends you've got."

"Wine would work," Marielle said. "I'm sure you'll get along great with them. They're good people."

Carl wished he could share her optimism. It felt wrong, though. She sounded genuinely happy about the idea, but there were too many unknowns, and the shadows of his previous life kept him on his toes. Marielle hadn't told him much about her friends in the city, and it was only recently that she'd started mentioning a woman who was dating the security director at her work. It had sounded like they got along well, but without meeting her, he had no way of knowing if the woman was another vampire like Marielle's ex-boyfriend.

He was all for letting her make her own decisions, but she had to make sure that she thought really hard about them, and about the people with whom she associated. It wasn't as if he thought all vampires were bad, but he knew the risks better than she did. The trick was to help her learn caution without throwing all of the secrets he'd learned out into the open.

Seven

Ian waited outside the door, listening to the conversation on the other side. Marielle was assuring Carl that his choice of attire was more than acceptable, and concern worked its way into his mind. Bringing her father along for the visit could lead to a disastrous outcome, and the moment the door opened, Ian leaned in to voice his thoughts quietly.

"Are you sure this is a good idea?" he asked.

Marielle glanced over her shoulder before stepping out into the hall, closing the door behind her. She understood why he'd worry, but she wanted to ease her way into honesty with her father. If that meant taking him to meet the vampires she'd had the opportunity to build a friendship with, then she'd accept the risks associated with it.

"It'll be fine," she said. "I have to tell him everything eventually. This seems like a good start."

"Have you thought about what could happen if he freaks out?" he pressed. "Marielle, I know he's your dad, but the Konistavs aren't like me and Euro. It's a lot harder for them to pretend to be human, and some of their traits make it damn near impossible. I'm not saying that you shouldn't try to talk to him about everything, but this is like throwing him right into the middle of it without any kind of warning."

"Ian," she began, resting a hand on his arm. The surprise on his features made her smile, and she gave a light squeeze. "Trust me, okay? I know my dad better than anyone. He won't freak out over it, I promise."

Carl opened the door behind her, and she let her hand fall back to her side as she turned to regard him. She couldn't read his expression, but it quickly vanished beneath a lopsided grin as he held up a paper bag containing a bottle of wine. His gaze lingered on Ian for a few seconds longer than necessary, and Marielle cleared her throat to break the tension.

"Are we ready?" she asked.

When both men nodded, she started down the hall to the elevators, and the ride to the ground floor stretched on in heavy silence. Her gaze darted between Ian and her father, trying to pinpoint the source of their mutual unease, but she came up empty by the time the doors opened again.

The cool evening air of spring greeted them, and she took a deep, steadying breath as she waited for the light to change so that they could cross the street. Following the path through Rittenhouse Square, she glanced up at the trees and the lights casting a soft glow on the grass and pavement, willing herself to relax as she silently repeated her belief that the night would progress without incident.

She greeted the doorman as they entered the building, guiding them to the elevators. Her nerves were on edge the closer they grew to their destination, and she glanced up at Ian for reassurance. His fingertips brushed the back of her hand, and she found the gesture comforting even as sparks danced along her skin from the contact. The second she realized it, though, she looked away, swallowing down the rush of latent feelings that she'd tried to move past since the night their relationship had ended.

"I know it's weird, but we're going to have to take the stairs from here," she said when the elevator stopped. "Ian, would you go on ahead? I need to talk to my dad before we head up, okay?"

He started to protest, but the pleading look in her eyes stopped him, and he simply nodded instead as he ducked into the stairwell. Taking a deep breath, Marielle turned to her father, meeting his cautious gaze nervously. She'd rehearsed what to say dozens of times, but it hadn't made the prospect any less intimidating.

"Marielle," he prompted. "Everything okay? We can go home if you're not feeling well."

"It's not that, Dad," she said. "It's just... There are some things you need to know before we go up there. My friends aren't from around here, and they may come across as a bit strange if you're not used to them. I really want this to go smoothly, and I don't want you to be uncomfortable, but I also want to make sure that you're not caught off guard by some of their mannerisms."

"Pretty cryptic of you," he drawled. "Why do I get the feeling there's more to this than you're saying?"

90

"It's really hard to explain," she said. "And every time I think I've figured out how to make it sound like it makes sense, it sounds even crazier. Let's just go up there and have a good time, and if anything bothers you, I'll answer anything you have to ask when we get home."

Carl's skepticism painted his features, but concern was etched into them as well. That she had an inkling of what her ex-boyfriend really was made itself apparent in the way she avoided coming right out and saying what was on her mind, but her warning was as clear as day. Whoever they were visiting had something to do with it, too, and he resisted the urge to insist that they return to her place and avoid the whole mess altogether.

"You're not caught up in any trouble, are you?" he asked.

"No, Dad, I'm not," she said. "Just trust me on this, okay? They're good people, and I want you to get along, but I also know how you can be sometimes. Don't worry about me so much. Just enjoy the visit, and like I said, we can talk later if you want."

After several long seconds of silence, he nodded, but his expression remained the same. If Marielle knew that she was dealing with the undead, and she actually trusted them, then things were far worse than he'd thought. Carl hadn't missed the way she and Ian still looked at each other, despite her insistence that they remained only friends and nothing more. He'd seen that look too many times for her to fool him, and the way she spoke of the friends who waited upstairs caused red flags to pop up all over the place.

Asking for trust felt like the theme of the night for her, and Marielle tried to offer a reassuring smile as she pushed open the door leading to the stairs. Four stories up, they exited into the corridor, where Ian waited for them. Carl forced his expression into something at least a little more welcoming as he approached the door, and Marielle gave both of them one last look before lifting her hand to knock.

Cassandra greeted them warmly, ushering them inside where the others were already waiting, and Carl's gaze immediately lifted to the small globes of light hovering around the ceiling. He missed the initial exchange between the two women, but a nudge on his arm brought his attention back, and he pasted a smile on his lips as he held out the paper bag.

"Couldn't show up empty handed," he said. "I appreciate the hospitality."

Lothan emerged from the kitchen, wiping his hands on a towel. He watched Ian move off into the living room with Sean and studied his new guest. To his credit, Carl kept his expression pleasant, despite the warning bells that sounded in his head when he took in the appearance of his host.

The man towered over him, and Carl estimated that he had to be nearly six and a half feet tall, with a physique that spoke of his years as a blacksmith's apprentice in a time long forgotten by most. It took quite a bit of effort to keep his heart rate from spiking when Lothan approached, experience aiding him in picking up on the lack of sound that should have accompanied footsteps.

"I heard that Miss Bonner would be bringing a guest," Lothan said, extending a hand. "You're her father, I presume?"

"Carl Bonner," he said, grasping his hand for a firm shake. As he'd suspected, the skin was cool to the touch. "Mighty kind of you to include me in the invitation."

"Lothan Konistav." Withdrawing his hand, he glanced over his shoulder before looking at him again. "And it's our pleasure. Marielle is a dear friend, and her family is always welcome. Make yourself comfortable, if you'd like. My wife is waiting for my assistance with the meal, but it should be ready shortly."

Carl swallowed hard as he watched the man return to the kitchen, realizing just how far out of his depth he'd gone. He could handle Ian – one punk vampire was easy – but he wasn't even sure what Lothan was. Feeling his daughter's gaze on him, he turned to look at her, and his expression must have betrayed some of his thoughts because she moved to his side instantly.

"Are you okay?" she asked softly. "There's nothing to worry about, Dad. I know it's different, but everything's fine. Just relax."

He wanted to snort at the suggestion. Relaxing was out of the question, but he didn't want her to worry. Outright fear for her safety plagued him, though, and he wracked his brain to figure out just how she'd managed to get herself so deep into such a dangerous situation. Sure, their host had seemed pleasant enough, but Carl would have bet his last breath that the man had more blood on his hands than any target he'd encountered during his years as a mercenary. He didn't have any proof, but his intuition seldom failed him.

"Marielle, you came!"

The new voice, holding the same accent as both Lothan and

Cassandra, carried through the room, and Carl watched the woman cross the distance to join them. Her genuine happiness showed clearly in the way she clasped Marielle's hands, practically beaming at her. Again, Carl wondered about what had transpired to bring his daughter into their present company, and he noted the same observations he'd seen on Lothan when violet eyes focused on him.

"Lalasa," Marielle began. "This is my dad, Carl Bonner. Dad, this is Lalasa Konistav. She and her husband are friends of ours."

"Pleased to make your acquaintance," Carl said, his jaw tight.

Lalasa's smile faded into concern, and she shot a questioning glance at Marielle, who tried to convey reassurance when their eyes met. Recovering, Lalasa regained her welcoming demeanor, and she gestured to the table in the next room.

"I believe we're waiting on one more person," she said.

"My brother couldn't make it," Cass said, joining them again. "He was called away for work, but he sends his regards."

Marielle tried not to let her relief show. She still had traces of lingering uncertainty when it came to Karian. Even though he'd apologized to her personally for the circumstances surrounding their initial meeting, the few times she'd seen him since then he seemed volatile. He'd been calm on the outside, but beneath the surface, she saw the coiled tension waiting to snap, and she had no desire to find herself in his presence when that happened.

Lothan emerged from the kitchen with a steaming platter, setting the roast on the center of the table. As promised, he presented the picture of hospitality, free of the questionable humor he'd offered in the past. Marielle was curious as to what exactly it had taken to convince him to behave. His mannerisms and off-color jokes had ceased to bother her – she'd learned that he didn't mean anything behind them – but her father's reaction would be unpredictable.

So far, the introduction into the finer details of her life in Philadelphia had progressed as smoothly as she could have hoped. Carl remained polite, if quiet, and he hadn't outright balked at the tingle of magic in the air. The tension in the air was palpable, though, and she braced herself for the worst when he began to speak.

"So, how did you come to be friends with Marielle?" he asked.

"We met with Ms. Evans last year but had to return home to handle some urgent business," Lalasa said. "Cassandra came here in our stead, and Marielle was kind enough to show her around and help her become acclimated to the area. They became fast friends, as have we."

It all came back to Rhonda Evans, he realized. The woman was an accountant, someone who dealt specifically with people's finances, but she had her hands in everything surrounding his daughter. He gave a brief look up at the lights before focusing on Lalasa again.

"And where are y'all from, if you don't mind my asking?"

"It's a very remote country," Lothan said. "Very few have even heard of it, so we'll spare you the boring details."

The evasive answer confirmed some of his suspicions, but it left him with even more questions. He eyed the empty spaces where the plates should have been in front of his hosts and Ian, noting a moment later that Cassandra watched him intently while she took delicate bites of her meal. He saw a warning in her green eyes, caution not to venture further down that path of curiosity, but he continued forward regardless.

"I used to travel a lot when I was younger," he said. "You might just find yourself surprised at the places I've seen."

"I'd love to hear about them," Lalasa said. "I'm sure you've visited plenty of interesting places. Do you still travel often, or are you settled in retirement aside from the occasional trip to this city?"

Marielle resisted a laugh at the smooth deflection. As much as she respected her father, he couldn't match hundreds of years of diplomatic experience. Lalasa's voice remained pleasant, her interest genuine, and Carl watched her quietly for a few seconds, unable to read her.

"My traveling days are long gone," he said, frowning. "I don't even manage to come up here as often as I'd like." Motioning to his plate, he arched a brow. "You aren't eating?"

"We have plans later," Lalasa said. "This was simply a chance to reconnect with friends. There's plenty here, so feel free to have as much as you'd like. Cassandra brought dessert as well."

"You sure you aren't planning on having one of us for dessert instead?" he asked evenly.

"Dad!" Marielle gasped, dropping her fork.

"The thought hadn't crossed my mind," Lothan said. "But if that's what you'd prefer…"

"Lothan," Lalasa warned. "Mr. Bonner, I would appreciate it if you would refrain from insinuating that our intentions are darker than a simple visit. Do you honestly think that we would have invited all of you here if we had plans to harm you?"

"So, you're admitting it?" Carl asked, setting his utensils on his plate. "I'm not blind, and I sure as hell ain't stupid. I've been worried sick ever since I had a little suspicion that Marielle had fallen in with the wrong crowd."

"There comes a time in every parent's life when he must realize that his child is grown and capable of making her own decisions," Lothan said. All pretense of civility began to vanish, and his dark blue eyes narrowed. "I would think that you would have reached that conclusion long before now."

"You want to lecture me about parenting?" Carl said, his patience thinning. "You think you know more about raising one than I do?"

"We have raised one," Lothan shot back. "And I'm very pleased with the result. We're both very proud of our daughter, but we also respect her decisions."

"And I'm sure she's growing up to be a nice little bloodsucker herself," he said dryly. Standing, he stalked away, pulling the door open. "Thanks for the invitation. Hope I never see you again."

Stunned silence followed his abrupt departure before Marielle rushed to her feet, apologizing on her way to the door. Her father stood by the elevator, barely sparing her a glance as she approached, and she stared at him in shock before she found her voice.

"What the hell was that about?" she demanded.

"You want to tell me why you're hanging around with those monsters all of a sudden?" He spun to face her, and she was again transported back to high school. "You're smarter than this, Marielle. Do you have any idea what they do to normal folks like us? Have you seen things like that in action? Because I have, and I'll tell you what, it ain't pretty."

"They're not like that!"

"Then you haven't looked hard enough," he said.

"Marielle, is everything alright?" Cassandra asked as she joined them in the hall.

"We're fine," she said. "We'll be back in just a few minutes."

"Like hell," Carl said. "I'm not going to go back and play house with a bunch of monsters. You think they're your friends, but they'll turn on you quicker than lightning if it suits them."

"Mr. Bonner," Cass began. Her voice was calm, but Marielle caught the undercurrent of anger coloring her words. "I'm not sure what stories you've been reading, but no one inside this residence has any intentions of harming you or your daughter. They extended an invitation in good faith, and you're throwing that in their faces."

"And I'm just supposed to take your word on that?" Sarcasm dripped from his voice as he shook his head. "I don't think so. You want to hang around with bloodsuckers, be my guest, but I'm not going to pretend that everything's fine while I wait for one of them to kill me."

"Mind your words, Mr. Bonner," Cass warned, green eyes fierce. "Those are my parents in there, the ones who raised me when I was orphaned. I will not have you speak ill of them when all they've done is offer you friendship."

"Friendship from things like them always comes with a price," he said. "Marielle, I want to go home now."

"Dad, would you please just listen?" she pleaded. "I don't know where this is coming from, but they're good people. Why can't you just give them a chance?"

"Because I know better," he said.

"How?" Marielle asked. "You keep saying that, but you haven't said anything else to explain how you know these things. What haven't you told me?"

Carl's lips pressed into a thin line, refusing to elaborate as he shook his head. He hated lying to her, hated the wounded look in her eyes, but there were so many things that she just couldn't know. The world was a dark and terrifying place, and she'd only just brushed the edge of it. If she knew the things he'd seen, the things he'd done, she'd never look at him the same way again. So, he remained silent, refusing to disclose even the tiniest detail of his old job, and he turned to the elevator again.

"Dad, please!"

"I'm going back to your place," he said wearily. "You coming?"

Marielle looked down, chewing her lower lip as her fingers toyed with the hem of her shirt. Family loyalty was one thing, but she knew that his actions and words were unnecessary. The decision tore her in two, between friends she'd never expected to meet, and her father who'd kept something from her until tonight. Following him home meant that maybe she could convince him to share his story with her, but she couldn't; she wasn't ready for her world to turn upside-down again.

"I'll be home later," she said quietly, handing him her keys. "Don't wait up."

He took them without comment, expression showing his disappointment, but that was enough for her eyes to sting with tears. As the elevator doors closed behind him, she felt a comforting arm wrap around her shoulder, and she leaned in to the touch, fighting back the surge of emotion. He'd told her nothing, but the hollowness of betrayal ached in her chest.

Carl nearly slammed the door when he returned to Marielle's condo, rage boiling in his veins. It was bad enough that she was getting close to Ian again, but the two he'd just met were on a completely different level. He'd only hear rumors about vampires like them, the ones with no shadows and silent movements, and for years he'd thought they were just a myth.

The girl was another mystery with the same strange accent as her supposed parents and a temper that he could see burning behind her passive exterior. She truly believed that they weren't monsters, and that made her dangerous. Whether they'd brainwashed her or convinced her by other means, she'd left no room to doubt where she stood when it came to them. He'd have to work quickly, and as he grabbed his phone and headed to his room to pack, he decided that all bets were off now.

Within five minutes, he was out the door, dialing a number he hadn't called in years but not knowing who else could help. He hadn't met the new owner of the business, but his ties with Boston ran deeper than any one person, and no matter who was running things these days, they couldn't turn away a former operative. It simply wasn't done.

"It's Reaper," he said when the call connected. "Tell the boss I want a meeting as soon as possible. I'm heading up from Philadelphia now."

It was time to come out of retirement.

*****

"Slow down and explain what the hell you're talking about," Alex said into the phone. "And try for English this time."

97

"I'm getting back in," Carl said. "This shit's deeper than I thought. It ain't just the vamp trying to cuddle up with her. There are some weird, really damn powerful ones involved, too. Never dealt with anything like them before, but they've got my kid convinced that they're just wanting to be friends. I ain't buying it."

"Listen," Alex said calmly. "I've met my fair share of corpses over the years, and some of them aren't completely psychotic. Are you sure you're looking at this rationally, or are you just worried that your daughter can't take care of herself?"

"Are you saying I should just let her hang out with these bastards and pretend everything is smiles and rainbows?"

"I'm saying that there are better ways to handle it," Alex said. "I told you, I'm working on sorting it out for you, but you're crossing the line between concerned parent and pain in my ass. You're retired. Keep it that way, or you probably won't have a chance to enjoy any more of your golden years."

The line was quiet, and Alex could practically hear the wheels turning in his head over the distance. Carl knew he was right; he just had to convince himself of it instead of rushing head first into a quick and violent death.

"Then tell me what you're planning." Carl sounded a little calmer than he had moments before, but there was still an edge to his voice. "Don't keep me in the dark on this, Malice. If you're handling it, then you owe me at least the peace of mind that comes with the details."

"It's like a chess game," Alex said. "I just need to maneuver all of the pieces in place and let the problem solve itself. This isn't my first time playing this game, so sit back and let me do what I do best. Cancel your meeting with Boston and go back to your daughter's place."

"Can't do that. She already knows something's up, and I'm not about to pull all of the skeletons out of my closet for her. I'll stay in town, but I'm keeping my distance."

"Smart move," Alex said. "I don't think you want to be anywhere near this when it goes down. Just sit back and enjoy the show."

*****

Ian walked her home, and Marielle kept her gaze downcast as they rode the elevator up to her floor. His silent concern carried its own comfort, and she found herself wishing they could go back to what they had before she'd learned the secrets hiding in the shadows. His hand rested on her shoulder when they reached their destination, gently guiding her forward as he fished out his keys with his other hand to open her door with the spare that she'd never demanded he return.

Flipping on the light, he locked the door behind him, and he placed her bag on the table before joining her on the sofa. More than anything, he wanted to fix this – the issues with her father, the latent fear that she still carried, them – but he had no ideas on how to help. He held her close, rubbing soothing circles on her back, and she leaned against him without flinching. She trembled at his side, obviously fighting back tears, and he stayed quiet until she was ready to speak.

The minutes ticked by as they sat there, and Marielle calmed in his presence. He asked for nothing, and his quiet comfort helped hold her world together when it threatened to fall to pieces. Lifting a hand to wipe her face, she slowly pulled away, swallowing down her emotions before they spilled over completely.

"I don't understand," she whispered, her voice threatening to break. "Why would he react that way? How did he even know? I never said a word to him about any of this."

Ian said nothing as she voiced her concerns, having no good answer to give. He wanted to share his suspicions, but this hardly felt like the right time. She needed a shoulder to lean on, not more questions piling onto the ones already circulating in her mind. He didn't doubt her strength, even though she might do so herself, but he could provide his own when she needed it.

"He's been acting strange ever since he got here," she continued as she looked up to meet his gaze. "It's like there's something he hasn't told me, and he doesn't want me to know. The things he said out in the hall before he left, it was like he'd known about your existence this whole time."

"Maybe he has," Ian said.

Something in his tone struck a nerve, and Marielle turned enough to face him, searching his features. When he said nothing more, she reached out to take his hand, once again torn between asking for the truth and remaining blissfully unaware. Her need for understanding proved stronger, and as her fingers linked with his, she gave a light squeeze.

"Ian, if you knew something, you'd tell me, right?" Her heart began to race, and she watched him swallow hard as he looked away. "I've been in the dark my whole life. Don't leave me there now. I thought we'd moved past that."

"I don't have any proof," he began. "Just a suspicion, but I don't think he is who he says he is. I noticed it when I first met him. He's had some serious training, the kind that stays with you even after you've moved on. I started looking into it, but I keep hitting dead ends."

She couldn't even feign outrage that he'd investigated her father. Maybe a few hours ago, she would have reacted with anger, but not anymore. Now, she was grateful for his instincts, and she placed her other hand on top of his, silently willing him to continue.

"I called in a few favors," he said. "Rhonda handles his money, and that's pretty damn out of place for someone who worked in some shop in Delaware. Turns out, the place doesn't even exist. She just got his account after a change with his old company at the beginning of the year. It's still only speculation, so I don't have anything solid yet."

"Have you talked to Rhonda?" she asked.

"Not yet. I was trying to do this without getting you involved. I know he's your dad, but I got worried. I didn't mean to go behind your back."

The understanding in her eyes soothed his worry, and she shifted her weight to lean against him again. She'd missed this, especially the companionship he offered. He'd never pushed her beyond her own comfort level – not intentionally, at least – and all of the feelings she'd suppressed since the night he'd confessed came rushing back full force.

"What if he doesn't come back?" she asked quietly.

"Do you want me to go find him?"

"I can't ask you to do that," she said, closing her eyes. "I can't ask you to get even more involved in my family drama. It's not fair to you."

"If it's important to you, then it's important to me," he said. "That's never going to change. If you want me to go after him, then just say the word and I'm gone."

"I just want to make sure he's okay." It was half true; she wanted to know that her father was safe, but she needed to know what he'd kept hidden from her all those years. "Are you sure you don't mind?"

Ian hooked a finger under her chin to lift her head so that he could look her in the eyes, and he didn't need words to convey that he was more than willing to help when she needed it. He could hear the frantic pounding of her heart, her pulse racing, but he wasn't prepared when she closed the distance and pressed her lips against his.

He froze, eyes wide as her hand rested on the side of his face, and if his heart could still beat, he was sure it would be ready to break out of his chest. Wrapping his arms around her, he returned the kiss with equal fervor, smiling at the way her face flushed when she pulled away.

"Thank you," she said.

"I'll bring him home," Ian promised. "Everything's going to be okay."

Eight

A lithe shadow slipped through the forest, her steps nearly silent on the leaves scattering the ground, and the young warrior dropped to a crouch to check for disturbances in the path. She'd wandered for miles, checking every broken stem she'd passed for a clue, but her quarry eluded her. Frustration was a luxury she could not afford; this final task meant too much, and failure was unacceptable.

Miria tipped her head to the side, listening, but only the soft sounds of the inhabitants around her disturbed the air. She'd already grown to dislike this place, although she'd spent only a handful of days away from home. The animals refused to speak with her, and she wondered if they even had the ability to understand her words like the creatures of Evemyst could. She suspected that they did, but they simply ignored her. The elf was a stranger to their realm, one who had not yet earned their trust, and whatever bonds her people had formed with the creatures of her homeland meant nothing to them.

Pale yellow eyes, the color of faded sunlight filtering through the trees, surveyed the area, and she darted forward again. The unfamiliarity of this place set her nerves on edge, sending a constant tingle of anxiety and anticipation through her body. None of it showed on her tanned features, though; her expression conveyed her determination.

A rustle of leaves a short distance away halted her in her tracks, one hand resting on the trunk of an ancient tree. Whatever was approaching was large, but its movements crashed through the brush clumsily. Having no desire to give away her presence, she sheathed her dagger and scrambled up the tree, decades of practice aiding her along the way. From her perch, hidden behind the leaves of another branch, she held her breath as a brown bear thrice her size lumbered into view, pausing every few seconds to sniff the air.

Tangling with the animal was at the very bottom of her list of priorities, so she remained above the ground, her feet landing lightly as she leapt from branch to branch. With the sun beginning to set, she needed to find a safe shelter for the night, and she climbed back to the ground, letting herself fall the final few feet. A small puff of dust caught in the air, clouding the dying rays of sunlight, and Miria wasted no more time.

The dense foliage around her hadn't been touched by man nor elf in at least several years, but carelessness meant death, so she picked her way along the overgrown path in hopes of finding somewhere suitable to rest.

After another mile, she saw the remnants of an old cabin, half-hidden beneath vines that climbed its outer walls and forgotten in time. Many of the windows were shattered, and thin slivers of glass dotted the ground surrounding the building. She approached with caution, her fingers curling around the hilt of one of her daggers as she slid it from its sheath without a sound. The walk around the perimeter revealed no threats, and she slowly stepped up to the door.

At first, the warped and weathered wood refused to budge, but with one last push that left her sweating and eager to catch her breath, it finally creaked open on rusted hinges. She opened it only enough for her slim frame to slip through the opening, her eyes adjusting to the darkness quickly. The door wouldn't close completely, but she thought it unlikely that anyone even knew of this place, so she left it slightly ajar as she ventured further into the cabin.

An empty oil lamp sat on the small table, both items covered with the thick coat of dust that blanketed everything else within the building, but the furniture looked mostly intact. The moth-eaten blanket draped across the bed against the wall was useless, and she set it down before it could fall apart in her hands. The fireplace sat empty as well, save for a scattering of ash, but she didn't dare light a fire; smoke could alert others to her presence, and she couldn't allow herself to be caught unaware.

A single candle would be enough for the time being, and she sheathed her dagger as she exited the cabin. Retracing her steps, Miria returned to the hollowed tree where she'd hidden her traveling pack, shouldering it as she hurried back to the relative safety of her temporary shelter. Until she had a better idea of where to go next, this would have to serve as her home.

By the light of her candle, she opened the roll of parchment, reading her assignment once more even though she'd already committed it to memory. An elf in exile, only a little younger than Miria herself, had fled to this world, and now they wanted her back. She didn't ask what the elders planned to do when she brought her lost kin home; it wasn't her place. Unrest brewed across Evemyst already, whispers and rumors stirring dissent between her people and the Empire, and her skills would be needed soon enough.

As a member of the Elite Guard, Miria would protect the Council, her home, and her people. If war breached the horizon, then she would fight, regardless of the cost. All of those plans hinged on her ability to complete this one task. If she failed, then her ambitions would be as useless as the broken pottery strewn across the edge of the floor.

*****

Karian had lost count of how many times Mikhail had suggested the purchase of a laptop, and every time, Karian had deliberately ignored him. It might have saved him a trip to Boston to collect the data for every new assignment, but he enjoyed the time on the road, and he had no interest in learning how exactly the computers worked. He'd survived his whole life without any of the technology that was prevalent on Earth; he'd continue to do so without it.

With his boots propped up on the table in his motel room, he flipped through the file, committing the details to memory. He understood why Mikhail had contacted him for this one, but something about it felt odd. If there were two elves roaming around the middle of nowhere USA, then it made little sense that he'd been tasked with finding only one of them.

Pulling out one of the documents, his brow furrowed in thought. Keeping his mark away from the other one couldn't be that difficult, but maybe someone else in his company was responsible for taking her into hiding. His employer danced around the subject when he'd asked, which made that option a dead end, but Karian hadn't left the compound without a good idea of where to look next.

He'd paid in cash for three nights at the run-down block of concrete at the edge of the city, buying himself time and privacy, but as soon as the sun dipped below the horizon, Karian gathered his things and secured them in the storage compartments of his motorcycle. The room wasn't expensive, and he could afford to let the owners keep the extra money he'd spent. Going back to argue for a refund would waste time that he could spend speeding back to Philadelphia, and his assignment took priority over a small scrap of cash.

His helmet shielded his face from the wind, and the modified engine of his Harley quieted to a low purr once he reached the comfortable speed of fifteen miles per hour above the posted limit. With the city lights fading behind him, he focused on planning, narrowing down the possibilities of where to start looking for his target.

By the time the Philadelphia skyline came into view, Karian had decided on a decent place to start. The two elves were connected, which meant the separate assignments to locate them could tie together as well. In most instances, he would have insisted that he worked best alone, but every now and then, he could see a reason to make an exception for the sake of efficiency.

He pulled up alongside the curb, letting the bike idle as he stared up at the hotel. If he had to, he could track down his colleague, but it was more effort than he was willing to put into it; he'd already made the trip down from Boston in record time and stalking through a hotel in search of a werewolf who might not want anything to do with him might just test the limits of his patience for one night.

Even through the visor of his helmet, he caught the strange scent growing stronger, and he turned his head slightly to watch the man approach. The slight narrowing of ice blue eyes didn't escape his notice, but Karian waited for him to stop a few paces away before reaching up to remove his helmet.

"I'm flattered, but you're not my type," Alex said as he stopped.

"We need to talk," Karian said.

"Not interested."

When Alex turned to enter the building, Karian killed the engine and moved to follow, catching up with him easily. He had nothing else to go on, and if they could share information about their respective assignments, then it would make both of their lives a little easier. The trick was getting his colleague to cooperate instead of pointedly ignoring him.

"I didn't ask if you were interested," Karian said, falling into step beside him. "This is business, Malice, and I'll be out of here a lot quicker if you stop acting like a dick and have a five-minute conversation with me."

Again, Alex ignored him, and a low growl rumbled in Karian's chest as he watched him step onto the elevator. To top it off, the bastard had the nerve to smirk at him just as the doors slid closed. Swearing under his breath, Karian ducked into the stairwell, pausing for only a second at each floor to try to pick up the distinctive scent. By the time he reached the top level of the hotel, his temper was on the verge of snapping, and he nearly ripped the door off its hinges as he stepped into the hall.

Alex spared him a glance, along with a roll of his eyes, but Karian pressed forward. He leaned against the wall as Alex slid a keycard out of his pocket, unblinking as he waited for some sign of acknowledgement. The quiet beep of the door unlocking crashed his hopes, telling him that it was pointless to even attempt to talk to Alex about any of this mess. They worked for the same company, but even amongst themselves, there was little trust between operatives.

"Will you go away if I throw a bag of O Negative down the hall?" Alex asked. He held the door open slightly but didn't enter. Karian only responded with a glare. "You're a pain in the ass. I hope you're aware of that."

"So, I've been told," Karian said dryly.

Alex considered him, weighing the risks of continuing their discussion. Whatever was on Karian's mind, the vampire felt it was important enough to persist, but Alex wasn't so sure. Too many inconsistencies had shadowed his experiences with his new employer, and he'd already considered making this his final assignment before parting ways with the company.

"Fine," he said. Pushing the door open fully, he stepped into the suite, and he let it fall closed on its own, giving Karian enough time to enter behind him. Once the door clicked shut, Alex turned to face him. "Make it quick."

"I need information."

"Don't we all," Alex said. "Where did you get the bright idea that I was the one who'd tell you anything?"

"It's just a feeling," Karian said with a shrug.

107

"Really?"

Alex stared at him, torn between throwing him back out the door or over the balcony. The latter sounded infinitely more satisfying, but Karian started speaking again before he grasped the opportunity to remove him from the suite.

"I'm not here to bullshit you," Karian said. "You're in Philadelphia on assignment. What exactly are you after?"

"I'm pretty sure that's none of your business," Alex said as his eyes narrowed dangerously.

"Humor me."

"Or you can piss off."

A sigh hissed through Karian's teeth, frustration clouding his judgment. He stepped forward, muscles tensing as his hands clenched into fists at his sides. Although Alex had several inches on him, Karian had no plans to back down or leave until he had answers.

"Maybe you can try pulling your head out of your ass long enough to answer a simple question," he said. "I have my suspicions, but without confirmation, I'm not sure if we're in a position to help each other."

"I don't need your help," Alex said, closing a little more of the distance. "And I'm not going to run around and do your job for you either."

Karian snarled as he turned to leave, anger boiling beneath the surface of his skin. Approaching Alex had been a long shot anyway, but he hated setbacks, and he bit back a retort as he pulled the door open. Before he made his exit, he paused, holding the door open just enough for him to fit through.

"Have it your way," he said. "I just know that elves are easier to find if you know where to look."

The parting remark had been a gamble; he wasn't even sure that Alex had been the one assigned to that case. All of the information in the files pointed to someone operating in the Philadelphia area, though, and it was the first link that had come to mind. If it turned out that his assumption was wrong, then he would lose nothing, but if not, then they both had more to gain by working as a team.

He took his time descending the stairs, letting his mind wander as he tried to find connections among the information he'd received. His short time with the company hadn't given him much of a chance to form any useful contacts, and he'd made the decision in the beginning not to involve his sister in anything regarding his work unless it became absolutely necessary.

His boots were silent on the marble floor of the lobby, and his anger began to cool as he exited the building into the night. To hell with him, he thought. Perhaps I'll get lucky and one of the elves will have silver-tipped arrows. A hint of a smirk twisted onto his lips, and he let out a short breath of a laugh before he willed away the mental image of the potential altercation.

Alex's size and skills – which Karian hadn't yet had a chance to observe for himself – might give him an advantage, but elves could be fierce opponents. They relied on speed and agility to incapacitate their enemies with deadly efficiency, and few could match the calculated strategies with which they fought.

With those thoughts in mind instead of the issues that should have occupied him, Karian swung a leg over his bike, but he gave one last look at the glass doors of the building as he held his helmet in his hands. A white brow lifted in both amusement and surprise as Alex crossed the lobby towards him, his expression betraying that he found the whole situation less than amusing.

"What do you know about it?" he asked, coming to a stop beside the motorcycle.

"More than you do," Karian said. "I thought you weren't interested."

A growl that could have matched his own filled the air between them, but Karian simply watched him, unimpressed. Both of them were dangerous, especially under the right circumstances, but neither was willing to give the other an advantage. Karian could wait until Alex brought his frustration under control, and he remained silent until Alex let out a long, steadying breath.

"Not only are you a pain in the ass," he said. "You're also an asshole."

"Believe me, the feeling's mutual," Karian said.

"We're not discussing this out here," Alex said, turning towards the hotel. "I'm going back to my room. If you have anything that's actually useful, then come on."

Once he was out of sight, Karian let amusement wash over him. Alex had taken the bait just as he'd anticipated, and he allowed himself a brief moment of victory. After parking the bike properly, he pocketed his keys and entered the building again, taking his time as he made his way to the stairs. He held the advantage now, and he was going to play it for all it was worth.

Alex stood outside of the door to the penthouse suite as Karian exited the stairwell with his helmet under one arm and a pair of files in his other hand, but his features hid his inner turmoil. He'd already decided that the vampire was connected to the one he'd met in Boston when he'd accepted the job, but it became even more obvious that those connections ran deeper than he'd initially thought. He wasn't naïve enough to think that Karian would share every detail he possessed, but Mikhail hadn't given him much more during their latest phone conversation.

As they headed inside, Alex studied him, tucking away all of the little details and quirks for later examination. Karian was decidedly different than the vampires he'd grown accustomed to meeting here and there, but the same traits that set him apart from them were identical to his client.

"I hope, for your sake, that you're not making this up," Alex said, locking the door behind them. "I've been running in circles trying to figure out where to go with this, and our employer hasn't been entirely honest with me. I'm not his lapdog, and I'm not going to chase my tail while I wait for him to decide that I might need the whole story in order to do my damn job."

Karian figured that he had a fair point. Withholding vital information not only made the ones out in the field less effective, it could also get them killed. If Mikhail thought that keeping details to himself was a means to make a point, then his methods were questionable at best and completely ridiculous at worst.

Dropping the files on the sofa, he placed his helmet on the floor and then slipped out of his jacket. He draped it over the arm of the sofa, but the shoulder-holster housing his nine-millimeter pistol remained in place. As he picked up the folders again, he sat down and leaned back, making himself comfortable and ignoring the glare sent in his direction.

Alex found himself reconsidering his earlier decision not to throw him off the balcony.

"How much do you know?" Karian asked. "It'll be easier to fill you in if I know where to start."

"Your boss didn't give me much," he said. "I called him again a few days ago, and he insists that this is important, but he seems to have the idea that I don't need to know most of the basic details about it. All I know is that this chick is five-foot-nothing, and blonde with orange eyes. In the last conversation, he let it slip that she's not human."

"That doesn't sound helpful."

"No shit."

Karian's brow furrowed in thought. Mikhail's actions made no sense, and he struggled to find some form of rationale behind them. The snippets of information were not nearly enough for Alex to complete his assignment, and if it were so crucial that he find the girl, then there was no reason to keep him in the dark.

"Lucky for you, I might be able to clear some of it up." He opened one of the folders, flipping through it before setting it aside, and then offered the second one to his colleague. "They don't have any photos of her, but this should help."

Suspicion returned to the forefront of Alex's mind, and he made no move to take the file. There had to be an angle here, something that Karian wanted in return for the seemingly altruistic offer of assistance. So far, the vampire hadn't hinted at anything, but he could be waiting until the timing suited him.

"What's the catch?" Karian had the nerve to look offended at the question, but Alex wasn't buying it. "I'm not an idiot, Silver. What's this going to cost me?"

"An agreement," Karian said. "I share information with you, and you share information with me. Our assignments are connected. Things will go a lot smoother if we work together instead of independently. Of course, that's if you think you can work with me at all. You don't strike me as a teamwork kind of person."

Alex snorted, biting back a retort. The idea wasn't entirely unpleasant, but Karian's assessment was accurate; he never had been known for playing nice with the other children. He enjoyed a moment of inner debate, more to leave his associate wondering than to really consider the options. As much as he wasn't thrilled with the idea, the prospect of having the tools with which to complete his assignment was attractive enough to tempt him.

Crossing the room, he snatched the folder away and put some distance between them. He skimmed through the documents, holding back his questions until he'd finished, and he had more of them than answers by the time his gaze met Karian's again.

"You seriously expect me to believe that he's got me chasing an elf?" he asked incredulously. "How much did he pay you to show up here with this crap?"

Without waiting for whatever line Karian planned to feed him next, he tossed the folder onto the floor and took a step forward, channeling his brewing rage. Muscle and bones strained, realigning as his figure grew, and his features distorted as they shifted into a snarling muzzle, glowing tattoos crawling over the short fur. Standing at over seven feet tall, Alex rolled his shoulders, and he stalked forward again.

Karian was on his feet in an instant, the whites and pupils of his eyes vanishing as the green of his irises began to spread over them. His muscles tensed as glowing eyes regarding the werewolf, but he declined to draw a weapon. Diffusing the situation would be ideal, but he mentally prepared himself to fall back on the defensive if it became necessary.

"A simple 'no' would have been sufficient." The sharpened tips of his fangs were visible as he spoke, but despite the tension in the air, he kept his voice neutral. "I don't have time to feed you bullshit, but if you don't want to believe me, that's your choice."

"Do you really expect me to believe that there's a goddamn elf from another planet running around the Philadelphia area?" His voice dropped several octaves, and a growl punctuated his words. "You have one more chance to tell me why you're really here."

Fight or flight instinct kicked in, and glowing eyes narrowed as his lips pulled back from his fangs in a snarl of his own. Karian refused to allow Alex to intimidate him, but letting the situation escalate into violence would hinder his plans. His voice was low, and his words were deliberate as he responded.

"What possible reason would I have to lie? It doesn't benefit me in the least, so there would be no point to it. If you choose not to believe me, then our business is finished here, but if you want a little bit of an advantage over the situation, then perhaps you should actually listen instead of threatening me."

"How did you manage to get the intel when he wouldn't tell me shit?" Alex growled.

"I asked nicely. Mikhail and I have an understanding. Maybe if you weren't actively trying to piss off everyone you meet, then he might have given you the same file willingly." Karian paused, gauging his reaction. "He doesn't know that I planned to share it with you."

With an incredible amount of effort, he forced his fangs to retract, and the glow faded from his eyes. He stepped forward, squaring his shoulders, and looked up to lock eyes with the menacing glare that fell on him.

"If you don't want to work together, then I'll take my files and leave," he said evenly. "Or, you can calm down and we can discuss this like civilized beings."

Alex regarded him, itching to just tear into him and rip him apart. He'd reached his limit with games, and he could think of nothing more satisfying than the feeling of rendering flesh to pieces with his claws. Karian didn't retreat, though, and the change in his features as they returned to something a little more human surprised him.

Several beats of silence stretched between them, neither willing to back down or give the other so much as a trace of an advantage. Karian waited, not even blinking as Alex weighed his options. Finally, Alex's features shifted again, and within moments, the transformation was complete. His clothes had shifted with him to cover his frame, and they were undamaged when he stood before Karian, his expression promising retribution if this turned out to be any more of a waste of time.

"No one's ever accused me of being civilized," he said with a humorless laugh. "I'll hear you out, but I want to know how you were so willing to believe that this is what we're dealing with."

"Unlike you, I'm quite familiar with the inhabitants of their homeland," Karian said. "My experience with elves is, admittedly, limited, but I know enough to realize that this isn't going to be easy."

"That's not an answer." Alex folded his arms over his chest. "Last chance before I toss you off the balcony like I've wanted to do all night. How do you know this?"

"Because it's my homeland, too," Karian said. "Think about it, Malice. How the hell else would I know half of the shit that I know? I can vouch for the accuracy of the intel when it comes to predicting what they're going to do."

"Then why didn't Mikhail make you find the runaway?"

"She's terrified of my kind," he said. "That's why she fled to Earth in the first place. They can recognize us for what we are – and I mean you as well – so if she's hiding from vampires, then sending one to collect her isn't the best idea."

"And sending a wolf is?" Alex asked, shaking his head.

"My people aren't the only ones who respect yours," Karian said. "The elves have a closer bond with your kind, almost like a kinship. When we have a very skittish elf who's afraid of vampires but trusts werewolves almost without question, then it's pretty obvious why you ended up with this job."

Alex couldn't deny the logic behind his words, and things became a little clearer with the new perspective. He still wanted to make his displeasure perfectly clear the next time he ventured up to Boston, but right now, his best lead lay in scattered papers across the floor.

"Where do you fit into this?" he asked. "What does he have you chasing if I'm supposed to find the runaway?"

"You're not the only one looking for her," Karian said, grabbing the second file from the sofa. "One of her people followed her to this world to find her. My job is to make sure that doesn't happen."

*****

Soph replayed the brief interaction in her mind, trying to find anything other than the few seconds when she'd heard the woman's voice that might tie the stranger to the elf in the backyard. She'd picked up a few other things, little details that didn't really make sense, but it had only given her more questions.

She hadn't heard a heartbeat, which told her that the woman was most likely a vampire as well, but there was more to it than that. There had been no sound when she'd passed her, not even the quiet footsteps on the tile, and Soph was certain that she hadn't seen a shadow. If the woman was a vampire, then she was different than any of the ones Soph had met in the past.

There was power there, too. An aura of it surrounded the stranger, and it had surprised Soph just as much as the sound of her voice. Glancing at the back door, she frowned. She wanted to climb up into the tree house and ask all of the questions floating around in her head, but doing so had the potential to frighten the elf into silence. If that happened, then Soph was

114

sure she'd be gone before the next sunset.

"What's wrong?" Trina's voice pulled her from her thoughts, and Soph pulled her gaze away from the door. "You seem a little out of it there."

"Just thinking," she said. "I want to find out if Krys knows anything about that chick we saw earlier, but I don't want to scare her off. Not really sure how to handle this."

Trina's arms slipped around her waist, and she leaned back, closing her eyes. They were quiet, and Soph found her presence comforting. Trina didn't always need words to convey her thoughts, and sometimes, all she had to do was be there while Soph worked things out on her own.

"I'm going to talk to her," Soph said. "Not tonight, though. I need to think of how to ask her without making her run away from me."

"Do you want me to give it a try?" Trina asked.

"Thanks, but I don't know if she'll talk to you," Soph said. "I've been dealing with her since she showed up, and she might trust me more."

The reversal would have been humorous if it weren't for the concern laced through her thoughts. Trina had always been the more diplomatic of the two; her calm, collected demeanor made it easy for others to open up to her, and Soph's volatile nature provided the exact opposite. Part of her relished the change, and she found a spark of pride in the knowledge that she was on her way to forming the start of a bond with someone before Trina.

There wasn't anything competitive about the situation – seldom did they try to outdo the other in their actions – but Soph hadn't really had this chance before now. Trina had her business connections, which were simply casual associates whom she contacted for work-related issues, but Soph had Trina, and that was it. She'd needed no one else, but with the opportunity to form a solid friendship on the horizon, she had to make sure she did things right.

"I don't know what to say to her," she admitted. "Never really been in this situation before."

"You'll figure it out," Trina said with full confidence. "I've never seen you fall short when you've set your mind to something, and you know I'm here if you need me."

Soph appreciated the assurances, and she rested her hands on Trina's as a smile curved her lips. She received a gentle squeeze in response, and she wondered for the hundredth time how she'd managed to keep her by her side. There was no chance of her complaining about it, but the knowledge that she didn't have to face anything alone sent a wave of warmth through her chest.

"Come on," she said after a few minutes of content silence. "Let's find some breakfast and have a night in. Gotta enjoy the time I have before you hit the road again."

*****

Krysanna returned to the safety of the treehouse much later than planned. During the day, she dared to venture out into the woods, learning her surroundings little by little, but once the sun began to set, fear chased her back to her sanctuary. With her legs folded beneath her, she risked the glow of a handful of tiny orbs, reading by the light they provided as she nibbled on the berries she'd collected.

Once or twice, her gaze strayed to the warm glow coming from the windows of the house, but she resisted the urge to approach. The offer to join the women inside had tempted her, but up in the tree, she knew she could flee at a moment's notice if she had to. The evening air was comforting, as were the trees a short distance away, and she decided that she'd be more at ease in her current position than trapped within the walls of the nearby building.

When the house went dark again, she strained to hear the sound of the front door closing, and she tensed at the growl of an engine in the driveway. She'd seen cars when she'd first arrived in the middle of the city, but she had no desire to get any closer than the distant sight provided. Alone with her thoughts, she considered exploring the residence, but she dismissed the idea as quickly as it had come. An offense such as that could destroy her chances of remaining in her safe haven.

She returned to her studies, trying to focus on finding a way out of her predicament. Removing the unwanted wings was the top priority, second only to making her way home. If she returned without the additional appendages, then perhaps they would lift her exile. Bitterness was a foreign emotion, and she'd managed to hold it at bay ever since the day she'd left Evemyst, but now, in the pale glow of her conjured lights, it wormed its way into her heart.

Nothing about the situation was fair. She'd only wanted to learn, and the pursuit of knowledge shouldn't have been a crime. Her magic wasn't as advanced as some of the more experienced practitioners, but that was why she'd been trying so hard to master it. The mistake had been minor, one that the Elders could have easily fixed, but instead, they'd chosen to make an example out of her indiscretion.

Setting the book aside, she drew her knees up to her chest, resting her forehead on them. Discontent gave way to loneliness, and her shoulders shook with quiet sobs as hopelessness ached deep within her. Golden-feathered wings wrapped around her slim frame, shielding her from the world as her grief spilled out in crystal clear tears.

Time passed without her notice, shaky breaths gradually evening out as her emotions eventually calmed. Instead of relief, she only felt misery, and the emptiness threatened to consume her. She longed for home, praying to whatever gods could still hear her that they would give her a chance to make things right. All she needed was the right spell, the right solution to fix everything so that she could live among her people again and face the world without the ever-present fear that kept her cowering in the shadows.

The creak of the wooden ladder startled her, and she pressed herself further against the wall, holding her breath. A crown of black hair appeared at the edge of her refuge, and she breathed a soft sigh of relief, willing the frantic pounding of her heart to slow. Her host's pale features were painted with concern, and Krysanna tried to offer a small smile that didn't quite reach her eyes.

"You okay?" Soph asked. She kept her distance, remaining by the entrance once she'd climbed into the treehouse, but she looked the elf over critically for any sign of injury. When Krysanna nodded and looked away, Soph took a slow step towards her. "Do you want to talk about it?"

Squeezing her eyes shut, Krysanna bit her lip. She wanted to talk, but how could she explain everything that had led her to this point in her life? If she broke her silence and told Soph what had happened, then she'd have nowhere to go if her generous host sent her away from there. A spark of hope ignited a need for understanding, and her eyes cracked open to regard her.

"I do not know what to do," she whispered, forcing the words past the lump in her throat. "I thought that I had a safe place to stay after my people sent me into exile, but I was so wrong. The ones who took me in were never unkind, and my cousin assured me that I could stay as long as I wanted, but then I discovered the truth about them."

Soph shifted just a little bit closer and sat down on the floor. She left enough space between them to ensure that the elf wouldn't startle at the proximity, but her posture indicated that she could offer comfort if Krysanna needed it.

"I should have noticed the signs," Krysanna continued. "Perhaps I was simply relieved to have somewhere to stay, but things were not as they seemed. I came to realize that, despite their kindness, the Empress and her husband were not as innocent as they would have me believe." Fear shot through her at the memory, and her wings closed around her body again. "They were Dusk Hunters – creatures of night who prey on the living. I cannot imagine why my cousin willingly kept their company. Surely, she knew what they were, but perhaps she'd fallen under their influence. It was unlikely – my people are quite resistant to any magic or skill that affects the mind – but I found no other possibility."

A string of curses raced through Soph's mind, but she managed to keep her expression from betraying her thoughts. She had a pretty good idea of what Krysanna meant by the term "Dusk Hunters", and a wave of guilt washed over her. There was no way she could tell the girl the truth about herself now without instilling more fear in her.

"How did you find out?" she asked.

"It was by chance," Krysanna said. "I had not noticed the differences until after I saw the truth with my own eyes. I decided to explore their castle one night; Abnalia told me of a second library containing spell books. It was my hope that I could find a way to remove the wings that I had acquired by accident. Somehow, I lost my way in the winding corridors and found myself in the dungeons."

A shudder coursed through her at the memory.

"I heard a voice up ahead, and I recognized the Emperor speaking. I should have turned back then; his business in the dungeons was not my concern. Curiosity pushed me forward though, and it was only by chance that he did not notice my presence." Tears welled in her eyes, her voice breaking as she forced herself to continue. "He… He was in one of the cells with a prisoner, too close for me to see what he was doing, but then he turned. The glow of his eyes… The blood…"

118

The vision was burned into her memory, haunting her whenever she dared to close her eyes. A shuddering breath preceded another wave of tears, fear and loss consuming her as she closed in on herself. Safety had become an illusion. Even in her temporary refuge, it was only a fallacy that she tried to convince herself was true.

"I want the fear to stop," she choked out. "I want to go home."

Soph wanted to close the distance, to hold her and tell her that she had no reason to fear anything anymore, but she remained in place. She struggled to find the words to make it better, every assurance falling short before she could voice it, and her silent heart broke as helplessness threatened to overwhelm her.

It was an unfamiliar sensation. Soph had spent decades focused only on what mattered to her and Trina; other people weren't a concern. The young elf trembling in her backyard had worked her way into her thoughts in such a short period of time that she had no idea how to handle it. Krysanna needed a friend, but as much as Soph wanted to provide that, her own nature made it impossible.

"Krys?" she asked softly. "I don't get it. You said there were signs, but don't they just look like everyone else?"

Sniffing and trying to bring her breathing back under control, Krysanna lifted her head. Her eyes continued to spill tears down her face, rolling over the reddened skin. It took several minutes before she trusted herself to speak, but she managed to shake her head.

"They are there if you know what to seek," she said weakly. "They are not of the living, and certain traits that humans possess are notably absent. They move without sound, not even the rustle of clothing, they have no reflection, and no shadow follows their path. I never noticed, but after I fled, I passed the Empress, and I saw the same things missing with her."

Understanding hit her like a speeding freight train, and Soph's eyes widened. The strange woman that she'd passed in the city was part of it after all. A sense of fierce protectiveness washed over her, and her expression hardened. The change was enough for Krysanna to shrink back against the wall, and Soph tried to give her a reassuring smile instead.

"No one's gonna hurt you here, Krys," she said. "I ain't gonna let that happen."

"They said the same," Krysanna said, on the verge of breaking again.

"They promised that I was safe, but it was never true. No one is safe around creatures such as them."

"I mean it," Soph said. "No one else knows you're here, and we're gonna keep it that way. Anyone tries to start shit, I'll handle it."

Nine

Marielle settled at her desk and unlocked her computer, reaching for a steaming mug while her email updated with any messages she'd missed. She nearly choked on her coffee when she read the subject line of the first email, and she placed the mug on the desk to keep from dropping it when part of the message loaded in the preview pane. Her mouth went dry as she read the bold headline twice; someone had copied a news article into the email.

She remembered the story from a few years ago – multiple murders in the Northeast – but she'd never seen this particular article. The photos edited only the victims' faces, leaving the lacerations in plain view, and she wondered how someone could have published it. Despite the growing horror, she scrolled down, her pulse pounding in her ears at the close-up shots of one of the deceased. The twin puncture wounds were prominent in the photo, and excerpts from the autopsy report followed the image.

The police had dismissed the supernatural elements, declaring that the bite marks were just a sick twist that the killer added for shock value, but the autopsy report noted the lack of blood. Again, the investigators attributed it to the other wounds, but the photos didn't support their theory. Deep lacerations covered the bodies, but little blood pooled on the ground around them.

When a hand fell upon her shoulder, she jumped, her heart racing as panic gripped her. Eyes widening, she dared to look up, trying to draw in enough air and only partially succeeding. Ian's worried gaze met hers, and she sat frozen as he slowly removed his hand.

"What happened?" he asked. "I've been trying to get your attention ever since I got off the elevator." When she gestured to the screen, his entire frame tensed. "What the hell?" The question was little more than a whisper, but he steadied his voice when he looked at her again. "Who sent this to you?"

"I don't know," she said. "I don't recognize the email address."

"We'll get the IT guys to trace it," he said as he closed the message and read the various subject lines on the other messages. At least six more had similar titles. "Don't open any of them, and anything else that comes from a weird address like that, send it right to IT."

It took a few seconds for her to process his instructions, and she nodded once before turning around to forward the emails. She couldn't imagine why someone would send her those articles, but then she sucked in a breath when a possibility came to mind.

"Ian?" she asked. "Do you think my dad has something to do with this?"

He couldn't answer her. Considering the recent confrontation with her father, it was possible, but sending her graphic articles was a terrible way to convince one's daughter to cut ties with people he thought were dangerous. During his interactions with the man, Carl seemed concerned, but he didn't seem like the type to go to that extreme.

"I don't know," he said. "I want to say no, but if he didn't send them, then maybe he knows who did."

She nodded, folding her hands in her lap. Her father hadn't answered her calls since the night he'd left, and concern for his safety was equal to the desire to make things right. They'd found nothing solid to fill in the gaps of his past, and most of the things she thought she knew about him had turned out to be completely untrue. He never worked in that shop in Delaware, and there were no leads to what he'd done prior to that, only that it had kept him on the road more than he had been home.

Ian's theory had merit, though, but she hesitated to reach out for confirmation. In a way, she wasn't sure if she wanted the truth, but wondering about it for the rest of her life wasn't an attractive option either. Knowing would at least give her a small measure of peace.

"I'm going to find him," Ian said, pulling her from her thoughts.

"What?" It didn't register, and she scrambled to her feet as he headed towards the elevators. "Ian, wait!"

"I'm just going to talk to him," he assured her. "That's it. If he's not behind this, then at least I can confirm it."

"And if he is?"

"Then I'll convince him to stop." He pressed the button to call the elevator. "I know he's your dad, and I really want to believe that he wouldn't try to scare the hell out of you just to make a point, but we'll feel a lot better once we know for sure."

She had no argument, but she reached up to rest her hand on his cheek. The images in the email haunted her, but she'd told herself the previous year that she was done being afraid. Whoever was playing a sick joke on her wasn't going to frighten her, and she managed a small smile.

"Just be careful, okay?" she said.

"Always."

His crooked grin was enough of a reassurance, and she watched the elevators doors close before she turned back towards her desk. She hoped that the technology team would be able to find out who had sent the messages, but even if they didn't, she wouldn't be caught off guard next time. As she slipped into her chair, she browsed the subjects again before deleting them one by one.

*****

Carl took Malice's advice about as well as he took anyone's, which was precisely why he was staring at the prepaid cell-phone in his hand as he sat on the worn mattress in a motel room that had seen better days. It would be smart to stay in retirement, but he couldn't find it in him to sit on the sidelines when his daughter was willingly putting her life in danger. He'd dialed the number several times, but now he finally hit the button to connect the call and brought the phone to his ear.

"Make it quick," the gravelly voice greeted on the other end of the call.

"It's Reaper," he said. "I want back in."

Silence answered him, and he wondered if the other man had simply hung up on him. The measured breaths told him otherwise, and he swallowed his doubts as he spoke again.

"I heard that you're the man in charge these days," Carl said. "So, I'm assuming you're the one to talk to about coming out of retirement."

"No."

He almost dropped the phone at the bland refusal, and he struggled for a decent retort. Maybe he was older than every other member of the organization, but he'd still trained with the best, and he had a specialty that he knew was useful.

"You're retired, Reaper," Mikhail said. "Most of us don't get that chance. I don't know what brought this on, and I really don't give a shit, but you're out, and it's going to stay that way."

"You're making a mistake." To his credit, he concealed the desperation in his voice, because this was his best chance at keeping Marielle safe. "I'm still damn good at what I used to do."

"Doesn't matter," Mikhail said. "I'm not giving you a different answer. Was there anything else you needed?"

"Yeah," he said. "There's a lot that I need, but it doesn't look like I'm going to get it from you."

"Enjoy your retirement, then."

The line went dead, and he almost hurled the phone across the room. He fired off a quick text to Malice, not expecting a response, and tossed the phone onto the small, round table. Closing his eyes, he let out a long sigh, trying to find a way to make Marielle see reason. She was in too deep, and he had to pull her out before she got herself killed. The cryptic voicemail she'd left before the holidays made sense now; he should have dropped everything and headed to Philly right then and there.

She was hurt now, but it was better for her to be angry at him if it kept her alive. She'd understand in time. His thoughts drifted to the strange dinner they'd attended a few nights prior, along with the unusual vampires who had hosted it. They hadn't threatened any of them, and Marielle insisted they were good people, but he just couldn't reconcile how the terms good and vampire could describe the same person.

The sharp knock at the old wooden door startled him from his thoughts, and he sat motionless, waiting to see if the visitor would just leave. When another set of knocks followed, he grabbed the pistol on the nightstand and checked the ammo before cautiously approaching the door. He made sure to load the gun with silver, and he took a deep breath before he opened the door just a crack.

His grip tightened on the pistol, and he fought the urge to take aim and empty the clip into the man waiting on the other side. Using his years of training, he kept his heartbeat even, taking measured breaths to remain calm.

"How did you find me?" he asked.

"I know people," Ian said with a shrug. "Can we talk?"

"I'm not inviting you in."

"You don't have to," Ian said. "I could just push my way inside if I wanted to, but that wouldn't really help anything, would it? I just didn't think this was a conversation you wanted to have out in the open."

Carl watched him, waiting for him to make a move, but Ian made no attempt to force his way into the room. He'd kept his hands in plain view, his expression neutral, but the display of honest intentions hardly quelled Carl's suspicion. Another minute ticked by before he stepped back, opening the door fully as he motioned with the gun for Ian to enter.

Blue eyes darted to the weapon before lifting to the man holding it, but there was no surprise in its presence. Ian walked past him, glancing around the room quickly before turning around to find the gun leveled at him.

"Give me one reason why I shouldn't shoot you right now," Carl said evenly.

"I'm not going to stand here and beg for my life," Ian said. "If you want to shoot me, then you're going to pull that trigger. I'm not going to try and fight you or do anything else that you might think of as a threat, if that's part of your problem. I just want to talk."

Neither moved at first, and they stared at each other, waiting for the other to decide how this meeting would go. True to his word, Ian gave no indication that he planned to attack. His eyes remained the same, and Carl didn't see even a hint of his fangs. Slowly, he lowered the gun to his side and tipped his head towards one of the chairs.

"I'm getting too old for this shit," he muttered. "Sit your ass down and talk."

Ian almost laughed; he would have if he didn't think doing so would get him shot. Instead, he sidestepped his way to the chair. The imminent threat of violence might have passed, but that didn't mean that he was comfortable turning his back on the man. Easing down to sit, he rested one arm on the table as Carl sat across from him.

"Marielle's worried sick," Ian said. "She doesn't know what the hell's going on with you, and she hasn't been able to reach you." He paused, glancing down for a moment before returning his attention to Carl. "I told her I would find you, but I haven't called her yet. She doesn't know that I'm

125

here, and if you don't want her to know, then I won't tell her, but you should at least let her know that you're okay."

He bristled at that. The last thing he needed was some bloodsucker lecturing him about his relationship with his daughter. Taking a deep breath, he calmed himself and tried to take the advice for what it was.

"I know you don't like me," Ian continued. "You don't have to, but I want you to know that I'd never hurt her. Ever."

"Don't tell me you're asking for my blessing," Carl said with a snort. "I meant what I said the other night. I've seen what your kind can do, and I don't want her anywhere near that. You want me to be okay with you walking out of here, then stay the hell away from her."

"She's an adult," he said. "And she makes her own decisions. When she broke things off last year, I was upset, but that was her choice. If she wants to try again, then I'm not going to tell her no. Believe it or not, I care about her – a lot – and I'm not about to push her away if there's a chance we might be happy."

"You really are as dumb as you look, aren't you?" Carl shook his head. "It doesn't work that way, Mackenzie. She's human and you're not. It's never that easy. It'll go one of two ways; either it'll end in heartbreak, or she'll become a monster just like you. So, how am I supposed to be okay with this, knowing how it's going to end?"

Ian didn't have a good answer. He'd considered those possibilities, and if he were honest about it, then if Marielle ever asked him to change her, he'd do it in a heartbeat. He'd never push the issue, though, and he'd never force it on her. If only he could make her father understand that. As it was, he was pretty sure that it was going to be a challenge to convince him of anything when there was a pistol between them.

"We're not all heartless murderers," he said. "The Konistavs were just hoping to include you when they invited you over to dinner. They aren't in town all that often, and their opinion was that any family of Marielle's was welcome at their table. It was kind of a dick move when you threw that in their faces." Turning just a little, he folded his hands on the table. "Marielle has some good friends looking after her, and I don't just mean me and the guys at work. She and Cass are really close, and it really hurt her when you stormed off the way you did. If nothing else, you should at least give her some kind of an explanation."

Carl was liking him less and less, and even more so, he hated to admit that Ian had a point. He couldn't accept the fact that Marielle was spending her free time with vampires, but he had to find a way to explain it in a way she'd understand. He still hadn't received an update from his colleague, and he had no way of knowing if there had been any progress on that front. Marielle meant the world to him, though, and it was his responsibility to do everything in his power to keep her safe and happy. Sometimes it wasn't possible to provide both.

"Do you have any idea what I did for a living before she was born?" he asked. "She doesn't even know, because I wanted to keep her as far away from that as possible. Do you know what it feels like to watch her walk into situations that I spent my life trying to keep away from her?"

Carl's words struck a chord, and Ian let out a humorless laugh. He knew the feeling all too well. No matter how much he'd wanted to keep her out of the line of fire, Marielle had refused to sit idle while everyone else put themselves in harm's way. She'd surprised him then, and she continued to do so almost every night.

"I have a pretty good idea," Ian said. "I haven't been able to confirm it, but all signs point to Jack-o-Lantern. I'm guessing that you put in for retirement when she was born, but still stayed at the edges of the business until you moved to Florida." The surprise on the other's face brought a grin to his own. "Let me tell you what I've learned about Marielle. She's got your drive to make a difference. She's one of the nicest people I've met, but she's also hell bent on getting involved if it means she can help someone. Once she has an idea in her head, there's no way to change her mind, no matter how frustrating it is. You should be proud of her."

Carl stared at him, jaw clenched. He couldn't bring himself to ask how the vampire knew about his former employer, but there was something in his tone that he hadn't expected to hear. There was no judgment when it came to his occupation, but beyond that, the way his expression softened when he spoke of Marielle surprised him. He hadn't thought Ian's kind was even capable of seeing a human as anything other than food, but even with his own experiences in mind, he couldn't deny the fondness in the way Ian spoke of her.

"I don't like you," he said flatly. "And I don't like the thought of you getting close with my daughter."

"I'm not asking you to," Ian said.

"I wasn't finished." Carl glared at him, the words tasting like bile as he forced them past his lips. "I'm also not going to tell her what to do. She's already made it clear that she's going to do whatever the hell she wants no matter what I say. So, I can do one of two things right now. I can step back and try to let her be happy, or I can fill you with silver and have some peace of mind that you can't hurt her."

If the threat worried him, Ian refused to allow it to show. His expression remained unchanged as his gaze flicked to the weapon and then back up to Carl, but the spark of amusement in his eyes was enough to throw off the former mercenary.

"I don't think you want to do that," Ian said. "My advice? Go with the first option."

The smug look on the vampire's face stirred the suppressed anger within him, and Carl leveled the pistol on him again. He disengaged the safety, waiting to see if Ian planned to move or attack, but they sat there staring at each other with mutual animosity.

His patience snapped, and he squeezed back on the trigger as the gunshot echoed in the small room. With the ringing in his ears, he didn't hear the expletive fly from Ian's lips, but he watched in satisfaction as the chair toppled backwards and sent his unwelcome visitor crashing to the floor.

He knew that he wouldn't have much time before Ian was on his feet again, and he jumped up to edge around the table, lowering the gun just enough to aim for the center of his forehead. Dark blood poured from the wound in the vampire's chest, staining the shirt, but Carl noted with disappointment that he'd missed the heart. In a few more seconds, it wouldn't matter, though; one more shot and it would be over for good.

The door slammed open behind him, shattering his concentration, and he spun to face the newest threat as he fired. Even without having a chance to aim properly, the bullet struck its mark, lodging itself into the muscle of the newest intruder's shoulder. It certainly helped that this target was larger than the other one, but his minor victory faded into terror when glowing blue eyes narrowed dangerously.

He pulled the trigger again, but Lothan barely flinched at the impact, and before he could react, Carl found himself face to face with him as the distance between them disappeared. He'd never considered himself to be a small man, standing at about six feet tall, but Lothan towered over him. Swallowing hard, Carl refused to retreat, and he started to bring the gun to bear again, only to find his wrist caught in a vice-like grip.

"I would suggest that you think very hard about the wisdom of continuing this," Lothan said evenly. The razor-sharp tips of his fangs flashed in the dim light of the motel room, but they were closer than Carl ever wanted them to be. "I'm going to release your arm, and you're going to put the weapon away, or I'm going to have to take it from you. Do we have an understanding?"

He knew better than to try to free himself, but he remained perfectly still as he tried to quell the fear that sent his heart rate skyrocketing. His breath came in short gasps, and all of his years of training fled his mind in the face of the ancient creature before him. Opening his mouth to speak, his words failed him, but he managed a quick nod.

Lothan released his grip but kept Carl within his sight as he stepped around him to check on Ian. Silver projectiles fell to the stained carpet as his body rejected the foreign material, and he pulled his attention away from his attacker only long enough to take stock of his friend's condition. Extending a hand, he helped Ian to his feet, and he shook his head slightly when Carl made a break for the door.

He barely made it halfway there.

Carl stopped in his tracks when he found his escape suddenly blocked, eyes widening again. He'd seen vampires in action, and he knew they were damn fast, but this was beyond his experience. Lothan didn't approach, his arms folding over his chest as he stood there, but Carl took a step back as he braced for retaliation.

Death hadn't frightened him. After the years he'd spent in dangerous and life-threatening situations, he thought he'd become numb to the thought, but staring at those eyes, which were glowing with malevolence, the fear returned like a sucker punch. No matter how hard he tried, he couldn't calm his racing heart, and he knew that the monsters that had him trapped on either side could hear it.

He didn't dare look behind him, sure that Ian was preparing to deliver the killing blow, but he refused to close his eyes. If they were going to kill him, then they would have to look at him while doing so.

"Are you finished?" Lothan asked, an edge of impatience in his voice.

Carl could only stare at him, not quite understanding the question. Of course, he was finished; the only thing left to face was whatever pain they planned to inflict. Lothan blinked once, and the glow faded from his eyes as a sigh hissed through his teeth. A thin sliver of hope fought to break through the paralyzing terror, but Carl still had trouble forming a response.

"I asked you a question," Lothan said. "Do not make me ask again."

"What the hell can I do now?" His voice wasn't nearly as steady as he'd wanted, but the bitter laugh that followed made his point well enough. "I'm good, but not good enough to get past both of you. So, go on. Let's get this over with."

"Do you honestly think we'd still be talking if I planned to kill you?" Lothan asked. "For someone as observant as you are, I would have thought you might have figured that out for yourself."

Carl bristled but didn't rise to the bait. He didn't quite believe that they would let him walk away after he'd shot them, but he wasn't going to argue if that ended up as the final decision. He caught the quick glance that Lothan sent to Ian, and he risked a look back to make sure that the other vampire wasn't coming up on him from behind.

Ian had pulled himself up to sit on the edge of the bed, one hand pressed against the wound on his chest. His glare promised revenge, but he'd made no move to follow through on it; Carl was pretty sure that it had a lot to do with the much stronger vampire blocking the door. He wasn't familiar with any hierarchy in the ranks of the undead, but there was definitely some form of respect there.

"So, you're just gonna let me walk away?" he asked. "Guess times have changed since I've been out in the field."

"You're getting ahead of yourself," Lothan said. "We're going to talk, and then we'll decide what the next steps should be."

It was better than immediate execution, but not by much. The chance that he'd find himself dead by the end of the night still remained, but the threat wasn't imminent anymore. He had no choice in the matter, though. They wanted to chat, and he wanted to live to see the dawn. His only chance to get what he wanted was to play by their rules. The mere thought of it left a sour taste in his mouth.

Lothan nudged the door closed behind him with the heel of his boot but remained in place, waiting for a decision. The only reason the man was still breathing was his relation to Marielle, and that was quickly becoming a weak reason to keep him alive. Ian was looking worse for wear, and the sooner they pulled the silver out of his chest, the better the night would be.

Getting staked had hurt like hell for the few seconds he'd felt it before paralysis had set in, but the burning pain of the silver beneath his skin had Ian clenching his jaw to prevent any sounds of it from escaping. It took all of his willpower to haul himself up onto the bed without crying out, and that strength rapidly faded while Carl and Lothan tried to work through their stalemate.

"Put down the gun before I take it from you," Lothan said. "And then have a seat. If you make one more move towards the door, then this little meeting will come to an abrupt and bloody end. Is that clear?"

"Crystal," Carl said.

He was certain that it wasn't an empty threat, and he edged backwards to place the pistol on the table before lifting his hands to keep them in view. He hooked the leg of one of the chairs to pull it closer to the center of the room, turning it so that he could keep both of them in view as he slumped down into it.

After reaching back to lock the door, Lothan crossed the room to assess Ian's wound. He pulled the other chair around so that he could have a closer look, his brow furrowed as he swore under his breath. Reaching to the side of his belt, he drew one of his blades – a smaller, thin knife that would be best for precision – and he met Ian's gaze evenly.

"It's incredibly inconvenient that your body cannot simply force the twice-damned thing out again," he said. "This is going to hurt, but it will be better than keeping the projectile in you."

Carl watched, not daring to speak, as the older vampire sliced through the front of Ian's shirt, peeling aside the fabric. Lothan gave him a moment to brace himself, and then slid the blade into the skin, widening the bullet hole that refused to mend while the silver was still present.

The low growl of pain sent a chill up Carl's spine, and his eyes darted to the door. With both of them distracted, he might have a miniscule chance at escape, but the warning he'd received moments prior echoed in his mind. If he made a run for it, he was as good as dead. His attention returned to the pair, and he focused on the determined crease of Lothan's brow as he carefully eased the bullet free.

It fell to the floor, rolling on the carpet, and Ian's shoulders slumped in relief. The wounds on his chest slowly began to heal, dark trickles of blood trailing down pale skin. Carl found it both fascinating and disturbing; no one should be able to walk away after taking a shot like that, and especially not after having their chest cut open to remove it.

When both sets of blue eyes turned towards him – one darker than what should have been possible, and the other as pale as the midday sky – he swallowed hard. His heart hammered in his chest, threatening to break free of his body, and a cold sweat formed across his skin.

"I'm only going to ask this once, so I advise you to answer truthfully," Lothan said. "What exactly is your reason behind responding with violence instead of words?"

Ten

Every now and then, he missed working in the field, but then he remembered how many times he'd nearly wound up dead and found a little more appreciation in his current position. Mikhail scrolled through the various updates from other operatives, deliberately ignoring the few pending contracts waiting in the tray on his desk for his approval.

He was starting to wonder what the hell was wrong with Philadelphia. Whenever an assignment cropped up in or around that city, it brought with it massive amounts of irritation and frustration. It hadn't helped that the most recent set of assignments involved his associates from Zalyndrya. His decision to give Malice the first one had been two-fold; his quarry was terrified of vampires, and Malice supposedly had superior tracking skills.

When it came to finding the other elf – the one who could pose an actual threat – Silver had been his best option. He hadn't called the vampire by name since he'd signed on several months back, and he saw no need to return to it. While they'd mostly kept their personal connection away from the business, Mikhail noticed after the fact that he'd given Silver a little more leeway than he would have given most of the staff.

The initial request for the companion file to his own case hadn't been surprising on its own; Silver wanted to know every detail about both elves that were wandering around Pennsylvania. As soon as Mikhail had turned to take a call, Silver had slipped out, taking both files with him. He should have called him back, demanded the return of the extra information, but he'd hesitated.

Now, with another sleepless night added to his calendar, Mikhail found himself sorting through the recent events. There had been no leads on the winged elf, but he had a feeling that Silver wouldn't be keeping the intel to himself. With reports of the second visitor making her way south from

133

the northeastern part of the state, it was likely that Silver would intercept her and send her along a different path, hopefully to some little mining town in the mountains.

It would buy them enough time to locate Krysanna.

Another issue gnawed at him, though. The recent phone call from a long-retired operative held more weight than he could see at face value. He hadn't had time to sort through all of the records since he took over the company, but he needed to make it a priority if he wanted to figure out that mystery. Most people in their line of work never made it to retirement, and it was unheard of for the few who actually did to request a return to the business. The whole mess screamed personal.

That was a surefire way to have things blow up in their faces. There were reasons why he maintained strict rules when it came to the personal lives of his staff. When they were off duty, they were off the grid. He could always find them if he needed to, but he rarely had to contact anyone during their time off from the job.

The phone on his desk rang, and he almost considered ignoring it. Technically, he should have left the compound hours ago, but he had more responsibility now than he'd had a year ago, and he wasn't the type to leave a job unfinished. It just so happened that this particular job was never finished. Downing the rest of his coffee, he reached for the phone and prepared himself for whatever fire was waiting on the other end.

*****

"Where are they sending you?" Soph asked.

"Dallas," Trina said, checking her ammunition supply. "I should be back in a few days, assuming I can get in, finish the job, and get out again. It doesn't look like a difficult assignment. I think he's just testing the waters to see if I'll follow through with it."

Soph sprawled out on the bed, clearly unhappy with the situation. She'd enjoyed the past few months, and she wasn't ready for Trina to leave again. Even if she'd be back soon, Soph wanted her to stay home. It was selfish – she knew that Trina was under contract – but while she had to accept the reality of her wife's employment, she didn't have to be happy about it.

"Maybe I'll bring you back a souvenir," Trina said. She paused in her task of ensuring her weapons were in working order, and her gaze trailed over Soph's form. "You know, you could join the company, too. We could even work as a team, then. It would be better than working alone, and then I wouldn't have to leave you here by yourself every time I get a new assignment."

"I don't think Mikhail would go for that," Soph said. "He still hates me."

"It's been seven years," Trina reminded her. "I'm sure he's moved on by now."

Soph envied her optimism, but she didn't believe it. There were some things that time couldn't fix, and her history with Trina's employer was one of them. The surprise on the man's face when they both showed up for the meeting was burned into her mind, and she knew better than to even suggest an interest in signing on with the organization.

"Maybe," she said. "I'm not good at taking orders."

Trina laughed as she finished packing her pistol and knives, and she cleared them off the bed so that she could stretch out beside Soph. Draping an arm over the other woman's stomach, she closed her eyes, relishing the moment that would be over far too soon. Knowing that Soph would be waiting for her at home would give her the incentive to finish her assignment quickly, and the soft kiss placed on the top of her head made her want to stay exactly where she was.

"I heard that it's supposed to storm before morning," Soph said quietly. "Make sure you keep the top up on your car."

Trina understood the undercurrent of concern in the remark. There was always a chance that a job could go wrong, and Soph wanted to make sure she knew that she was expected to make it back home. She'd been lucky so far; she'd only been shot a couple of times over the past couple of decades, and thankfully, never with silver. Eventually, that luck might run out, but she fully intended to keep the streak going for as long as possible.

As much as she wanted to stay there in bed, she needed to cover as many miles as possible before dawn. The sooner she made it to Dallas, the sooner she could come home. Reluctantly, she rolled over and stood, missing the close contact the second she moved.

"Call me when you stop for the day," Soph said, propping herself up on her elbows. She was obviously sulking, although she'd never admit it, and she tried to keep her unhappiness from showing on her features.

"Of course," Trina said.

They'd never been fond of emotional goodbyes, so Trina offered a reassuring smile and shouldered her bag as she turned towards the door. Soph watched her leave, and she waited until she heard the door close before she stepped out of the bedroom. She closed her eyes at the sound of the engine starting, tires on pavement signaling Trina's departure.

Her steps brought her to the back porch with a book in hand, but she couldn't focus on the words. The script on the pages failed to hold her attention, and her gaze lifted to the sky. Dark clouds rolled in, obscuring the moon and stars as a gust of wind sent her hair flying across her face.

She had to trust in Trina's abilities. She'd been in the business since before they'd even met, back when they were both human. Her skills had only increased with her additional speed, strength, and reflexes. She'll be home soon enough, she told herself. You won't even have time to miss her.

It was a hollow thought, one that lacked the conviction she wished she felt. She needed to keep her mind occupied, but studying wasn't helping, and she was at a loss for how to pass the time. The faint glow of light spilling from the treehouse drew her gaze, her brow furrowing in concern.

The storm already looked like it was going to be rough, and the thought that Krys would be stuck outside in the middle of it brought another wave of worry. Setting the book aside, she stepped down from the porch and crossed the yard to look up at the tree. Wind continued to pull at her clothes and hair, but thankfully, it hadn't started raining yet. That could change at any moment, though, and she quickly climbed the ladder.

The elf was huddled in the corner, trying to avoid the gusts of air that blew through the opening behind Soph, and orange eyes were wide with the fear she tried to ignore. Slowly, Soph approached, dropping down to a crouch about a foot away from her, and she held out her hand.

"Krys, there's a bad storm coming," she said. "I know you said you don't want to be a pain, but why don't you come inside until it's over?"

Krysanna stared at her, biting her lower lip as indecision held her in place. She'd weathered storms back home, but the dense forests of Evemyst surrounded her then, shielding her from the worst of the rain and wind. Here, though, the meager shelter of the treehouse left her exposed to the elements. The woods outside of her haven were thinner than what she'd grown accustomed to, but the thought of imposing any further had a refusal on the tip of her tongue.

"Please," Soph pressed. "I told you I'd keep you safe, and I can't do that if you're stuck out here. Just come in for a little while, and if you want to come back out here once it lets up, then that's up to you. I'm not gonna make you stay in the house if you don't want to."

A few long minutes passed, neither of them moving, Soph's hand still outstretched with the offer. Krysanna gave it a quick glance before meeting grey eyes to gauge their sincerity. She read honesty in them, and she tentatively reached out her hand to take Soph's. With a barely perceptible nod, she stood when her host pulled her to her feet.

Turning, she gathered her belongings, carefully placing them in her traveling pack as quickly as she could without damaging them. A rumble of thunder preceded a flash of lightning, and she cringed. The weight of her bag lifted, and she looked at Soph in confusion, receiving a comforting smile as the woman took her hand again and led her to the opening, her belongings resting carefully over her host's shoulder.

With a small smile of gratitude, Krys glanced up at the sky before jumping out of the treehouse, her wings spreading behind her to slow her descent. She landed lightly, folding her wings over her back as she turned to watch Soph climb down the ladder. The crossed the yard together, but Krysanna hesitated when they reached the back door of the house.

The homes of Evemyst coexisted with the great trees, and most of the buildings incorporated the living wood in their construction. Giant oaks provided comfort and a connection to the earth around them, but the house before her held no similar qualities. The wood was far removed from the source, and the shape of the two-story building was even more unnerving up close. Even the towers of metal and glass in the city hadn't shaken her this much.

"Hey," came Soph's soft voice. "It's okay. You've never been in one of these, have you?"

Krysanna shook her head, but another crash of thunder as rain began to splatter the edge of the porch made the decision for her. It was just a building. Yes, it was nothing like her homeland, but she had to push her uncertainty aside for now. Until she found a way back to Zalyndrya, she had to adapt as best as she could.

When Soph opened the door, the elf walked forward, her steps cautious as she looked around the unfamiliar residence. As soon as the door closed behind her, she heard the sky open up with a downpour. Relief and gratitude coursed through her, and her shoulders relaxed as she ventured further into the house.

There were so many sights to take in, but she was able to find similarities between the different items in the kitchen and living room and the homes of her beloved forests. Perhaps they had more in common than she'd thought, and she took a small measure of comfort in the realization. Even so, she decided that she would only remain in the house until the storm passed.

Her bag rested beside a plush chair, and a reassuring nod from Soph gave her the courage to move forward. Pulling off her boots, she settled on the chair, drawing her feet up to rest beneath her. The soft material was comfortable, and she found her voice after a few minutes of listening to the rain pour down outside.

"Are all houses like this one?" she asked.

"I guess," Soph said with a shrug, dropping down onto the sofa. "I mean, there are houses like this one, out in the middle of nowhere, and there are ones closer to each other. Most of those are close to the city, and then you have buildings that have a lot of separate rooms that people rent out; they're called apartments. I had one years ago before we bought this place. It's kinda nice being out here away from everyone."

Krysanna hummed in thought. The close proximity of the woods was indeed nice, but she missed the regular interactions of people. There had been a sense of community, and being in a house so far away from others felt lonely. Maybe in time, if she failed to find a way back, she would learn to accept it.

*****

Alex checked the address one last time, glancing between the documents and his laptop. It was the first actual solid piece of the puzzle that he'd found, but figuring out what to do with it was a problem. His quarry had first appeared in a private residence in Center City, one whose owner was unlisted, which meant that they had enough money to keep their real estate interests private.

There was one interesting detail he found, though – all inquiries regarding the property were directed to Evans International. At first glance, few would find that suspicious; people with that kind of money could afford to have their accountant handle the day-to-day business of property management. In this case, however, it provided yet another clue.

Closing his laptop, he grabbed his jacket and left the suite. His destination wasn't far, and the walk would give him a chance to gather his thoughts. He still couldn't figure out why Silver wanted to help him – the explanation that their assignments were connected felt like a weak excuse – but he wasn't about to complain about it. The vampire had his own motives, Alex was sure, and he would have to figure them out before he found himself in a difficult position. No one, especially not someone in their line of work, could be that altruistic.

The night air was cool, a spring storm closing in on the city, and he set a brisk pace as he headed towards Rittenhouse Square. He hadn't heard anything concerning the stream of emails he'd sent that morning, but it would only be a matter of time before he would increase the pressure. For now, he had a job to finish. Screwing with another vampire could wait.

He entered the lobby as if he owned the place, ignoring the main desk as he stepped into the elevator. As the doors closed, he pressed the button for the top floor, scowling when it failed to respond. There was no sign of a card reader, but the next two buttons provided the same result. He finally found one that lit up, and the elevator began its ascent.

Climbing the next four flights of steps was an inconvenience, but if this outing proved useful, then it would be worth the effort. He closed the door to the stairwell as quietly as possible, keeping his movements nearly silent as he neared the condo. Straining to hear the voices on the other side, he noted the familiarity of one of them, but he couldn't understand the language.

The conversation stopped abruptly, and he stepped back, preparing to disappear into the nearest shadow as the door opened. He stared at the woman, suspicion dancing up his spine, but she regarded him with calm curiosity as she seemed to wait for an explanation for his presence.

"I should've known," he muttered.

"Is there something I can help you with, Malice?" Lalasa asked.

"I was following a lead, which brought me here," he said. "So, unless you're keeping the girl you have me chasing locked in a closet, then no."

Understanding flashed across violet eyes, and she stepped aside, gesturing for him to enter. Alex hesitated, his mind screaming that this was a trap, and he failed to hide a growl. Lalasa was unfazed, but he couldn't find it in himself to be surprised. He could practically feel the power emanating from her form, despite her lithe frame. After another moment, he stalked forward into the condo, his senses alert for anything the might indicate an impending attack.

Another woman regarded him with green eyes, and Alex stopped, glancing between the two. Lalasa closed the door, walking past him into the kitchen and returning with a glass of water. He eyed it with growing suspicion when she held it out to him, but he reluctantly accepted it, feeling more and more like he'd just walked into the most screwed up situation he'd ever encountered.

"Malice, this is Cassandra," Lalasa said, motioning to the woman who offered a smile. "We were just catching up since I've been away for a few months. Since you're here, perhaps you could share your progress?"

He was only half-listening, his attention focused on Cassandra. The resemblance between her and Silver was undeniable. He had the feeling that he'd somehow wandered into a bigger mess than he'd thought when he accepted his current assignment. The connections just kept coming, and there were too many coincidences for him to simply dismiss them.

"My progress would be moving forward if I actually had all of the information from the start," he said, pulling his gaze away from Cassandra to regard Lalasa coldly. "You knew he was holding out on me, but you didn't say shit about it."

"Mikhail will run his business as he sees fit," she said. "I interfere only when I must."

"And giving me the info I needed to find her didn't warrant your interference?" He made no attempt to hide the venom in his voice. "Do you want me to do this or not, because I'm getting really tired of running in circles about it."

"Is that why you're here?" she asked.

"I'm here because the info Silver gave me pointed me in this direction." He didn't miss the flash of recognition in Cassandra's eyes, but he had more important matters to discuss; he filed it away for later. "She was here, and I think you know where she went, so why don't you stop bullshitting me."

Glass cracked in his hand, spilling water over his fingers and onto the hardwood floor. His patience was already past its limit, and the glowing tattoos that usually only revealed themselves when he was in his other form began to crawl across his features. A brief tingle danced against his skin, and the glass mended itself in his hand, but the impassive expression on Lalasa's face only served to frustrate him.

"She was here," Lalasa said. "The spell that she used to leave our world brought her to its last destination, which was my Philadelphia residence. If I knew where she went from here, then I would have had no need to hire you, so I would appreciate it if you kept your temper in check."

She turned, her footsteps eerily silent as she opened a drawer on the other side of the coffee table. When she returned, she grasped a clear plastic bag, golden feathers carefully gathered within, and she turned it over in her hand.

"This is what we've been able to find, but I'm not sure how helpful you'll find it," she said. "These were scattered around the room when I arrived. Perhaps they will assist you in tracking her to her current location."

With his free hand, he took the bag, barely giving it a second glance. Only then did he notice the absence of the steady hum of common appliances. The air inside the condo was static, alerting him again of the presence of magic, and he tore his attention from Lalasa to locate the source.

Traces of it surrounded him, from both women in front of him, to the small globes of light floating around the ceiling. Magic flowed through the entire condo, and the reason for the elevator's malfunction became strikingly clear. Magic and technology seldom coexisted; it made sense that someone had taken precautions to prevent any incidents involving the two crossing each other.

"My guess is that she would have traveled west," Cassandra said, finally speaking up. Her accent was the same as the one he'd heard from both Lalasa and Silver, solidifying his suspicions that none of them were from this world. "She'd want to find the closest thing to a forest around here, and in order to do so, she'd have to go to northern New Jersey or further into Pennsylvania."

The pine woods of New Jersey were a possibility, but an elf would have better luck heading towards the less populated areas of Pennsylvania. Unless she'd continued to travel by magic, then she would be on foot. Or in the air, he realized as he considered the gathered feathers. It was another lead, at least.

"Give my brother our regards when you see him next," she said. Something akin to regret passed across her features before she forced it away, a sad smile on her lips.

Alex took a moment to process her words before their meaning clicked into place, providing him with more information that he figured she'd intended. He said nothing as he stepped forward, placing the remains of the glass on the table, and he left the condo without another word.

The threads were weaving together, connections continuing to form as he examined what he'd learned. Something had happened between all of them, and his employer was also involved. His client had referred to the man by name, familiarity in her voice, and he wondered just how deep this hole led.

The remark from Cassandra brought a little more information regarding his colleague. If they were siblings, then Silver had likely been turned recently, which gave Alex even more confidence in his own abilities if their working relationship turned sour. He had no desire to cross Lalasa – although he would if it came down to it – but even with the similarities between the two vampires, Silver wouldn't be nearly as powerful as she was.

So far, though, none of them had been overtly deceptive, and he continued to sort through the details as he descended the stairs, declining to take the elevator after the fourth flight. As he reached the ground floor, he withdrew one of the feathers, catching the scent of woodlands as he closed his eyes. Finding the wayward elf would be much easier now, and he allowed a grin to spread on his features.

*****

Karian picked his way through the woods, the shadow of the nearby mountains looming over him. Dropping to a crouch, his fingertips brushed across the dirt, finding light footprints that others might have missed. Green eyes snapped up, darting around as he listened for movement, but he heard only the sounds of nocturnal animals roaming the land.

He was on the right track, at least, and he straightened to start forward again. The silence of his movements was worthy of his gratitude; it made his job easier, and he could stalk his prey without revealing his presence. Every dozen or so paces, he paused, checking for tracks or other

142

evidence of passage, his confidence growing when the signs started to grow fresher.

His instructions were clear – locate and deter, but do not engage – and he was confident that he could follow them to the letter. He'd found stealthier targets than one elven warrior.

The more time he spent on Earth, the more he realized that he'd made the right decision. Zalyndrya held nothing for him anymore. His people wouldn't have accepted him once they discovered his condition, and it would be pointless to try; Dravias was no longer there. There were too many memories that would threaten to overcome him, experiences that he only acknowledged on nights when he'd shut himself away in his new home.

Those thoughts were no help when it came to accepting everything that had changed, and he still struggled to come to terms with everything that had happened since he'd first set foot on this world. All of the changes threatened to break him, to shatter him beyond what he'd already become, and he pushed them down into the deepest recesses of his mind in order to survive. He wasn't sure if he'd be able to resist the pull of the dawn if he allowed them to resurface.

Adaptation was his only hope for survival. He'd learned enough about this world in the time he'd been here, although many finer points of technology escaped his comprehension. His cell phone was useful, more complex than he'd estimated, but the ability to communicate instantly without the aid of magic certainly helped. He'd always focused on physical combat, ignoring the opportunities to study the arcane arts, and even with his new life and the expanse of time stretching before him, he saw little need to change the habit.

The ground was still wet from the storm that had just passed, threatening to wash away the remaining tracks, but he could find them again. He knew the direction they were heading, and he estimated that he'd find the elf within two nights at the absolute latest.

He could feel the sunrise approaching, and he turned to retrace his steps, careful to avoid damaging the evidence of previous passage. As the sounds of the occasional late traveler reached his ears, he fished his keys out of his pocket and pushed his motorcycle out of the brush and back onto the road.

Driving across slick pavement, he made his way back to the poorly maintained motel. Several of the letters on the sign had long since burned out, and the Vacancy indicator flickered as it tried to cling to life. The interior was marginally better, but the lingering scents of mold and bleach made a convincing argument for him to simply avoid breathing.

Karian sent a quick text to update Mikhail on his progress before unfolding a sheet of parchment from his bag. He'd already sketched several landmarks onto the paper, and he added more to the map, relying on memory for accuracy. The project served as a means to pass the time, as well as a chance to utilize his less violent skills. Not to mention that the various maps he'd drawn helped him learn the land and find his way in his various travels.

He recalled a remark from Sean that had informed him that he could have bought any number of maps from gas stations and other stores, but he continued to dismiss the idea as forcefully as he'd done at the initial suggestion. Karian preferred not to rely on another's interpretation of different locations. By drawing them as he'd seen them, he could verify their accuracy.

His phone vibrated across the table, breaking his concentration, and he set his pencil aside to read the message that flashed across the screen. Apparently, he was making better progress than Malice was. He expected that to change with the file he'd provided, and he was only mildly surprised that Mikhail had declined to mention its absence after their last meeting.

The vague praise didn't warrant a response, so he stood to check the curtains instead, ensuring that no light would enter the room. Satisfied that he was relatively safe from the prospect of waking up as a pile of ash, he carefully folded the half-finished map and placed it back into his bag. He could afford a few hours of rest in order to approach his continuing task with a clear head.

*****

The storm hindered her progress, and Miria watched the raindrops trail down the remaining glass in one of the windows. Flashes of lightning grew further and further apart, and the wind ceased its pounding against the cabin, but a few trickles of water still fell outside. Turning away, she returned to her seat on the cushions she'd be able to salvage.

Her mission was vague at best. Locating her kin was enough of a challenge, but she had no idea what she was supposed to do next. The elders

144

hadn't specified if she was to check on her well-being, bring her home, or kill her. Perhaps that was part of her task – in order to achieve the rank of Elite Guard, she was supposed to trust them without question. It would have been nice if they'd provided just a little more guidance.

She supposed that they would tell her when the time came, and she ignored the doubts that told her that they were uncertain of her ability to find Krysanna in the first place. She'd worked hard for the honor of joining the ranks, and she couldn't allow insecurity to stand in her way. Whatever they wanted from her, she would provide it, even if it meant eliminating one of her own people. She hoped that it wouldn't come to that, but she had to prepare herself for the possibility.

The first few rays of the rising sun filtered through the window, painting rainbow patters on the floor as they passed through the lingering drops of water in their path. She wouldn't stray too far from her shelter, but she hoped to find at least some evidence to prove she was heading in the right direction. Avoiding the populated areas felt like the wisest choice, but her chances of hearing any rumors that might assist her were nonexistent if she continued to follow that path.

If she were being honest, the thought of trying to move about within the general population made her apprehensive. To the best of her knowledge, they were all humans, many of whom had never seen one of her people before, and she had limited experience when it came to interacting with humans in general. She'd only ventured outside of Evemyst once prior to this mission, but while she'd encountered no trouble then, Earth was vastly different from Zalyndrya.

Even at night, she could see the glow of lights against the sky in the distance, and the scraps of information she'd gathered about this world told her that the way of life in general was nothing like how her people lived. The technology as they called it, was completely foreign to her, and she was hesitant to use even a small amount of magic lest she invite disaster.

Miria settled for a light breakfast, using some of her rations, and went about tidying the cabin. She would search where she could, but she wanted to be able to return if necessary, and even if she never saw the place again, perhaps another wanderer could find it useful. Restringing her bow, she stood in the doorway, gazing out at the forest, and with one last look at her temporary shelter, she left the cabin to continue her search.

The morning passed fruitlessly, and a sense of foreboding cast a shadow over her thoughts. She couldn't place its source, but unease caused her steps to falter, wariness keeping her alert. The woods were quiet, the sounds of birds and other wildlife strangely absent. She tried to assure herself that it was only her imagination playing tricks on her; maybe the storm during the night had sent the animals to safer territory.

A twig snapped under her foot, startling her, and she chided herself for allowing her paranoia to get the better of her. She was a warrior, yet she was acting as if the shadows beneath the trees held invisible enemies that could reduce her to nothing. Shaking her head, she squared her shoulders, moving forward with purpose.

By midday, she heard unusual sounds, and she slowed her pace to approach them with caution. The trees thinned around her, and a path cut through the woods. She focused on keeping her breathing steady, each footstep deliberately placed, and she used the shadows to her advantage as she neared the darkened ground separating both sides of the forest.

Her eyes widened and she jumped back, clamping a hand over her mouth to keep any sound from escaping, and something large and fast passed through her vision along the path. A few seconds ticked by before another object followed the same path as the first, but she kept her distance, searching her memory for anything that would tell her what they were. A few more sped by, and she swallowed hard as she summoned her courage to walk towards the edge of the tree line.

The intermittent passes of the objects kept her tense, but she managed to get a closer look, surprise finding a home on her features when she saw people inside of them. She'd made it to the edge, her feet barely inches away from the odd material, and she nearly shrank back into the trees when one of the contraptions slowed to a stop after passing her. She held her ground, though, her fingers curling around the dagger at her hip as the thing began moving back towards her. When it stopped, the glass separating her from the woman inside lowered, and she turned the ring on her right index finger to activate the language enchantment.

"Are you okay?" the stranger asked, concern evident in her brown eyes, along with suspicion.

"I am," Miria said, keeping her voice steady. "I seem to have lost my way, but I will find it again."

The woman studied her, taking in her appearance as she debated with herself. Picking up strangers was beyond dangerous and definitely ill advised, but the girl was on her own as far as she could see. Although it was only early afternoon, once the sun set later, she could find herself in trouble.

"Are you out here by yourself?" she asked, receiving a nod in response. Her heart sank at that, and she wondered who would let someone who barely looked old enough to be an adult wander around the woods on her own. "Where are you trying to go?"

Miria hesitated, her own suspicion growing. Humans, especially ones on this alien world, could be deceptive, and despite the stranger's worried expression, Miria wasn't willing to walk into a trap. She'd been warned that there were those who would seek her failure, who would stop at nothing to keep her from her goal, but she saw nothing that would indicate that this human was one of them.

"Philadelphia," she said after a moment.

"I think you're more than a little turned around," the woman said, shaking her head. "We're a few miles outside of Milford. Philly is at least two and a half hours from here. How were you planning to get there?"

The question stunned her. How else was she supposed to make it to the city if she didn't walk? Was there another way that she hadn't discovered? The answer sat right in front of her as she realized that the quickly moving objects were vehicles, and she looked away as she spoke.

"My intention was to travel on foot."

When she received no response, she risked a glance at the stranger, catching the look of sheer surprise. Meeting her gaze evenly, Miria silently challenged her to say something, to question her intelligence or sanity, but the woman snapped out of it quickly. There was a soft click, and the human motioned to the side of the car closest to the elf.

"It'll take you forever to get there if you're planning on walking," she said. "I can give you a ride as far as Allentown, but you'll have to find your own way from there."

Again, Miria made no move to accept the offer. Part of her was certain it was a trap, but if accepting assistance would bring her closer to her destination, then she would be foolish to refuse. Adjusting the position of her bow, she took a cautious step towards the vehicle, eyeing it warily as she found the handle to open the door.

"You can put your things in the backseat if you want," the woman said.

Miria nodded, her hand moving to the back door, and she carefully placed both her bow and her traveling pack on the seat before closing the door and sliding into the front passenger seat. The vehicle didn't move, and she sent a questioning look at the stranger, noticing the strap across her chest and lap. Finding a similar one to her left, she realized she was expected to pull it across herself as well. It took a moment for her to figure it out, but when it clicked into place, she offered a small smile.

"I thought the Renaissance Faire wasn't going to be open until later in the year," the stranger remarked. "Or are you one of those kids who's into that whole LARP thing?" When Miria simply stared in confusion, she shook her head. "I guess it's not important. You can call me Alma."

"Miria," she offered. Reaching up, she adjusted her hair to cover her ears, and she held her breath when the vehicle started moving. "How long will it be before we arrive?"

"About an hour and a half, unless the traffic gets bad," Alma said. "Is there someone you can call? I can let you use my cell phone."

"I am traveling alone," she said. "My cousin is near Philadelphia, and I am trying to find her."

It was close to the truth, and Miria couldn't reveal exactly why she was traveling towards the city. She could feel Alma watching her out of the corner of her eyes, but she kept her gaze forward, her fingers gripping the side of the door as the vehicle's speed increased. Thankfully, the subject ended there, and any other questions Alma might have had remained unspoken.

"Many thanks," Miria said after a few minutes had passed. "For helping me," she clarified. "It would have taken days for me to reach the city."

"Just promise me that you're not a runaway," Alma said. "Are your parents looking for you or anything?"

"My parents do not live in this country," she said, shaking her head. "I traveled here alone, and I assure you, I am not running from anything or anyone."

Eleven

Sleep eluded her, and Marielle turned over under the covers again, trying to gain even a few minutes of slumber. She'd heard nothing from Ian or her father, no word of whether the latter had even been located. Ian usually called by now. Worry kept sleep at bay, and the look on her father's face when they'd left the dinner continued to haunt her.

Checking the time, she sighed. It was late afternoon, and she had to work in a few hours, but even exhaustion wasn't enough to quiet her mind. Deciding that any further attempts would be useless, she climbed out of bed and made her way to the kitchen to start a pot of coffee. With the night's schedule, she'd need as much caffeine as she could get.

She'd spent plenty of time alone, but the place felt empty now. Carl had left before they'd even returned from the Konistav's dinner, and she'd hoped for even a single text from Ian to let her know that he was okay. Her thoughts were still a mess when it came to the vampire, but although she wasn't sure where things were heading between them, she needed to feel confidence in his safety.

Returning to the living room, she curled up in the corner of her sofa and flipped on the news, hoping for something to distract her from the complicated thoughts running through her mind. Six months prior, she'd sat in that very spot, feeling beyond useless, and had made the decision to change that. Of course, she'd found herself locked in the trunk of an old Cadillac for her efforts, but at least she lived to tell about it.

Looking back, the experience had changed her perspective on several things. She was no longer afraid of the clients who came to the office to meet with Rhonda, and her smile became genuine as well as professional whenever she greeted them. The fear that had insisted that she send Ian away the night he'd confessed the truth had dissipated, and she found herself looking at him in the same manner she had before she'd learned what he really was. She could read the longing look in his eyes, even though he never pressed the issue, and now maybe she was ready to let him back into that part of her life.

Before those events had turned her life upside-down, she'd never imagined that she would count vampires amongst her friends – she'd never even known of their existence – and beyond that, one of her closest friends these days wasn't even from the same planet. Everything had changed, beyond just her own perception of reality, but she wouldn't have done things differently if she had the chance to go back and try again.

The sound of her phone brought her back to the present, and she opened her eyes to see that the sunlight had all but faded. At some point, she must have dozed off, her coffee forgotten on the table beside her. Blinking a few times to gain some semblance of awareness, she reached for her phone and breathed a sigh of relief when Ian's name flashed across the screen above his message.

He'd found her father, along with some answers, but he hadn't made it home before sunrise. He didn't specify exactly where he'd spent the day, and she responded with a quick message to thank him for everything he was doing to salvage the situation. She could ask him for specifics at work later.

By the time she exited the elevator and crossed the tiled floor to her desk, Marielle was in much better spirits. The anxiety that had twisted in her gut had loosened into a barely noticeable twinge of concern. She needed to see Ian, to know for certain that he was fine. The text messages had helped, but there was something to be said about confirming it for herself.

Rhonda's schedule was almost as packed as the night before, but Marielle had a system in place, one that streamlined the process for new clients and provided all of the information necessary for potential clients. All in all, she was proud of herself for her organizational skills, and the raise Rhonda had given her at the start of the year told her that the accountant had noticed, too. She had a feeling that some of it came from how she'd handled the situation before the holidays, but as long as she kept her wits about her, she had no concerns about her ability to perform her job.

When the elevator doors opened, the soft chime signaling their arrival, she looked up from her computer screen and smiled at the sight that greeted her. Ian's crooked grin sent her pulse racing, and the arch of a blond eyebrow told her that he'd noticed. Clearing her throat, she tried to convince her heart to return to a normal pace – with limited success – but she couldn't deny that she was happy to see him.

"So?" she asked. "Was he okay? What happened?"

"He was well enough to shoot me," Ian said, his grin vanishing. "Lothan showed up before he could do anymore damage, and he ended up with a bullet in him, too, but that was the end of it. Your dad knows how to take us down; he was using silver." He paused, trying to read her expression. "You know what that means, right?"

Marielle didn't want to admit it, but the truth was staring at her, and it couldn't have been more obvious if her father waltzed into the building wearing full gear for an operation. It still threw her, though. She couldn't quite reconcile the kind man from her childhood with an unapologetic killer, especially one who seemed to know enough about vampires to know how to kill them.

"I know," she said quietly. "Is he...?"

"Alive," Ian said. "We're not going to kill your dad, even if he doesn't plan on giving us the same treatment. He asked me not to tell you, but he knew he was wasting his breath. He retired from Jack-o-Lantern right after you were born, and he isn't too happy with the idea of the two of us being friends."

Logically, she knew that Ian wouldn't cross that line. She wasn't so sure about Lothan. His rules meant that those who were "innocent" were safe from him, but a former assassin was far from innocent. She had to trust that they were in agreement on the subject, and she leaned back in her chair as she tried to figure out how to process the truth about her father and how to keep their family intact.

"Hey." His voice was gentle, and she looked up to read the concern in his eyes. "It'll be okay. We'll figure this out, and everything will turn out just fine. Trust me."

She did trust him, which was part of the problem. Ever since she learned the truth, she didn't want to trust him, but she did anyway. He'd done everything he could to keep her safe, and he'd more than earned her trust again. He could have killed her father – had it been anyone else pulling the

151

trigger, he probably would have – but he wouldn't let it come to that.

Marielle nodded, offering a small smile as his hand rested on her shoulder. Reaching up, she placed her own on top of it, giving a quick squeeze, before she returned her attention to the information on the screen. He didn't withdraw his hand, and his presence helped remind her that she could get through this.

*****

The trail vanished at the edge of the woods, and Karian swore under his breath. There were no tracks on the other side of the road, but he found it difficult to believe that someone would pick up a stranger so far from any major town. Then again, an elf wouldn't strike an imposing figure; she'd probably been mistaken for a lost teenager, and apparently, she was intelligent enough to use that to her advantage.

He looked down both sides of the road, weighing the odds of which direction she would have gone. Whoever picked her up was probably heading south, judging by his current position. The elf wouldn't have crossed the road to approach a car, so her new ally must have pulled over to speak through the passenger window.

Racing back through the forest, he retrieved his bike and sped back to the motel, gathering his few possessions before returning the room key to the front desk without a word. She had a sizable lead, and he'd have to push the limits of the motorcycle to gain back the ground he'd lost. He trusted his reflexes, and the ground had long since dried, but he was still working on guesses and assumptions.

Completely ignoring the speed limit, he flew down the road on the bike, frustration echoing with a low growl deep within his chest. She'd want to avoid the larger cities, even if she had information pointing to Philadelphia, but she'd also be at the whims of the person who'd offered her a ride.

The melody of an incoming call surrounded him in the helmet, and he tapped the side of it. His employer had insisted on the Bluetooth extension, stating that if Karian traveled by bike, he still needed to be reachable.

"I heard you lost something," Mikhail said once the call had connected.

"Word travels fast," Karian said. "Do you have anything on this or

152

did you just call to give me shit?"

"Ten miles north of Allentown," he continued. "Got a call from one of my informants. She said that she saw someone that looked out of place getting out of a red sedan. I ran the license plate, and I'm sending the address to your GPS. Handle it."

The line went dead, but Karian had what he needed. Step-by-step directions filtered through the speakers, guiding him to his next stop. Even if the elf wasn't at the location, whoever was there had something to do with how she'd made it closer to Philadelphia. All he had to do was figure out which method would provide the desired results; he could decide whether or not to tie up the loose end afterwards.

He parked two blocks away from the apartment complex, leaving the helmet with his bike as he checked the details on his phone. With any luck, he'd be in and out before the engine had a chance to cool, and he slid his hands into his pockets as he walked the remaining distance. He spotted the car in the parking lot, telling him that his unknowing contact was indeed home.

The door to the building was propped open – likely by someone who wanted to return without going through the hassle of entering the code – and he made sure to keep it that way when he stepped inside. Climbing the stairs to the second floor, he read the numbers on the doors before finding the one he needed, his knuckles landing on the wood in quick succession. Following the sound of approaching footsteps, two sets of locks clicked open, and a woman peered out through the small space of the open door, a chain keeping it from opening further.

"Can I help you?" she asked.

He could already catch the scent of fear, faint but present, and he offered a disarming smile as he reached up to smooth down his hair. His leather jacket remained closed, hiding his weapons, but he knew enough about the people of this world to know that few of them would greet a stranger at their door without suspicion.

"Ms. Herrera?" he asked. "My apologies for disturbing you so late, but I've been trying to find my cousin, and I was wondering if you might have seen her recently?" The woman didn't respond, but she didn't slam the door in his face either, so he continued. "She's a bit on the eccentric side, probably still wearing her archer costume. I'd say she's about a head shorter than I am. She's only just turned eighteen, and she was supposed to meet me in Philly two days ago."

Alma hesitated, unsure of whether or not to trust the stranger at her door. He seemed harmless – it wasn't as if he'd threatened her – and his accent was the same as the girl she'd helped earlier, but something about him set her on edge. Her instincts warned her not to trust him, even though she couldn't find a solid reason, but she was never one to ignore her intuition.

"I'm sorry," she said. "She doesn't sound familiar, but I hope you two find each other."

Karian's smile faltered, but he kept it in place. Even without the hereditary talent that he and his sister shared, other physiological signs made the woman's deception obvious. A white brow arched as the door began to close, and he stopped it from completing the motion, the side of his boot blocking its path. Now, he could definitely smell the fear permeating the air, although he made no further move to enter the apartment.

"Are you certain?" he pressed. "Because it's very important that I find her quickly. Her safety is at risk. She's on her own out there, and she's not entirely in touch with reality. Surely, you wouldn't want to place her in more danger by declining to assist someone who can help her, would you?"

Her initial distrust multiplied tenfold when he insisted on preventing the door from closing, and she summoned her courage to meet his gaze. His words sounded genuine, but his eyes told the truth; she read no concern in them, only cold and calculating darkness.

"I think you should go," she said. "I'm closing the door, and if you don't leave, then I'm calling the police."

The smile vanished altogether, and Alma tried to remember how to breathe. His pleasant façade changed so quickly that she knew she had to get away from him before the situation escalated. His boot remained lodged in the small space of the open door, and he seemed to have no intention of removing it, but she held herself together until he started speaking again.

"That would be unwise." This time, his voice carried an unspoken threat. "You have information, and you're going to provide it. I've asked nicely twice, which is more than I usually do, so perhaps we could come to an agreement."

His movements were quicker than she could follow, his fingers snapping the chain as if it were cheap plastic, and before she had time to

154

react, he was in front of her. The door shut behind him, and his hand clamped over her mouth as he reached back with the other one to turn the lock. Fear held her in place, her heart racing as she silently screamed at herself to do something, to move, to fight back.

"Ms. Herrera," he said, his voice dangerously low. "I'm going to remove my hand, but if you scream, then this will not end well for you. Do you understand?"

At that, she nodded slowly, eyes wide as he withdrew his hand and took a step back. Her gaze darted to her cell phone, wondering if she could reach it before he could stop her, but the memory of just how fast he moved only seconds ago kept her from following through on the idea. All she could do now was hope that he let her go without hurting her.

"Now then," Karian said, leaning back against the door as he folded his arms over his chest. "Where is she?"

"I... I don't know," Alma said. There was a tremor in her voice, and she fought to keep tears at bay. "She was all alone and didn't have anyone else to help her, so I gave her a ride. All she said was that she was trying to get to Philly. I swear, that's all I know!"

Karian said nothing, and she would swear that he didn't even blink as he stood there weighing her words. She shrank under that stare, praying that he believed her. There was nothing else she could say, no other information she could offer, but she feared that what scraps she'd given him wouldn't be enough to save her life.

"How long ago did you two part ways?" he asked finally. "Did anyone else pick her up?"

"It was a few hours ago," she said. "I dropped her off at a gas station, but the last I saw her, she was heading towards the woods again."

He nodded, his expression turning thoughtful, and Alma allowed herself to breathe a little easier. There were no other threats, direct or implied, but she didn't dare to hope that she was in the clear just yet. When he unzipped his jacket and reached inside, the fear returned, but he only withdrew a scrap of paper instead of a weapon.

"I want the exact location," he said, holding out the paper.

Slowly, she approached, but he didn't close the distance between them. As soon as her fingers closed on the paper, she retreated again, leaning it on the wall to scribble the name of the gas station and the cross streets. As she reached out to return it, she saw him hold out a folded set of cash with another slip of paper on top of it.

"To cover the broken chain," he explained. "If you see her again, call me."

Alma risked a glance at the money but didn't count it yet, focusing on the phone number with the word "Silver" scrawled above it. The glance she managed to get of the payment showed that at least the top bill was worth one hundred dollars, and she realized that it was as much to buy her silence as it was to replace the hardware.

"I could still call the police, you know," she said, regaining a small measure of courage.

"And I could still kill you," Karian countered. "But I'm trying to avoid that. Remember what I just said, though. This woman is not as harmless as she seems. You're lucky that she accepted a ride from you without pressing for more."

She swallowed a humorless laugh. He'd forced his way into her apartment, but he wanted to warn her against the dangers of a young woman half his size? It was ridiculous. Her incredulity was short-lived when she considered the events of the day and evening, though. Taking another look at him, she found herself wondering what exactly was going on between him and Miria.

"You're not going to hurt her, are you?" she asked.

"I'm not planning on it," he said. "But it depends on if I can bait her away from the city." His impassive features grew serious. "Ms. Herrera-"

"Alma," she interrupted. "I'm probably twice your age, but you already know my name, so just call me Alma."

"Alma, then," he said, tipping his head in acknowledgment. "What do you do for a living?"

"I'm a nurse," she said. The question surprised her, and she tried to figure out how it was relevant to the current conversation.

"And I assume that your job has certain requirements that you must adhere to," he continued. "My job is to solve problems. This young woman is looking for someone in Philadelphia, and my job right now is to keep her as far away from the city as possible until my colleague can find this other person and ensure their safety."

His words provided a different perspective, but she still had trouble

156

seeing the woman she helped as someone dangerous. Then again, the bow she'd carried looked much more functional than a simple prop, and she was almost certain that she'd seen some kind of knife on Miria's hip. Alma was quiet for a moment before she spoke up again.

"How did you kids get involved in something like this?" she asked, earning her an arched brow. "You can't be older than your early twenties, and you said yourself, she's only eighteen. So, how can you both be stuck in something that sounds so dangerous?"

"I lied," Karian said. "She's older than she looks."

He couldn't come right out and reveal the elf's true age, and he could read the skepticism in Alma's expression. It took another handful of moments for him to gather his thoughts and form something close to an explanation, although he owed the woman nothing.

"Where I'm from, you're considered and adult when you reach your sixteenth year," he said. "I've lived six more since then. There are factors in play right now that leave me in a precarious position, and my aim is to guide everything in the right direction without it blowing up in my face. I can't ask you to trust me – especially considering the circumstances surrounding this conversation – but at least believe me when I say that the less you know, the safer you'll be."

She tried to read his expression, but she caught a rare glimpse of honesty, and she looked away. Whatever he and the young woman were involved in, it had to be worse than he was letting on, but did she have any right to interfere? She was a nurse, living on her own after a mostly drama-free divorce, and her grown son was away at college. Looking at Karian again, she realized that he would be at an age where he could have been finishing up college for himself, but his path had led him elsewhere. She couldn't find it in herself to follow any further.

"Can I ask a favor?" she asked, waiting for him to nod before she continued. "When it's over, I want to know how everything turned out. It's not really my business, but something tells me that things could go wrong for you two if you're not careful."

"If you're lucky, you'll never see me again," Karian said. "But if that's what you want, then I'll try to get word to you regarding the outcome." Reaching back, he unlocked the door. "Thank you for your time, Alma."

With that said, he was gone, leaving her in the silence of her

157

apartment to ponder the strange turn her night had taken. She should have called the police, pressed charges in hopes that they would find the strange man who had briefly taken her hostage, but she simply stared at the closed door as she willed her pulse to return to a normal speed. Her life had brushed the edges of a world she could not hope to understand, but a twinge of worry and dread settled around her heart.

That night, she dreamt of forests and fields, of two opposing forces meeting only to bring about mutual destruction. She wouldn't remember it when she awoke, but in those hours of slumber, she witnessed magic and monsters battling for advantage, only for it to end in blood and flames.

*****

He couldn't place what had brought him to the middle of the woods at three in the morning, but he pressed forward nonetheless. Maybe it was some sixth sense that had lain dormant for most of his life, or the shock of a connection that ran deeper than time that surged through him the second his fingertips brushed against the feathers when he pulled one from the bag. Whatever it was, Alex wasn't sure that he liked it, but he'd followed his intuition as it led him away from the city.

The scent had faded, but he could still pick up traces of it – ancient forests and a hint of honeysuckle – and he followed it further away from the crowded metropolis. The scattered leaves on the worn path were still wet from the previous night's rain, hidden from the sun by the canopy above, but the occasional squish beneath his boots didn't bother him nearly as much as the unnerving feeling that he still couldn't place.

Alex was used to solitude, he'd accepted it from the moment his pack had rejected him all those years ago, and he honestly preferred it. To feel the overwhelming need to find and protect a stranger was an alien concept, one that he tried to ignore with minimal success. He tried to tell himself that it was just the urgency of the job, that once he'd finished the assignment and returned to his flat in London, the feeling would vanish. He only half believed it.

He came to the edge of the woods, the strength of the scent almost overwhelming his senses, and his eyes narrowed as he scanned the area. The glow of lights from within the house across the large yard held his attention for only a moment, his gaze settling on the treehouse in his path. It was dark inside of it, but he stalked out of the shadow of the trees, listening for any signs of occupation as he stood at the bottom of the ladder.

Climbing up, he confirmed what he'd already guessed; the treehouse was empty, but she'd been there recently. He peered out the small window towards the house, but he didn't approach. Instead, he climbed back down and headed back into the woods.

Within seconds, he emerged from the shadows in the corner of the penthouse suite, the sounds of the city around him assaulting his ears in sharp contrast to the near silence of the forest. Crossing the room, he shrugged off his jacket and dropped down onto the sofa, reaching for his laptop. He could find the location again easily enough, and he had a feeling that the elf wasn't going to stray too far from the seclusion that the property afforded.

He could have simply strolled up to the house and taken her away, with or without her cooperation, but the other scents that he caught warranted caution. The pair of vampires who were present at the recent meeting had been there as well, and while he wasn't sure if both of them had been home, he wanted to plan his next actions carefully.

There might have also been a part of him that wanted the elf to come with him willingly. She startled easily from what he'd learned, and kidnapping her from a place where she must have felt safe would only frighten her. He didn't want to have to track her down twice; once was enough of a pain in the ass.

That was what he told himself, although he knew it was only partially true. He wanted her acceptance, as absurd as the notion was. He wanted her to trust him instead of fearing his presence. If coaxing her away from that place without taking her by force was what it would take to achieve that, then he would take whatever steps were necessary.

"I've found her," he said into his phone once he'd made the call.

"If you'd called me at this hour to say anything else, I might have had to fire you," Mikhail said, his voice thick with fatigue. "Where?"

"I'd have to check a map for the exact area, but she's not alone," Alex said. "Our two favorite corpses are there."

He heard shuffling in the background, along with a string of expletives, and he knew that the information was vital. His employer was suddenly alert, his voice sharp, but Alex remained quiet until he was addressed again.

"You're sure?" Mikhail asked.

"Unless there's another pair of them that have the same exact scent, then yes," he said. "She's alive, so that's not a concern. It looks like she's been staying in a treehouse in the back yard, but she was inside their house when I got there."

"Get her out of there, but be careful about it," Mikhail said. "Try to approach her when they're not around. I don't want to risk them getting pissed and killing her."

"That was my plan. This is just a courtesy call. Some of us actually share information when we have it. Luckily, I seem to have made friends with one of my coworkers, so I was able to get what I needed anyway without your help."

"I had my reasons," Mikhail said.

"Apparently, the elf's safety wasn't one of them," Alex said dryly. "If I have to stake one of them, I'm charging extra."

He didn't wait for Mikhail to respond. Ending the call, he set his phone on the cushion next to him and settled down with his laptop. With one problem on its way to a solution, he still had the other one to deal with, but even with the possible entertainment that it could involve, his thoughts kept straying to golden feathers and honeysuckle.

Twelve

The sound of the television filtered through the condo, and Marielle opened her eyes slowly. The clock on her nightstand told her that it was mid-afternoon, and confusion chased away the lingering pull of sleep. She stood quickly, cautiously moving to her door and opening it slowly to keep the wood from creaking. The door to the guest room was still closed, which told her that Ian was still in there, but that didn't give her any clues as to who was sitting in her living room watching what sounded like the news.

Holding her breath, she padded closer, trying to calm the pounding of her heart. Logically, a burglar wouldn't have stopped to watch television, but that did little to settle her nerves. She risked a glance around the corner, surprised at the identity of the visitor, and the knowledge only put her more on edge.

"Dad?" she asked, her brow furrowed. "What are you doing here?" How did you even get in? The unspoken question lingered in the air, and she couldn't' read his expression when he turned his head to regard her. "How long have you been here?"

Carl muted the television, standing to approach, but she took a step back as he neared. The distrust in her eyes was obvious, and he couldn't say that he didn't deserve it. Everything he'd wanted to keep her from was out in the open now. He was sure that the second Ian and Lothan had left the motel room, the former had told Marielle everything.

"I can explain," he said.

"Go ahead," she replied. "I hope it's good, because as far as I can tell, you have a lot to cover."

He sighed; he definitely deserved that one. Stepping back, he returned to his seat on the sofa and gestured for her to join him. She

161

hesitated, but followed after a moment, sitting as far away from him as possible. The betrayal in her gaze hurt just as much as the anger, and he couldn't think of a single reason for her to feel anything other than those two emotions.

"I retired early," he said. "I didn't want to miss your childhood by either being away working or getting killed. It wasn't something that I wanted you to know – ever – but I still had enough connections to keep you safe. That's all I ever wanted."

"What were you so afraid of?" Marielle asked. "Did you think that knowing what you did for a living would change the fact that you're my dad and that you raised me?"

"Would you really have looked at me the same way, knowing the things I've done?" he countered. "You can't even do it now."

"You lied to me, Dad," she said. "I don't care what you used to do, but you never trusted me with the truth. And then, on top of that, you used the truth that you never told me to justify the way you treated my friends."

"You don't know what they're capable of," he said.

"I don't?" she shot back. "You don't even know whether I do or not. You're assuming that because you never told me about it, I couldn't find out on my own. I'm not a child anymore. I know how things work, even if I didn't six months ago. I learned, and I've had time to process it and make my own decisions. You don't get to decide what's best for me just because you don't think I'm capable of judging a situation before heading into it."

Carl took a moment to let her words sink in, seeing his daughter in a new light. The message she'd left him before the holidays had only been a glimpse into her life. He'd heard both fear and determination in her tone, but it had stirred paternal worry within himself. The change he'd heard then had only continued since that night, and the young woman sitting at the other end of the sofa had learned and adapted to the things she'd learned.

She had a point, he admitted begrudgingly, but that didn't erase the need to ensure her safety. Maybe he couldn't make decisions for her, and maybe he had to take a step back and let her succeed or fail on her own, but when it came to the ones she called her friends, failure could mean death. He'd seen it enough times, and he couldn't just sit back and watch his only daughter fall prey to the monsters who claimed the night for themselves.

Despite the conviction in her voice, he realized that she hadn't let it

162

rise in anger. That hadn't lessened the impact of her words, but it added another item to the equation, and he glanced over his shoulder towards the hallway. Returning his attention to her, he read the apprehension in her expression and let out a long sigh.

"He's here, isn't he?" he asked, already knowing the answer.

"In the guest room," she said. There was no hesitation; there might have been a challenge instead. "We're not back together."

"Yet," Carl said. "Don't give me that look. I may be old, but I'm not blind. Whatever you two have isn't over." Another sigh, this one full of resignation, escaped him. "Don't ask for my approval or blessing or any of that. I think it's a bad idea. Hell, there are a dozen reasons why you should keep him at arm's length, but you're going to do whatever it is you want to do, so all I can do is voice my opinion and hope that you make the right decisions."

Marielle had expected more of an argument than that. In fact, when she'd admitted that Ian was in the guest room, she'd expected her father to storm in there. He hadn't moved, though, and if anything, he seemed to finally understand that his preferred methods weren't going to work this time. She wasn't prepared for grudging acceptance, though.

Recovering quickly, she nodded, relief flooding through her. She had no idea what her future with Ian might entail, but she was done running from it. The shock of learning what he was had long since faded, and the draw she'd felt towards him before was returning. She'd made it obvious in her words and actions, but she would still take it one step at a time.

"I'll be careful," she said. "But we're still not finished the discussion about you. I know most of it, I think, but I want to hear it from you."

"Fair enough," he conceded.

*****

For the second night in a row, Krysanna remained inside the house. The warmth and comfort were too tempting to ignore, and the lack of conversation was anything but awkward. She read in peace while Soph watched television, but the silence was calm and comfortable. She didn't inquire about Trina's absence, and her host declined to mention it. Krysanna had no complaints, though; she had a feeling that Trina wasn't exactly fond of her.

"I'm heading out for a bit," Soph said. "Haven't gone grocery

163

shopping, so there's nothing in the fridge to eat. Anything in particular you want me to get?"

Krysanna glanced up from her book, confusion on her features. In her short time on Earth, she'd learned that people generally bought food from large stores – as opposed to gathering it themselves from the surrounding areas – but she still didn't know what options there were. Her own diet wasn't too limited, except when it came to meat, which she only ate once every few weeks. Now that she thought about it, the protein would be welcome.

"I do not eat much," she said. "If they have fresh vegetables, like you brought me before, I would appreciate that, and maybe some venison?"

"I'll see what I can find," Soph said. "No wild parties while I'm out."

Soph could tell that the joke was lost on the elf, but she laughed quietly to herself as she grabbed her keys and left the house. Once she started the car, her humor faded. Where the hell was she supposed to find venison? It wasn't like the local stores carried it on the shelves at any given time. She'd just have to find a substitute and hope that Krysanna found it edible.

Which is exactly why she found herself staring at the selection of meats in the middle of an all-night grocery store, no closer to making a decision than she'd been when she'd left the house. Picking out food had never really been a common experience for her, not even when she was human, and she could only imagine how the options must have increased over the decades since then. It was just her luck that no one seemed to be working in this particular section to help her.

Grabbing a small pack of sirloin steaks, she dropped it into the basket and made her way over to the produce section. Again, the multitude of options left her with little guidance, but she picked a few different things that looked like they'd go well together and decided that it would be good enough. She'd deal with the daunting task of actually cooking a meal when she returned to the house.

As she placed the bags in the back seat of her car, she froze. She sensed the presence before she saw him, and she straightened. The figure leaning against the hood of her car regarded her with thinly veiled amusement, and she wanted nothing more than to wipe that smirk right off of his face.

164

"Get your ass off of my car," she spat.

"Not happy to see me?" Alex asked, arching a brow. "I just found it strange that you'd be out shopping for groceries when you're on a liquid diet."

"Not that it's any of your business," she said. "Maybe I have a friend staying for a few days. You know, some of us actually have friends. I'm sure it's something you're not really used to, but it happens."

"With an attitude like yours, I'm shocked," Alex said.

"What do you want, Malice?" she asked, growing tired of the exchange.

"I heard Duchess was out of town and thought you might be lonely," he said with a shrug. "But if you already have company, then I guess I shouldn't intrude. I am curious, though; who's spending time at your place? I wasn't aware that there might be someone other than her who can stand hanging around with you for more than a few minutes."

"Also, not your business," she said. "So why don't you piss off and go back to whatever rock you crawled out from under?"

Alex laughed but made no move to leave. As Soph bristled at his continued presence, he watched her posture, gauging how she would react if he clued her in that he knew where she lived. Deciding not to tempt fate, he rolled his shoulders in a shrug.

"Or you could invite me over," he said. "I love meeting new people."

"It'll be a cold day in hell when that happens." Leaning on the open door of her car, she fixed a glare on him. "Now move before I run you over."

He flashed a grin, leaning down so that his fingertips brushed the side of the tire a second before his nails grew into claws to pierce the rubber. Straightening, he gave a half-hearted wave and moved away, and as he crossed the parking lot, he let the shadows swallow his form.

Slashing the tire bought him some time, and as he emerged out of the darkness to approach the house, he allowed himself a small measure of pride at the victory. Alex smoothed down his hair as he climbed the stairs to the front porch, and he listened for any sounds of inhabitation before knocking lightly on the door. A quick shuffle on the other side alerted him to the presence inside, and he knocked again, a little louder this time.

"Krysanna?" he called. "It's alright to open the door. I need to talk to

165

you."

Maybe addressing her directly was a gamble, but it was also his best shot at gaining entry. If he could convince her that he was there to help, then the rest of his job would be easy. Light footsteps approached, but the door remained closed. He waited for another few minutes, his patience starting to fail him; he only had a limited amount of time, and he needed to make it count.

"How do you know my name?" a voice asked through the wood. "I cannot allow you to enter. I was instructed not to open the door for anyone."

"Sophia is having some car trouble," he said. "I just wanted to check on you to make sure nothing happened while she was out. Everything's alright, isn't it?"

When he heard the reluctant turn of the lock, he knew that he'd won again. He schooled his expression into one of concern when orange eyes peeked out through the small opening to regard him. He could only do so much to make himself appear less intimidating, but the way her brow furrowed in thought as she gave him a long look told him that something was telling her to trust him.

"Who are you?" she asked, her voice filled with timid curiosity.

"Just a friend," Alex said. "I'm not here to hurt you, I promise."

It was an assurance that she'd heard more often than she wanted to recall, but despite his imposing stature, she believed him. There was something strange about the man, something she couldn't quite place, but it marked him as something other than human, something more. It wasn't the instant fear that she'd felt upon discovering that she'd been among undead – he looked very much alive – but there was an air about him that demanded her trust.

"Have I met you before tonight?" she asked.

"No, but I'm better at keeping you safe than most," he said. "If you don't want me to come in, would you at least step outside so that we can talk?"

Again, she couldn't answer. Out on the porch, they were exposed, and while the house was a fair distance from the main road, she wasn't aware of the frequency of travelers in the area. Biting her lower lip, Krysanna glanced around, looking behind him to ensure that he was alone, and slowly nodded.

"There is a small house up in a tree by the woods," she said. "Meet me there."

*****

One of the advantages that he'd discovered with his condition was speed. Karian covered ground quickly, and once he'd picked up the trail, he tapped into the instincts that he still didn't completely understand in order to close the distance. He grew closer as he ran through the forest, the thrill of the chase bringing a sense of excitement that he tried to temper it with reason. Losing control wasn't an option.

He had two hours before he'd have to seek shelter from the sun, but he was confident that he could find the elf with time to spare. Pausing, he dropped to a crouch to brush his fingers along the dirt. Her scent was stronger here; he was close.

His pace was slower when he started forward again, keeping at a light jog before gradually slowing again to walk. After another few minutes, he could pick up the sound of a heartbeat, and he stopped, listening carefully to pinpoint the source. It hadn't come from one of the animals who made the area their home; subtle differences made that clear.

No sound came from his footsteps as he ventured closer, one hand reaching into the folds of his jacket to draw his pistol from its holster. Using one of the large trees for cover, he finally caught sight of his prey in the middle of a small clearing, but instead of resting, she stood alert. Her gaze scanned the area, an arrow notched in her bow.

Her posture complicated things; he wasn't supposed to engage her. Leaning back against the tree, his mind raced for an idea on how to proceed. If he left her to her own devices, then he'd have to find her again the next night, but he was faster than her. He could reclaim lost ground easily if necessary.

The thud of her arrow striking the other side of his tree made the decision for him, and his muscles tensed as he listened to cautious footsteps approaching his position. If he moved now, she'd see him, but if he remained in place, she'd discover him just the same.

Holstering his gun, he turned, but he didn't step into the open. His fingers found impossible holds on the bark of the tree, and he scrambled up it until he was sure he was out of view. Climbing onto a sturdy branch, he grasped it with one hand as he crouched, staring down through the leaves as

167

the elf reached his former hiding spot only to find herself alone.

The frustration on her delicate features would have been amusing had he not been in his current predicament. She didn't seem inclined to lower her guard, and he had to start heading back to safety soon. Still, he was high up enough that he could move through the trees from branch to branch without her seeing him, except that he had never attempted that sort of aerial maneuver before.

Glancing down, it was obvious that she was planning on remaining awake to survey the area, and his options dwindled down to confrontation or the questionable plan of using the tress for his escape. Damn it all. He looked around, settling on a branch not too far away for his first try, and a bit of confidence returned when he landed silently. Maybe this idea would work after all.

He managed a few more successful leaps, checking the ground after each one to ensure that the elf hadn't caught on to his actions. The next branch was a little further, but the previous two had been increasing in distance, and he had no reservations about bridging the span between his current one and the next.

Until the one he landed on snapped beneath his weight, and gravity did the rest.

Karian landed in the dirt with a muffled curse, thankful that the silence surrounding his form had given him a chance to escape discovery. The sharp crack of breaking wood was enough to alert her to his presence, and as he waited for the broken bones in his arm to mend, he found himself staring at the sharpened tip of an arrowhead. The woman glaring down at him did not look amused.

"I'm fine," he said dryly, speaking in their shared language. "Thanks for your concern."

Her eyes widened at that, but her aim didn't waver. If anything, her suspicion grew. Sighing, Karian tested the movement in his wrist and slowly sat up, nudging aside the arrow with less concern than he probably should have had. Then again, he'd been shot with far worse than that.

"*You were following me,*" Miria said evenly. "*Why?*"

"*Considering that your people aren't exactly common around here, I wanted to see what you were doing.*" Using the tree beside him for support, he pulled himself to his feet, arching a brow when she adjusted her aim to keep the weapon trained on him. "*If you're hoping that's going to intimidate me, then I have some bad news for you, elf.*"

"*I'm not afraid of you, Dusk Hunter,*" she countered, her glare returning. "*Where did you learn my language?*"

"*You have a lot of questions,*" he said. "*And I'm really not in the mood for them tonight. So, put the bow away, and I'll leave you alone for now.*" When she made no move to comply, he rolled his eyes. "*Do you think I'd be talking to you if I planned to kill you? Really?*"

"*Leave.*"

"*That's the plan,*" he said. "*I'm sure we'll meet again. Be careful out here. Earth isn't like Zalyndrya, which I'm sure you've already discovered for yourself.*"

Karian flexed his fingers, noting that the bones healed without issue, and he brushed some of the dirt from his clothes. With a mock bow, he turned, heading back through the woods, but he listened for any footsteps that would indicate pursuit. Certain that the elf had remained at her camp, he quickened his pace again, racing the impending sunrise.

*****

She returned to an empty house and a strikingly familiar scent. Dropping the groceries on the floor, Soph searched the rooms, finding them unoccupied, and turned her attention to the back of her property. The treehouse was once again lit with a soft glow, and she raced outside, panic guiding her as she stopped at the base of the ladder.

"Krys!" Concern colored the name, and the sounds of movement above were not comforting. "Krys, are you up there?"

"We're having a chat," Alex said, leaning out through the small window. "Come back later, preferably after sunrise."

"You son of a bitch," she snarled. "Where is she?"

"I told you," he said. "We're talking. It's rude to interrupt."

"I'm coming up."

"Do you have an appointment?" he asked. Landing in a crouch beside her, he heard Krysanna walk to the edge of the treehouse to watch them. "I said, we're busy."

"Are you okay?" she called up, ignoring him for the moment.

"Is it true?" Krysanna asked, her voice subdued. "Are you really one of them?"

"Krys, honey, I can explain," Soph said, grasping for a way to salvage the situation. "It's not what you think."

"Of course, it is," Alex said. "Think about it, Krysanna. She doesn't keep any food in the house, and have you ever seen her out during the day?"

"Shut the hell up, Malice," Soph snapped. "Get off my property

169

before I turn you into a throw rug."

"Soph," Krysanna interrupted, hurt and betrayal in her eyes. "He told me what you are. You let me trust you, knowing that I have my reasons for staying far from your kind. You were dishonest with me."

"It's not like that, I swear!" Her voice was pleading now, and the smug grin on Alex's face made it difficult to keep from lashing out. "Please just hear me out?"

Krysanna shook her head, but she summoned her courage to step off of the edge, landing lightly behind Alex as her wings folded behind her back. One hand grasped the sleeve of his jacket, giving her something tangible to help her remain out in the open, and she risked a glance around him to see the desperation on Soph's face.

"He's not human either, you know," Soph said. "Did he tell you what he really is, or did he just sit up there talking shit about me?"

"She knows," Alex said. "There's a bit of a difference, though. At least I'm actually alive."

"Krys, he's dangerous." She had to change tactics, grasping for anything that might turn the encounter in her favor. "I know I didn't tell you everything, but I didn't want you to be afraid of me."

"And such a great job you did there," Alex muttered.

"Oh, just fuck *off* already!" Her hold on her emotions slipped, her words coming out as another snarl, and a pang of guilt hit her when the elf ducked behind him. "Just hear me out, okay? Did I do anything to make you think I'd hurt you?"

"You are a Dusk Hunter," Krysanna said from behind Alex. "Your kind exists by hurting others." Her next words were quieter, addressed to the man standing between her and the vampire. "I want to leave this place."

It was all he needed to hear, and Alex offered Soph a smirk as he stepped back, one arm wrapping around Krysanna's shoulders. He knew better than to turn his back on a pissed off vampire, so he stepped back, guiding the elf with him towards the mass of shadows at the edge of the woods.

"Close your eyes," he said, his voice unusually soft. "There are things in the darkness that you don't want to see."

*****

Karian made it back to the relative safety of his motel room with a few minutes to spare. While the bones in his left arm had healed, it hung at an awkward angle, and he winced as he shrugged out of his jacket around the dislocated shoulder. He couldn't show the pain in front of his target, but in

170

the privacy of his solitude, there was no need to pretend.

Rubbing his shoulder, he wondered how long it would take it to realign, and he groaned when he heard the vibrations of his cell phone from inside his jacket pocket. He had no desire to talk to anyone, but on the off chance that it was his employer requesting a report, he fished out the device, confusion creasing his brow when he didn't recognize the number.

"Silver," he greeted sharply, putting the call on speaker as he set his phone on the small table.

"You sound like shit." It took a moment for him to place the caller's voice, and the knowledge only brought unease. "I figured I should at least thank you for that file. I'm tying things up on my end. Did you find yours yet?"

"That's one less thing to worry about," he said. Malice wasn't the worst person he'd dealt with in their organization, and he saw no need for hostility. "I found her, but there were complications."

"You didn't kill her, did you?"

"No, but she knows I'm following her." He sighed, testing the give in his shoulder; maybe he could pop it back into place to save himself from waiting for it to fix itself. The movement resulted in another shock of pain, and he swore under his breath. "It's an inconvenience, but not enough to scrap the operation."

"Did she get a few hits in on you?" Alex asked.

"No, I misjudged distance," he said. "I broke a couple of bones in my arm – they're fine now – but the dislocated shoulder is not exactly pleasant."

"Where are you?"

Karian didn't respond. Giving away his location, even to a colleague, was a quick way to get himself killed permanently. It was one of the rules – trust no one, not even your coworkers. He heard a sound of frustration on the other end of the line.

"Do you want help with that shoulder or not?" Alex asked.

"And risk you throwing open the curtains on me?" Karian countered. "Thank you, but I'll pass."

"Don't be an idiot, Silver," he said. "If you think I couldn't find you on my own, then you're dumber than Duchess' girl."

Again, Karian said nothing, but he conceded that the man had a point. Even with his limited time working for the company, he'd heard the rumors surrounding Malice's unrivaled tracking skills. He prided himself on his own – another reason he'd been given his current assignment – but even if he didn't want to be found, he knew that he wasn't completely safe.

"Allentown," he said after another moment of silent debate. "I'll text you the address."

Only a handful of minutes passed between the time he sent the message and the knock on his door. Standing, he approached, drawing his pistol with his right hand as his finger disengaged the safety. It was a small favor that this motel had the small holes in the door through which he could see the visitor, and he switched the safety back into place before unlocking the door.

"Let me move into the next room," he said.

He sought refuge in the small but functional bathroom, calling out again once he was behind the safety of the wall. The sound of the door opening and closing didn't ease his caution, but he glanced out from behind the corner to ensure that he wasn't about to turn into a pile of ash. Satisfied that his colleague wasn't there to betray him, he stepped out into the main room, but his gun remained in his grasp.

"You look like shit too," Alex said, taking in his appearance. "Should I even ask?"

"No."

"Too bad," he said. "How the hell did you manage that? Aren't you supposed to have superior agility or some crap like that?"

"It might have involved a tree and a thirty-foot drop to the ground," Karian said, holstering the pistol. "Believe me, it wasn't intentional."

To his credit, Alex made it a full ten seconds before he started laughing. The glare he received in response only fueled his humor, and it took a few minutes for him to calm himself. Shaking his head, he hung his jacket over the back of one of the chairs and stepped forward. He didn't miss the tension that held Karian in place, nor the open suspicion in his eyes, but he continued until he stopped close enough to be somewhat useful.

"This is going to hurt." The warning was unnecessary, but Alex felt the need to voice it.

He waited for Karian to nod in acceptance before reaching forward, checking the position of his shoulder. Without waiting for any further signs of unease, he gave a quick push, and the sound of the joint falling back into place told him that he hadn't caused more damage.

The string of expletives spilling from Karian's mouth, however, proved his earlier warning. Karian staggered back, grasping his shoulder, as his jaw clenched in pain. He wouldn't cry out, and the sensation started to fade within moments, but it certainly wasn't an experience that he wanted to

172

repeat anytime soon.

"Thank you," he said, forcing the words past his teeth as he gave the shoulder an experimental roll. "It would have eventually moved back into place on its own."

"You're new at this whole walking corpse thing, aren't you?" Alex said, ignoring the words of gratitude.

"Why did you really come here?" Karian asked. "I didn't need the help."

"I don't like being in anyone's debt," he said. "You also didn't have to give me that file, but you did anyway. I'm not going to try to guess your motives, but it helped me do my job, so I'm not going to take it for granted." Pulling over a chair, he turned it to sit backwards, his arms resting on the back of it. "I don't know you, and you don't know me, but you had the bright idea to work together, and it wasn't completely pointless."

Karian dropped down on the edge of the bed, leaning forward to rest his forearms on his knees. Reading between the lines, he could tell that there was more to this than a simple social call to offer assistance, but he couldn't quite figure out his colleague's true motives. He wanted something – that much was obvious – but he seemed to be taking his time in getting to the point.

"Where's your elf?" Karian asked.

"I have her tucked away some place safe," Alex said. "You might want to call Boston and see if he wants to change your instructions now that we have one of them in custody."

"She shouldn't be a prisoner," he pointed out.

"She's not," Alex said. "She asked me to get her out of there." He paused, studying Karian for a moment. "You know more about this than just another operative. When I met the client, she had the same accent, and the information you gave me led me right to her door. Your sister says hi, by the way."

Green eyes flashed, glowing dangerously as those words sent ice through him. The reminder that he couldn't trust the man before him crossed his mind, and his hands clenched into fists as he sat up straighter. As he reached for his pistol, his upper lip curled, revealing razor-sharp fangs.

"Stay away from her," he growled.

"Relax," Alex said. "I'm less worried about you than the rest of the company she keeps. It's not my fault she was hanging out with the client when I showed up." He waited for the glow to fade from Karian's eyes before continuing. "So, how do you tie into all of this? How deep does this

173

rabbit hole run?"

"I'm not the person you should ask," Karian said. "We all have our secrets, Malice. Don't expect me to share mine. As you said, we don't know each other."

"Fair enough." Even with the concession, they both knew the discussion wasn't over yet. "I'll let Mikhail know where the situation stands. He might just tell you to get rid of the other one and call it a day."

Karian nodded, his expression pensive. He hadn't really considered how everyone tied together with the others involved in this mess, and he wasn't thrilled with the knowledge that Malice had met his sister.

"Do you remember hearing anything about what happened in Boston last year?" he asked, meeting Alex's gaze. "I was there, as was my sister, and your client. I wasn't able to do much during the worst of it, but that's where I died. So yes, I'm not entirely used to my condition yet, but I'm learning."

"But you're all from the same place, aren't you?" Alex asked. "Then maybe you can tell me why I feel the need to protect this girl when she should be just another assignment."

"I told you that my people have great respect for your kind," Karian said. "It runs deeper with the elves. Your kind were considered guardians of their forests, and they developed a sort of kinship with the elven nations. It's rare to see your kind these days, though; many of them were wiped out in the days leading up to the Midnight Wars, but those who remain generally stick to the forests of Evemyst. I'm not sure if any have sought refuge in Evesrun. Their borders have been closed for centuries."

"So, because of some kind of bond that the elves have with werewolves back wherever the hell you lot are from, I actually feel like I should give a damn about her," he said, shaking his head. "This wasn't part of the deal."

"Shit happens," Karian said with a shrug. "I didn't ask to get killed, but here we are."

Thirteen

As soon as dawn broke over the horizon, Miria packed up her camp. The encounter with the vampire had shaken her, but she refused to allow it to deter her from her path. Once everything was in order, she pulled a small scroll from her belt, along with the quill tucked beside it. There was no need for ink, and as she scrawled her report across the parchment, the lettering glowed before vanishing. Several minutes passed before new words formed on the page, and she read her instructions carefully.

Find her quickly, and bring her back. The Council wishes that she be captured alive, but if it proves impossible, then do what you must.

The words were chilling, and she read them again before they faded into nothingness, leaving her staring at the blank scroll. They were insinuating the unthinkable. She knew how to fight, could handle herself well in battle and on the training fields, but to take the life of one of her kin was asking too much.

It's a last resort, she told herself. If she could just find Krysanna and capture her, then she could avoid bloodshed.

The thought of what she might have to do haunted her as she started heading south, and she tried to reconcile the demand with her own motives. She'd spent too many hours training for this opportunity, and failure could very well put her in the same position as the one she sought. Not only would she lose the opportunity to serve as a member of the Elite Guard, but if she couldn't complete this task, she could find herself exiled or, at worst, executed.

And then all of your efforts would have been for nothing.

It was more than she could accept, and she squared her shoulders as she raced through the brush, adrenaline and determination solidifying her resolve. If it came down to a choice between her own life and that of an elf who had broken the laws of their people, then it wasn't that difficult of a choice. There were consequences for every action, and if she had to be the method of delivery for them, then so be it.

She maintained a brisk pace throughout the morning, stopping only when necessary to eat or fill her waterskin. Time was against her, and every minute that passed was another opportunity lost. She refused to think about the possibility of Krysanna finding an escape or a safe haven to keep her hidden from discovery. Even if that turned out to be the case, she couldn't hide forever.

The Council's message spoke of impatience, though, and even with the centuries that spanned her lifetime, she knew that she couldn't keep them waiting. If she didn't produce results, then they'd send another candidate. That thought alone provided another burst of motivation, and any doubts that she wouldn't be able to follow through with the worst-case scenario fled her mind. She had to prepare herself for the reality of taking another elf's life. There could be no room for doubt or hesitation.

*****

The hotel room was almost as large as the first floor of the house she'd just left, and Krysanna cautiously explored it in Alex's absence. She found so many things she'd never seen before, and her eyes were wide with wonder as she circled the large bath. It had been days since she'd had the opportunity to bathe, and the residual dirt and grime of her travels was beginning to bother her, but the different knobs were daunting.

She reached a tentative hand out to turn one, jumping back when water began to pour from the faucet, and she gave a nervous laugh when she realized that there was nothing to fear. Through trial and error, she found a comfortable temperature, sitting on the edge of the tub while she waited for it to fill with water. Turning off the flow was just as simple, and she smiled at the small victory as she stripped off her soiled clothes.

Settling down in the warmth, a soft sigh of contentment escaped her, and she closed her eyes. She couldn't remember the last time she felt safe enough to truly relax, but the present opportunity was welcome. They weren't fully in the clear – Alex had explained that they would be leaving the city again for somewhere much further away – but she knew that he could protect her.

Krysanna wasn't sure how much time passed. The water was still pleasantly warm, and she saw no reason to leave the comfort while she had the room to herself. She'd left the bathroom door open, though, and the sound of someone entering the suite startled her back to awareness. Her gaze darted around for an escape route, but she breathed a sigh of relief when she

176

caught a glimpse of Alex walking through the other room.

He stopped in the doorway, and she offered a small smile. His presence put her at ease again, chasing away the lingering fear of what she'd experienced, but she caught a trace of discomfort in his posture. As soon as he'd seen her, he'd looked away, and he seemed reluctant to meet her gaze.

"I'll wait in the other room," he said.

"Is something wrong?" she asked, concern in her voice. "Have I upset you?"

"No," Alex said. "Not at all. People don't usually watch their guests taking a bath. Something about boundaries and privacy. We can talk when you're done."

She blinked a few times as he retreated, curious at his behavior. With a sigh, she decided it must be a cultural difference between her world and Earth, and there was little she could do to change that. In time, she would learn the subtle intricacies of social interactions and rules, but for now, she wanted to enjoy her bath for a little while longer.

The wolf's home was far different than the places she'd stayed before, smaller and in a building with other, similar residences, but Krysanna wasn't going to complain. It was cozy, and it was safe; for that, she was grateful. He'd left shortly after they'd emerged from the shadows in the alley outside, giving her a chance to settle in what would be her home for the foreseeable future.

Wings shifting at her back, she padded through the flat, pausing here and there to examine anything that caught her eye. The décor was sparse, but the furniture looked comfortable, and she eventually relaxed on the sofa as fatigue began to get the better of her. Her people didn't require the same amount of sleep as humans, but the events that led her to this moment had left her feeling drained, her eyes drifting shut as one of her wings covered her side.

She couldn't have been asleep for long, and she stirred at the sound of the door opening. Sitting up, she blinked a few times before she recognized the approaching figure. Krysanna managed a small smile as she sat up, pulling her knees up to her chest as she rested her head on them, but she remained silent, unsure of how to approach conversation with him.

"You can go back to sleep if you want," he said, shrugging out of his jacket. When she simply shook her head, he sighed. "I'm not used to having guests, so don't expect much from me on this. There's a spare room, and you have free reign of the kitchen, but if you need anything else, you're going to have to tell me."

"Who are you?" she asked, her voice quiet. "You brought me here, away from the Dusk Hunters, but I don't even know your name."

She didn't even know where *here* was, but she was certain that it wasn't *there*, where she'd been hiding from the very creatures that lived on the same property the whole time. It didn't matter where she was now. She knew that she was safe here, under the protection of a werewolf who didn't really seem sure of how to approach the situation either.

Alex stayed silent for a moment. Giving his code name was habit, something that had been ingrained in him for decades, but the elf wasn't a colleague. Magic or not, she trusted him to keep her safe, and knowing how frightened she must have been, he couldn't justify deceit.

"Alex," he said finally. The name felt strange as it left his lips, something he used only when he was pretending to live as a normal Londoner. Taking a seat on the other end of the sofa, he turned his body to watch her. "The people I work with call me by another name, but I think you'd prefer my real one."

She repeated the name, trying to find some familiarity in it, but it was foreign to her, like so many other things she'd seen on this world. Still, his willingness to provide it was a show of trust, perhaps in exchange for the trust she showed him. Despite how shaken she still felt now that awareness had returned, she was confident that she would come to no harm in his presence.

"We're in London," he continued. "There's an entire ocean between us as the place you were staying, so you don't have to worry about them finding you here."

Silence fell between them, and it didn't take long for it to become awkward. They were strangers, but Krysanna would be spending plenty of time around him, and their interactions would be easier if she could just open up the door. Too many things held her back, though. He wasn't from her homeland, and even though her people held a bond with his, things on Earth were not the same as they were in Evemyst.

"What happens now?" she asked, almost fearing the answer.

Maybe she had gone from one dangerous situation to being his prisoner. She could only guess at his motives, but he hadn't threatened to harm her. Then again, the vampires hadn't made any threats either.

"It's like I already told you. You're my guest."

"Guest or captive?" she dared to ask.

If he was offended, he didn't let it show. Instead, Alex studied her, contemplating his answer. He couldn't very well allow her to wander around the city on her own, and turning her loose in a world that she didn't understand could only lead to more trouble. Keeping her under lock and key seemed almost cruel after what she'd been through, but it was the only way to ensure her safety.

"That depends on your perspective," he said. "I'm not going to sugar coat things and tell you that you'll be fine out there if you wanted to leave. I don't know where you're from, but it's probably a lot different than here, and until you learn those differences, the safest place for you to be is here. Am I going to let you wander the streets of London and make your own life out there? No. At least, not yet. I'm not going to lock you in a room and pretend that you don't exist either."

So, she wasn't a prisoner, but she wasn't free either. Hugging her knees closer to her chest, she tried to fight back the tears that began to sting her eyes, but the first ones began a path down her cheeks.

Alex froze, unsure whether to keep his distance or make a sad attempt at comfort. This wasn't what he signed up for; he was supposed to find her and keep her safe until the client decided whether or not they wanted her back, not act like a stand-in therapist for someone he hardly knew.

Living a life of relative solitude had helped him avoid moments like this, and he couldn't remember a single instance when one of his colleagues might have started crying in front of him. His organization was comprised of seasoned fighters and ruthless killers, not fragile elves who had lost everything they'd known for who knows how long.

Words failed him, and he stood to make his way to the kitchen, returning with a glass of water. He could read the sorrow in her eyes when she looked up at him and took the glass with a murmur of thanks, but his expression showed no reaction. Whatever things were like where she was from, he needed to make it clear that she couldn't expect him to just jump into whatever kind of friendship she expected.

"Get some rest," he said. "I'll be out more often than I'll be home over the next few days, but I'll make sure to buy groceries so that you don't starve. Don't answer the door for anyone while I'm gone."

Some would call it cowardice to escape an uncomfortable moment like that, but Alex called it preserving his own sanity. Besides, Krysanna needed some time on her own to figure out what she wanted to do once everything was said and done. He didn't expect her to live with him forever, and there was no sense in accepting her offer of friendship when she probably wouldn't stick around later.

*****

Night fell in Philadelphia, the city lights replacing the glare of the sun against towering glass buildings, and Marielle looked up from her laptop as she heard the door to the guest room open, her smile guarded even as she tried to hide it. Her father's words returned to her, despite her efforts to shove them back down, but there was no way that he could predict the future.

Looking at Ian as he joined her in the living room, blond hair still a mess from sleep, she wondered if maybe Carl had been on to something. She'd been terrified when Ian had told her what he was, so much that she was afraid to reject him, afraid that he wouldn't accept it and slake his thirst with her blood. He'd been hurt, of course, but he'd never so much as hinted that he'd harm her in any way.

Even afterwards when Mikhail had abducted her for information, Ian was only concerned for her well-being. She'd been unfair to him, but he hadn't been completely honest with her either. They both had their faults, she realized, but maybe there was a chance that they could still salvage what they'd once had.

"I can't look that bad."

His voice stirred her from her thoughts, and she realized that she'd been staring. Looking away quickly to hide the heat rising to her cheeks, she busied herself with a sip of tea, even though she knew that she couldn't hide such reactions from him.

"You don't," she said before she could stop herself. Taking a deep breath, she focused on the screen in front of her, clicking through another email. "I'm off tonight, but I have a few things I need to check before I can do much else."

"No problem," Ian said. "I need to step out for a while, anyway. I'll be back, though, if you want me to come back, I mean."

Just like that, he reminded her that he wasn't as human as he looked. He didn't have to tell her his plans outright; she could read between the lines well enough. Ian would walk out that door, find some unfortunate stranger, and then it would be a toss-up if his breakfast would live to see another day.

It wasn't as if she could overlook that. Even if he'd never given her a reason to suspect that he'd do the same to her, she wasn't sure if she could pursue something more than friendship anymore. He'd killed before, and maybe he was more careful about it now, but he was a predator by nature.

"I don't have any other plans tonight," she said, avoiding his gaze.

180

"I'll be up for a little while if you want to come back."

Ian paused at the door, turning his head to regard her. Something was definitely wrong, and he had an idea of why her demeanor had changed, but he couldn't just avoid what was necessary for his survival. Walking out the door without trying to smooth things over probably wouldn't be a good idea, either.

Instead of turning the knob, he headed back into the living room, taking a seat on the opposite end of the sofa. He recalled how well she'd reacted to the news of what he was, and he wanted to avoid a similar discussion. Honesty was the best route, he'd learned, but there was no easy way to help her understand.

"You know I'm not doing this because I enjoy it, right?" he asked. "There really isn't much of a choice here."

Marielle wanted to argue with him because there was *always* a choice, but she said nothing. Her logic was flawed; Ian never had a choice when it came to losing his humanity. That had been taken from him the night that his so-called friend had made him a vampire.

"Then why do you keep other supplies?" she asked, still keeping her gaze on her laptop. "Euro sells blood to you, so why can't you just use that?"

Why do you still have to hurt people?

"Sometimes, it's not enough," he said patiently. "It helps, and it keeps me from having to go out and feed off of some poor bastard every night, but it doesn't keep me going for long. I can go three, maybe four days at most, but after that, I start to get edgy. I don't want to risk putting you in danger by trying to give up fresh blood completely."

It wasn't the answer that she wanted, but she couldn't argue his reasoning. His motives shouldn't have been about her, about his concern for her safety – especially from him – and she wished that she could come up with a counterargument.

He didn't ask for this, she reminded herself. *What right do I have to judge him for something he can't control?*

"Marielle, please look at me."

Reluctantly, she turned her head, looking at him as she set her laptop on the coffee table. His expression said enough; even after a few decades, he still wasn't happy with the way his life had changed.

"I know that it's not easy to understand, but if I could survive on a couple bottles a night, then I would," he said. "I try not to kill people, and I know that you hate this, but I can't change the way things are. I've had to accept it, even if I'm not thrilled with it."

181

She nodded slowly, looking down as she considered his words, and she realized what he must have gone through to reach this point. It must have been horrible at first. Even now, she believed him when he said that he didn't enjoy hunting humans, but there was still a barrier that she couldn't bring herself to cross.

"Just be careful," she said.

"I will."

Focusing on work became impossible once he'd left, and Marielle closed her laptop with a sigh. Her thoughts ran rampant through her mind, justifying and contradicting each other, but she failed to find even a tiny bit of sense in them. It had been obvious to even her father that she still had feelings for Ian, and he made no secret of how much he wanted to bend the bridge between them, but her stubborn sense of morality prevented her from taking the first step.

There were practical reasons for her reluctance, too. Ian was immortal; he'd never grow old, while the years would continue to change her. Even if she found it in herself to try again, it would only be temporary. He could make any promise that he wanted, tell her that he'd stay by her side until she grew old and died, but it was easy to say something like that now while she was barely into her thirties.

He could also take another approach, one that frightened her not just because of how it would change her life, but because of how she might respond. If she were to be honest with herself, Marielle couldn't deny that the idea of spending eternity with him hadn't crossed her mind, but she'd always pushed those thoughts far away from herself.

She didn't want to become like him, she didn't want to have to live off of the lives of other people, and she wasn't sure if she'd be able to go through with it if he ever made that offer. It was unlikely that he would, though. He'd spent so long trying to convince her that he'd never ask her for something she couldn't give, and he'd never even suggested that he might want to feed from her.

There was no way that she was going to make any sense out of it tonight. She'd had this inner debate too many times over the past six months, and she was no closer to a solution. What she wanted and what she knew she had to do were two completely different things, and no matter how much it tore at her heart whenever she looked at him, she couldn't allow herself to fall for him again.

She didn't want to admit that it was too late for that. Marielle reached for her phone and scrolled through her contacts, deciding that there was at least one person she could call who might be able to help with her dilemma.

"Hi, Cass, it's Marielle," she greeted once she heard the other woman answer. "I need some advice."

*****

The call went to voicemail again, and Soph threw her phone across the room. Trina wasn't answering, just when she needed to talk to her. Soph wanted to scream, to slam her fist through the nearest wall, or to walk into the dive bar in town and slaughter everyone. Her lips pulled back from her fangs in a snarl, rage boiling within her.

Her cell phone rang, surprising her and causing her to spin to face the sound. Honestly, she'd thought that she'd broken the damn thing in her anger, but she rushed across the room to retrieve it, a small measure of relief finding her as she read the name on the cracked screen.

"Soph, I'm working," Trina said. "So, why did you have to call me sixteen times in a row?" A gunshot sounded in the background, followed by a muttered curse and more gunfire. "This isn't a good time."

"You think?" Soph snapped. "The elf is gone."

"And?"

"And what?" Soph nearly shouted into the phone. "Some asshole werewolf showed up out of nowhere and told her that we were vampires, and then they just disappeared! They know where we live, Trina. What if they send a bunch of vampire hunter wannabes here?"

"Then you'll deal with them," Trina said. It had grown quiet in the background, and her voice remained calm. "Do you really think that a few humans are a threat to you?"

"If they show up during the day, like any smart human would do."

"People, in general, are idiots," Trina assured her. "Every now and then you meet someone who has more than two brain cells to rub together, but don't give them more credit than they deserve. I'll be home in two days, and we'll talk about your elf when I get there." She paused, hoping that her words would help calm her. "Go find something to eat and try to keep yourself occupied."

Soph was far from placated, but at least she resisted the urge to hurl her phone at the wall again once the call had ended. She'd never had any reason to hate werewolves, but the one who had shown up on her property to abduct the elf who had sought sanctuary had hit every mark on her list.

Grabbing her keys, she left her phone behind, and she slammed the front door on her way out, her features set in a scowl as she stalked to her car. She rarely cared about the speed limit on a good night, but it wasn't even

183

an afterthought as she sped towards the Philadelphia skyline. Malvern wouldn't satisfy her tonight.

It took a few passes down Columbus Boulevard before she settled on one of the several night clubs, finding one that still had the goth-themed night once a week. Music had come a long way since the seventies, and even if the bass was too loud for her, she needed a chance to lose herself in the life surrounding her.

The man at the door barely glanced at her ID before motioning for her to enter, and Soph offered a wink as she passed. Inside, the lights flashed around the room, pulsing in time with the beat of the current song, and she closed her eyes to drink it all in. She ignored the bar, throwing herself right into the middle of the dance floor as she let the music guide her.

It was the perfect place to blow off some steam and find a decent meal, and her gaze roamed the crowd as her hips swayed. The attention she was gaining would have made her uncomfortable years ago, but she'd been human then, just trying to survive for one more day. Now, every set of eyes that fell upon her was an opportunity, and she had her pick of eager humans who tried to get closer.

She entertained a few of them, one by one, but the man with short-cropped dark hair held her interest in the end. It was almost too easy, and she turned around to lean back against him as they moved together. Even as one song bled into the next, she stayed close to him, watching him grow more and more hopeful that his evening wouldn't end with just a few dances.

It would have been cruel to crush his dreams, and her gaze flicked to the side, towards the restrooms as she arched a brow. He picked up on her meaning quick enough, and she wove her way through the crowd while he trailed behind her.

Even inside the ladies' room, the beat of the music thudded against the walls, and she turned the lock as she watched his gaze rake over her body. It was almost too easy, even if there was a bit of risk involved with cornering him in a public place, but now that she had him in front of her, she didn't hesitate to close the distance.

Soph left him on the cold bathroom floor, his sightless eyes staring at nothing, with a gash down the side of his throat from her pocket knife to disguise the twin puncture wounds. There was no reason to stick around; it wouldn't take long for someone to discover the body, and she wanted to have at least several miles between herself and the club before they did.

She had to admit that she felt a little better. The night out had done her some good, and the fresh meal helped to calm her temper. She was still furious about the situation, but thoughts of turning the werewolf into a throw rug helped placate her during the drive back to her house.

With music pouring from the speakers, she sped down the highway, planning her next moves. There was no way that she could just let that asshole turn Krysanna against her, but without any idea of where he'd taken her, rectifying the situation was going to be almost impossible. She knew bits and pieces about him, but not enough to take action.

Trina had connections, people who could find just about anyone, and her boss might be the key to picking up the trail. That was a problem in itself, though. Soph remembered the times they'd met in the past, and Mikhail's reaction when he saw her at the meeting at Evans International told her that he hadn't forgotten either.

There was little she could do until her wife returned from Dallas, and she reminded herself that this was one of those unfortunate instances where she'd have to be patient. It wasn't her strongest trait, but without the resources to act, it was all she could do.

It wasn't just that she could have learned a lot from the elf – although Krysanna's knowledge would have furthered her studies more so than she could have done on her own. She barely knew Malice, and their previous meetings hadn't given her a positive opinion about him. It was entirely possible that the elf was in even more danger with him, and no one even knew where to find them.

She told herself that she wasn't invested in this just because of her own selfish reasons, and she was genuinely concerned for Krysanna's safety, but she couldn't deny that she was taking the turn of events personally.

Fourteen

Miria knew she wouldn't find sleep that night. Her encounter with the vampire had shaken her more than she would allow herself to admit, and knowing that he could come for her at any time had her constantly on her guard. Every movement in the shadows became a potential threat, but whenever she turned her head, everything was still.

Her quest was supposed to be dangerous. Very few earned the opportunity to join the Elite Guard, and this was her final trial; once she completed her task, then she could return home to take her place amongst seasoned warriors. She doubted that encountering a Dusk Hunter had been part of the Elders' plans, though.

Covering as much ground as possible, she stopped only to eat a light meal and refill her water before she was on the move again. He could still pick up her trail, which meant that she had to find an alternate means of travel, something that he couldn't track so easily. She still wasn't sure how he'd found her in the first place, or how he'd known her language, but she couldn't allow him to catch her again.

It was a small comfort to know that he'd chosen to let her live, and that alone added to her confusion. Dusk Hunters were known for their cruelty, and he'd made no secret of the fact that he could have killed her before she'd even noticed his presence, but she wasn't foolish enough to think that he allowed her to walk away out of the goodness of his heart.

He wants something, she decided.

Whatever it was, she would give him nothing. One act of charity was not enough for her to find any sense of debt towards him. She was losing daylight, though, and exhaustion was seeping down to her bones. Eventually, she would have to stop to rest for longer than a fraction of an hour, but even though she'd left the forest and kept just outside of the areas of civilization,

187

staying in one place once the sun set could bring her another encounter with him.

If he decided to seek her out again, then she wanted to be prepared. It would be better if she could find a place that wasn't out in the open, but she had no means to secure lodging for the night. She had no local currency, which was required to seek shelter at an inn.

She'd have to stay awake again. Three days was average for her people, but she had already pushed herself longer, and fatigue pulled at her eyelids, drawing her further from awareness. Lying down, she pulled her cloak over her body, using her traveling pack as a makeshift pillow, and Miria told herself that an hour or two wouldn't hurt.

The sun had long since set when she awoke, refreshed and ready to travel, but as her eyes opened, she realized that she was not alone. Scrambling into a crouch, she drew the knife from her belt, sending a glare at the figure leaning against a tree only a few paces away.

Karian didn't approach, and he watched her with a hint of amusement as she took a defensive stance. It wouldn't have helped her if he'd intended to attack, but if it made her a little more comfortable, then he wasn't going to argue the point.

"What do you want?" Miria asked, suspicion masking her fear. The stories claimed that he'd be able to smell it on her regardless, but she had to at least appear confident.

"Conversation," he said with a shrug. *"And answers."*

"Leave. I want nothing to do with you, and I have no intentions of answering any of your questions."

At that, he straightened, taking a step forward, but he kept his weapons out of view. If it came down to a fight – which he hoped she was smart enough to avoid – then he wouldn't need bullets to kill her. Humor vanished from his features, his expression hardening as he regarded her.

"I don't think you understand," he said. *"I'm not here to negotiate with you. I want information, and I know you have it. You can either sit down and talk, or I can find more creative ways to get what I want."*

She paled visibly, her heart pounding in her chest as she stared him down in spite of the chill that coursed through her. There was no doubt that she was outmatched, but telling him anything significant could jeopardize her mission. Then again, she couldn't very well complete it if she was dead or worse.

Miria stood and backed away from him, wondering if escape was possible. She couldn't outrun a vampire if the tales of his speed were true, and there were too few trees around for her to use them to her advantage.

"*Listen*," he continued. "*If I wanted to kill you, I would have already done so.*"

"*It sounds like the only reason you haven't is because you want something from me. That doesn't inspire much trust.*"

He closed the distance in one quick movement, seeming to appear directly before her. Debating the issue would garner no results, and the elf didn't seem to be very forthcoming with information.

"*I don't give a damn if you trust me,*" Karian said. "*The only thing I care about is results. You can act stubborn all you want, but I'm not exactly a patient man.*" There had to be another way to get through to her. "*You know shit about this world. I'm willing to bet that you have no money, and unless you're holding out on me, you probably don't even know the language. I can help you with both of those, but I'm not going to give you anything for free.*"

There it was. While it was a small relief that he wasn't going to torture her, his offer only caused more warnings in the back of her mind. She wouldn't admit aloud that he was right, and if she was going to be stuck here for much longer, then she would need to have the means to survive.

"*Tell me how you think you can help, and I'll consider your offer.*" Accepting anything from him would indebt her to him, but only if she failed to deliver on her end of the bargain. Without knowing what he wanted to ask, she couldn't make an assessment on whether or not it was worth it to accept his terms.

"*I have money,*" he said. "*I'd be willing to buy information from you, if you'd prefer that instead of my other ideas.*" There was a slight curl of his lips, the smallest hint of a cold smile. "*If you're lucky, I might just explain a little about what you can expect on this world.*"

It was tempting, and for a few minutes, Miria found herself seriously considering it. The money he'd mentioned would make her time on Earth easier, but it seemed like far too much to exchange for whatever he wanted to know. There had to be more, some kind of catch that she was still missing.

"*You can't expect me to believe that you'd just give me these things when all you're asking is for me to answer your questions. What else do you want? I will not live in your debt, so we will settle this tonight, or we will not be making any deals.*"

"*That all depends on what you can tell me,*" he said.

Honestly, he was surprised that she was speaking with him at all. Surely, she would have tried to fight or run, even if it would have ended poorly for her, but instead, she'd taken the smarter route. Karian had to appreciate her ability to weigh her options and her odds of surviving this

189

encounter.

She didn't cower before him, as some would have when faced with someone they knew could kill them before they had a chance to react. Miria kept her fear carefully hidden beneath a mask of strength and determination, and she maintained civility in spite of the way the balance of power was in his favor.

"And if I tell you nothing?" she asked, as if she didn't already know the answer.

"Then this might get a little messy."

The brief but bright flash of his eyes made his response perfectly clear, and she found herself faced with another decision. Had she studied magic beyond the basic requirements, then she might have another way to even the playing field, but her focus had been on combat skills, and they would do her no good against him.

She certainly believed that he would make good on his threat; after all, his kind were known for their violent tendencies. Her pride kept her from agreeing completely, though, and even as she lowered the knife, she met his gaze without hesitation.

"I am not afraid of you," she said, even though it was only half true. Most of her people were terrified of the Dusk Hunters, and that fear was ingrained in her, but she couldn't allow that to show.

"Is that a no?" Karian asked, a predatory grin settling on his lips. *"I sometimes wonder what elven blood tastes like. Is it sweeter than a human's?"*

Miria took a step back, finding it more difficult to hide her fear in the face of a creature that would drain her without concern for morality. She pulled her gaze away from him, her eyes darting around for a path of escape, and her pulse raced as adrenaline coursed through her.

"You know that you can't outrun me, elf," he said. He took a step towards her to match every step of her retreat, the glow returning to his eyes, and she caught a glimpse of sharp fangs when he spoke again. *"I'm giving you one last chance to accept my offer."*

It was an impossible choice – compromise her mission by answering his questions, or face a slow, painful death. Miria told herself that her own life wasn't as important as what she was there to accomplish. If she fell, then Evemyst would send another to complete her work, and she was willing to give her life for the good of her people, but she couldn't hold firm to that when she was staring at the face of her potential killer.

"Alright!" she said quickly, failing to calm the pounding of her heart. Fear hadn't paralyzed her, but she could feel it coiling around her chest,

making it difficult to breathe. "*I accept. Show me what you have, and I will tell you what I can.*"

*****

Ian considered just going home after he'd tracked down some breakfast, but he couldn't just leave the tension that had formed between him and Marielle. He was still crazy about her, and every night he wished that things would settle between them so that they could pick up where they'd left off, but he couldn't pursue his attraction to her if she wasn't willing to give him another chance.

Crossing through the park, he glanced up to see that her light was still on, and he maintained his course towards her building. The ride up the elevator gave him more time to lose himself with his thoughts, filling his head with both possibilities and regrets.

He couldn't blame her for maintaining the distance. She was human, had never known that vampires were real until six months ago, and had learned the truth about Rhonda's clientele when she couldn't have even imagined that possibility. Finding out that she was dating one had only been the first step down that path.

The doors whispered open with the soft chime to announce his arrival at her floor, and he ran a hand through his hair as he started down the hall to her door. Even if things could never go back to how they'd been before she learned the truth, he was grateful that she hadn't shut him out of her life completely.

Marielle opened the door after the first knock, and Ian's eyes widened a little in surprise. She seemed more relaxed than she'd been before he'd left earlier, and a small smile greeted him as she stepped aside for him to enter. It was a step up from the discomfort she'd shown before he'd left, and he headed into her apartment feeling a little better than he had on the ride up.

He hadn't been gone for more than an hour, and he glanced around as she moved back to the sofa, a grin finding his lips when he saw the pizza box on the coffee table. Damn, he missed pizza, but he could at least enjoy the smell of it.

"You're not the only one who has to eat," she said as she pulled a slice from the box. Humor laced her tone, and he wondered what had caused the change in her demeanor during the short time he'd been gone. "I even made sure they didn't put garlic on it."

Ian had to laugh at that. Garlic wasn't really a problem for him, not as much as it was for his Zalyndryan counterparts, but he appreciated the thought nonetheless. The atmosphere was light, where he'd been expecting

191

more tension to be waiting for his return. He couldn't resist commenting on it.

"You look like you're in a better mood," he said.

"I'm feeling better," she said before taking another bite of pizza, and she waited until she finished the slice before continuing. "It's been a lot to take in. Up until the end of the year, I thought I was just working for a really good accountant, and it blew my mind when I found out what was really going on."

Ian could understand. He'd never known about what was waiting in the dark until the night he'd been shot, and realizing that he'd become one of them was just as jarring. It had taken years for him to come to terms with it, and he couldn't expect her to reach the same conclusion after half of one.

"It makes sense when I think about it, though," Marielle said. "I mean, look at what she's paying me and all of the perks that come with it. I should have known something was going on. Sean had an idea about it before I did, though, and I didn't want to hear it at the time. I think it's better that I know now, though. I'd rather know what I'm working with instead of staying in the dark."

Turning on the sofa to face him, she relaxed against the cushioned arm and took a sip of water. Her conversation with Cassandra had helped put things into perspective, and she almost wished she'd called her sooner. After all, who would know more about vampires than someone who was raised by them?

She looked him over as she fell silent, her friend's words repeating themselves in her mind. *He's still the same person you were dating before you learned what he is. The only thing that's changed is that now you know that he isn't human, but that doesn't make him any different at heart.* She'd wanted to argue, because how could he not be different when his survival depended upon human blood? He'd been that way when they'd first met, though, and even after he'd told her, she still felt safe with him.

It was crazy.

"I'm trying, Ian," she said. "I miss how things were between us, but it's hard to accept the possibility of starting again when I don't know how it could possibly work. I don't think that I can let those worries lead me to a decision I might regret later, though."

Confusion clouded blue eyes as Ian stared at her, not daring to hope that she was implying what he thought she was. There was no way that she could really be considering giving this another shot, and he wondered if he might have consumed some tainted blood and was hallucinating. Ignoring the

192

absurdity of that thought – substances, even in blood, couldn't affect him – he stayed quiet, waiting for her to clarify her thoughts.

Instead of speaking, Marielle closed the distance between them and pressed her lips to his, one hand lifting to rest on his cheek. He didn't react at first, frozen in shock, but before she could pull away to second guess herself, he threaded his fingers through her hair, and his lips parted for her.

Her body was warm against his, her pulse thrumming beneath his palm as she shifted her weight to settle on his lap. For six months, he'd been hoping for a moment like this, but he'd kept his distance, giving her the chance to reach a decision on her own. Ian couldn't deny that he'd missed the feeling of her lips on his, of her heart pounding against his chest, and he recalled all the times that he'd backed off before they could go any further.

He told himself that it was for her safety, but as true as that was, he didn't want her to find out about him in a moment of passion. Marielle was aware of his condition now, though, and she'd cast aside her doubts and fears to seek his touch. He wouldn't argue with that.

His hands traveled down her back to slide up under her shirt, and he relished the soft gasp she gave at his cool touch. She didn't withdraw, though, and he could feel hunger and desire in her kiss. The small roll of her hips against him nearly caused him to give in, to cross the line that he'd drawn when they'd first started dating, and he pulled back to meet her gaze.

Her face was flushed, her eyes burning into his, and her lips were red from where they'd met his. As he read the expression on her face, he wanted nothing more than to pull her close again, but this was the part where he'd always brought things to a halt.

"Marielle," he breathed, his hands rubbing circles along her lower back. "Are you sure about this? I don't want you to regret it later."

"Do you know how many times I wanted this?" she asked. "We can stop if you want to, but I promise, I'm sure."

She wasn't going to let herself hide behind the concerns that had haunted her for the past several months. There was no way she could deny what her heart was telling her, and the heat pooling in the pit of her stomach as her hips shifted against him again rekindled the fire that they'd once shared.

Stopping was the furthest thing from his mind, but he had to make sure that she wasn't having second thoughts. Her words warmed him, and when he pulled her close again, his kiss conveyed the passion he still maintained for her. Complications be damned, they were adults, and they wanted each other; he was done denying them what they'd been craving for so long.

Adjusting his grip to support her weight, he stood, and her legs wrapped around him as he carried her down the hall to her room. She discarded her shirt along the way, aching for the contact of his skin against hers, and their kiss grew more desperate before he pulled back to gently lay her on the bed.

Her breath had already grown heavy, and the rise and fall of her chest made him pause to let his gaze wander over her. She was gorgeous, her lidded eyes watching as his shirt fell to the floor, and he held back only a moment longer before he settled on the mattress above her.

*****

Alex had finally managed to grab a few hours of sleep. Helping Krysanna settle in had taken some time; the elf had asked so many questions about every little detail. It annoyed him, but he could understand that she knew next to nothing about this world. It was only natural that she had questions.

His thoughts had kept him awake even longer, and they forced him to examine his own perspective. He'd lived alone for more years than he'd bothered to count. Having someone else in his flat was new, and he wasn't exactly thrilled with the idea. He liked his privacy, preferring solitude to the company of others, but he couldn't bring himself to remain irritated at her constant curiosity.

Her explanation of their supposed connection was another issue. Just because the elves were friends with werewolves where she was from, it didn't mean that the same was the case here, and he adamantly denied that any sense of companionship could exist when they barely knew each other. His unprecedented need to protect her said otherwise, but he held fast to the notion that he could overcome whatever latent feelings tried to surface.

A shriek and what sounded like a small explosion snapped him awake far too soon for his liking, and a growl found its way up to his throat as he jumped out of bed. He could already smell the smoke clouding the kitchen when he rushed out of his room, and he halted in the doorway to get an idea of what the hell was going on.

Krys was huddled in on corner, her eyes wide as she stared at the sparking remains of his microwave, and Alex felt a scowl forming as he looked between them. Grabbing the small fire extinguisher, he held his breath as he smothered the smoldering appliance, and once he was satisfied that they were in no real danger, he turned to her.

"Should I even ask?" he said.

She backed further into the corner, her attention shifting from the smoke to his features. He was certainly upset with her, and she felt tears stinging her eyes. It had been an accident, but she'd managed to destroy a piece of his property within the first twenty-four hours of her stay. Surely, he would decide that she was too much trouble and find somewhere else for her to hide.

"I'm sorry," she whispered, curling in on herself. "I didn't mean to…"

Alex regarded her for a minute, his frustration fading as he studied her posture and reaction. *Just what the hell happened to her?* He didn't have any answers, but she shouldn't have been cowering away from him when he needed her to believe that he was going to keep her safe.

"I know," he said. He didn't approach, but he tried to soften his tone so as not to frighten her further. It was an uncomfortable attempt, and he was sure that he was only barely pulling it off, but she risked a glance up at him. "Just tell me what happened."

He only caught about half of what she said as words spilled out of her, but from what he could piece together, she had tried to heat up some vegetables, and instead of just using the buttons on the microwave to start it, she'd used magic. Of course. A string of apologies followed her explanation, and he heaved a sigh as he looked at the charred clump that had once been one of his most-used kitchen appliances.

"It's fine," he said, leaning against the doorway. It wasn't exactly *fine*, but if she thought he would hurt her over the issue, then they had a long way to go. "I can always buy another one, and at least it didn't set off the smoke alarms and wake up the whole damn building. Are you hurt?"

She shook her head but refused to meet his gaze again. Alex only knew bits and pieces of why she was on the run, but *something* had ingrained the fear in her that she would be evicted over the slightest transgression. He found himself looking at her wings, wondering if they had something to do with her situation; he'd never heard of winged elves before.

Then again, he'd never really dealt with her people before either.

"Krysanna, come here," he said.

It was almost impossible to keep his tone gentle, and the way she flinched at the command spoke of his failed attempt. She obeyed, though, pulling herself up from the floor as she slowly crossed the kitchen, her eyes cast down as if she were afraid to even look at him. *That* actually made him feel bad, and he held out a hand to her.

"I'm not angry with you," he said. Her trembling hand rested in his,

195

and he led her back to the living room. "Accidents happen, but next time, don't try to use magic on the appliances, alright?"

Again, she nodded, but her gaze remained on the floor. Even though he was trying to sound understanding, she'd received the same tone from her tutor before he turned her over to the Council for judgement.

"I'm not going to kick you out over a mistake," Alex assured her. "I told you that you'd be safe here, and I'm not taking that back."

He needed her to trust him, and if there was even a trace of fear when she looked at him, then he had to find a way to eliminate it. Until he knew exactly what was going on, she was his ace in the hole. As long as she was staying with him and believed that he wouldn't hurt her, then he had more bargaining room whenever the client decided on what to do with her.

"I'm sorry," she whispered again.

"Stop apologizing," he said, and she pulled her knees up to her chest. Damn, he really needed to work on his tone with her. "You're not hurt, and I can replace a microwave. It could have been worse, so let's just take this as a learning experience and move on."

There had to be a way to change the topic, to bring back some level of comfort, but it was too soon to start delving into the mystery that was her past. Instead, he focused on the present, turning slightly to face her, and he silently hoped that a calm conversation would help her relax.

"I have to take care of some business later, but would you like me to show you around London when I return?"

Krysanna lifted her head, turning to look at him finally, and she tried to gauge the sincerity of his words. It made little sense that he would make such an offer if he were planning to send her on her way, but it took a few tries before she could find her voice.

"I think I'd like that," she said.

"It might be easier to show you things if I knew a little more about you," he said, hoping it would help. "I'm sure it's safe to say that you're not from Pennsylvania, either."

She shook her head, unsure of whether or not she should tell him the truth. Still shaken from the unfortunate experience in the kitchen, she was silent for a few moments longer, but he deserved to know what he'd signed up for, and denying him that opportunity would only tell him that she still didn't trust him completely.

"I'm… I'm not from Earth," she said, looking away from him. Krys wasn't sure what to expect in terms of his reaction, but she felt safer with her gaze averted. "I grew up on Zalyndrya, in the Elven Nation of Evemyst."

Alex considered her words to decide whether or not he should believe them, but she had no reason to lie to him, especially about something like this. Pieces started to click into place – his colleague's accent that was so similar to Krysanna's, the strange attire his client had worn when they'd met, and the elf's confusion when it came to things that should have been common knowledge.

Silver wasn't from Earth, and neither was their client. Leaning back against the sofa, he let everything sink in, but it also brought of host of new questions. Mikhail seemed pretty comfortable with Lalasa, which meant that he'd known her for more than just a few days.

His mind traced back to the incident in Boston six months prior, and Silver's admission that he'd died there told him that these aliens weren't exactly new to Earth. He could only guess how long they'd been traveling between the two worlds, but they'd been discreet enough to keep their presence from the general public. The tabloids would have a field day if someone ever let it slip that there were beings from another world routinely visiting this one.

"Alex?" Krysanna's soft voice pulled him from his thoughts, and he focused his attention on her. "Have I said something wrong?"

"No," he said. "It just isn't the kind of answer I was expecting."

Truthfully, he had no idea *what* he'd been expecting, but her admission that she was an alien hadn't been it. Maybe that wasn't the best term to use. When he looked at her, he didn't see the green or grey caricatures that had become a stable part of pop culture. She was an elf, not some weird creature that sucked people up into flying saucers to probe them.

Alex almost laughed at the absurd thought, unable to even picture her in that situation, but she was still staring at him with anxious eyes, her lower lip caught between her teeth. Considering another's feelings hadn't been one of his frequently used skills, preferring to look out for himself when he had no one else there for him.

"Right, so you're from another planet, this Zalyndrya was it?" he began, trying to make sure he had the facts in order. "But something happened there, and of all places, you came to Earth." He shook his head. "Wouldn't have been my first choice."

"It wasn't a choice!" Defiance slipped into her tone, and her eyes widened again at her own outburst. "I just wanted to escape the castle. I had no idea that it would send me to this world, but I tried to accept it. I thought that maybe I could find a way to live here without worrying about encountering more Dusk Hunters."

"You missed the mark on that one." He sighed and shook his head. "What about your country? Just find a way to go home, and you'll be fine."

Her next words were too soft for even him to hear, but her posture said everything. He'd caught wind of her situation, but in a business where even his own employer withheld the truth, he needed to hear the truth from her.

"I was exiled," she said. "They accused me of using magic above my station, and the Council chose that as my punishment. If I try to cross the borders, then I'll be executed."

"Just because you used magic you weren't supposed to?" His surprise was obvious; there had to be more than she was telling him. "How many people were hurt?"

"Just myself," she said. "It's how things are there. The laws are strict, but they benefit everyone." The explanation sounded hollow in her ears, and before she could stop herself, words spilled out of her. "It was just a simple mistake. I had asked my tutor if he knew of any spells that would give the illusion of wings, and he sent me to a section of one of the Great Libraries to find a certain book."

Alex could tell where this was going, but he let her continue anyway.

"He found me unconscious in my room," she said. Her voice had grown quiet, tears trickling down her cheeks. "The pain had been so much that I must have blacked out, but he was gentle when I awoke. He assured me that everything would be fine, that he would help me find a way to reverse it. Not even two hours later, I was arrested. He testified against me at the trial, and even my own parents, who are on the Council, accepted his words as truth."

"He set you up," Alex said.

He could only shake his head when she nodded. In the short time he'd known her, it seemed impossible that Krysanna would intentionally harm anyone, and to find herself without the home she'd had for however long she'd been alive was grossly unfair. Life wasn't always fair, though. It tended to give one a sense of false security only to pull the rug away, and then kick them while they're down.

"I don't understand," she said, her breath catching in her throat. "I never did anything to him, and he turned against me when I was only following his suggestion."

Before he had a chance to react, Krys had closed the distance and buried her face against his chest, her body shaking with sobs. He remained still, trying to wrap his mind around the latest development, but after a few

198

seconds, his arms wrapped around her.

He had no words to comfort her, but he simply held her while she cried, finding a rare sense of compassion for the elf. Alex knew what it was like to have his family turn against him, but he'd arguably deserved it. Krysanna, however, didn't seem to have the slightest trace of a malicious streak.

At that moment, the urge to track down her tutor and make him answer for his actions was strong, and he swallowed down the growl that threatened to escape. Maybe it was whatever bond she claimed existed between them, or maybe it was just that she hadn't deserved what she'd been through, but he was more irritated than anything about the situation.

"My cousin is one of the Imperial Advisors," she said once her sobs had quieted. "Abnalia spoke with the Empress and Emperor, and they offered me sanctuary at their castle. It was wonderful at first. Of course, I missed my home, but they were kind to me, and my cousin took time from her duties to help me adjust.

"My people don't sleep as often as humans, and there were times when I'd simply explore the castle during the night. There were always members of the Royal Guard present, so I had no need to worry about my safety, but one night, when I passed by the entrance to the dungeons, the Emperor was on his way back up the stairs."

Her head still rested against his chest, but he could hear the fear in her voice as she spoke. He almost assured her that she didn't have to continue; she'd said enough already.

"He had blood on his face, and I thought he'd been hurt by one of the prisoners," she continued. "But then I saw that his eyes were glowing, and when he spoke, he had fangs." Leaning back just enough to look at him, her eyes told her vivid recollection of that night. "Both the Emperor and the Empress are Dusk Hunters, vampires as the people on this world call them."

"So, you found a way to escape," he said. "By magic, of course."

"I found one of Lady Konistav's spell books, and I gathered a few enchanted items that I thought I might need to keep them from finding me, but when I spoke the incantation, it brought me to a foreign city."

"Philadelphia is a bit strange." His humor went unanswered, but he was already filling in the blanks with the new knowledge that she presented.

It was safe to assume that his client was likely the Empress herself, but even as a vampire, she didn't seem like she wanted the elf harmed. There might have been some genuine concern for her well-being, but she'd also mentioned her missing property, which he'd already concluded were the items Krys said she'd brought with her.

"Where are these enchanted items?" he asked, trying to keep his voice from raising her suspicion.

"They're back at that house," she said. "I need to get my books and my bow, but I don't think I can go back there."

His job was to retrieve both her and whatever she'd taken, but without her as a guide, he had no idea what he was looking for. Books would be easy to find; all he had to do was grab anything that wasn't written in any language known on Earth.

Forcing her to accompany him would shatter whatever fragile trust she had in him, and after what she'd experienced, it would be cruel to drag her back to a place that housed a pair of vampires, one of which was definitely not happy with him at the moment.

"I'll find a way for you to retrieve them," he said.

He had to contact Silver. Even if it meant revealing what he'd just learned, he needed answers on what the hell he could expect if Krysanna refused to let him hand her over to their client. Alex wasn't keen on the idea of fighting someone in such a powerful position, but what remained of his conscience wouldn't allow him to betray the elf when it seemed he was the only one she had.

Fifteen

Mikhail looked up from one of the files that were scattered across his desk, his expression nowhere near amused as he watched Alex stroll in as if he owned the place. As far as his calendar showed, there were no appointments scheduled, and while he tried to make time for his operatives, everything about this one managed to get under his skin.

"I'm busy," he said flatly.

"I know, you're meeting with me." The grin that Alex flashed was nowhere near friendly, but Mikhail refused to rise to the bait. Instead, he simply glared at him, waiting for him to get to the point. "We need to talk."

"And here I thought you were just here to shoot the shit."

"You withheld information that I could have used to do my job," Alex said. His tone was casual, but the anger beneath it was unmistakable. "If you had told me that I was supposed to find an elf with *wings*, then I could have located her that first night, and my expense report would be much lower."

He fell silent, regarding his so-called employer with open disdain. This wasn't supposed to be some game; they were professionals, and if he planned to stay with this company, then Alex needed to know that this new boss would have his back when it counted. So far, he wasn't convinced.

"You found her, though," Mikhail said. "Otherwise, I want to think that you'd have enough sense not to barge in here and start bitching. Where is she?"

"She's safe," he said. "That's all you're getting. What do you know about this client?"

"Client information is confidential. As long as you've worked here, you should know that by now." He wouldn't deny that he wasn't thrilled at the way Alex was hiding his own information, but he begrudgingly admitted

201

that he might have deserved it.

"Last time I checked, we didn't take clients who aren't from Earth. Our little blonde friend was pretty talkative last night, in between being scared half to death because she's hiding from a pair of vampires from her own world." Alex leaned forward, resting his elbows on the desk.

"I noticed something else when you called me in for this assignment," he continued. "This client just so happens to have a very interesting accent, and I'm sure you already know this, but she's not exactly on this side of the living. It doesn't take a genius to see how things add up."

"I'm not paying you to get involved," Mikhail warned. "Your job was to find the elf and wait for further instructions. Whatever happens next is up to the client."

"I'm not turning her over to someone she doesn't want to be involved with," Alex said, matching his tone.

"That's not really your call, now is it?"

For a moment, Mikhail thought that Alex was going to jump over the desk and escalate their discussion beyond a few sharp words. Sharp claws would be even less pleasant, and he slid the hidden pistol from its position under the desk. He knew that Alex would be difficult to control, and he also knew that he'd been with the company far longer than Mikhail himself, but Alex wasn't the one in charge here.

"Before you follow through with that idea, you might want to remember who's signing your paycheck," Mikhail said. "You're working under contract here, Malice, and you're not going to ignore standard procedure just because some pretty blonde ruffled your fur. So, here's how it's going to be. You said you have her somewhere safe, and that's fine, but the second our client decides that she wants to meet with her, you're going to bring her wherever the hell I tell you we're meeting, and you're going to act like a goddamn professional about it."

"And if I don't?"

"You know what happens when an operative goes rogue."

The low growl echoed in the office, but Alex made no move towards violence. He'd worked for this organization for decades, and he'd been called to track down a rogue on more than one occasion. Usually, the new targets had come unhinged, tossing aside the rules they'd lived by in favor of chasing whatever thrill they'd failed to find during their employment.

He sure as hell didn't want to be lumped in with that lot, but he also couldn't allow someone to take Krysanna back to the very place from which she'd fled. Not to mention that his occupation helped provide him with a

202

very comfortable lifestyle. Alex couldn't deny that money went a long way to help him put up with the occasional inconvenience, but there had been at least some measure of trust between him and Jack, and the man sitting across from him was almost nothing like his predecessor.

The game had changed, and until he had an idea of what that might mean when it came to his future with the company, he'd have to play his part carefully. He still had one of their former colleagues on his side, and even if Reaper was retired, Alex knew he could count on him if things went to hell before he could stop it.

"Maybe you should think about what happens when the boss can't trust his people," he said finally. "If you want me to keep putting my ass on the line and follow your orders, then you might want to make sure you're not screwing me over in the process. You used to be out there, and I'm pretty sure that the time you've spent behind this desk isn't enough for you to forget what it's like."

"Then stop acting like you're some alpha male jackass," Mikhail said.

"You're the one who kept important details from me. I'm not going to work with some asshole who thinks that I don't need to know something that would help me do my damned job."

They were going in circles, and Mikhail could feel a headache brewing behind his eyes. He didn't like the werewolf, and it was obvious that the feeling was mutual, but he had a business to run. Arguing like children wasn't going to solve anything.

"Is this a bad time?"

Both sets of eyes snapped over to the door; neither of them had heard it open, and it was possible that it hadn't. Lalasa stood just a pace or two into the room, watching the exchange with growing concern.

"Speak of the devil," Alex muttered.

"Just hashing out some issues," Mikhail said, ignoring him. "It's good that you stopped by, though. Malice found your missing elf."

Violet eyes immediately focused on Alex, and he leaned back in his chair as he met her gaze evenly. Empress or not, he was absolutely not in the mood for any form of superiority complexes. Her expression, however, looked nothing short of relieved, and he recalled her demeanor during their first meeting.

Shade was absent this time, and Lalasa's attire was more suited to this world than her own, leading him to believe that she had other plans when she'd finished this meeting. Whatever her reasons, they weren't his business, and he couldn't bring himself to care.

"Is she unharmed?" she asked.

It was an interesting first question, he had to admit. She hadn't demanded to know of Krysanna's whereabouts, and she actually seemed genuinely concerned for the elf's well-being. Alex gave a shrug.

"She was a little shaken up, but she's not hurt." He glanced over to address Mikhail. "Duchess' wife is pretty pissed at me, by the way. Good luck with that one."

"We have her in protective custody," Mikhail said before Alex could say anything that would make the situation worse. "She'll be safe as long as she's with us."

"Good." Lalasa accepted the answer without question, and Alex noted once again the trust that existed between the two.

Something had to have happened for them to have that level of faith in each other, and he recalled the reminder Silver had given him about what had taken place within the compound. He had yet to learn all of the details, but he knew that it ended with Mikhail becoming his new boss, and some kind of connection with extraterrestrial royalty.

"And of my belongings that she had taken with her?" Lalasa asked.

"Still working on that," Alex said. "It shouldn't take me long, especially if she cooperates."

There was a challenge in his voice, almost daring her to ask where he was hiding Krysanna, but she was unwilling to broach that subject. Lalasa felt the same hostility he'd displayed before, although it was magnified by whatever had just transpired between him and Mikhail.

As accustomed as she was to offering counsel, this was one area which she planned to avoid. Mikhail was her friend, but the dynamic between him and the wolf was outside of her control, and it would be best for them to settle it without her interference. The tension in the air was palpable, as was the silence that fell between the three.

"Has there been any word on the other elf?" she asked.

"Silver's last report put her somewhere in the Allentown area," Mikhail said. "He's still tracking her, but that's all I have. We're not sure what her motives are, but if she's still in Pennsylvania, then we'll have no problem keeping them apart."

She offered a nod, but didn't press further, and Alex took that as his cue to leave. He'd already had enough irritation for one night, and spending any more time in that office was going to test his patience more than the conversation already had.

As he stepped out of the Central Command building, he checked his phone, finding a missed call and a text with an address. After only a few seconds of debate, he moved around to the side of the structure and allowed the shadows to surround him. He could afford to spend another hour or two on this side of the pond.

*****

The seconds ticked by, and Karian felt his patience slipping away as he stared at the man who had opened the door. It was no secret that Sean still hated him, but at the moment, he was preventing Karian from visiting with his sister, and the vampire would not tolerate that for much longer.

It wasn't as if Sean would try to tell Cassandra that her brother wasn't welcome, but after nearly dying by Karian's hand, he reserved the right to make things as difficult as possible. He was tempting fate, knowing that Karian was deadlier now than he'd been that night in a dimly lit motel parking lot, but he also trusted in the thought that he'd suffer nothing more than a few threats as long as Cassandra lived with him.

"I don't need an invitation, you know," Karian said.

"And I can call the cops on you for trespassing. You're on my property, and I shouldn't have to tell you that I don't like the thought of you coming into my house." Sean's tone was harsh, revealing the lingering resentment. "But I'm not enough of a dick to try to come between you and Cass. I care about her feelings a hell of a lot more than I care about yours."

"It's out of respect for her that I haven't moved you out of my way," Karian said.

Their standoff continued for another handful of minutes until Cassandra stepped up to stand behind her boyfriend. The scene was common, and a sigh of exasperation hissed past her teeth.

"Would you two at least try to get along?" she said, shaking her head. "Honestly, you're both adults, and you're acting like children."

"He *did* try to kill me," Sean said.

"Once," Karian shot back. "And I haven't made an attempt since."

"Stop it." Cassandra's expression had gone from mild annoyance to complete irritation, and she nudged Sean aside so that she could address both of them. "You don't have to like each other, but I expect some level of civility."

At that moment, Karian could see how much she'd grown since they'd been separated as children, and it was obvious that the influence of her adoptive mother had taught her how to command almost any situation. He admired her, even if he still harbored less than friendly feelings towards her choice of suitor, and he gave a curt nod as he fell silent.

She was right, though, too. The initial meeting between the two men had landed Sean in the hospital, fighting off an unknown poison, and it had taken a fair measure of convincing for Karian to provide the antidote. They would probably never be friends, but adolescent jabs at each other would only damage their chances of coexisting in her life.

Even so, neither of them would be the first to extend a hand in an attempt to put the tension to rest, and it was a continued source of frustration for Cass. She allowed the matter to drop as her attention focused on her brother, and she rested a hand on Sean's arm in an attempt to calm him.

"I'll behave," he assured her. *As long as he does the same,* remained unspoken, but he was sure that she understood.

With one last tense moment slipping by, Sean turned and headed back into the house, leaving the pair at the door. Cass shook her head as she motioned her brother inside, and her frustration melted away when he sighed and ran a hand through his hair.

"Something's wrong," she said.

"I wouldn't say wrong, exactly, but I think I need to get your thoughts on something," Karian said.

He followed her into the living room, sliding off his jacket and setting it on the arm of the sofa before he sat. His shoulder holster was still in place, housing the nine-millimeter pistol that had become a permanent part of his attire.

"Has Lalasa said anything to you about an elf running around on Earth?" he asked.

"Abnalia's cousin," she said. "I know some of the details, but not much. She told me that she spoke with Mikhail, and he has someone searching for her. If I'm not mistaken, it's the werewolf that stopped by to speak with her a few nights ago."

"It is," he said. "There's another elf looking for Krysanna, though. I found her near Allentown, but she claims that she hasn't been told what to do if she finds her. From what I've heard about the current Council of Evemyst, I don't think that this one's intentions are going to be harmless."

He paused, gathering his thoughts. Karian wanted to say that he trusted his twin completely, but he couldn't ignore her ties to the Empire, and it was possible that whatever he said in her presence would make it back to Lalasa and Lothan.

"I need to know what Lalasa plans to do once Malice finds Krysanna," he said. "From what I've heard, she's terrified of my kind, and I

206

suspect that's the main reason she fled Zalyndrya. Knowing my colleague, he'll take her somewhere safe until our employer gives the word to bring her in for a meeting, but I doubt that he'd follow orders if he thinks that she's going to have to go somewhere against her will."

"I don't think Lalasa would make her go anywhere," Cassandra said. "That's not her way, but if this elf has stolen from her, then at the very least, she'd want her property returned. Other than that, I would imagine that she wants some sort of assurance that Krysanna is unharmed and will be able to live safely."

"That's good to know," he said. "Now I need to figure out what to do with the other one. She claims that she's training to be a high ranking soldier, and finding Krysanna is her final test. You're more familiar with Evemyst's politics. Any thoughts on what they might want with her? After all, they did kick her out in the first place."

"It's difficult to tell when it comes to elves," she said. "I learned much from Abnalia, and although exile is rare, they never reverse it. If they've sent a soldier to find her, then I'm almost certain that they aren't going to ask for a peaceful report."

"They want her dead."

"That would be my guess," Cass said. "And if that's the case, then it's imperative that they never meet face to face."

Karian stood, grabbing his jacket as he turned towards the door, already dialing a number on his phone. When the call rang and then went to voicemail, he muttered a curse and tried again with the same result. He settled on a text message, and then he turned his head to regard his sister.

"I have to go," he said. "Thanks, Cass. You've helped me figure out what my next steps should be."

"Anytime," she said. "Just be careful out there."

"You know how I am," he said, flashing a grin. "I'm already dead, so they can't do worse."

*****

Alex sat on the edge of the reflecting pool, watching the few late-night passersby in the park of Rittenhouse Square. With the sounds of cars passing on the city streets, he listened for that of a motorcycle, turning his head when one idled at the curb before silencing.

"What's so bloody important?" he asked, standing when Karian came into view.

"I have information," Karian said, as he stopped before him. "And I need to meet with your elf."

207

"Considering her thoughts on vampires, that's not going to happen."

"I'm not sure that's really your decision to make," Karian said evenly. "This affects both of our assignments and her safety."

"What about your elf?" Alex asked.

"We made a deal," he said. "Information in exchange for some cash. And no, I didn't just let her go so that she could try to stay off of my radar." Pulling out his phone, he tapped the screen a few times and then turned it so that his colleague could see. "There's a tracker sewn into the little bag that has the money in it. She has no reason to think that it's there, but I'll know where to find her again when I need to."

"So, you *can* plan ahead every now and then," Alex said. "For a while there, I wasn't sure."

Karian ignored the jab as he slid his phone back into his pocket. His senses were alert, picking up every heartbeat in the immediate vicinity, but his attention remained on the wolf.

"Let me talk to Krysanna," he said. "You can even babysit if you think it's necessary, but there are things that she needs to know."

"Fine, but I'm going to get something in return." Alex watched him nod before continuing. "She left a few things at the last place she was staying, and we're going to get them back."

"Fair enough," Karian said. "Where do you have her hidden?"

Without waiting for an answer, Alex smirked and grabbed him by the arm to pull him back into the shadows. He heard the vampire swear, but he made sure that there was no time for Karian to pull away before the darkness swallowed them. Only a few seconds passed before the grass beneath them gave way to concrete, and once they were clear, Alex withdrew his hand.

"Was that really necessary?" Karian snapped.

It was nearing dawn in London, and his expression registered alarm when he glanced up to the gradually lighting sky. A thin layer of fog blanketed the streets, and his gaze returned to his colleague, a demand for an explanation on the tip of his tongue.

"I'm not going to let you burn," Alex said, although his grin wasn't exactly reassuring.

Leading the way out of the space between the buildings, Alex unlocked the door to the one on their right, holding it open for Karian to enter. Once the door closed, he could see the vampire's shoulders relax in relief, and he couldn't help a quiet laugh. It was tempting sometimes to toe the line, but they were supposed to be working together, and taking the time to watch the first bits of flame form on the other's skin would hinder their progress regardless of how amusing he might find it.

"Wait here," he said, leaving his guest in the entryway.

*****

Krysanna was seated on the sofa, staring intently at the television as some game show played out on the screen. She seemed fascinated by the device itself, but the images that held her attention were equally as intriguing. Catching movement out of the corner of her eye, she turned her head as Alex returned, a million questions about to spill from her lips until she saw the expression on his face.

"Is everything alright?" she asked, her smile fading at the edges.

"I have someone with me who wants to talk to you," he said. "He has information that he thinks you should know, but if you don't want to see him, then I'll get rid of him." He crossed the room to sit beside her. "Before you answer, you need to know the details."

Alex turned off the television, removing the distraction as he watched concern and confusion settle on her features. Fear would come next, but he'd already given her his word that he'd keep her safe, and there was a sliver of hope that she'd still believe that as he spoke again.

"We work together, but he isn't human either," he continued. "He's a vampire." As he'd suspected, her eyes widened and she started to shake her head. "Krys, listen to me. I wouldn't have brought him here if I thought he'd hurt you, and I'm not going to let him even think about it. I'll stay in the room with you two the entire time if you want me to."

She looked away, fighting down the fear that threatened to choke her. Alex hadn't given her a reason not to trust him, but if he'd been keeping company with a Dusk Hunter, then how could she be certain of his assurance of safety? He'd already acknowledged that she would likely find discomfort in a potential meeting, and he'd also left the decision in her hands.

"You're stronger than your fear, Krysanna," he said, his voice unusually gentle.

"Are you sure that it's important?" she asked, unable to look up. "And you'll stay here with me?"

"Silver seems to think so, and yes. I'm not leaving you alone with him."

She didn't speak for a full minute. She wanted to refuse, but if the vampire had information for her, then Alex wouldn't have brought him to her unless it was important. Trying to calm herself, she finally found her voice and nodded.

"I'll speak with him," she said.

Alex watched her for another few seconds, waiting to see if she changed her mind, but when she didn't retract her decision, he returned to the entryway. He knew that Karian had heard their conversation, and his expression showed his annoyance.

"You shouldn't have told her," Karian said, keeping his voice quiet.

"She trusts me," Alex hissed back. "If she figured it out on her own and realized that I brought a bloodsucker here, knowing damn well that she's terrified of you lot, then she'd try to run from me, too. Can't let that happen."

Karian had no argument for that. As long as they knew where Krysanna was, they could make sure that no one came after her, and if keeping her trust meant revealing what he was, then he'd simply have to accept that.

The pair returned to the other room, Alex leading the way, and Karian could smell the sickly-sweet scent of fear as soon as he crossed the threshold. Stopping for a moment, he regarded the elf from a safe distance, but he gave her some space while his colleague spoke.

"This is Silver," Alex told her. "He's a bit of an asshole, but he won't hurt you. I'll be right here with you."

Krysanna looked between them, her eyes wide and features pale when she regarded Karian. He hadn't moved towards her, and she tried to accept Alex's assurances that the vampire would remain on his best behavior, but it was different when he was standing in the same room.

Just by observing her, Karian knew that this was going to be a challenge. The poor girl was obviously frightened, and he decided it would be best to speak his piece and leave. There was no sense in lingering if his presence alone was enough for her to curl up with her back against the opposite arm of the sofa.

His movements were deliberately slow as he took a few steps forward, his hands clearly visible, and he gestured to the side of the sofa closest to him before speaking. This was a delicate situation, and he hoped that maybe a trace of familiarity would help ease her nerves.

"*Well met, Krysanna,*" he said, speaking in the language of their world. "*May I sit?*"

Alex should have been surprised at the change of language, but it only confirmed his suspicions. Krysanna, however, stared at Karian. It was obvious that she hadn't expected him to address her in that manner, and she remained still for a moment before she remembered that she had the ability to move.

With a glance at Alex, she carefully removed the ring from her index finger and set it aside, but she couldn't speak. The vampire before her knew her language, and questions flooded her mind. He was still waiting for an answer, though, and she managed to look at him again with a small nod.

As Karian took a seat, he noticed her move back just a little more, even though she was already pressed as far back as possible. Again, he made no sudden movements, unwilling to startle her when she was terrified enough already.

"*My name is Karian of the Silver Tiger,*" he said. "*Your friend knows me as Silver, and I'd like to keep it that way. I'm telling you so that maybe you'll be able to trust me enough to know that I'm not going to hurt you. I give you my word as a Traveler, you're safe with me.*"

Krysanna had heard of his people, groups of humans on the northern continents who held no loyalty to the Empire, and the knowledge helped her sort the information into perspective. He was from her world, but even though he wasn't human anymore, it was unlikely that he would rush back to the empress to reveal her whereabouts.

Silence fell between them, and she realized that he was waiting for a response. Without her ring, they would be able to speak privately despite Alex's presence in the room. She felt a small twinge of remorse, knowing that it might come across as rude, but the measure was necessary.

"*Well met,*" she said finally, her voice quiet.

"*I've learned a few things recently that you should know,*" Karian said. "*I'm aware of your situation, and we're going to do whatever we can to help you.*" He paused, casting a glance at Alex before returning his gaze to her. "*There is another of your people on this world. Do you know an elf by the name of Miria?*"

She shook her head. Evemyst was by no means a small country, and it would have been impossible for her to meet every elf who resided there. He seemed to understand this, and she watched him give a short nod.

"*She said that she's training to be a member of the Elite Guard,*" he continued. "*Her final test was to come to Earth and find you. She claimed that she hasn't been told what to do if that happens, but I have my suspicions.*"

That was enough for her eyes to widen again, and Karian took note of her reaction. He recalled his sister's words, understanding the truth behind them, but his expression remained neutral.

"*She doesn't know where you are,*" he said. "*She's in Pennsylvania still, and I'm keeping track of where she goes. Unless you want to speak with her, there's no chance of her finding you.*"

Krysanna wanted to believe him, and his knowledge of the situation certainly helped, but it was difficult to look past what he was in order to take his words as truth. He'd given his word on the name of his people, and that was something that she could not take lightly.

"*If she finds me, then she will try to kill me,*" she said, drawing her knees up to her chest. "*My people rarely leave Evemyst, but if the Council sends the Guard after someone, it's for that reason alone.*"

"*Then she won't find you,*" he assured her.

"*Please don't kill her,*" she said, forcing herself to look at him. "*She cannot change the decision of the Council, and if she doesn't even know why she's searching for me, then she doesn't deserve to lose her life.*"

"*I wasn't planning on it,*" he said. The possibility had crossed his mind, but he had no intentions of seeking her out for that purpose alone. "*My job is to keep her from finding you, while his job,*" he gestured to Alex, "*is to keep you safe. We're working together on this, and between the two of us, no one is going to hurt you.*"

As he continued to assure her, she found herself relaxing little by little. She trusted Alex, and if he trusted Karian, then perhaps she could give him a chance. It didn't change what he was, and it didn't eliminate the fear she felt by knowing that, but it kept her from slipping into paralyzing terror.

When he didn't prepare to leave, she realized that there was more than he'd just shared. He'd already given her information that she didn't know yet, but she had a feeling that he had questions of his own, and her unease began to grow again.

"*We know that Lady Konistav is looking for you as well,*" he said, watching her expression closely. "*As far as we can tell, she doesn't have a way to find your exact location, and neither of us has plans to tell her. From what I know of her, she doesn't have any intention of harming you, but there was mention of some things that she's missing.*"

"Silver," Alex warned, watching Krysanna's demeanor change.

She shifted uncomfortably at his words, unable to meet his gaze. Her pulse quickened, fear rolling off of her in waves. There was no room behind her for her wings to move, but they twitched nervously as she sat silently.

"*You don't have to meet with her,*" Karian said, ignoring his colleague. "*I think that as long as she knows that you're alright and her property is returned, then she'll return to Zalyndrya and leave you to live your life in peace.*"

"*How can you be sure?*" she asked, her voice barely audible.

"*I've heard many things about her, but I've never heard anyone accuse her of cruelty. I know she's a Dusk Hunter, just as I am, but not all of us are heartless murderers.*"

212

Maybe that assessment belonged to him regardless. He'd been a killer before he became a vampire, and even though he resisted at first, he'd fallen into the role without much trouble. Karian did what was necessary to survive, and if someone had to die so that he would live, then he had no reason to put any more thought into it. He was sure that his colleague knew this, but it was likely that Alex understood nothing of their conversation. Had he spoken in English, then it was possible that Alex might have said something to contradict his assurances, even though it would be counterproductive to their cause.

"*I told your friend that I would help both of you collect your things from the last place you were staying,*" he continued. "*If you don't want to go back, then just tell us what we're looking for, and we'll bring everything to you first.*"

Krysanna finally lifted her head to regard him, trying to read his features. His expression hadn't changed, though, and she absently wondered if revealing nothing of his thoughts had become second nature to him. Rarely had she seen anyone, even of her own people, who could easily hide their thoughts, and it did nothing to help put her at ease.

Even a glimpse of emotion might have given her more faith in him, but the only thing she had was Alex's promise that she would remain unharmed. If she found herself alone with the vampire, however, it was possible that everything would change, regardless of his words.

"*I'm afraid,*" she admitted, but this time, she kept her gaze on him. "*The place where I was before, the two women who live there are the same as you, the same as the emperor and empress. No matter where I go, your kind is always there.*"

Finally, Karian's expression softened. He understood her all too well; he'd faced similar troubles when he'd first come to Earth, when he was still human. Everywhere he turned, he'd find them, and he could only kill so many before he nearly died at their hands. If it hadn't been for a chance meeting, he wouldn't even have lived as long as he had.

"*I know you are, Krysanna, but your friend was right earlier,*" he said, his tone unusually gentle. "*You are stronger than your fear, and you don't have to be afraid around him or me. It's easier said than done. I'm sure you've seen or heard terrible things about my kind, and many of them are likely true, but even if you don't trust me, trust him to keep you safe.*"

The change in tone wasn't lost on Alex, even if he didn't understand the words. In the short time he'd known Karian, he'd never seen his professional mask slip, not even during the snarky exchanges that had passed between them. It would appear that the vampire wasn't as cold as he pretended to be, and Alex found himself assessing him all over again.

213

Krysanna relaxed just a little bit, the change almost unnoticeable, but whatever Karian had said had put her at least somewhat at ease. Alex didn't expect her to act as if she didn't fear him or any other walking corpse, but at least she was able to hold a conversation with him without falling into a panic.

Karian was silently grateful for the language barrier. He and Alex had an understanding; they worked together, and they could even act almost friendly with each other, but trust wasn't built in only a few short nights. He had to build on Krysanna's trust for the werewolf, though, and if that meant speaking highly of him, then he had no choice but to do so. At least Alex had no idea what he'd said.

There was the possibility that the elf would tell him later, but by then, Karian would hopefully be back in Philadelphia. He could only imagine the smug grin that he'd have to face, and then he would have to resist the urge to punch him just to remove it.

It wasn't that he had any real animosity towards Alex, but their professional relationship had its own nuances, and Karian preferred not to change that. They didn't get personal with each other; it was strictly business. Neither of them had joined the company to make friends, and there was no reason to start now.

"Are you finished?" Alex said, failing to hide the impatience in his voice. "I don't need you hanging around here all day, Silver."

"Almost," Karian said. "Find yourself a chew toy if you're bored."

Karian couldn't resist the hint of a grin as Alex glared at him, even if the expression lacked any real threat. It was part of their game, and at least it put them back on even footing after he'd let his usual façade slip.

"*Thank you.*" Krysanna's voice pulled him away from his exchange with Alex, and he regarded her with mild surprise. "*I hope you understand that I can't just pretend that I'm not afraid of you, but I appreciate that you're willing to help me. I don't want to meet with them, and I'd rather not go back to that house, but I'll give you both full descriptions of what I left behind.*"

"*Then we'll make sure to retrieve them,*" Karian said. "*You can sort through them once we bring them to you, and we'll go from there. Don't worry about the empress or Miria. We will not let them find you.*" He paused, almost leaving it at that. "*And thank you, for agreeing to meet with me. I know this was difficult for you, but I appreciate that you could give me a chance.*"

She nodded, almost managing a small smile, but it faded almost instantly. The sooner Karian left, then better she'd feel. Speaking the thoughts aloud would never happen, though, and she glanced up at Alex as she slipped her ring back on her finger.

"I think we're finished," she said, hoping that he could understand her desire to be free of the vampire.

"We are," Karian said. He didn't miss the way she flinched when he stood, and he took a step back in an attempt to keep her calm. His attention shifted to his colleague. "I hope you have a way to take me home that doesn't involve going outside."

"As if I would let you spend the day here," Alex said, rolling his eyes.

He didn't wait to see if Karian was following, and the other's silent footsteps gave no indication either. It was safe to assume that his colleague knew that his prolonged presence would only cause the elf more distress, and even if he was a pain in the ass, even Karian wouldn't be that cruel. At least, Alex thought he wouldn't.

The light from the living room cast enough shadow in the kitchen for his needs, and he took Karian by the arm to pull him back into the darkness. Grass replaced linoleum, the towering buildings of Philadelphia creating a stark contrast to the comfortable flat in London, and Alex noted the way Karian relaxed once back in the city.

"Your elf is braver than she knows," Karian said. "Let me know when we're going to retrieve her belongings. I'll need a night to prepare in case we have problems."

"We're going to be dealing with two corpses," Alex said. "And they're not going to be happy to see us."

"Us or you?"

Alex only grinned.

Sixteen

Marielle awoke to the sound of a series of knocks on her front door, and she opened her eyes slowly. Ian was still beside her in bed, blue eyes meeting hers as she smiled at him, ignoring the visitor vying for her attention.

"Morning," Ian said.

"Is it?" she asked.

"Close enough."

Glancing past him at the clock on her nightstand, she read the display to learn it was only a few minutes past noon. Considering the schedule she kept for work, it wasn't as bad as sleeping until dinner time. Another knock, louder this time, made her sigh, and she dropped her head onto his chest.

"It could be important," he said.

"They should have called first," she mumbled.

She rolled over to grab her phone, seeing the series of missed calls, and she sat up quickly when she saw the name of the caller. With a curse, she jumped out of bed, grabbing the first thing she saw, which was his discarded t-shirt, and her jeans.

"It's my father," she said. "Just stay here, and I'll have him come back later."

Rushing from the room, she grabbed the few pieces of scattered clothes along the way and tossed them into the spare bedroom, and she ran her fingers through her hair in an attempt to make it presentable when she reached the door. She took a deep breath, just as another knock came, and she turned the lock to greet him.

"Dad?" she asked, hoping he would think that she was surprised to see him.

"I tried calling," he said. "You going to let your old man in or not?"

"This really isn't a good time."

Carl looked at her skeptically, taking in her appearance, but he made no move to leave. He didn't have to guess why she wanted him to leave; her expression and attire said enough.

"Your shirt is on backwards," he said. "Doesn't even look like yours either."

This was *not* a conversation she wanted to have right now, especially when any of her neighbors might walk by and hear them. Reluctantly, she stepped aside for him to enter, closing the door behind him.

"I know you're grown and can make your own decisions, but-"

"I really hope you don't plan on finishing that sentence," Marielle said. "I'm a grown woman, and yes, I can make my own decisions. Did you come over here just to make sure that you approve of them?"

Carl sighed, dropping down to sit on the sofa. He still wanted to see the little girl she used to be whenever he looked at her, and his concern for her safety over everything else made it difficult to stay out of her business.

"Is this where I get to say 'I told you so'?" he asked. There was little humor in his tone, though, and she knew that he wasn't happy with the development.

"Not to be rude, but why are you here?"

"You weren't answering you phone." It was a weak excuse, and he didn't need to see her expression to know that she wasn't buying it. "I found out what happened in Boston. Marielle, what were you thinking? You could have been killed."

"I haven't had nearly enough coffee for this conversation," she said, turning towards the kitchen.

The last thing she needed was another lecture. She was sure that he meant well, but it was already done, and there was no going back and changing anything. Even if she could, she was sure that she would have made the same decisions.

None of that deterred her father from trying to persuade her to cut ties with Ian or any of the people she'd grown close to over the past several months. Her routine of working, going home, and the occasional date with Ian had been disrupted with the initial arrival of the Konistavs, but she could now say that she had friends to go with her career.

"I also looked into the company you work for," Carl said, joining her in the kitchen as she set the coffee to brew.

"Do we really have to do this?" she asked, exasperated.

"Marielle, I just want what's best for you. I want you to be safe."

It was what any parent would want for their child, but Marielle mentally prepared herself for his arguments. Her job had its risks, but she'd long since decided that they were worth the benefits and experience she gained through it.

"I want you to come to Florida with me," Carl said. "I could use some help around the shop, and you'd be safer there than you are here."

"What? No."

Marielle stared at him like he'd lost his mind; she wasn't sure that he hadn't. Turning to face him, she shook her head, unwilling to even consider the idea.

"I have a life here," she said. "I have a career, friends, and a boyfriend. I'm not just going to drop everything because you don't like it."

"And you're risking losing your life by staying," he countered. "Your boss deals with bloodsuckers every night, half of your friends aren't even technically alive, and don't get me started on that boyfriend of yours."

"Rhonda's family has been running that company for generations," she said. "You don't get to decide who I can and can't have as friends, and you really don't get to decide who I'm dating." Checking the coffee, she pulled the pot from the machine once there was enough for a cup, but she kept speaking as she filled her mug. "Is that all you came over here for? You just wanted to give it once last try to see if I'd walk away from almost everything I care about so that you can sleep better at night?"

"I don't want to get a phone call in the middle of the night telling me that there was an *accident*," Carl said. "I spent half of my life facing those murderers, and I'm not just going to step aside while my daughter is sleeping with one."

"That is *none* of your business," she snapped.

"Like hell it isn't!"

Both of their voices had risen in anger and frustration, but Marielle had no intentions of relenting. She'd spent too long staying quiet and trying to process everything that had happened since the night she'd found out that Ian wasn't human, but enough was enough. As much as she loved her father, she couldn't let him have this one.

"I've worked my ass off to get where I am," she said. "And I'm damn good at my job. Yes, maybe it's a little dangerous at times, but I've also made some very good friends, and I'm not about to throw all of that away just for your peace of mind. I know the risks, and they're not enough for me to cut ties with the people I care about."

"Then I guess it's time for me to sell the shop and move back up here," he said.

219

Marielle almost dropped her mug, her eyes widening as she stared at him. She wasn't sure how to react to the idea; she wouldn't mind seeing him more often, but she could tell that his primary motive was to keep an eye on her. It was ridiculous.

"No," she said after a moment. "I'd love to have you visit, but I don't need a babysitter, and I don't need you thinking that I can't make my own decisions."

Carl was stunned into silence. He'd expected her to try to compromise with him, but her adamant refusal was something that he never would have seen a year ago. She'd changed, he realized, and her resolve was stronger than he'd given her credit for, but that didn't erase the concern he held for her well-being.

Maybe he had overstepped his boundaries. He was still her father, but she'd been living on her own for years now; she didn't need him barging in and trying to make decisions for her. It was a difficult pill to swallow, one that he realized he couldn't fully stomach, and an argument was already forming when she stopped him.

"I don't want to spend the entire time you're here arguing," Marielle said with a sigh. "We used to get along so well, and ever since you came up this time, all we've done is fight. I know you're worried, but I'll be okay. I need you to trust me on this."

It wasn't that he didn't trust her. It was the ones she surrounded herself with that worried him. There was the possibility that having several vampires as friends could work in her favor, but all it would take was for one of them to lose control, and she'd be gone. Right now, her boyfriend was the biggest concern among them.

She'd made it clear that she wasn't going to heed his warnings, no matter how much he tried to make her see reason, and he couldn't just force her to leave with him. Well, he could, but she'd never forgive him for it.

Several minutes passed, and Marielle sipped her coffee while Carl was lost in thought. He didn't want to keep arguing with her either, and he heaved a sigh as he watched her. Moving back to Philadelphia wouldn't solve anything; it would only give him a front row seat to every instance where she'd put herself in danger, and he knew that he wouldn't be able to keep quiet about it.

"My plane leaves the day after tomorrow," he said. "I'd like to have a nice dinner with my daughter before I leave, maybe that restaurant down near Penns Landing that looks like a boat." He paused before adding, almost as an afterthought, "Bring that boyfriend, too."

"He has a name," she said, although she managed a hint of a smile.

"Well, I could come up with plenty of names for him, but you wouldn't like them."

The tension started to recede, and she rolled her eyes instead of offering a retort. He didn't have to like her friends, or Ian, but at least he seemed willing to stop trying to change her mind. As he turned towards the door, she walked beside him, standing in the doorway once he'd stepped out into the hall.

"I have to work tomorrow night, but we can do dinner tonight if you want," she said. "I'll see if I can get reservations, and I'll let you know what time, alright?"

Once she closed the door, she turned around to lean back against it. That was possibly one of the worst ways her father could have woken her, second to him walking in on her and Ian in bed. She'd dared to hope that they'd made some progress after their last discussion, but he seemed determined to make her question her decisions, and after the way the previous night had gone, she could do that well enough on her own.

"Everything okay?" Ian asked, coming into view.

He'd pulled on his jeans, but it took her a moment to remember that the reason he was shirtless was because she'd grabbed his t-shirt when she'd jumped out of bed. She didn't doubt that he'd heard the entire argument, and she gave a light shrug. Things weren't completely okay, but maybe they would be going forward. She had to hope that would be the case.

"My dad really doesn't like you," she said with a laugh and a shake of her head.

"Yeah, I kind of figured that," he said. "He's not the one dating me, so he'll get over it." Ian paused, suddenly uncertain. "We are dating again, right?"

Marielle wanted to laugh again, but for someone who was physically stronger than any human she knew, Ian looked strangely vulnerable. It was a reminder that just because his heart didn't beat, it didn't mean that it couldn't hurt.

Instead of responding, she set her coffee down and closed the distance between them, her arms looping behind his neck as she leaned up to kiss him. They would still have issues along the way, but she was willing to face them now instead of worrying about everything that could go wrong.

"Yes, we are," she said.

*****

Soph was fully prepared to spend the day in bed, still fuming over the

221

turn of events and Krysanna's disappearance, but the sound of movement from downstairs dashed her plans. Growling in annoyance, she tossed aside the covers and stalked to the door of her room, vowing to murder whoever thought that breaking into her home was a good idea.

She didn't need a weapon as she moved through the house, following the disturbance, and she was halfway down the stairs when she saw the blond figure crouched down in front a pile of books.

"What the hell are you doing?" she demanded.

She'd lost the element of surprise, but she knew that Malice would have heard her coming anyway. Descending the rest of the stairs, uncaring that she was still in her pajamas, she settled a glare on him, eyes flashing in anger.

"Get out."

"I'm just picking up a few things," Alex said, barely sparing her a glance. "Go back to bed so you can get your beauty sleep."

"Okay, let me put it in terms you understand," Soph said. "Get the hell out of my house before I mount your head on my wall."

Alex wasn't nearly as impressed as she'd hoped, but her recollection of the few times they'd met should have made her realize that before she'd even spoken. Still, she certainly didn't want him in her home, and she wasn't sure she even wanted to know how he'd gained entrance in the first place.

"What's that?" he asked, finally looking up. "You want me to open the curtains? I think that's a fantastic idea. We should brighten this place up a bit."

"Don't you dare."

His grin infuriated her, and razor-sharp incisors dug into her lower lip as she stalked forward, the dim red glow of her eyes promising murder. In response, Alex stood, arms folding over his chest as amusement flashed in his eyes.

"Let me make this easy then," he said. "Give me the elf's belongings, and I'll leave you to whatever you were doing upstairs before you interrupted me."

Soph snarled as she darted forward, reaching for him, but his speed matched her own, and he stepped aside before her nails could find purchase. Still, that irritating grin remained on his lips, as if he were having the time of his life, and she wanted nothing more than to rip it off of his face.

As she spun to face him again, his features shifted out of place, and she paused to watch as his height increased. His face reformed into a dark muzzle, glowing tattoos crawling on the surface as clawed fingers spread out.

His scar remained as a thin line devoid of fur, and his eyes took on a glow as he responded to her snarl with one of his own.

"Do I need to repeat myself?" His voice had dropped an octave, laced with a growl as stood up to his full height, nearly eight feet in total.

"If you shed all over my carpet, then I'll skin you alive," she warned.

Any surprise she might have had at his shift in appearance lasted only a few seconds. He was still in *her* house, and more than anything, she wanted him gone. It didn't matter that he towered over her, or that his claws could have taken a decent sized chunk out of her; Soph would *not* let herself be intimidated in her own home.

"Tell Krys if she wants her stuff, she can come get it herself," she said. "I'm not gonna let you ransack the place just because she's too scared to pick up her own crap."

Alex was not above using violence to achieve a goal, but he also knew when to pick his battles. Even with their differences in size, Soph would be no easy foe, and he had no desire to explain to Krysanna why he'd returned bruised and bloody. He took a menacing step forward anyway, glaring down at her with his teeth bared, and his voice rumbled from deep within when he spoke.

"Gather them up, and I'll be back for them," he said. "I don't need your permission to come in here, and I wouldn't mind showing up in the middle of the day again just to let the sun burn you to a crisp."

"Trespassing is a crime, asshole," she spat.

"So is murder, but you're not in prison." His features twisted into a caricature of a grin, but he didn't press the issue any further.

They simply glared at each other for a few more moments, neither willing to back down first, but eventually, Alex let his body relax as he shifted back to a more human appearance. There was plenty of fun to be had with her, but he'd learned enough.

Seventeen

Dropping a few names had been the only string she'd had to pull in order to secure reservations at the restaurant, and Marielle looked over at Ian as he handed his keys off to the valet. She had to admit that he cleaned up rather well – he looked fantastic in the dark suit, the light blue tie bringing out the color of his eyes.

Even with the promise of amazing food, her stomach was in knots as they made their way into the restaurant. With the way things had been going with her father, she wanted the evening to go smoothly, and she hoped that he could remain civil towards Ian for the duration of one meal.

Ian rested a hand at the small of her back, offering a reassuring smile as they reached their table, and she returned the expression warmly when he pulled out her chair for her to sit. They hadn't been on a date in ages, and since they were officially back together, this was the perfect place to change that. Of course, that meant that Carl had to maintain the peace during their meal.

They had a few minutes to themselves to browse the wine list, but they waited until the familiar figure came into view before Marielle opened her menu. Ian rested a hand on hers, giving a light squeeze as he watched her father approach, and he tried to keep his expression friendly as the man sat across from him.

Awkward didn't even begin to describe the silence that fell between them. Between Marielle's nervous fidgeting, Ian's attempt to remain civil in front of someone who surely hated him, and Carl's calm assessment of the situation, it was a welcome relief when their waiter reached their table to request their wine order.

Marielle selected a bottle of pinot noir, and once the three of them were left alone again, she tried to find a way to start the conversation. There was little common ground between her boyfriend and her father, but she opted for another subject after they'd had a chance to peruse the menu.

"How are things going with your shop?" she asked, looking at her father. "You haven't said much about it during your visit."

It was a safe subject, one that didn't involve her job or his former career. It also steered clear of anything regarding her current circle of friends, and she hoped that it would serve as a good ice breaker.

"I have my regulars," Carl said. "I think I spend more time talking to them than selling anything, but it keeps me busy and gives me a chance to socialize every now and then. Retirement can get boring if you don't have anything to keep you out of trouble."

"What kind of shop is it?" Ian asked.

"Mostly antiques," he said, opting for civility. They were in public, after all, and the staff at such an upscale restaurant would likely take issue with their dinner turning into a war. "Just things that I've picked up on the road here and there, and some other pieces that I bought at estate sales. I'm sure some of it's worth a pretty penny, but I'm not in it for the money."

They fell silent again as the waiter returned and poured them each a glass of wine, leaving the bottle beside the table for them. Ian waited until the man had left to pour the contents of a small vial into his, and he swirled the contents to mix them, feeling Carl's gaze on him the entire time.

"And what is it that you do for a living?" Carl asked.

"I'm part of Ms. Evans' personal security detail," Ian said.

"I imagine that's necessary, considering what kind of people she deals with every night," he said, tasting his wine. "Probably not a bad idea to have a bodyguard on hand. You keep an eye on anyone else there?"

"My job is mainly to make sure things don't escalate if they get heated," Ian said, refusing to take the bait. "People tend to get pretty uptight when it comes to their money, and since most of her clients are on the upper end of the tax brackets, they really want to make sure that their finances are being handled the way they want them to be."

"Ian provides an extra layer of security in addition to our regular staff," Marielle said. "He and Sean also work together to assess any possible risks that our company might encounter to ensure that all transactions take place in a calm and safe environment."

"So, basically, you make sure the boss doesn't get eaten," Carl said.

"If you want to take it down to the basics, then I guess so," Ian said. "Ms. Evans isn't my only focus when I'm there, though."

226

"Slacking off and flirting with my daughter when you're on the clock?"

Marielle nearly choked on her wine, and her gaze snapped to her father. There was a smile on his face, but little humor in his calculating eyes. A glance at Ian confirmed that he hadn't missed the detail either, but his grin remained in place even as his eyes narrowed ever so slightly.

"Keeping her safe is part of the job, too," he said. "Marielle is the first point of contact for our clients, so it's probably a good thing that I'm out there near her desk when they come in for appointments."

Ian hid a smirk behind his glass as he took a sip of wine, his attention never leaving Carl. He knew the man was baiting him, but he was going to show that he could remain calm, polite even, regardless of what he had to endure.

He probably liked Carl about the same as the other liked him, and he'd only agreed to this dinner for Marielle's sake. She wanted them to at least try to find some common ground, even though it was practically nonexistent. If it made her happy to have the two most important men in her life attempt to play nice, then he'd deal with whatever her father wanted to throw at him.

It would have been nice if the meeting they'd had in the shady little motel room had made a difference, but even after Carl had taken the first shot and lived to regret it, he didn't look like he was going to change his stance anytime soon. Ian guessed that it was likely due to what he'd done for a living before retirement.

There was a lull in the conversation once their food arrived, and it was almost peaceful at the table. Tension still hung in the air between them, but no one had tried to use the flatware as a weapon yet, so the evening was going smoother than expected.

Marielle watched the two of them as she ate, wishing that she knew how to bridge the gap between them, but nothing viable came to mind. Both of them were frustratingly stubborn, and both were set in their ways. The only common thread between them was her, and she didn't like being in that position.

Once dinner and dessert were finished, Marielle could finally start to relax. Aside from a few goading remarks, her companions had been on their best behavior, and there wasn't much time left of the evening for them to cause too much trouble.

It was nice to enjoy time with both of them at the same time, and a smile had settled on her lips as she leaned back in her chair, cradling her wine glass. She cared deeply for them, thankful that they both remained a part of her life, and she silently hoped that the relative peace of this outing would continue into further gatherings.

Splitting her time between them, especially around the holidays, would put a strain on the relationships she shared with them. After all, they both held special places in her heart, and she wouldn't choose one over the other when it came to making plans. If they could make it through one night without trying to kill each other, then maybe there was hope for a happy ending after all.

*****

Trina had a vague idea of what she was walking into when she returned home. Soph had always been volatile, her emotions as unpredictable as an approaching storm. One could hope that it would pass without too much damage, but there was always a chance that it would wipe away everything in its path.

She'd seen her wife on the edge of fury before, and it was likely that Soph was in a similar state now, even if she'd had a little bit of time to calm herself. The house was still standing, and there didn't appear to be any damage to the property, but Trina braced herself as she opened the door and stepped into her home.

For a moment, she wondered if the place was empty, but she saw the half empty bottle sitting on the coffee table and realized that neither of them would have left the house with something like that out in the open. Letting the door close behind her, she took a few steps forward, listening for any signs of another's presence.

"Soph?" she called. "I'm home."

It took only a few seconds for her to receive a response, and tension eased from her shoulders when Soph came into view, a small stack of books in her arms. As much as Trina hated being away for more than a few hours at a time, returning home after being gone for a day or two never failed to remind her what was waiting for her.

Dropping the books in a pile near the sofa, Soph rushed over to her, and they shared an embrace that they both desperately needed. It was clear that she was still upset over the whole ordeal with Krysanna, but Trina was just happy to be home.

"I missed you," she said. "I'm sorry I wasn't here when you needed me."

It was all she could offer. Soph had dealt with the problem on her own, and there was no changing it now, but at least she could be there to help her through whatever happened next. As she pulled back a little, she brushed a strand of dark hair away from Soph's pale face.

"Come sit down and tell me what happened," Trina said softly.

She hated the defeated look on the other's face almost as much as she'd been concerned about walking into a mess brought on by rage, and she sat beside her with barely a glance at the books scattered on the floor.

As Soph explained the situation, Trina found herself torn between anger, frustration, and a small measure of relief. She hadn't been thrilled with the elf sharing their property, but it had made Soph happy. Without Krys in the picture, maybe things could get back to normal for them. She would love for her wife to have friends, but Soph's circle had always been incredibly small.

Something about the elf never sat right with her, though, and she couldn't quite put her finger on it. It was strange enough for Krys to show up out of nowhere, but Trina had never seen Soph take to someone that quickly. She could dismiss her thoughts as simple jealously, but there was more to it than that, and she was silently glad that she wouldn't have to deal with the winged trespasser anymore.

All she had to do now was help Soph deal with the absence. She listened calmly as her wife explained what had occurred while she was in Dallas, and her hopes started to fade when she heard the name of her colleague.

"Malice was here?" she asked.

"Twice," Soph said. "He showed up out of nowhere and took Krys with him, but then he came back today in the afternoon. No idea how the hell he got in, but he said that he wanted her stuff. I told him she can come get it herself if she wants it that badly."

"He was in our house," Trina said, scowling.

Unacceptable was too light of a word for her stance on the matter.

On a professional level, no one within the organization was supposed to know personal details about their colleagues. It was one of the main reasons why they used code names and met on neutral ground. When a group of armed, fully trained killers occupied the same area, then there was too much potential for a minor disagreement to escalate, and then someone usually wound up dead.

Personnel files were stored behind layers upon layers of security, financial and personal data was encrypted, and no one could access it without the head of the company knowing. She didn't see Malice as the type to hack into a network to find her address. Even if he had the skills to manage it, it would have taken time, and he didn't strike her as the patient type.

On a personal level, this property was supposed to be the one place in the world where she had a solid separation from her work. She could have her own life here with the woman she loved, and no matter where her assignments led her, she would know that Soph was safe.

That was gone now.

"Pack up," Trina said. "I don't want you staying her alone if I have to leave again."

Soph stared at her, shock melting into anger as she stood.

"This is our home," she said, barely holding her temper in check. "I'm not going to hide just because some overgrown fleabag broke in during the day. Not a goddamn chance in hell."

"I'm not saying that you can't take care of yourself," Trina said patiently. "I know you can, but he's had training that you haven't, and I don't want you to get hurt. We're going to be relocated when I report this anyway, so it doesn't hurt to be prepared."

"What?"

"What part wasn't clear?" Trina asked. "Malice just trampled over multiple company policies, and Mikhail isn't going to sit back and let it happen again. I might not be thrilled with my new boss, but he's still the one signing my paycheck, and it's in his best interest to make sure that we're both in a safe location that won't be compromised."

"No," Soph said. "I'm not moving. We've put too much into this place to just give it all up over this bullshit."

"We're not going to have much of a choice."

"Then don't report it," Soph said. "If you don't report it, then we won't have to leave. I can handle one stupid wolf if he shows up again."

Trina fell silent, assessing their options. She didn't want to have to start over somewhere new either, but she couldn't let her colleague think that he could trespass on their property without consequences. From what Soph had told her, when he'd left before, he'd simply vanished into the shadows, which meant that a new security system wouldn't prevent him from coming into the house again.

"How much have you learned from those books you've been reading?" she asked.

"I'm not an expert, but I've been able to pick up a few things here and there," Soph said. "The bracelet I got from Krys helped with some of the ones she brought and some of the older ones since they're not in English."

"Do you think you know enough to defend yourself if you have to?

Maybe you could see if there's anything in there that will help protect the house or stop someone from just waltzing in here whenever the hell he feels like it."

"I'll see what I can find." Soph's mood lifted somewhat. She had a distraction, one that would make her feel useful, and even though she wasn't willing to leave the matter of the elf alone, the more she learned, the more she could start planning on how to get her back.

*****

"Where do you keep going when you leave here?" Krysanna asked.

They stood in the kitchen, Alex preparing something to eat on the stove while the elf watched his every move. He hadn't replaced the microwave yet – he wanted to give it some time instead of risking another unintentional explosion – but he knew his way around the kitchen well enough. Glancing at her as he stirred the vegetables in a pan, he considered giving her an excuse.

"I'm still on the job," he said, opting for honesty. "As long as you're here, I have work to do. I'm waiting for a clear answer on what my client wants with you, and there's still the matter of the things you left at your last stop."

Her brow furrowed in thought as she processed the words, but some of them had no translation in her language, and her ring failed to provide any insight. She understood most of his response, and it brought more questions to mind.

"Your *client*?" The word was unfamiliar on her tongue, and she was sure that she'd mispronounced it, but Alex seemed to understand her meaning.

"I don't know if you think that I brought you here because of whatever bond you think we're supposed to have, but I wouldn't have even known about you if I hadn't been paid to find you," he said. "My client is the one paying for my help. That's how this works, but I'm not going to just hand you over unless I know what she wants with you. Silver seems to think that she doesn't want to hurt you, but he's just as tied up in this mess as you are, seeing as how none of you are even from this planet."

Out of the corner of his eye, he watched her step back, realization dawning on her delicate features and betrayal in her eyes.

"You're working for Lady Konistav." Her voice was barely a whisper as she shook her head in denial.

"Not directly, but that sounds about right." Turning off the stove, he turned to face her. "You're safer here than anywhere else, whether you still

231

trust me or not. Silver is going to help me collect your things, and then I'm going to call a meeting with the client. You'll be staying here the entire time, so you won't be in the line of fire if things don't go as planned."

"And if I want to leave?" Krysanna anticipated his answer even as she spoke, but she had to know how far he would go to ensure payment for his services.

"Then you're going to be disappointed," he said. "I told you when I brought you here that you'd be staying in my flat until we have everything settled. This shouldn't be a surprise."

"I trusted you."

"Now you know better," he said. "I'm not here to tell you that everything is smiles and rainbows; I'm here to do a job."

"I can escape." Defiance settled on her features, her shoulders squaring as she stared up at him.

"And I can find you wherever you hide," Alex countered. "You don't want to play that game with me, Krysanna. You won't win." Sliding some of the vegetables onto a plate, he spared her a glance. "Eat something. I'm not going to let you starve."

"I find myself suddenly not hungry," she said, backing away from him.

"Krysanna, listen to me." His patience was fading, and his demeanor had gone from casual to annoyed fast enough to make her nervous. "You can be a guest or a prisoner, your choice."

"There doesn't seem to be a difference."

"That depends on your perspective," he said. "As a guest, you have free run of my flat. You can live comfortably for as long as you're staying here, but if you choose to be a prisoner, then I'm not above locking you in a room and bringing your meals to you."

Krysanna's world began to shatter, tears stinging her eyes as she tried to find something in his voice and expression that might tell her that he had a shred of compassion. He'd been so accommodating up until now, and she couldn't find a reason why that would change without warning.

Finding nothing resembling warmth, she rushed out of the kitchen. For a second, she almost considered running out the door, but she didn't doubt that he'd be able to find her again. Instead, Krys returned to the guest bedroom and closed the door harder than she'd intended.

She'd dared to hope that she'd found a friend, someone who cared and would keep her safe, but instead, she'd fallen for another ruse. The gods had a cruel sense of humor, she thought, dropping down onto the bed. She was alone again, unable to trust anyone on this strange world, not even the wolf who she'd felt drawn to from the start.

This wasn't Zalyndrya, and whatever existed between her people and his kind did not extend beyond the borders of Evemyst, especially not as far as an alien planet. It was heartbreaking, chipping away at the little piece of solace she'd found when he'd first taken her away from the home of vampires. For a moment, she had the ridiculous thought that the Dusk Hunter he'd brought to speak with her seemed more trustworthy than Alex himself.

Alex dropped the pan back onto the stove with a curse. He hadn't wanted that conversation to happen at all, let alone in that manner, but it was for the best. There was no point in allowing himself to get close to her when his assignment could change at any moment. He would keep her out of danger, but the more he entertained personal questions, the more this arrangement would become a conflict of interest.

He eyed the vegetables with distaste, but instead of throwing them in the trash bin, he covered the plate and placed it in the refrigerator in case Krysanna came to her senses and decided to eat later. Whatever trust she had in him had been shattered, much like her trust in everyone else she'd met since her exile, and it left a sour taste in his mouth.

Guilt was an unfamiliar pill, and it twisted in his stomach as he moved through the flat and stopped to look at the closed door of the guest bedroom. Decades had passed since he'd last felt anything resembling remorse, since he'd given a damn about the look of betrayal in another's eyes.

Maybe he was getting soft. After several months without an assignment, this one was hitting him harder than it should. It wasn't the first time that he'd had to find someone and return them safely, so this shouldn't have been any different.

He almost knocked on the door, but then he withdrew his hand, doubting that the elf would want his company. He'd give her some time to calm down, and he would talk to her when he was sure that she would be willing to listen.

*****

Miria read the message for the third time, even as the intricate lettering began to fade. She was no closer to finding Krysanna than she'd been when she'd first arrived on this world, but now her orders were clear. Her stomach turned as she crumpled the scrap of parchment, and she leaned back against the headboard of the bed.

233

With the money she'd received in exchange for information, she'd purchased a room at a relatively quiet inn, and after some much-needed rest, she'd found the note pinned to her traveling pack. She'd expected the Council to instruct her to bring the missing elf back home. Maybe they would reevaluate their decision to exile her, but now, Miria knew that a pardon wouldn't be possible.

This was what she'd been training for, her final test before she joined the ranks of the Elite Guard, and she couldn't falter now. She had no choice; if she didn't complete her mission, then she faced exile as well, and all of her effort would have been for nothing.

If she failed, then they would only send someone in her place. It didn't make their decision easier to accept, though, and indecision gnawed at her. With no one to help her sort through the dilemma, she struggled to figure out what her next steps should be.

She thought that she'd been prepared for whatever they asked of her, but she never even considered the possibility that she would have to kill one of her own people. The note could have been a test, though, something to gauge how she would react to their decision, but she'd watched the council meetings plenty of times. She'd been present when they'd exiled Krysanna, and she knew that this wasn't a test.

They wanted Krysanna dead, and Miria was to be their weapon of choice.

For a brief moment, she almost wished for the company of the Dusk Hunter – Silver, he'd called himself – but she dismissed the thought immediately. He was the only one who had offered her help, and while she knew that it was for his own benefit, at least he knew her language and could offer perspective.

She must be growing desperate if her thoughts had strayed to him, of all people. A humorless laugh escaped her as her head rested back against the wooden surface, questioning her resolve. The natural course to take would be to complete her mission and return home, and as important as success was to her, she shouldn't have even given her orders a second thought.

It bothered her, though. It was one thing to face someone in battle and take a life to protect her own, but tracking down a fellow elf and killing her felt too close to outright murder, and that was something her people had always spoken against. They'd expressed time and time again that their opinions on other species, vampires especially, were because of the tendency for the others to murder without remorse, but following through would make her no better than them.

Sitting around with conflicting thoughts racing through her mind would do her no good, and she stood to leave. The evening air was warm, bringing a hint of approaching summer, and she took a deep breath. Everything was so *different* here, a sense of homesickness building in her chest, but she forced herself into motion as she left the motel behind.

Her traveling pack remained in the room; she'd only be gone for a short while. Hoping that the fresh air would help clear her head, she started walking with no destination in mind, and her thoughts roamed freely as she tried to consider the different angles of the issue.

She should have seen their decision coming, planned for it as she'd tried to plan for everything she might encounter along the way, and their verdict had been final, so she had no right to question it. Questioning the will of the Council was frowned upon, to say the least, but this was the first time they'd given her something that caused conflict with her morality.

Her steps were even, light upon the pavement, and she almost froze when she caught movement to her right, too close to be coincidental. Turning her head, she recognized the figure who had fallen into step beside her, every movement silent in answer to her own quiet footsteps.

Even as she tried to hide her surprise, she felt her pulse quicken in response to danger in such close proximity, and she could have sworn that he nearly smiled, but he had the decency not to comment. They walked in silence for a few minutes, neither willing to disrupt the peace just yet, but Miria couldn't ignore the unease building within her.

"I thought our business was finished," she said.

"I just wanted to check on you," Karian said. "You seem to be making good use of your new resources."

"You did not come out here just to have a casual conversation," Miria said, stopping as she turned to face him. "What do you want?"

It was almost frightening how he'd shown up after he'd crossed her mind earlier, and she almost wondered if he could read her thoughts. He was obviously following her, though, but she couldn't figure out how he'd managed to do so without her knowledge.

"And here I thought we were past the hostilities," he said, feigning offense. "How are you doing with your search for your friend?"

"Is that really any of your concern?"

This time, Miria clearly saw the grin that settled on his lips, and her eyes narrowed. It couldn't be a coincidence that he continued to show up the longer she spent on this world, but aside from his request for information

235

when they'd last met, she couldn't determine his motives. That alone was unsettling, almost as much as his interest in her.

She had the persistent feeling that he knew much more than what she'd told him, that perhaps he was simply playing her for a fool, but without knowing which questions to ask, she had no way of knowing why he was there. Surely, he could find some other way to occupy his time instead of wasting hers.

"It was a simple question, Miria," he said. "There's no need to be defensive."

His use of her name felt wrong, like he'd soiled a part of her that she'd never be able to clean, and she wanted him out of her sight, out of her life. It wasn't right that his kind should pretend to have morals, to actually care about the living.

She had a moment of weakness, though, and despite her dislike of him and everything he represented, her shoulders dropped in defeat. There wouldn't be much harm in asking his perspective; after all, he was a killer, so perhaps he'd have some insight that she hadn't considered yet.

"I think it might be best if I don't find her," she said quietly, turning as she started forward again. "My people want me to kill her."

Karian nodded, her words confirming his suspicions, but she seemed conflicted about it, and that was a good sign. Maybe he wouldn't have to eliminate her after all.

"You don't seem to like their decision," he said, keeping pace with her.

"I tried to understand when they exiled her, but even then, it didn't seem right," she said. Even voicing the thoughts aloud brought discomfort, and she'd never dared speak them within the borders of Evemyst. "She broke one of our laws, but no one was hurt, and she doesn't deserve to die for it."

"I assume that you can't just tell them that," he said.

"If I gave them reason to suspect that I questioned their will, then I would lose any chance that I have of joining the Elite Guard," Miria said. "They expect me to follow their orders without fail, and there will be consequences if I don't."

"Then which one is more important to you, sacrificing the morals that I think you have in order to reach your goal, or staying true to what you believe is right by refusing to murder someone who has done nothing to warrant it?"

He'd managed to articulate her exact problem, but she had no answer. She'd spent decades training for her final test, but now that she faced it, she wasn't sure if she could complete it.

"I suppose it would be useless to ask for your opinion," she said with a sigh.

"I was human once," he said. "And it wasn't very long ago, either. If you want my thoughts on the matter, then I'll answer honestly."

It couldn't hurt, she decided. If she could believe him, then maybe he could provide a human perspective, but she was well aware that she would have to take his words with a grain of salt. She didn't trust him, and she doubted that she ever would, but she would take any help that she could find.

"What would you do in my position?" she asked.

"I would consider my options first," Karian said. "Both choices have consequences, and I would have to decide which ones would be easier to accept. If this elf has done nothing wrong, and your moral compass tells you that you're not the type to kill an innocent, then she should live, but if you value ambition above your conscience, then the logical choice would be to kill her.

"Personally, I'd walk away. I made the mistake of nearly killing an innocent man, because I thought that he was holding my sister against her will, but once I learned that the situation was much different than I'd thought, I handed over the antidote to the poison that had coated my knife. I'm not going to bullshit you by telling you that I've never killed anyone who didn't deserve it, but once you cross that line, then you can't go back. You'll spend the rest of your very long life knowing that you've cut down someone who had never willingly hurt anyone."

She hadn't expected him to speak so plainly, but she was pleasantly surprised that he'd given her a chance to examine the situation from a different angle. His words rang of truth, of experience, and she was grateful for his willingness to speak on the matter.

"From the time we are young, they tell us that we cannot trust your kind," she said. "They tell us that you envy the living, that you hate that we are alive when you are not, and that envy and hatred cause you to seek nothing but our destruction. I spent three centuries with that as the only truth that I knew."

Karian stopped, unsure of where she was going with that line of thought. Her teachings were nothing new; even humans shared similar stories. When she stopped and looked up to meet his gaze, he saw the confusion written in her eyes, the conflict that was surely tearing her apart at the seams, and his expression softened.

"I don't trust you," she said. "I've never even spoken to one of your kind before I found you following me, but I don't think that the stories are entirely true. You must have your own reasons for helping me, and even if I haven't figured them out yet, I will. You've also had the opportunity to end my life on multiple occasions, but you haven't."

"I have no reason to kill you," he said. "I won't tell you that things might not change, but right now, I can't justify taking your life."

"I'm beginning to understand that," she said. "You're the only person on this world that I've spoken to on more than one occasion, but maybe that's because we share a homeland. I cannot simply forget what I've been told throughout my entire life, but I'm willing to look past that. We don't have to be enemies, Silver."

They were hardly friends, but her words surprised him, and it showed in his expression before he schooled his features back to a mask of professionalism. It was possible that they would find themselves on opposite sides in the future, but if she wanted to call a truce before the chance for violence became a reality, then he could see the potential benefits to such an arrangement.

"You're running in circles, aren't you?" he said. When she looked away, he had his answer. "Go back to your room and gather your things. You can stay with me until you figure out what you're going to do."

The surprise on her face would have made him laugh if he wasn't being serious. It would be easier for him to keep an eye on her if she were closer than Allentown, and she wouldn't be out here on her own without even a clue as to where to search. It was a mutually beneficial suggestion.

"Why?" she asked.

"Would you rather wander around a place you don't know without anyone to help you?"

"Why would you help me?" she pressed. "I could understand our previous trade, but how would you benefit from this arrangement?"

"Maybe I'm just feeling generous," he said with a shrug.

She shot him a skeptical look, a delicate brow arching at the grin he offered in response. Trusting him was dangerous, potentially deadly, but she couldn't deny that having someone on her side on this world would be nice. If he wanted to take her suggestion for peace seriously and extend an offer of peace, then the benefits might outweigh the risks.

"I haven't tried to hurt you," he reminded her. "Give me a chance to show you that not everyone with my condition is a heartless beast."

His terminology gave her pause, and she regarded him for a moment.

238

Her people had never spoken of the people who had become monsters, of the lives they'd led before darkness had taken them, and it made it easy to see them as mindless killers. Silver was the first one she'd met, and he'd given her reason to question the things that she'd been certain of throughout her life. He spoke of it as if it were an ailment, something that he hadn't chosen, but that didn't make him any less of a killer.

Once again, she found herself torn by indecision, but this time, it was a matter of her own safety that was called into question. She was lost with no clear path to her goal, and Silver was making her an offer that seemed too good to be true. Even with the danger he presented, she was making no progress on her own, but maybe a chance to face her challenge with someone at her side would help her figure out what she should do.

There would be a price; she wasn't going to pretend that he wouldn't ask for something in return at some point. She only hoped that she would be able to pay it when the time came.

"Very well," she said.

The walk back to the motel was quiet, giving Miria a chance to reevaluate her decision. The occasional car and her own footsteps were the only things that broke the silence, and the lack of sound from her companion's movements chipped away at her nerves. It was a steady reminder that she could not allow her guard to drop in his presence, regardless of how friendly he might be for the moment.

They parted ways at her door, and she waiting until he was out of sight before she stepped inside, giving the room a sweeping glance. She could stay here, try to complete her mission on her own, or she could accept the help of someone who could kill her at any time. She'd already made her choice, though, and trepidation brought tension to her shoulders as she quickly repacked her bag.

Silver was waiting for her outside, leaning against a machine of metal and chrome, his arms folded over his chest. It wasn't the same type of vehicle she'd ridden in when she'd accepted a ride from the human woman, but it looked less confining.

"Go check out while I take care of your pack," he said.

Handing over her bag, Miria gave him a long look before heading towards the office to return her key. When she returned, Silver had secured it to the back of his vehicle, and he handed her a rounded helmet. She turned it over in her hands, examining the smooth surface. It certainly wouldn't be fit for battle, and she glanced up at him.

"It will protect your head if we have any trouble," he said. "You'll need that more than I will."

She flinched when he started the engine, but she hesitated only a moment before she slipped the helmet over her head and climbed on behind him. The motorcycle rumbled beneath her, and she met his gaze when he turned his head to regard her.

"Hold on tight," he said. "I drive fast, and I want to make it to Philadelphia quickly."

As he backed out of the parking space, she reluctantly wrapped her arms around him. She wasn't fond of this position, but if it kept her from falling off the back of his vehicle along the way, then she would accept her situation.

It was akin to riding behind someone on a horse, and she wondered if that was why he'd chosen this method of transportation instead of the enclosed ones that she'd seen more frequently. Once they reached the highway, her grip tightened, and she wasn't sure if she felt him laugh or if it was just the way the bike moved beneath them.

When she finally dared to look up, she saw distant lights reaching towards the sky, and her eyes widened. She wasn't sure how long they'd been traveling, but they grew closer to the city quickly, and he only slowed down once they were in the heart of the towering buildings.

Miria had more questions than she could voice at once, and with the wind still whipping through her clothes, she had to keep them to herself. It was the first human city she'd seen on this world, and while it was far different than the cities of Evemyst, the towers of glass and metal were breathtaking.

By the time Karian had pulled into an underground garage, Miria could barely contain her excitement. All of her training was forgotten as she took off her helmet and jumped off of the bike, and she nearly raced back out of the garage before she managed to restrain herself.

"What is this place?" she asked.

"Philadelphia," Karian said, suppressing a laugh. "They call it the City of Brotherly Love. It's not a bad place to live once you get used to the constant noise. It's quite a change from Zalyndrya, isn't it?"

"And you live here?" Disbelief was clear in her voice, and she thought she saw a genuine smile grace his lips as he killed the engine and stepped off the bike.

"It seemed as good a place as any," he said. He untied her bag from the back of the bike and started towards one side of the garage. "I plan on taking the stairs, but the elevator will get you there faster. Twenty-six flights of stairs won't bother me." Seeing her confusion, he shouldered her pack and turned to face her. "The elevator is a device that will carry you up to your preferred level of the building. The walk can be a bit much for some."

"I'll walk," she said.

She regretted her words as the stairs seemed to go on forever. A glance at the wall when they passed yet another door provided no insight, the characters foreign and useless to her. Her legs burned, but she refused to voice any complaint. She was a warrior, and she would not show weakness in front of anyone.

"We're almost there," Karian said.

Relief flooded her when he finally opened one of the doors, leading them into a corridor. A few more steps brought them to yet another door, and he unlocked it so that she could enter.

Karian flipped on the light as an afterthought, remembering that she would need it more than he would, and he watched her expressions change as she took in the interior of his home. His salary had afforded him a penthouse condo in the heart of the city, and he'd chosen the furniture carefully for both appearance and functionality.

On one wall of the living room was a half-finished mural, something that he toyed with during his spare time in between assignments, and he set her bag down beside the door as he motioned her to follow him further into the room. Across the room, two sliding glass doors led to the balcony, and he glanced over his shoulder as he stepped outside.

"You'll want to see this," he said.

Her initial distrust had faded into memory as she followed him out onto the balcony, and her hands gripped the railing as she took in the view. Below them, the park of Rittenhouse Square caught her attention first, followed by the buildings that surrounded him when she looked around.

Never had Miria imagined such a place could exist, and as cars moved on the streets below them, she wondered what it would be like to live here. Reality brought her back to the present, though, and she took a step back. This was temporary; she couldn't stay here indefinitely.

"I'll show you to your room."

Karian broke the silence again, and she followed him inside so that he could slide the door closed again. A small corridor revealed several doors, and he stopped in front of them as he opened it, motioning her inside. "You can rest in here. I'll ask my sister to bring some regular food over for you in the morning. Just so that you're prepared, I have a security system in place to keep me safe during the day, so don't panic when the windows and

241

door are covered once dawn arrives."

Miria watched him walk away, her mind piecing together the strange events of the night. It made little sense that she would willingly find herself keeping company with him, but she was grateful for his generosity. His words brought another concern to mind, though; come dawn, she would be trapped inside his home with no escape.

Eighteen

Krysanna waited until the sound of footsteps faded, sitting up on the bed as she watched the door just in case he decided to try again. She was tired of running, but she couldn't trust him, and she couldn't stay in his flat much longer.

His words echoed in her mind – she had no doubt that he'd try to find her – and she stood and began to pace. There had to be a way out, a way to escape without him noticing her departure, but his senses were sharp. She couldn't very well just walk out the front door, especially since she knew nothing of this city.

Stopping in her tracks, an idea came to mind, one that might just give her a way out of this situation. The spell that had brought her to this world was still fresh, the words embedded in her thoughts, and she caught her lower lip between her teeth.

A knock on the door pulled her from her thoughts, and she jumped, startled by the sound. Remaining in place, Krysanna held her breath, hoping that he would simply leave, but when another knock accompanied a call of her name, she knew that she was running out of time.

"Krys, open the door. We need to talk."

She didn't want to talk. She didn't want to see him or hear his voice, but the longer she tried to ignore him, the more persistent he became. It would only be a matter of time before he opened the door without an invitation.

Closing her eyes, she blocked out the noise, allowing it to fade into the background as soundless syllables fell from her lips. Magic tingled along her skin, its familiarity wrapping her in warmth, and she opened her eyes again to catch a brief glimpse of him before the room around her vanished.

Her new surroundings came into focus, but despite the sunlight filtering at the edges of sturdy curtains, the room was shrouded in darkness. It only took a second for her to recognize the same place she'd appeared when she first left Zalyndrya, fear spiking as she looked around quickly. She heard nothing to indicate that the residence was occupied, but she felt no desire to remain there.

Turning towards the drapes covering the sliding glass doors, she rushed across the living room, reaching out to pull them aside. A cool hand closed around her wrist just as her fingertips brushed against fabric, and Krysanna bit back a scream as she tried to break free from the unyielding grip.

"*Don't scream.*"

She trembled at the voice, hot tears stinging her eyes, but she didn't dare disobey. Every mistake she'd made came rushing back to the forefront of her mind, bringing her to the present where she was trapped in the grasp of the reason she'd fled her own world.

Lothan Konistav, the Emperor of Zalyndrya and the source of her deepest fears, held her firmly, and he guided her away from the curtains. Resistance would be useless, likely bringing about the end of her life quickly, but she couldn't hide the way her body shook as she tried not to trip when he led her to one of the sofas.

"*Sit,*" he said. "*You've caused quite a bit of trouble, little one.*" Thankfully, he took a seat on the adjacent sofa instead of right beside her, and once he turned on the dim light on the end table, his features came into focus. "*If you decide to speak, be quiet about it. I'd rather not wake my wife just yet.*"

Krys said nothing, her breath coming far too quickly as she edged further away from him. If only she could turn back time, she would have opened the door in that London flat and listened to whatever Alex had to say. Instead, her attempt at escape had led her to the very one who'd caused her to run in the first place.

"*Abnalia has been beside herself with worry.*" His voice was stern, but he gave no indication that he intended to move closer. "*We even enlisted the aid of one of our associates to find you. I must say, I didn't expect you to just drop right into my hands like this.*"

"*Please, just let me go.*" Her voice was barely a whisper, broken by ragged breaths as she fought back her tears. "*I won't cause you any more trouble, I swear. Tell my cousin that I am safe, and you won't have to worry about seeing my ever again.*"

"*It's not that simple,*" Lothan said. "*You have something that is not yours, and there will be no agreements until you return it.*"

Of course, things were never as simple as she would like. She paled at his words, lowering her gaze as they sealed her fate. He would demand an answer if she remained silent, but it took every ounce of willpower she possessed to speak.

"*I don't have it.*" She squeezed her eyes shut, waiting for the inevitable. If she couldn't provide what he wanted, then she was of no use to him. "*I left it behind when I ran.*"

Lothan watched her, his expression softening despite his displeasure. The poor girl was terrified, and he worried for the thoughts that were plaguing her. Judging by her posture, he wondered what he had done to give her the impression that he would take her life over a misplaced book, but then he recalled the night she'd left the castle.

With a sigh, he leaned back against the cushions, searching for words that might put her at ease but finding none. Lalasa was better at this sort of thing than he was, but he stood by his decision to let her rest.

"*I'm not going to hurt you, Krysanna,*" he said. "*I never intended for you to see me when I returned from the dungeons, but whatever opinions you hold regarding that night, remember that not once have I done anything to you that would give you a reason to fear me.*"

"*You're a Dusk Hunter,*" she said, pulling her knees up to her chest. "*You kill for your own survival, and whether or not you wanted me to see evidence of that, I did. How can you expect me to ignore that?*"

The boldness of her words surprised them both, and he watched her eyes widen even as a hint of a grin began to form on his lips.

"*I'm not asking you to ignore that,*" he said. "*Simply consider that we offered you a safe place to stay. You are under no obligation to explain your decision to leave, and once this matter is settled, then you can go along your way, but until this book is found, I'm going to have to keep an eye on you.*"

Lothan had a feeling that she knew exactly where she'd misplaced it, but Krysanna seemed to have no intention of revealing that knowledge. It was a delicate situation; he couldn't just allow her to leave, but if he kept her here, then they would accomplish nothing. Going with her, especially during the day, was out of the question.

Frustration began to build inside of him, but as he watched her, he understood that his own annoyance was nothing compared to the terror she must have felt at that moment. Leaning forward, he rested his elbows on his knees, letting out a deep sigh.

"*I can only give you so many assurances that you will come to no harm in my presence,*" he said. "*I'm not going to force you to stay here, but consider your own safety if you walk out that door. There are many things about Earth that you have yet to learn, and should the humans discover your presence, your troubles will only be beginning."*

Krysanna lifted her gaze to meet his, fighting down the urge to bolt as soon as he confirmed that she wouldn't be his prisoner. His warning was enough for her to wait, to hear him out before leaving. The humans on this world were not like the ones on Zalyndrya; these humans were unaware that they were not alone in society.

She jumped at the sound of a door opening, her attention turning towards the sound, and she curled in on herself when she saw the empress emerge from one of the other rooms. Surely, Lalasa would be angry with her, and even if Lothan had tried to maintain peace, his wife had reason to react differently.

"Krysanna? Thank the gods, you're alright."

The speed in which Lalasa moved to cross the room had the elf trembling again, fear rolling off of her in waves, and her heart threatened to escape her chest. She didn't quite register what had been said, but the way Lalasa's expression shifted from frantic worry to gentle concern told her that she wasn't about to face retribution.

Lalasa stepped back to give her some space, moving to sit beside Lothan, but her focus remained on Krysanna. It pained her to see the discomfort in the girl's posture, the way her wings had wrapped around herself defensively, but she would keep her distance if it would help.

"I want to leave," Krys said, lowering her gaze again.

"Where will you go?" Lalasa's voice was soft, but she had to ask. *"At least allow us to find you someone to stay with you and teach you the things you need to know about this world."*

"Someone like yourselves?" She didn't intend the words to come out as harsh as they did, but she looked at them without regret. *"Or someone you've paid to find me? I trusted him, and then he told me the truth."* Gathering her courage, Krysanna stood, her wings folding over her back. *"I can find my way on my own. I'll find your book, and then we will part ways."*

"I'm not concerned about the book," Lalasa said. *"We hired him only to locate you, not to take you in, but you're not safe out there on your own."*

"I'm not a child!" Krysanna shouted, her small hands closing into fists. *"I've seen two hundred and seventy-nine summers. I'm not a helpless youth who cannot survive without your help."*

"No, you're not," Lothan said, standing. Even with the small distance between them, he towered over her, but his voice was calm when he spoke. *"We do not doubt your ability to protect yourself, but that will only take you so far. The humans of this world are not prepared to face differences even among themselves, and our concern is for how they would act should they discover you.*"

Krysanna was torn by the truth of his words. She wanted nothing to do with the two of them, but what would she do if the people of this world tried to capture her? As different as she looked compared to them, it was likely that she would become as much of a prisoner here as she would have been had she remained in London, perhaps worse.

Lalasa stood as well, but she didn't move forward. From her pocket, she withdrew a small, silver chain, a warm smile settling on her lips.

"*May I approach?*" she asked.

It was a strange request, Krys thought. To hear the empress ask permission was unexpected, but she found herself nodding even as she tensed.

Slowly this time, Lalasa closed the distance, carefully taking the elf's hand to guide it up before clasping the bracelet around her wrist. Krysanna stared at her in confusion before Lalasa motioned behind her, and as she turned her head, she saw her wings begin to fade until no trace of them remained.

She couldn't even feel their presence anymore, and her eyes flicked between the bracelet and the woman before her.

"*This will only hide them,*" Lalasa said. "*When you remove it, they'll be visible again, but it should help you remain unnoticed in your travels.*" She stepped back again. "*If you need a place to stay, our daughter lives not too far from here. She's human, and she'll gladly take you in should you ask.*"

*****

"What the hell do you mean, you *lost* her?" Karian snapped into the phone. "You're supposed to be the best at finding people, so what happened?"

Miria overheard his side of the conversation as she peeked out into the hallway. She heard no one else speaking, and she wondered if he was simply talking to himself in the other room. As she crept towards the living room, she heard him speaking again.

"Everything's handled on my end. I'll make some calls in case anyone has seen her around here. It'll be difficult for her to blend in with the crowd." He paused, apparently listening to something only he could hear. "I wouldn't. He doesn't need to know every little detail along the way."

Glancing around the corner, she watched him pull a rectangular device away from his ear, setting it aside as he picked up a paint palette instead. Bits of color speckled his pale skin, his shirt discarded on the sofa,

247

and he moved the brush with precise strokes against the wall. The first hints of a picture were beginning to form, a vague shadows of a landscape, and she took a few steps into the room.

"Is there someone else here?" she asked, glancing around and seeing no one but him.

"Phone call," he said, adding one more detail to his project before setting his paints aside and turning to face her. "I'll explain later."

His response only confused her further, but the promise of answers kept her silent. Miria's gaze moved from him to the painting on the wall, marveling at the skill of his art. To think that a creature who survived on the lives of others could create something of beauty was unimaginable, and even with the evidence before her, she found it difficult to understand this new reality.

Her people had spoken of his kind as nothing more than heartless monsters, beasts that would gladly kill anyone simply for the pleasure of causing pain, and yet the man before her had dismissed several opportunities to harm her. She wasn't foolish enough to think that he was kind and innocent; by his very nature, he had to find some way to keep himself alive at the expense of others. He'd offered her sanctuary, though, and while her first thoughts were that this would be a trap, the vampire had made no move to even approach her, let alone torture her for information.

"Are you hungry?" he asked. Gathering his supplies, he turned, glancing at her before he started towards the kitchen. "My sister should be here any minute."

"A little bit," she admitted. Miria trailed behind him, keeping a couple of paces between them.

She stopped in the doorway, watching as he pulled a bottle from the fridge and twisted off the cap. The moment he brought it to his lips, she knew what it contained, but she managed to hide her revulsion as she swallowed thickly. A knock at the door drew her attention, her muscles tensing as she turned towards the sound.

"That would be Cass," Karian said, walking past her.

Miria remained in place, apprehension coiling into a knot in the pit of her stomach, but one glance at the metal barriers over the window as the one over the door slid open gave her at least a tiny sliver of information – his sister wasn't like him. To her credit, the elf resisted the urge to reach for a weapon; vampire or not, the addition of another stranger could leave her facing two adversaries if things went sour.

"Thank you for coming," Karian said, stepping aside for the woman to enter. "I know it was short notice, but you know how quickly things can change."

The elf regarded the stranger with guarded curiosity, noting the similarities between the siblings, as well as the differences. Cassandra was very much alive, as evidenced by the sun-kissed tan of her skin and the way she carried herself. She wasn't a predator like her brother, but that made her no less dangerous as far as Miria was concerned.

Both sets of green eyes settled on her, and the elf nearly took a step back from their attention. She felt exposed, vulnerable, and defenseless, but she squared her shoulders and stepped forward instead. There was no chance that she would show any indication that she was intimidated. Miria was a warrior, and she would conduct herself as such.

"You must be Miria," Cassandra said. Her smile was gentle and disarming, her expression warm, and the elf felt a little more at ease.

Miria only nodded, but she stepped forward with a silent offer to take some of the bags in the woman's hands. Her expression betrayed nothing of her thoughts as she glanced between the pair again, dozens of questions coming to mind that she didn't dare voice. Her situation was uncertain at best, and although neither of them had threatened her, she knew better than to trust them completely.

"Any news?" Cassandra asked, her attention on her brother.

"Malice lost the other one," Karian said. "He thinks she's coming to Philly, which means it's possible that she'll run into the Konistavs or Duchess' wife. I don't need to tell you which one is preferable." His twin nodded in understanding. "I have more pressing matters to deal with right now, though. I'll explain while I'm fixing something for Miria to eat."

Taking the remaining bags, he headed into the kitchen, sorting through the contents before settling on a few ingredients. He was quiet as he started cooking, but once everything was where he needed it to be, he spoke again.

"Miria was sent to retrieve or kill Krysanna," he said. "It seems that her people have decided on the latter, and they've outlined consequences if she doesn't handle this."

"They'll execute me if I fail," Miria said. "Even if I don't believe that she deserves death."

"I have an idea on how to make this work," Karian said, glancing at his sister. "But we'll need your help."

Nineteen

She couldn't quite place it, but something was odd about the way that they were allowing her to simply leave on her own. Krysanna hesitated at the door, glancing down at the bracelet on her wrist with her brow furrowed in thought. There had to be more to the seemingly plain piece of jewelry than the single enchantment that Lalasa had told her, but she wasn't about to spend more time in their presence than absolutely necessary.

With one last glance over her shoulder, she opened the door and stepped out into the hallway, every nerve on edge as she started towards the set of closed doors to her left. She made it about halfway there when she heard the door open behind her, and she froze in her tracks as her muscles tensed. It was foolish to think that she was free.

"I won't keep you very long," Lothan said, slowly approaching her. He stopped several paces away, giving her some space, and he waited a moment to see if she would wait or flee. "Would you talk with me for a moment?"

"Do I have a choice?" Krys tried not to sound bitter.

"There's always a choice."

Her shoulders dropped as she slowly turned to face him, swallowing thickly as she looked up at him. Even if he were human, she'd have little chance of besting him in battle without the use of her magic, and even then, she'd likely call upon her knowledge to escape rather than fight.

"I'm not going to hurt you," he assured her.

"How can I believe you?" Her voice sounded small, even to herself, and she couldn't hide the fear that crept into her words. "I saw you. The night I left, I saw what you did in the dungeons. I know that you're a Dusk Hunter, that you kill to keep yourself alive. Why would you spare my life when it was so easy for you to take the life of that prisoner?"

251

"There are rules," he said, trying to keep his voice as gentle as possible. She seemed like she was on the verge of running again, and the last thing he wanted was for them to part ways with her fearing him. "We're not permitted to harm innocents, Krysanna, which means that you're safe from us. Your only crime was borrowing something that wasn't yours, and you're going to rectify that. I have no reason to hurt you."

She remained unconvinced, unsure of what to believe. On the one hand, he'd had ample opportunity to hurt her, and he'd shown nothing than hospitality, but on the other hand, she'd seen him kill, and that image still haunted her nightmares.

"I'm afraid," she admitted quietly.

"I know," he said. "But sooner or later, you have to stop running from your fears. There are people who are willing and able to help you, and you can't keep shying away from them simply because they're not perfect. Things are different on this world, and I worry that you're ill prepared to handle the challenges you'll face alone."

That gave her pause, and Krysanna studied him for a moment. While she questioned his motives, his concern felt sincere. She was terrified of heading back out into this world alone, but she had little choice in the matter.

"The first person I trusted here turned out to be a Dusk Hunter, and the second one only helped me because you paid him," she said.

"I can't speak for the first one, but Malice was only paid to find you. He took you in and protected you on his own."

Her eyes widened at the revelation, and guilt settled in the pit of her stomach. Perhaps Lothan was right; she had been quick to judge instead of giving Alex the benefit of the doubt, and now he was no doubt searching for her.

"Can you get a message to him?" she asked.

"I can try."

"If you can, tell him that I will be where he found me last time. I must go."

"Be safe out there, Krysanna," Lothan said, taking a slow step towards her. When she didn't immediately retreat, he pulled a slip of paper from his pocket. "I have full confidence that he can find you again, and when he does, ask him to show you how to use a phone." Holding out the paper, he took another step forward. "Our daughter is human, and she lives not too far from here. If you ever need anything, she'll know how to help."

Krys hesitated for a moment before taking a tentative step closer, and she moved only close enough to accept the slip of paper. The numbers

252

meant nothing to her, but she didn't dare question him further. Her outburst only moments ago had tempted fate enough for one day.

She managed a quiet *thank you* before retreating several steps again, unwilling to remain close to him, but Lothan didn't seem offended by her actions. He didn't attempt to move closer to her again, and silence stretched between them for several long seconds.

Again, she wanted to leave, but there was something still unsaid, something that nagged at her, and Krys bit her lower lip as she tried to figure out how best to phrase her thoughts.

"Do all Dusk Hunters follow the same rules?" she asked.

"No," Lothan said. "My wife and I are bound to certain guidelines, but I haven't met any others of our kind who have to follow them. Some do, simply because they feel it's the best way to handle their situation, but others take their meals wherever they can." He paused, considering something for a moment. "If you ever wish to return to Zalyndrya, you're still more than welcome to stay at the castle. You have my word that no one there would harm you."

"Thank you for the offer, but I don't know if I could stay there again," she said honestly. "To be quite honest, I'm afraid of you, and while you seem kind right now, I know more than I should."

"Fair enough. Just know that you have a home if you find yourself lost."

She offered a nod before backing away, turning only when she neared the doors. Ignoring the buttons on the wall, she pushed open the door with the picture of stairs beside it, and she started heading up instead of towards the downstairs exit. Krys knew the way by flight, but not by road.

It took some creativity, and a little bit of magic, but she managed to open the door to the roof without setting off an alarm, and she hurried to the edge as she pulled off the bracelet. Slipping it into her pocket, she stretched her wings behind her, feeling the breeze ruffle the feathers, and she stepped off to catch the wind currents.

Sunset was approaching, and part of her wished that Soph might still be asleep. It would be easier to slip inside and retrieve her belongings than to hold an awkward conversation with a potentially unhappy vampire. She shivered as her wings carried her out of the city, but she told herself it was the chill of the wind and not the possibility of facing Soph again.

She'd taken Lothan's words to heart, though. Perhaps she'd been too quick to judge, too quick to make rash decisions, and too quick to turn away from someone who hadn't threatened her even once during her short stay at the house. If Soph followed at least some form of morals, then maybe Krys wouldn't be in danger in her presence. Trina was a wild card, though. The elf couldn't get a good read on the other woman, but she hadn't seemed thrilled with Krysanna's previous arrival at their home.

Shaking her head slightly, she pushed those thoughts aside as the sun dipped below the horizon. The woods below her were familiar, and it took only a little longer for the property to come into view. She began her descent carefully, avoiding the last few trees in her path before she landed on the ledge of the tree house.

The lights were on inside the house, and a chill went up her spine. Despite her desire to give Soph the benefit of the doubt, she couldn't dismiss the reality ahead of her. Soph could easily kill her and keep her possessions, and there would be little that the elf could do about it. Taking a deep breath, she spread her wings again and glided down to the grass, and she steeled her resolve as she started towards the house.

*****

Karian set his paint brushes aside, glancing towards the doors to the balcony as the steel barriers covering them lifted. With dusk spreading shadows across the city, it was time to return to work, and he started towards the kitchen to clean his supplies. Flecks of paint speckled the pale skin of his chest, but a quick shower would remove most, if not all, of it.

A knock sounded on the door when he was halfway to the kitchen, and he set his supplies down on the dining room table as he shot a glance at Miria. With a quick motion for her to retreat to one of the bedrooms, he grabbed the pistol hidden beneath the table and stalked towards the door.

Glancing through the peephole, he swore under his breath, and he considered not answering it at all. His uninvited visitor would know that he was home, though, and he held the pistol at his side as he tapped a code on the keypad to unlock the door.

"What do you want, Lothan?" It was all the greeting he was willing to offer as he looked up at him.

"I need a favor," Lothan said. "May I come in?"

"This should be good," Karian muttered, stepping aside. He glanced out in the hall to see if anyone had followed and then closed the door, locking it again.

"You have a way to contact your colleague Malice, correct?"

"Why?" Instantly suspicious, Karian set the pistol aside and folded his arms over his chest.

"I have a message for him from Krysanna." Dark blue eyes shifted

254

away from him, glancing past at the figure at the edge of the short hallway. "And who is this?"

"She's not your concern," Karian said as he moved to stand between them. "Let's hear this message."

"If she is who I think she is, then she damn well is my concern," Lothan said. His demeanor changed, his casual tone changing as it grew firm. "Evemyst sent her after Krysanna, and you've been hiding her in your own home. Whose side are you on, Karian?"

"I'm on the side that pays me," he snapped. "My job was to keep them apart, and as long as I know where Miria is, then I'm doing my job. I have the situation under control."

"You'd better know what you're doing, Traveler." Shaking his head, his gaze then returned to the younger vampire. "Tell Malice that he'll find his elf in the same place he found her last time."

Lothan gave Miria one last look before turning to leave, and once the door closed behind him, Karian swore again. He hated dealing with the emperor, but sometimes, he realized, he couldn't avoid it. It was unfortunate, but then again, so was his entire situation. All he could do was deal with it and keep moving forward.

"It's alright," he assured her. "Lothan isn't going to get any more involved than he already is."

Miria stepped out of the hallway, studying Silver – no, Karian – in a different light. She'd learned more about him in the past few minutes than she had in the entire time she'd spent with him. He was understandably secretive, and perhaps his past wasn't any of her business, but she couldn't help the curiosity and the questions that came from the exchange.

"Was that...?" she asked, unsure of how to finish the question.

"Lothan Konistav," he said. "The Emperor of Zalyndrya, and a complete asshole."

The bad blood between them was obvious, but Miria had never expected to witness someone speak to the emperor so boldly without consequence. There had to be more to their ties than she was willing to ask.

"I need to shower, and then we'll put our plan in motion," he said, changing the subject. "There's food in the refrigerator if you're hungry. I won't be long."

*****

"Understood. I'm there now."

Alex slid his phone back into his pocket as he approached the door. He was tempted to use the shadows and make himself at home, but if Krys

255

was inside, then she could be in danger. To his displeasure, he was forced to use more conventional means to gain entry, and he knocked on the door before taking a step back to wait.

As the door opened, Soph took one look at him and started to close it right in his face, but his foot stopped it from closing completely.

"I'm not in the mood for your shit tonight," she said.

"Well, isn't that unfortunate," he said with a grin. "Where is she?"

"The hell are you talking about?"

"Krysanna," he said, holding his hand out. "About this tall, blonde, has wings. Don't tell me you've forgotten her already."

"I know who she is. She ain't here."

"My sources tell me otherwise."

"You might want to check your sources, then. Now piss off."

"Listen, Sophia, we can do this one of two ways. If she isn't here now, she will be shortly. So, you can either open the door and we'll wait for her, or I can come in anyway and collect her things." His grin faded as he grew serious. "She's pissed at me and terrified of you, so as much as I enjoy this game, we're going to have to put it aside for now."

She hated to admit it, but he had a point. Soph wasn't thrilled about having him in her house, but it made more sense for him to wait inside instead of out of the front porch, especially if Krys was upset with him.

"What did you do?" she asked, finally opening the door fully for him to enter. "She doesn't seem the type to get pissed at anyone easily."

"Now, that is none of your business."

Rolling her eyes, she closed the door and led him into the living room. It wasn't long before another knock sounded, and Alex stayed back as she went to answer it.

She could see the fear in those sunset eyes, although Soph had to admit that Krys was holding herself together pretty well. She felt bad for the elf, and her expression softened as she moved aside with a gesture for her to enter.

"Your friend is here, too," Soph said. "You, um, want to come in?"

Krys nodded once but hesitated before she stepped inside. She'd been welcome in this house before, and nothing had changed except that now she knew what inhabited it. Knowing that Alex was there made her feel a little better, but it didn't completely erase her unease.

As she stepped into the living room, she could feel his gaze upon her, but she couldn't meet it. She'd wronged both of them, but she didn't know how to make it right.

"My apologies," she said quietly, staring down at her hands. "I suppose I'm better at running than listening. Soph, I shouldn't have left the way that I did. I should have given you a chance to talk instead of leaving. And Alex, you did not have to do half of what you have done for me, but you did anyway, and for that, I am grateful."

Silence fell around them, and Krys finally looked up at them. She saw no anger in either of their expressions, and relief washed over her. At least they didn't seem angry with her. Even with Alex's neutral demeanor, she could see the concern in his eyes, and Soph simply seemed relieved that she was there with them.

"I'm not here to catch up, though," she continued. "Soph, I need some of my belongings back, or at least one book in particular. It was not mine to give, and I must return it to its rightful owner."

Soph said nothing, but turned to head upstairs, returning a few minutes later with Krysanna's traveling pack and bow. With a sigh, she handed them over, and she glanced at Alex for a moment before she took a step back.

"It's all there," she said. "I made some copies of some of the stuff in those books just in case you came back for them." Her gaze lifted to regard Alex again. "I know we don't like each other, but I have a favor to ask."

"I never said I didn't like you," he said with a shrug. "It's just too easy and amusing to get a reaction out of you. What's this favor of yours?"

"I'm tired of Trina being away all the time, but I don't want her to be the one to talk to Mikhail. I thought that maybe you could put in a word for me so maybe I'll be able to go with her on some of these trips she takes."

"So you want in," he said. "I'll see what I can do. The lad will probably call another meeting sooner rather than later. Show up and act like an adult and he might be willing to hear you out."

He glanced down at Krys, and he could tell that she was ready to leave. With a nod to Soph, he placed a hand on the elf's back and guided her towards the door. He waited until she'd stepped outside to glance at Soph one last time.

"You'll keep her safe, right?" she asked. "You won't let nothing bad happen to her?"

"Anyone who wants to hurt her will have to go through me first," he assured her. "And because I'm so nice, I won't even slash your tires this time."

"Wow, thanks," Soph said, fighting down a laugh. "I feel like shit that she's scared of me now, but maybe she'll come around someday." Looking

257

past him, she called out through the open door. "Hey, Krys! Don't be a stranger, okay?"

*****

Miria ran through the woods, glancing back over her shoulder every few seconds. She couldn't hear any signs of pursuit, but that didn't mean that she wasn't being followed. Her breath came in gasps when she finally stopped, and she looked around quickly before rummaging through her bag for a small gem.

Placing it on the ground, she whispered a few words, her impatience clear as she waited for the enchantment to activate. She straightened when an image began to form above the gem, and her expression was one of relief when the view of the Council became clear.

"I don't have long," she said, trying to catch her breath. "I've been discovered, and I'm certain that I was followed. There are Dusk Hunters on this world, and they are everything we've been taught to fear. One has been chasing me for the past few nights."

"What of Krysanna Owlwhisper?"

"I believe he's already killed her." Miria turned her head to examine the tree line. "Please, bring me home before he finds me again."

"It's funny how you thought you could keep evading me," a voice said behind her.

Miria froze, her eyes widening. She couldn't tell whether her heart was racing from exertion or fear, but she knew what those words meant.

"You had to know that I'd eventually grow bored of toying with you," Karian said, stepping out from behind a nearby tree. "It's over, elf. You can't run from me."

There was still a chance that someone on the Council could summon her home, but they seemed just as frozen as she was. She doubted that any of them had ever dealt with a vampire in their lives, and yet she stood there with one closing the distance between them.

"How fitting that we have an audience," Karian mused. "I hope I didn't ruin your plans by killing the other one, but elven blood is impossible to find on this world."

In one swift motion, he was beside her, green eyes taking on a deadly glow as his grin revealed the tips of razor-sharp fangs.

Turning her back around to face the image of the Council, he wrapped one arm around her to pin her arms at her sides. His other hand came up to her head to tip it to the side. Karian expected her to fight back, regardless of their agreement, especially since the terror she displayed was all

258

too real. Miria seemed frozen in place, her eyes pleading with the spectators to do something, anything that might save her life.

With his gaze locked on the image of the Council, his teeth pierced the tender flesh of her throat, and hot liquid filled his mouth. It was then that Miria started to struggle, but his unyielding grip held her in place. Karian drank quickly, although part of him wanted to savor the sweet taste, and her attempts to break free ceased as she grew weaker.

Once he was finished, he dropped her limp form to the ground, and he stepped over her to crush the gem beneath his boot. The image of the Council vanished, and he turned to scan the trees around him as he dropped to a knee beside Miria. Her heartbeat was weak and her breathing shallow, but she was still alive.

"Cassandra!" he called out, reaching out to check the elf's pulse. "We need you!"

Twenty

"What will happen to me now?" Krys asked. She was seated on a bench beside Alex in the middle of Rittenhouse Square, waiting for the Konistavs to arrive. It was difficult to sit still, her fingers fidgeting from nerves and unease, but she refused to run anymore. The bracelet on her wrist hid her wings, and to any passerby, she could pass for human.

"Isn't that up to you?" Alex said. "You can still return to your own world, right? You can still go home."

"I'm not going back." She shook her head, her voice firm. "I can't go back to Evemyst, and I do not feel safe at the castle anymore."

"What happened in Evemyst?"

Krysanna looked up at him, unsure of how to respond. She wanted to tell him, but what if he didn't understand? What if he blamed her just as her tutor and the Council had? Taking a deep breath, she looked down, and she folded her hands in her lap.

"The laws in Evemyst are strict when it comes to magic," she said. "It is forbidden to permanently alter your appearance, with the exception of imbuing tattoos. I had asked my tutor for a spell that would give the illusion of wings, but he gave me the wrong one, and the ones I have are no illusion. He denied it when I was brought before the Council, and since he is of a higher standing than I am, they believed him without question."

"So, they sent you packing," Alex said.

She nodded, not meeting his gaze. The betrayal still stung. Krys had trusted her tutor, had followed all of his instructions to the letter, and then when he turned on her, she was left questioning everything she'd ever known about him. Still, it was in her nature to trust others until they proved themselves undeserving, and even then, she believed in second chances.

261

"Come back to London with me," he said. "I still have the spare room, and you'll be safe there. I'm not saying that you need to spend the rest of your life there, but it'll give you a chance to learn about Earth without risking discovery."

Before she could answer, a pair of figures approached, their movements silent on the sidewalk. Krys felt herself stiffen when she noticed the lack of shadows under the street lamps, and she glanced up at Alec as she bit her lip nervously.

He wasn't the type to offer reassurances, but he stood and placed himself between the two and Krysanna. If this meeting went south for any reason, then at least he could buy her time to escape. His arms folded over his chest when they neared, and he heard her stand behind him.

"Well met," Lalasa greeted, stopping a few paces away.

"Right," Alex said. "Krysanna has your things, so that should take care of your problem."

"You've done well," Lalasa said. "Mikhail will handle your payment." Her gaze turned to the elf, who was peering out from behind Alex.

Despite their last meeting, Krys was still fearful of them, of what they could do if provoked, and she wanted this finished as soon as possible. Taking a deep breath, she stepped out from behind him and held out the bag.

"Everything is inside," she said. "My apologies for taking it. It wasn't my place to go through your things and steal them."

Lothan took the bag from her but didn't check the contents. With a glance, something passed between him and his wife, and it was Lalasa who spoke again.

"I've been told that Miria decided to abandon her mission," she said. "I believe they faked her death in order to save both her and you, and I plan to offer her sanctuary once we return home. The offer stands for you as well."

"Many thanks, but I'm going to be heading to London," Krysanna said.

Alex hid his surprise, but he was glad that she'd accepted his offer.

*****

"I'm surprised you agreed to meet with me."

Soph had made the drive to Boston alone, wanting to meet with her potential employer without the support of her wife. It was strange to sit across from Mikhail after their initial meeting years ago, but hopefully, he'd let the past stay there.

"I'm surprised you're not trying to kill me again," he said.

"That was one time," she countered. "And you and your partner were trying to kill *me*."

They both remembered the incident well, a case of mistaken identity that had ended with one of the operatives dead and one running for his life. Duchess had raised hell afterwards, and Mikhail had gotten an earful from Jack for his troubles.

"I was told that you had a point for this meeting."

Soph rolled her eyes but kept the next snarky comment to herself. Yes, there was a point, but they weren't off to a great start, and she expected him to refuse her request.

"I want a job," she said.

"Go online," he said. "I'm sure you can find plenty of jobs there."

"I want to be able to work with Duchess." Before he could say anything, she continued. "Look, I know you and I aren't exactly the best of friends, but just put the bullshit aside for a few minutes and give me a chance. I have the same skills she has, and we can do jobs that would take a full team of humans with just the two of us. You don't have to like me, but you can't say that this wouldn't be beneficial to your company."

He was quiet for a minute or two, considering her words, but then he nodded and grabbed a manila folder from one of the drawers of his desk. Setting it down in front of her, he handed her a pen.

"Paperwork first," he said. "Then, we'll see about starting your training. You'll have to spend a couple of weeks here, but then we'll pair you with Duchess for field training and future assignments. Do not make me regret this, Sophia." He paused, resting his elbows on the desk. "You'll need a name for while you're working. Pick a good one, or I'll choose one for you."

*****

In the end, Karian decided to take the news to Allentown in person. Knocking on the door to the apartment, he waited silently for the door to open, and when it did, he noticed the new chain in place. A hint of a grin settled on his lips, and he offered a nod to Alma before she closed the door and unhooked the chain.

"I don't need you breaking another one," she said, opening the door fully. As she stepped aside, she motioned for him to enter, and she noticed that his smile faded. "It isn't good news, is it?"

"I'm afraid not," he said. Stepping inside, he waited for her to close the door, and he turned to face her. "Miria is dead."

Alma looked down, only a little surprised at the news. It hurt to know that the girl she'd helped had passed, but she had to believe that it had been unavoidable. Lifting her gaze, she met his.

"How?"

"When I found her, she turned violent," he said. "I tried to stay on the defensive, but you need to understand that she was a trained fighter. I didn't intend for it to end that way, but there was little else I could do."

"So, you killed her?" Alma asked. Now, surprised showed on her features, and she took a step back, putting a little bit of distance between them. "Are you here to kill me, then?"

"To be honest, I considered it." Karian didn't approach, and he let out a quiet sigh. "You're a loose end, Alma, one that I can't really afford to leave like this, but I can't justify taking your life. Miria's people will likely retaliate over her death, and they'll come looking for anyone that she'd met while she was here. I can help you relocate, if you'd like."

Alma considered the offer, but she already knew her answer. This was her home, and she had no intention of leaving it.

*****

Miria awoke slowly, her head still foggy as she opened her eyes. It took a moment, but she recognized the room as the one she'd stayed in previously before...

Her hand went to her throat, feeling for the twin puncture marks as the memory of the previous night came rushing back to her. She was breathing, and she still had a pulse – she could feel her heart racing in her chest as she sat up – but dizziness forced her to lie down again.

The fear from that moment returned, her eyes darting about only to discover that she was alone in the room. Through the closed door, she heard footsteps approaching, and her muscles tensed as she sat up again to lean against the headboard. Without a weapon in sight, she had no means to defend herself if Karian decided that he fancied elven blood more than human.

It was Cassandra who entered, though, after a light knock on the door, and Miria wanted to be relieved. The tension wouldn't ease from her tired body, but she managed a ghost of a smile as Cass came to the side of the bed.

"How are you feeling?" Cassandra asked.

"As if I've been run over by a carriage, but I'm still alive."

Miria knew how close she'd come to death, and even though they'd discussed the plan beforehand, she couldn't fully trust Karian. She'd never dismissed the possibility that he would have taken her life, and the thought frightened her more than she was willing to admit. It was only by chance that he'd stuck with their initial agreement and spared her life.

"I brought you some soup and another potion," Cass said. "You should be fully healed within a day or so."

Thanking her, Miria smoothed out the blanket around her waist, sniffing appreciatively as Cassandra handed her the bowl. It was a light broth with vegetables, and the scent teased her senses, prompting a protest from her stomach. The first taste felt like her first meal in ages, the flavors dancing on her tongue, and she offered a nod towards Cassandra.

"This is perfect," she said.

"Good," Cassandra said. "I'll be back in a little while to check on you, but you should try to rest some more. You lost a lot of blood last night."

Despite her hunger, the reminder soured her stomach, and she set the spoon down for a moment. She wondered if she would still be able to face the vampire, even though she was once again a guest in his home.

Perhaps she was overthinking things. She still drew breath, and she was on the med after they'd executed the deception flawlessly. Evemyst believed she was gone, so all she needed to do was figure out where to go from here.

"You look lost," Cass said.

Looking up from where she was staring at her soup, Miria met her gaze, but said nothing at first. Her future was uncertain, and she had no home to which she could return.

"I feel lost," she said. "I cannot go back home, but I'm not sure where else to go. I'd stay here, but I know little of this world, and I do not know what I would even do with my time here."

"I'll be opening a café in the coming months," Cass said. "I could use the help if you're interested. It'll be similar to a tavern, but we'll serve tea and coffee instead of ale."

Miria considered the offer, but then she nodded. A fresh start was exactly what she needed.

Epilogue

For a long time, I'd always wondered what it would be like to explore the world outside of Evemyst, but I never imagined that I would be forced from my home. The prospect of exploring Zalyndrya had excited me years ago, but I never worked up the courage to leave on my own. Perhaps I should have. Then, I would have had a better idea of what areas to avoid.

Times have changed, though, and I now know that staying on that world would have ended in disaster. The Council had already sent one warrior to find me, and it was only by chance that she had a change of heart before she was able to find me. I wonder if I have Karian to thank for that.

If I returned to any place on Zalyndrya, surely, they would send others after me. That's part of the reason I decided to stay on Earth. Alex promised to keep me safe, and I believe him without a doubt. He may be a little rough around the edges, but I can see beyond the tough exterior. Maybe he's done things that I shouldn't be proud of, but he's stayed by my side throughout this ordeal.

The first couple of months in London passed without incident, and with the bracelet to hide my wings, I've been able to leave his flat to explore the city more and more. I can't let fear hold me back for the rest of my life, and the gods know I have so much of my life yet to live. The only way forward is to swallow that fear and keep looking towards the future.

Alex once told me that I'm stronger than my fear, and I'm trying every day to prove him right. He must have seen something in me that I hadn't discovered for myself. For so long, I spent my time afraid, and all it's done is hold me back. While I can't bring myself to remain in the company of Dusk Hunters for an extended amount of time, I'm trying not to react with terror whenever I know one is around.

London is a far cry from the way things were back home, but I've grown accustomed to the differences, and I'm learning more every day. English has been a challenge to master, and I still stumble over my words here and there, but soon enough, I won't need my ring to translate the language.

Sometimes I toy with the idea of going home, of presenting myself to the Council so that I could try again to explain myself, but I know that they would only order my execution. Evemyst is lost to me now, and I've somehow managed to come to terms with that.

I'm not sure how long I'll stay in London. Maybe I'll decide to explore this world once I have a solid grasp on the English language. Then again, Alex told me that different countries have different languages. How difficult it must be to communicate with others around the world when there are so many differences in words.

This city has grown on me, despite my strong ties to my homeland, and while I've learned to love England, I can't help the pull of the open road. Alex received a phone call for me the other day from the empress' adoptive daughter, offering me a job back in America. It's tempting, but the elf who was sent to kill me is also employed there. I worry that she might change her mind in an attempt to earn the good graces of the Council. Karian assured me that they believe she's dead, but I know just how hard it is to leave our home and start over. Not everyone can handle it.

I think in time I might make my way there, but for now, I'm content to stay here. Alex has been kind and generous to me, and I can find it in myself to leave him here alone. This is my home now, and until the call of the road becomes too much for me to ignore, this is where I'll stay.